VAULT
VAULTCOMICS.COM

PUBLISHER
DAMIAN A. WASSEL

EDITOR-IN-CHIEF
ADRIAN F. WASSEL

ART DIRECTOR
NATHAN C. GOODEN

VP BRANDING/DESIGN
TIM DANIEL

DIRECTOR OF MARKETING
KIM MCLEAN

PRINCIPAL
DAMIAN A. WASSEL, SR.

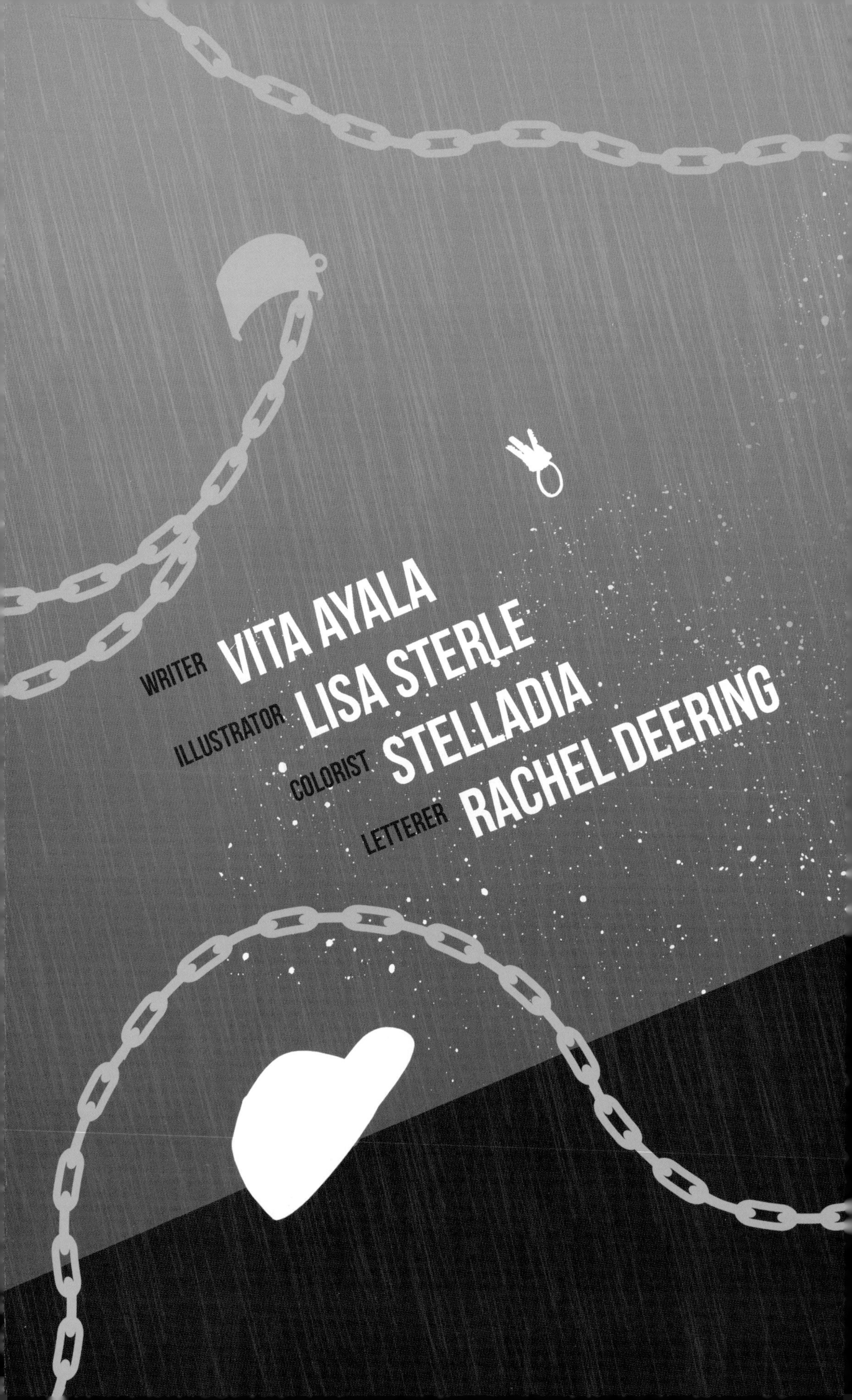
WRITER VITA AYALA
ILLUSTRATOR LISA STERLE
COLORIST STELLADIA
LETTERER RACHEL DEERING

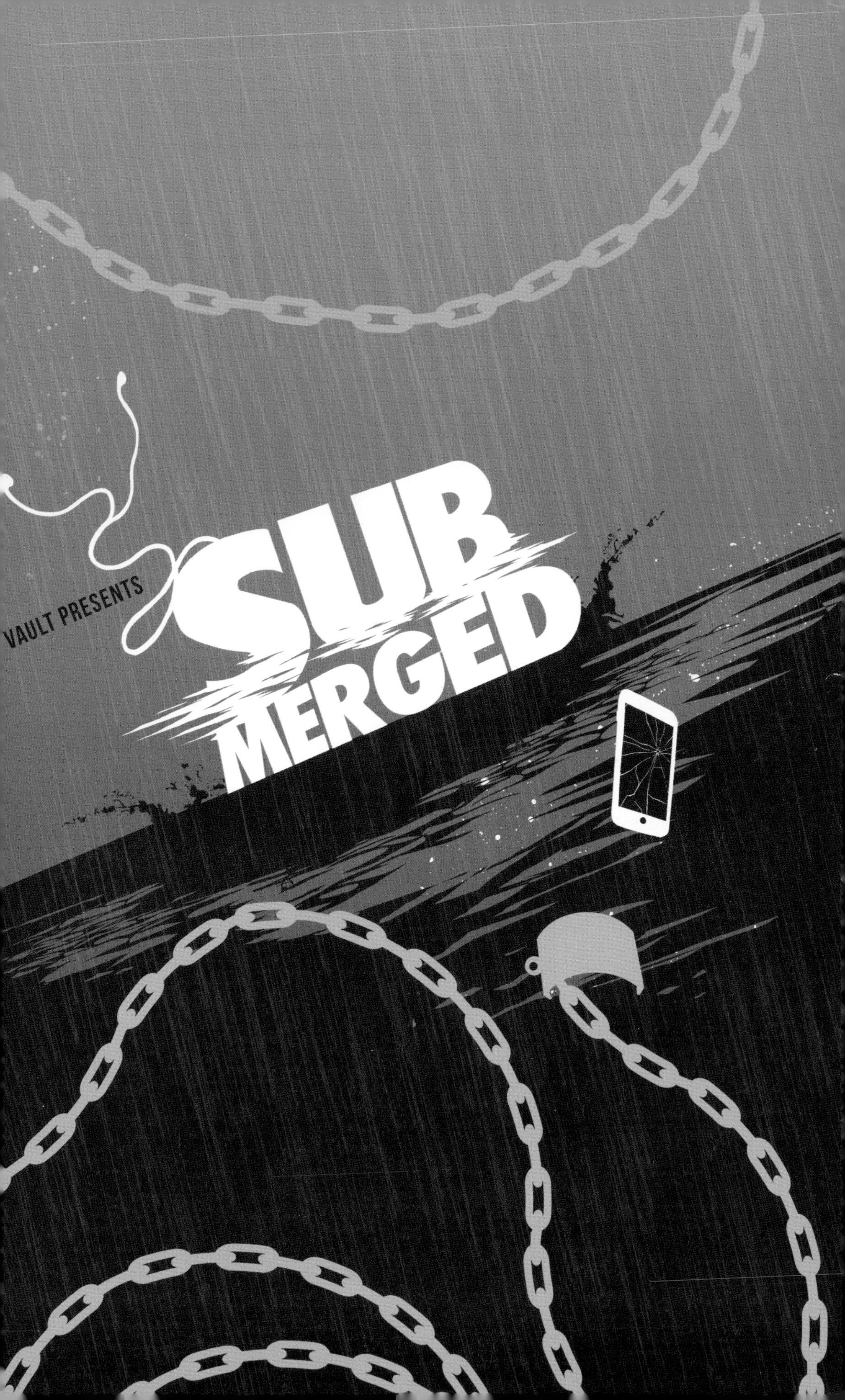
VAULT PRESENTS
SUB
MERGED

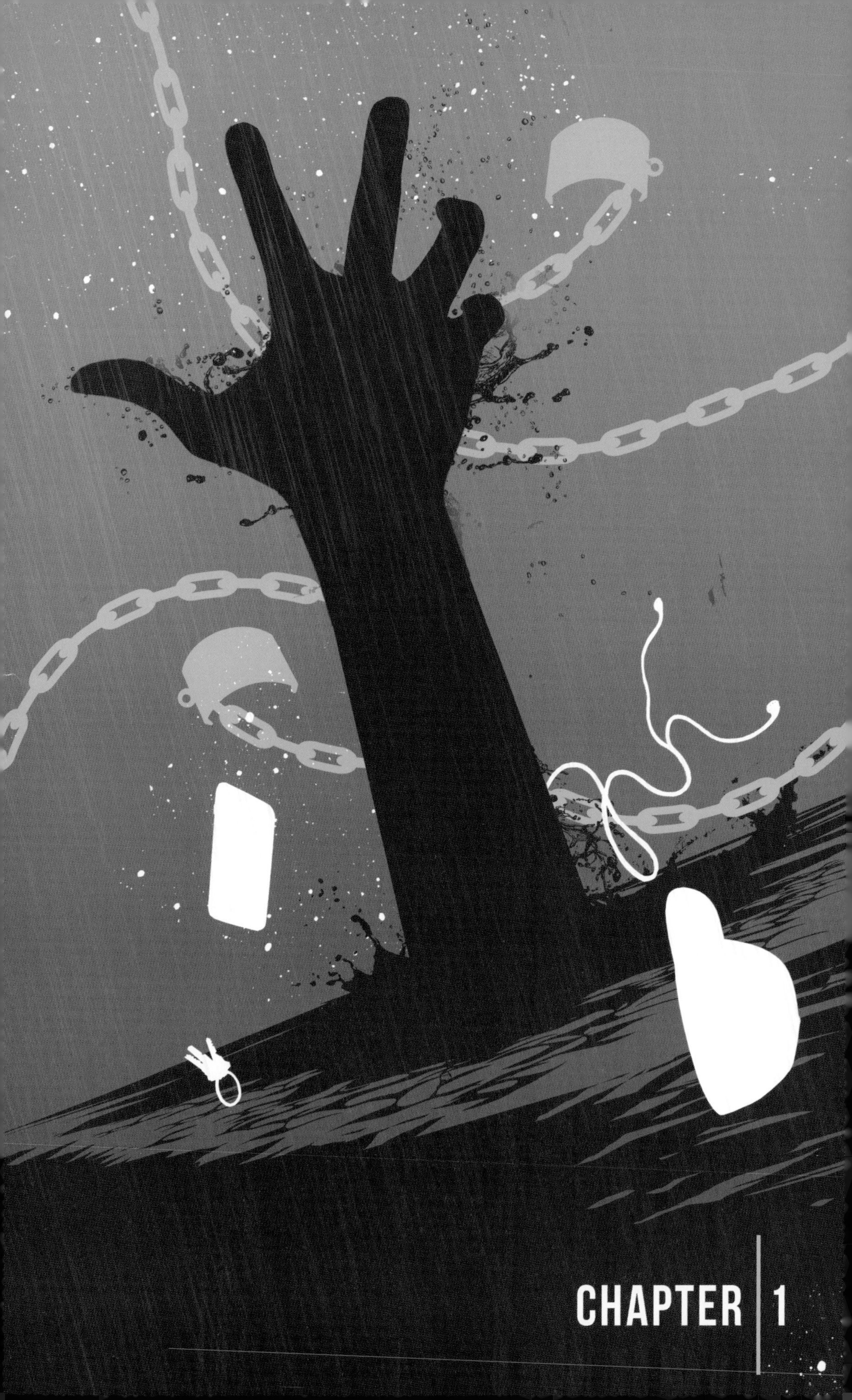

CHAPTER 1

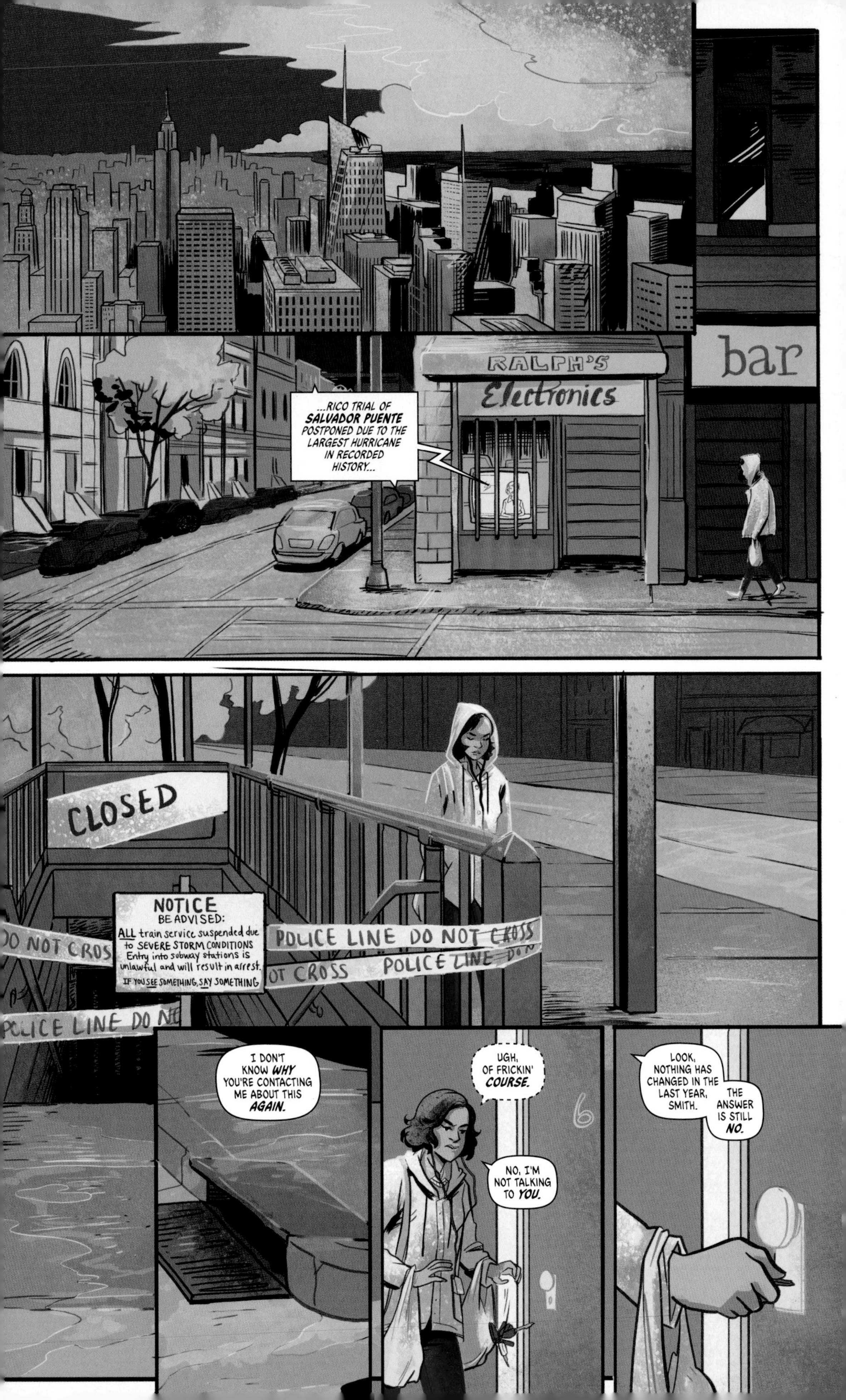
RALPH'S
Electronics
bar
...RICO TRIAL OF SALVADOR PUENTE POSTPONED DUE TO THE LARGEST HURRICANE IN RECORDED HISTORY...
CLOSED
NOTICE
BE ADVISED:
ALL train service suspended due to SEVERE STORM CONDITIONS Entry into subway stations is unlawful and will result in arrest.
IF YOU SEE SOMETHING, SAY SOMETHING
POLICE LINE DO NOT CROSS
I DON'T KNOW WHY YOU'RE CONTACTING ME ABOUT THIS AGAIN.
UGH, OF FRICKIN' COURSE.
NO, I'M NOT TALKING TO YOU.
LOOK, NOTHING HAS CHANGED IN THE LAST YEAR, SMITH.
THE ANSWER IS STILL NO.

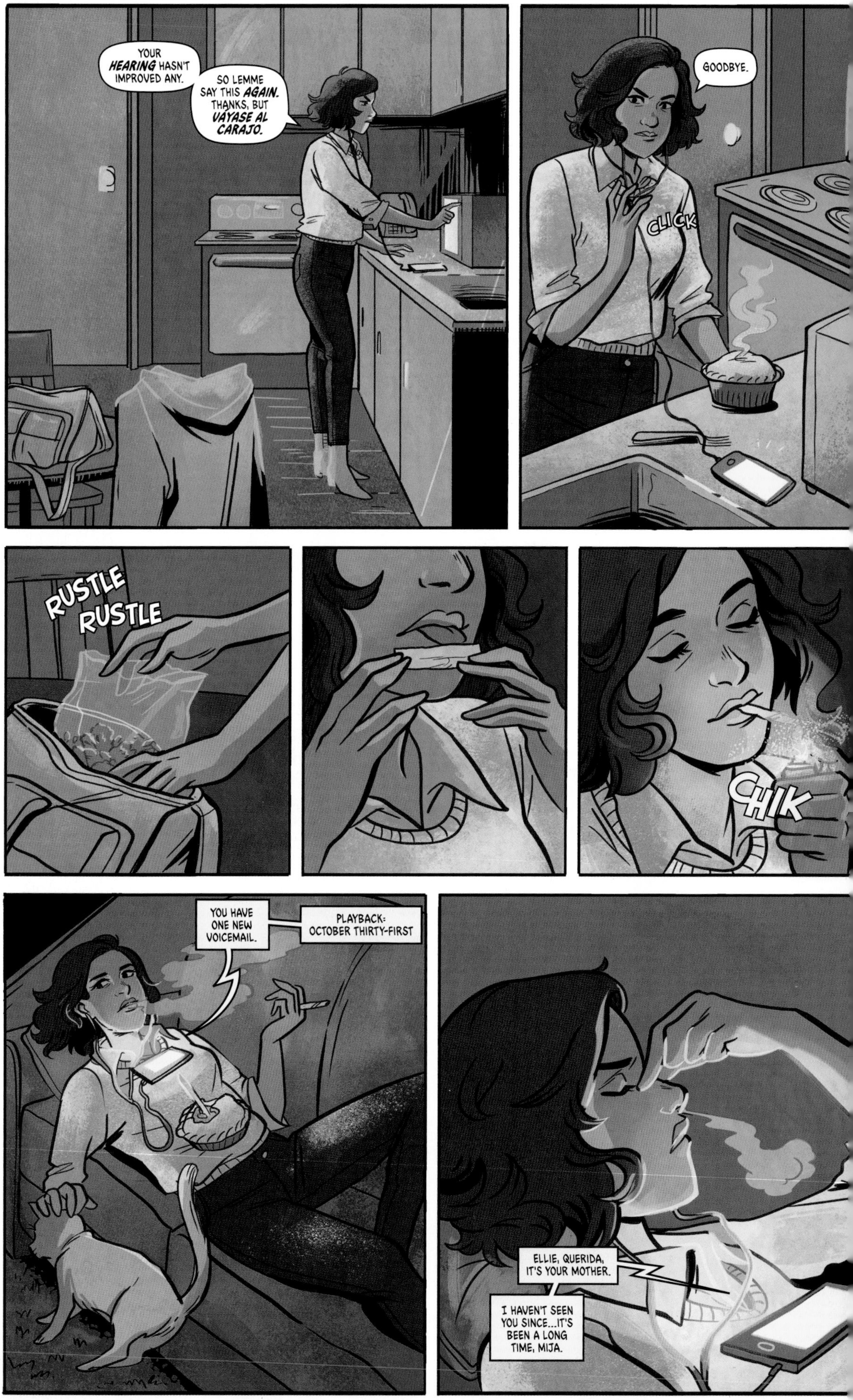
YOUR HEARING HASN'T IMPROVED ANY.
SO LEMME SAY THIS AGAIN. THANKS, BUT VÁYASE AL CARAJO.
GOODBYE.
CLICK
RUSTLE RUSTLE
CHIK
YOU HAVE ONE NEW VOICEMAIL.
PLAYBACK: OCTOBER THIRTY-FIRST
ELLIE, QUERIDA, IT'S YOUR MOTHER.
I HAVEN'T SEEN YOU SINCE...IT'S BEEN A LONG TIME, MIJA.

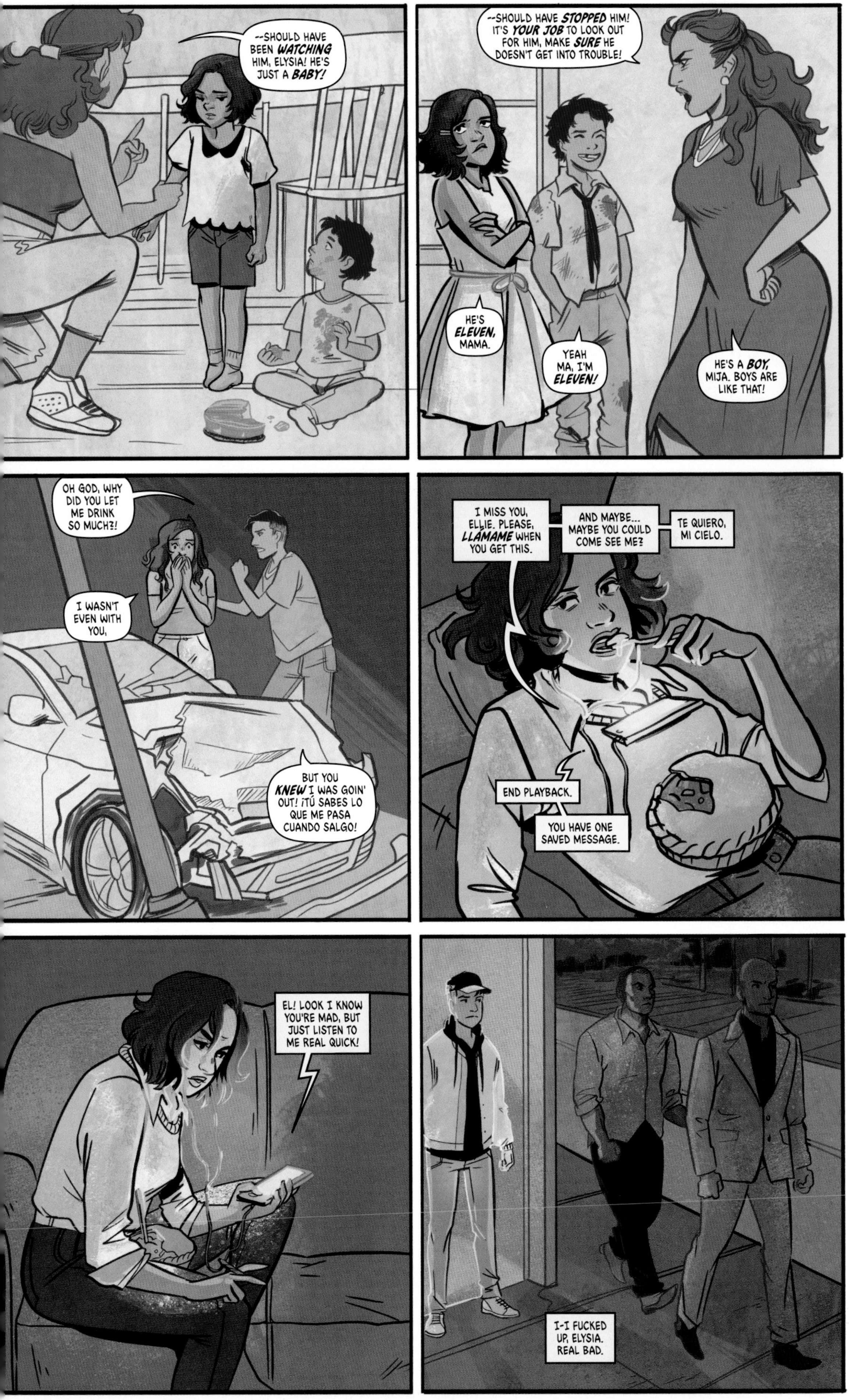
--SHOULD HAVE BEEN WATCHING HIM, ELYSIA! HE'S JUST A BABY!
--SHOULD HAVE STOPPED HIM! IT'S YOUR JOB TO LOOK OUT FOR HIM, MAKE SURE HE DOESN'T GET INTO TROUBLE!
HE'S ELEVEN, MAMA.
YEAH MA, I'M ELEVEN!
HE'S A BOY, MIJA. BOYS ARE LIKE THAT!
OH GOD, WHY DID YOU LET ME DRINK SO MUCH?!
I WASN'T EVEN WITH YOU,
BUT YOU KNEW I WAS GOIN' OUT! ¡TÚ SABES LO QUE ME PASA CUANDO SALGO!
I MISS YOU, ELLIE. PLEASE, LLÁMAME WHEN YOU GET THIS.
AND MAYBE... MAYBE YOU COULD COME SEE ME?
TE QUIERO, MI CIELO.
END PLAYBACK.
YOU HAVE ONE SAVED MESSAGE.
EL! LOOK I KNOW YOU'RE MAD, BUT JUST LISTEN TO ME REAL QUICK!
I-I FUCKED UP, ELYSIA. REAL BAD.

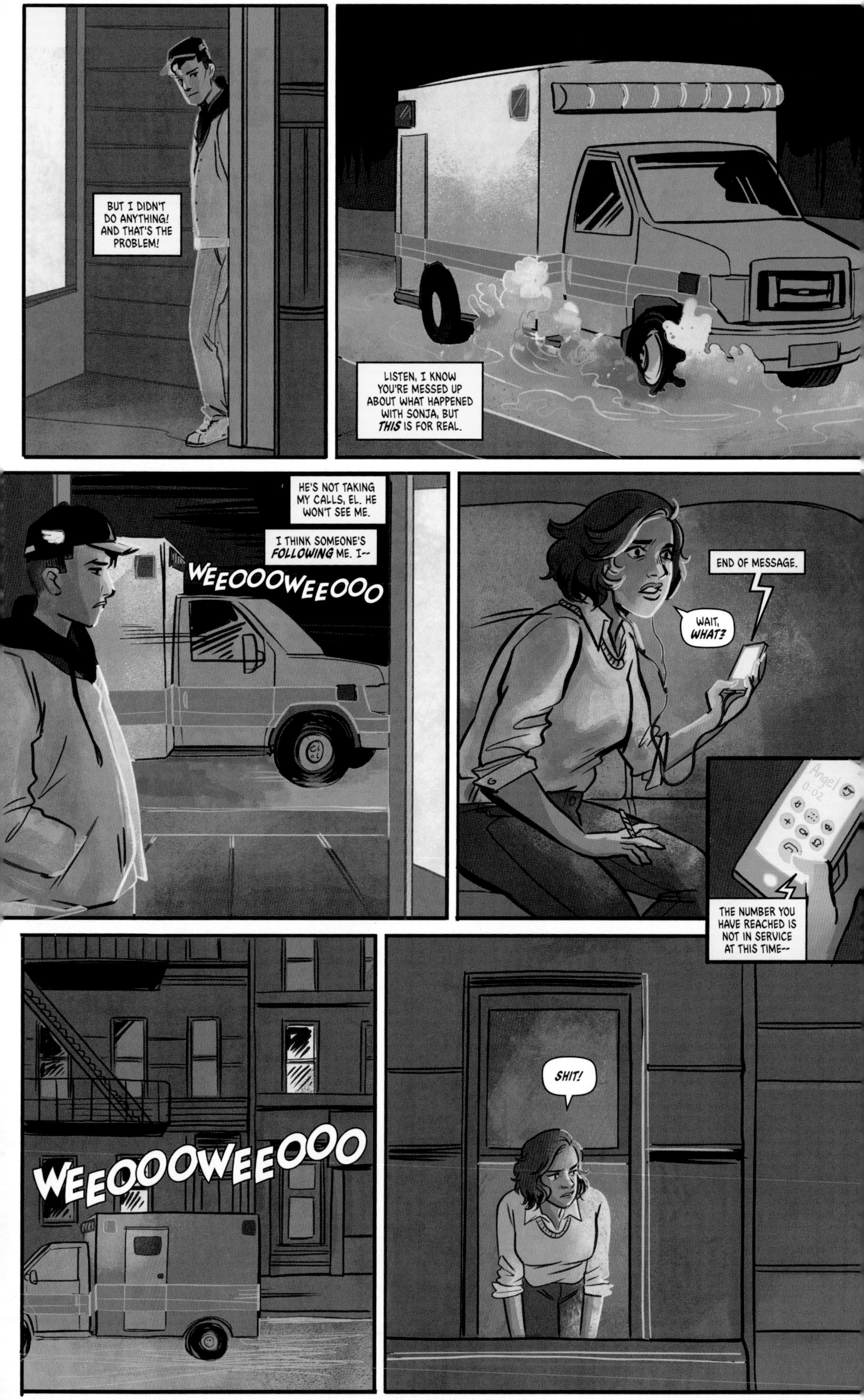
BUT I DIDN'T DO ANYTHING! AND THAT'S THE PROBLEM!
LISTEN, I KNOW YOU'RE MESSED UP ABOUT WHAT HAPPENED WITH SONJA, BUT THIS IS FOR REAL.
HE'S NOT TAKING MY CALLS, EL. HE WON'T SEE ME.
I THINK SOMEONE'S FOLLOWING ME. I--
WEEOOOWEEOOO
END OF MESSAGE.
WAIT, WHAT?
Angel
0:02
THE NUMBER YOU HAVE REACHED IS NOT IN SERVICE AT THIS TIME--
WEEOOOWEEOOO
SHIT!

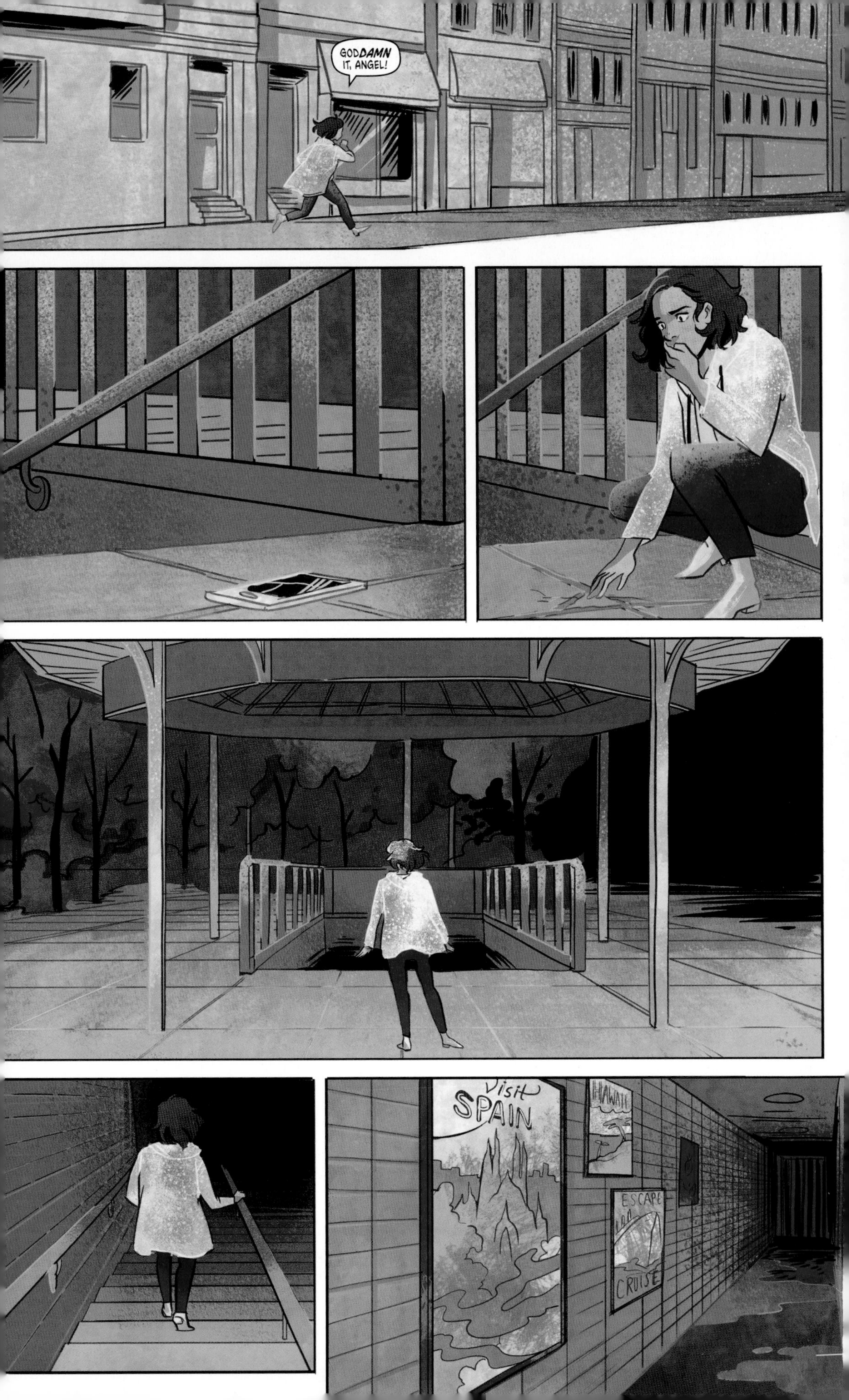
GODDAMN IT, ANGEL!
Visit SPAIN
HAWAII
ESCAPE
CRUISE

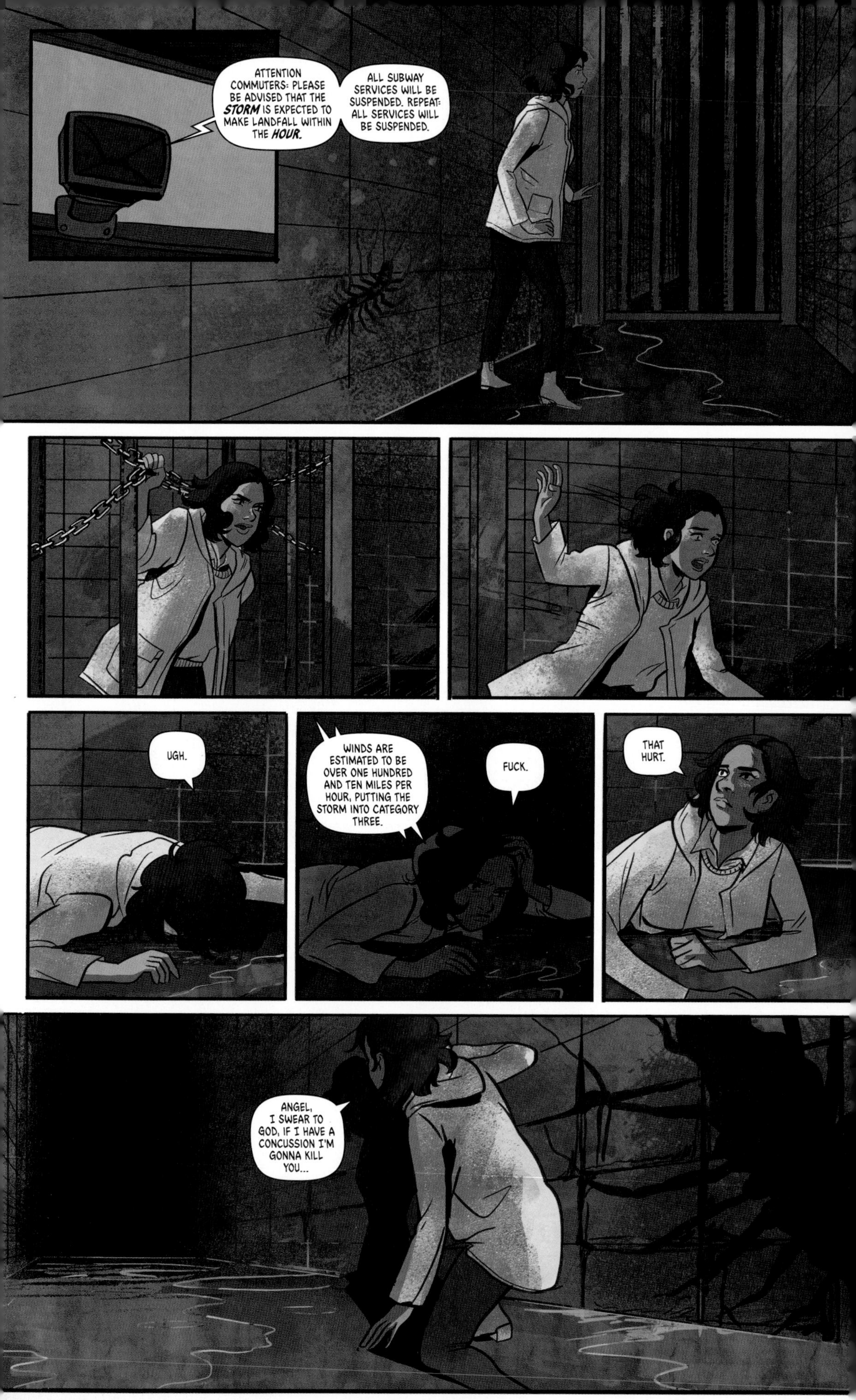
ATTENTION COMMUTERS: PLEASE BE ADVISED THAT THE **STORM** IS EXPECTED TO MAKE LANDFALL WITHIN THE **HOUR.**
ALL SUBWAY SERVICES WILL BE SUSPENDED. REPEAT: ALL SERVICES WILL BE SUSPENDED.
UGH.
WINDS ARE ESTIMATED TO BE OVER ONE HUNDRED AND TEN MILES PER HOUR, PUTTING THE STORM INTO CATEGORY THREE.
FUCK.
THAT HURT.
ANGEL, I SWEAR TO GOD, IF I HAVE A CONCUSSION I'M GONNA KILL YOU...

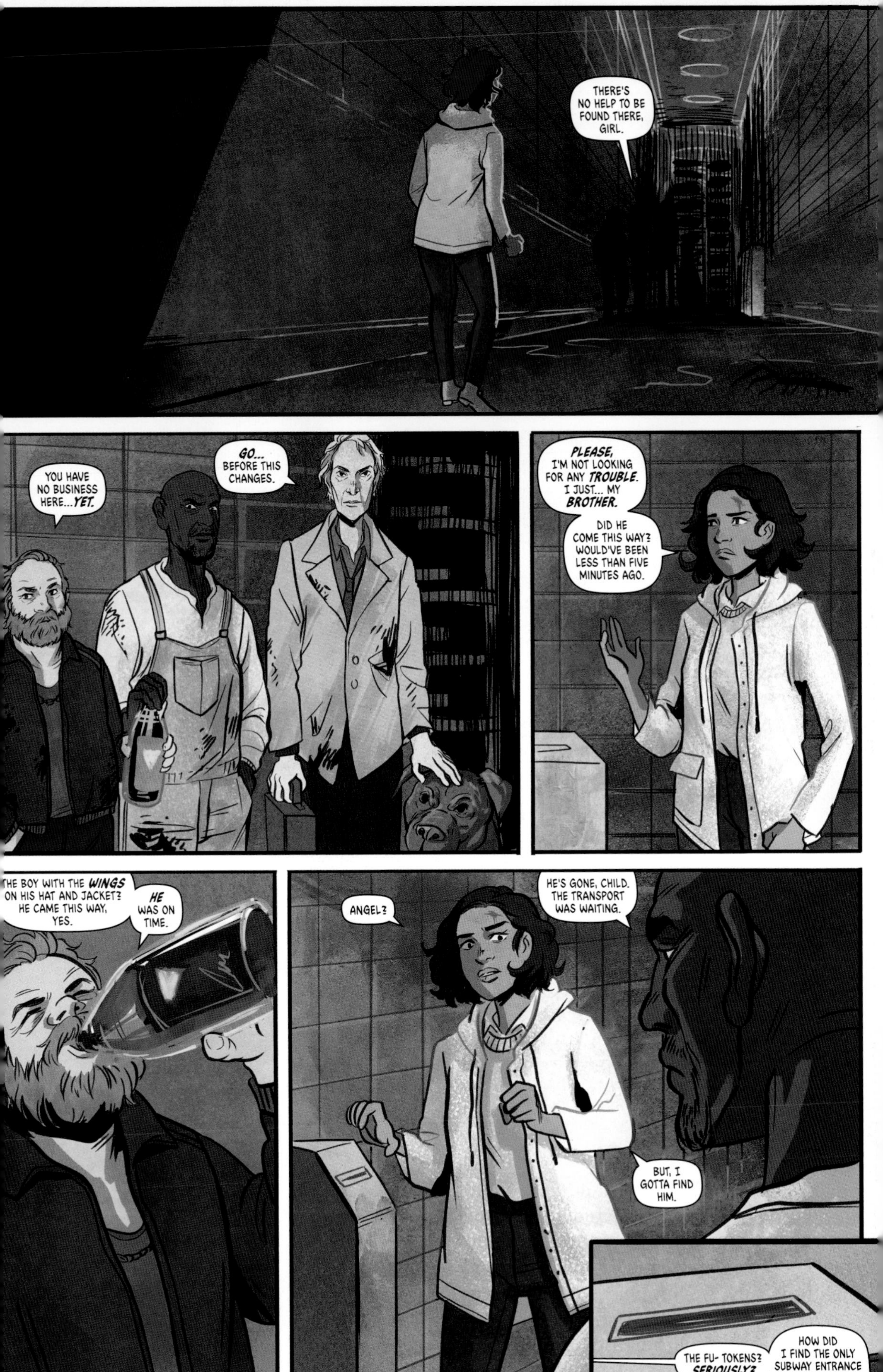
THERE'S NO HELP TO BE FOUND THERE, GIRL.
YOU HAVE NO BUSINESS HERE...YET.
GO... BEFORE THIS CHANGES.
PLEASE, I'M NOT LOOKING FOR ANY TROUBLE. I JUST... MY BROTHER.
DID HE COME THIS WAY? WOULD'VE BEEN LESS THAN FIVE MINUTES AGO.
THE BOY WITH THE WINGS ON HIS HAT AND JACKET? HE CAME THIS WAY, YES.
HE WAS ON TIME.
ANGEL?
HE'S GONE, CHILD. THE TRANSPORT WAS WAITING.
BUT, I GOTTA FIND HIM.
THE FU- TOKENS? SERIOUSLY?
HOW DID I FIND THE ONLY SUBWAY ENTRANCE IN NEW YORK THAT STILL TAKES TOKENS?

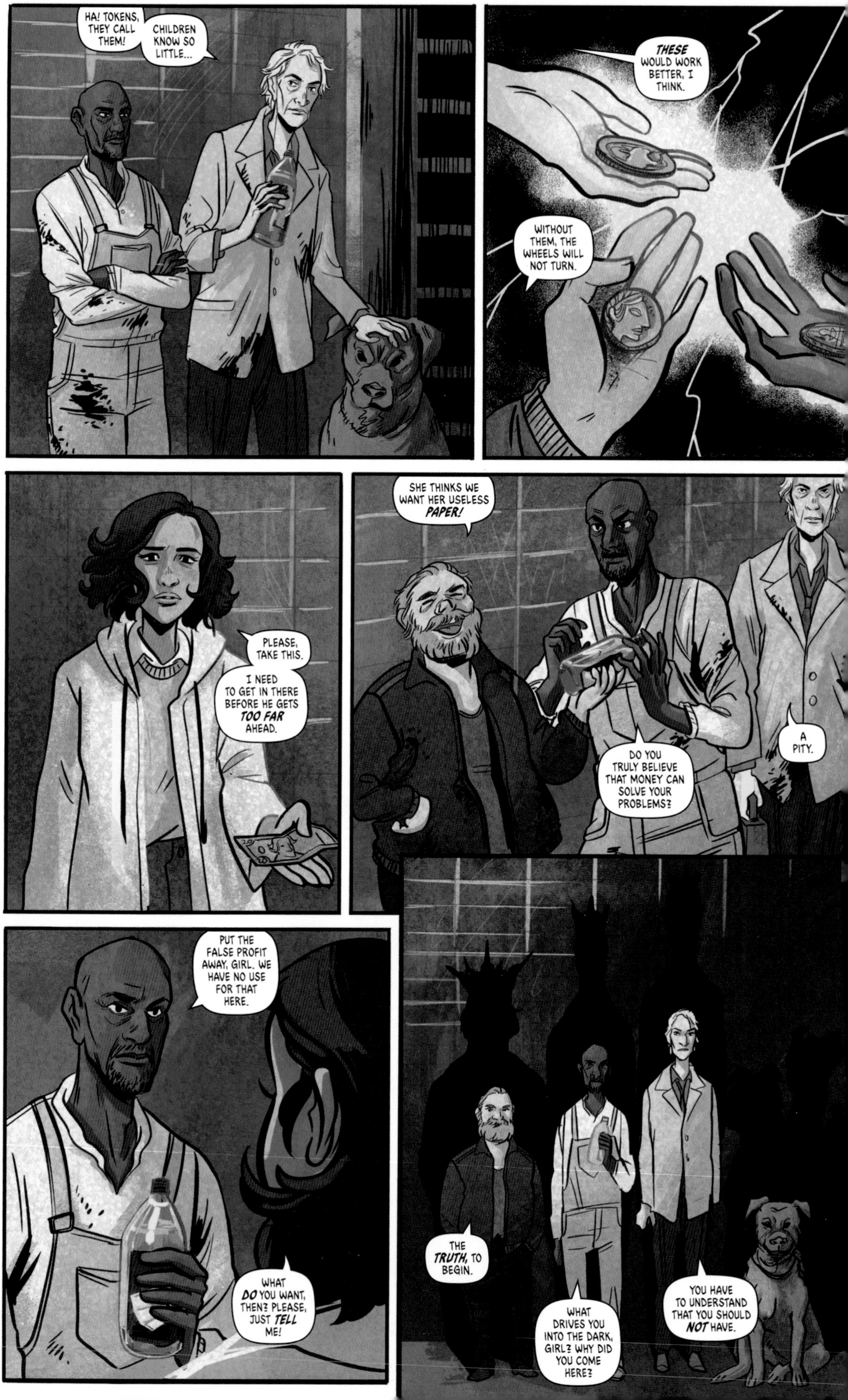
HA! TOKENS, THEY CALL THEM!
CHILDREN KNOW SO LITTLE...
THESE WOULD WORK BETTER, I THINK.
WITHOUT THEM, THE WHEELS WILL NOT TURN.
PLEASE, TAKE THIS.
I NEED TO GET IN THERE BEFORE HE GETS TOO FAR AHEAD.
SHE THINKS WE WANT HER USELESS PAPER!
DO YOU TRULY BELIEVE THAT MONEY CAN SOLVE YOUR PROBLEMS?
A PITY.
PUT THE FALSE PROFIT AWAY, GIRL. WE HAVE NO USE FOR THAT HERE.
WHAT DO YOU WANT, THEN? PLEASE, JUST TELL ME!
THE TRUTH, TO BEGIN.
WHAT DRIVES YOU INTO THE DARK, GIRL? WHY DID YOU COME HERE?
YOU HAVE TO UNDERSTAND THAT YOU SHOULD NOT HAVE.

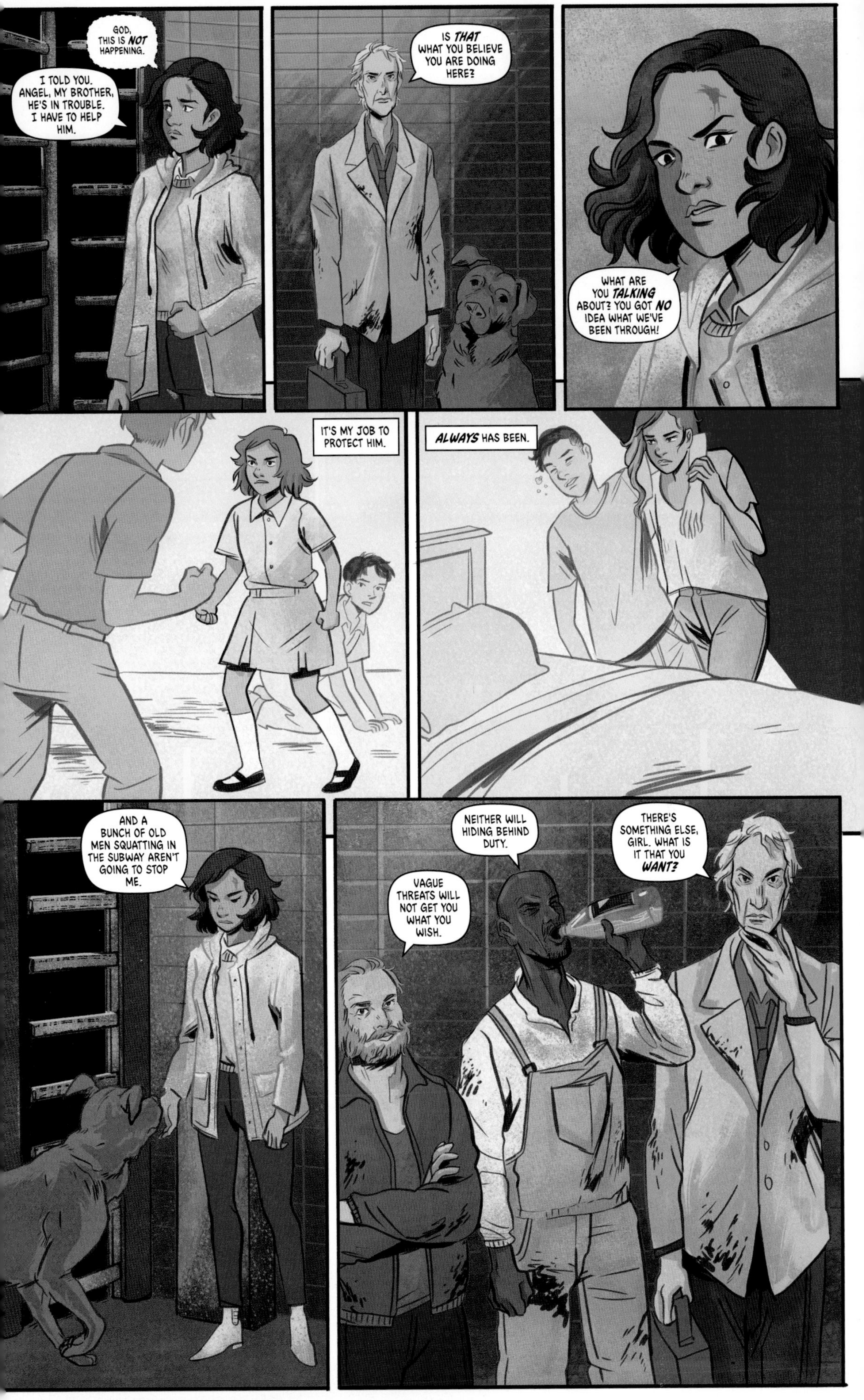

GOD, THIS IS NOT HAPPENING.
I TOLD YOU. ANGEL, MY BROTHER, HE'S IN TROUBLE. I HAVE TO HELP HIM.
IS THAT WHAT YOU BELIEVE YOU ARE DOING HERE?
WHAT ARE YOU TALKING ABOUT? YOU GOT NO IDEA WHAT WE'VE BEEN THROUGH!
IT'S MY JOB TO PROTECT HIM.
ALWAYS HAS BEEN.
AND A BUNCH OF OLD MEN SQUATTING IN THE SUBWAY AREN'T GOING TO STOP ME.
NEITHER WILL HIDING BEHIND DUTY.
VAGUE THREATS WILL NOT GET YOU WHAT YOU WISH.
THERE'S SOMETHING ELSE, GIRL. WHAT IS IT THAT YOU WANT?

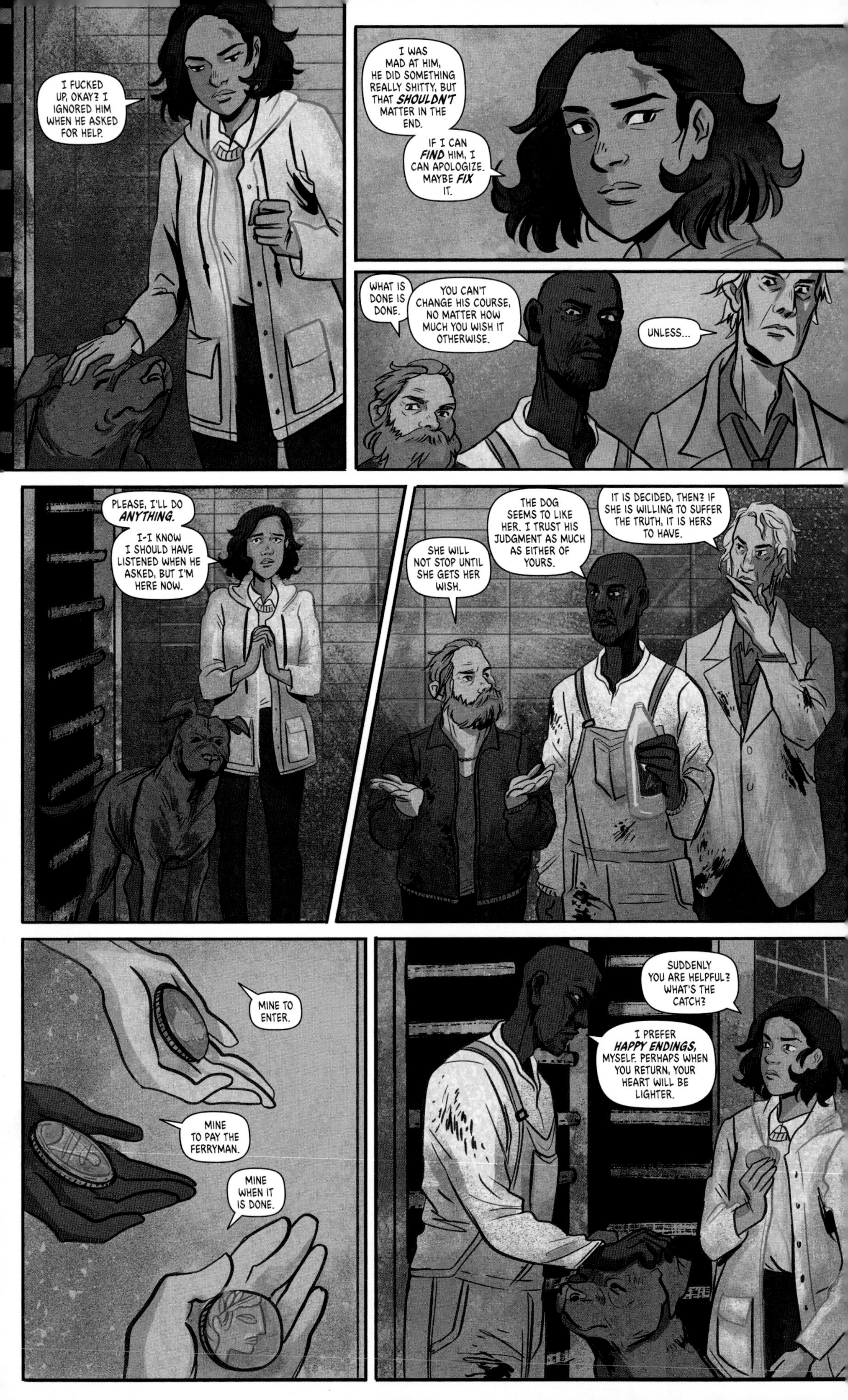

I FUCKED UP, OKAY? I IGNORED HIM WHEN HE ASKED FOR HELP.
I WAS MAD AT HIM, HE DID SOMETHING REALLY SHITTY, BUT THAT SHOULDN'T MATTER IN THE END.
IF I CAN FIND HIM, I CAN APOLOGIZE. MAYBE FIX IT.
WHAT IS DONE IS DONE.
YOU CAN'T CHANGE HIS COURSE, NO MATTER HOW MUCH YOU WISH IT OTHERWISE.
UNLESS...
PLEASE, I'LL DO ANYTHING.
I-I KNOW I SHOULD HAVE LISTENED WHEN HE ASKED, BUT I'M HERE NOW.
SHE WILL NOT STOP UNTIL SHE GETS HER WISH.
THE DOG SEEMS TO LIKE HER. I TRUST HIS JUDGMENT AS MUCH AS EITHER OF YOURS.
IT IS DECIDED, THEN? IF SHE IS WILLING TO SUFFER THE TRUTH, IT IS HERS TO HAVE.
MINE TO ENTER.
MINE TO PAY THE FERRYMAN.
MINE WHEN IT IS DONE.
SUDDENLY YOU ARE HELPFUL? WHAT'S THE CATCH?
I PREFER HAPPY ENDINGS, MYSELF. PERHAPS WHEN YOU RETURN, YOUR HEART WILL BE LIGHTER.

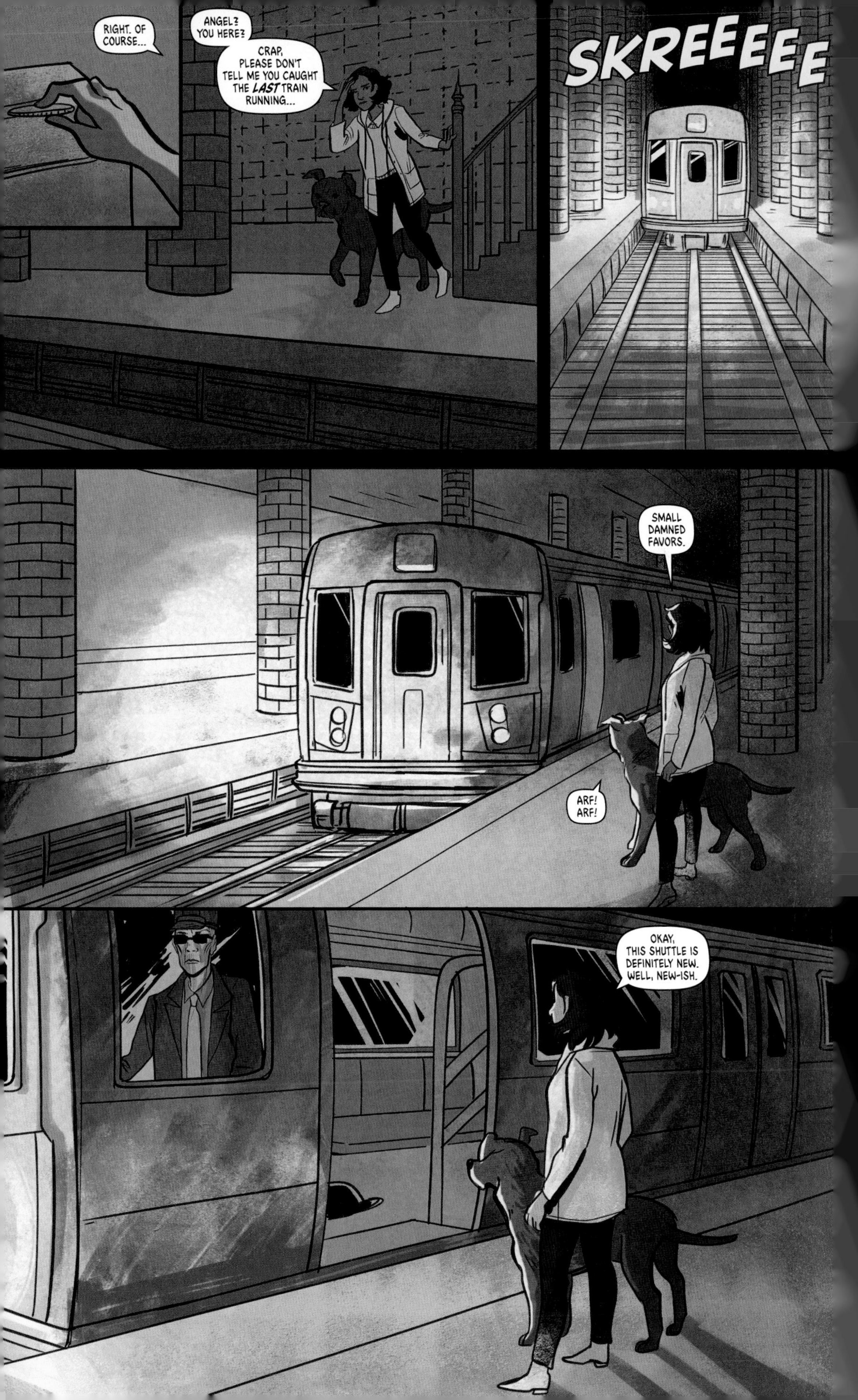
RIGHT. OF COURSE...
ANGEL? YOU HERE?
CRAP, PLEASE DON'T TELL ME YOU CAUGHT THE *LAST* TRAIN RUNNING...
SKREEEEEE
SMALL DAMNED FAVORS.
ARF! ARF!
OKAY, THIS SHUTTLE IS DEFINITELY NEW. WELL, NEW-ISH.

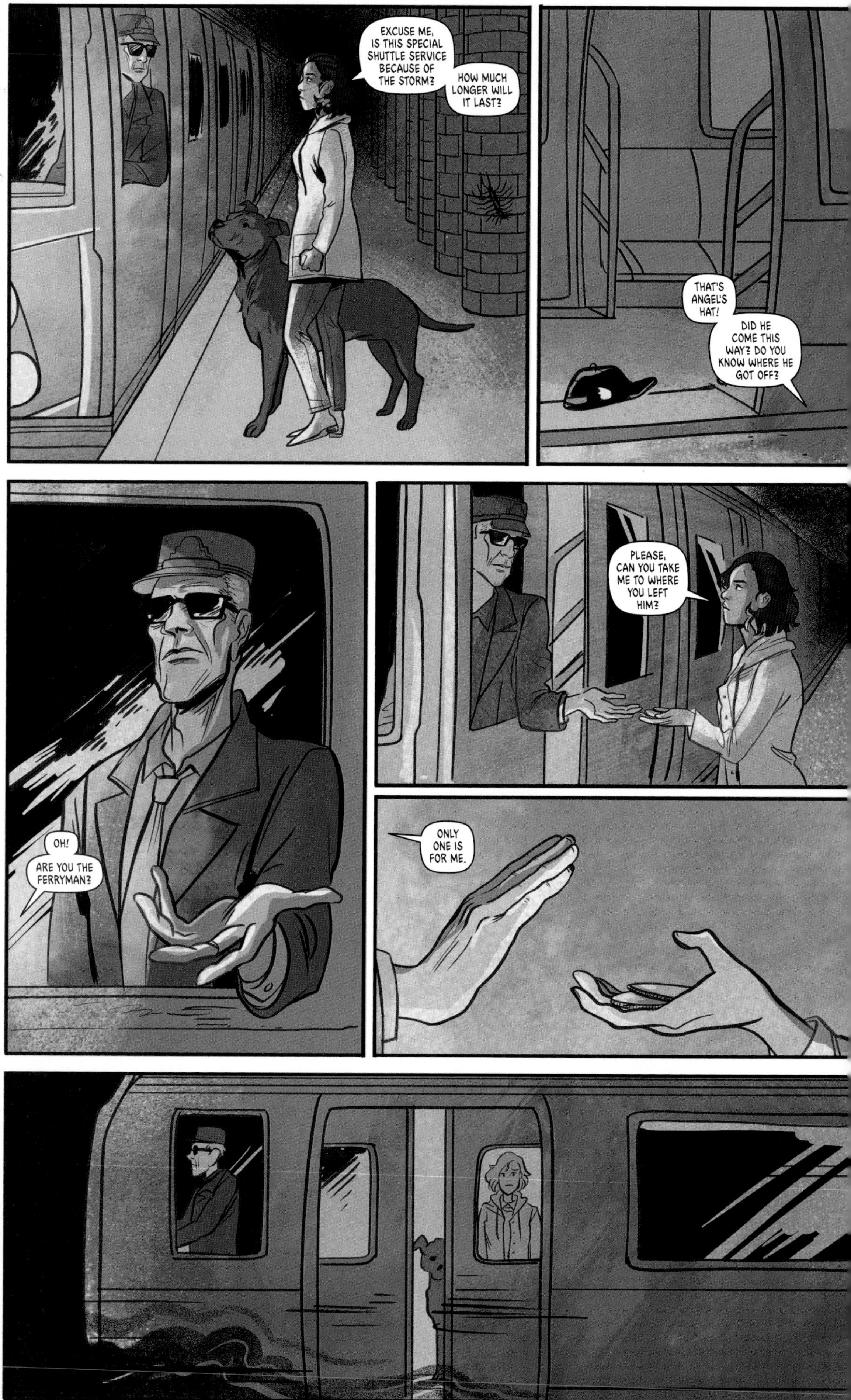
EXCUSE ME, IS THIS SPECIAL SHUTTLE SERVICE BECAUSE OF THE STORM?
HOW MUCH LONGER WILL IT LAST?
THAT'S ANGEL'S HAT!
DID HE COME THIS WAY? DO YOU KNOW WHERE HE GOT OFF?
OH!
ARE YOU THE FERRYMAN?
PLEASE, CAN YOU TAKE ME TO WHERE YOU LEFT HIM?
ONLY ONE IS FOR ME.

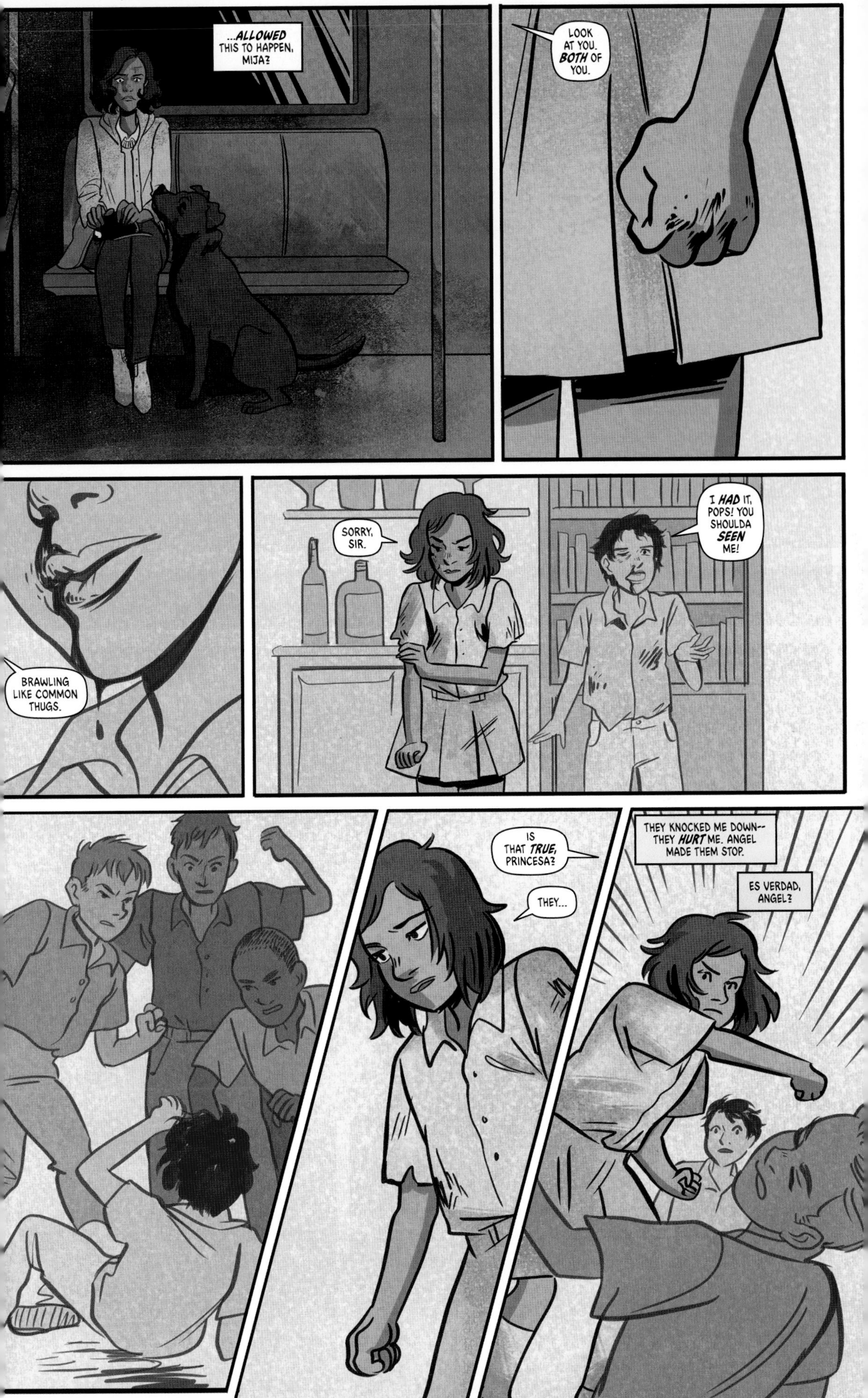
...ALLOWED THIS TO HAPPEN, MIJA?
LOOK AT YOU. BOTH OF YOU.
BRAWLING LIKE COMMON THUGS.
SORRY, SIR.
I HAD IT, POPS! YOU SHOULDA SEEN ME!
IS THAT TRUE, PRINCESA?
THEY...
THEY KNOCKED ME DOWN-- THEY HURT ME. ANGEL MADE THEM STOP.
ES VERDAD, ANGEL?

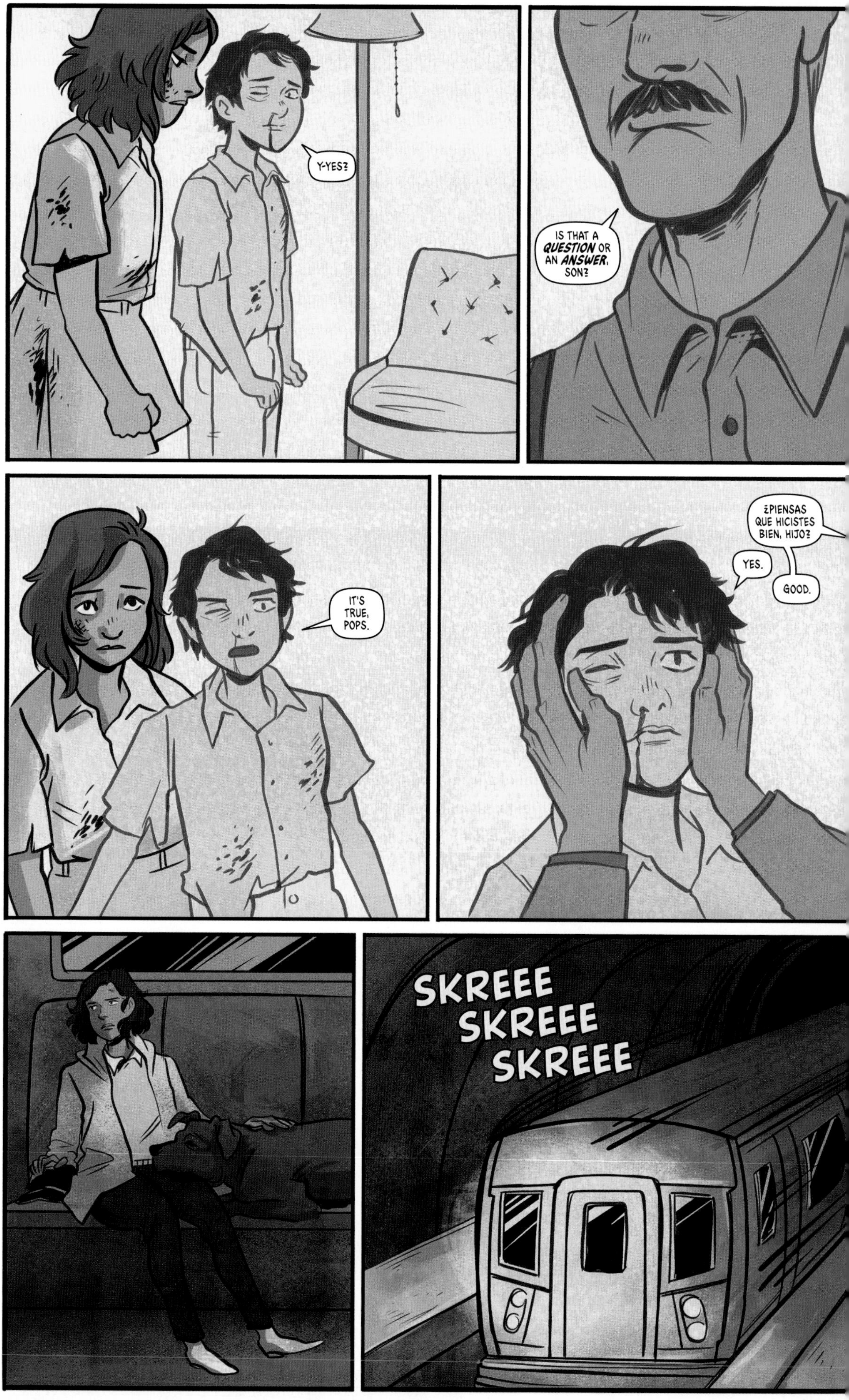
Y-YES?
IS THAT A QUESTION OR AN ANSWER, SON?
IT'S TRUE, POPS.
¿PIENSAS QUE HICISTES BIEN, HIJO?
YES.
GOOD.
SKREEE
SKREEE
SKREEE

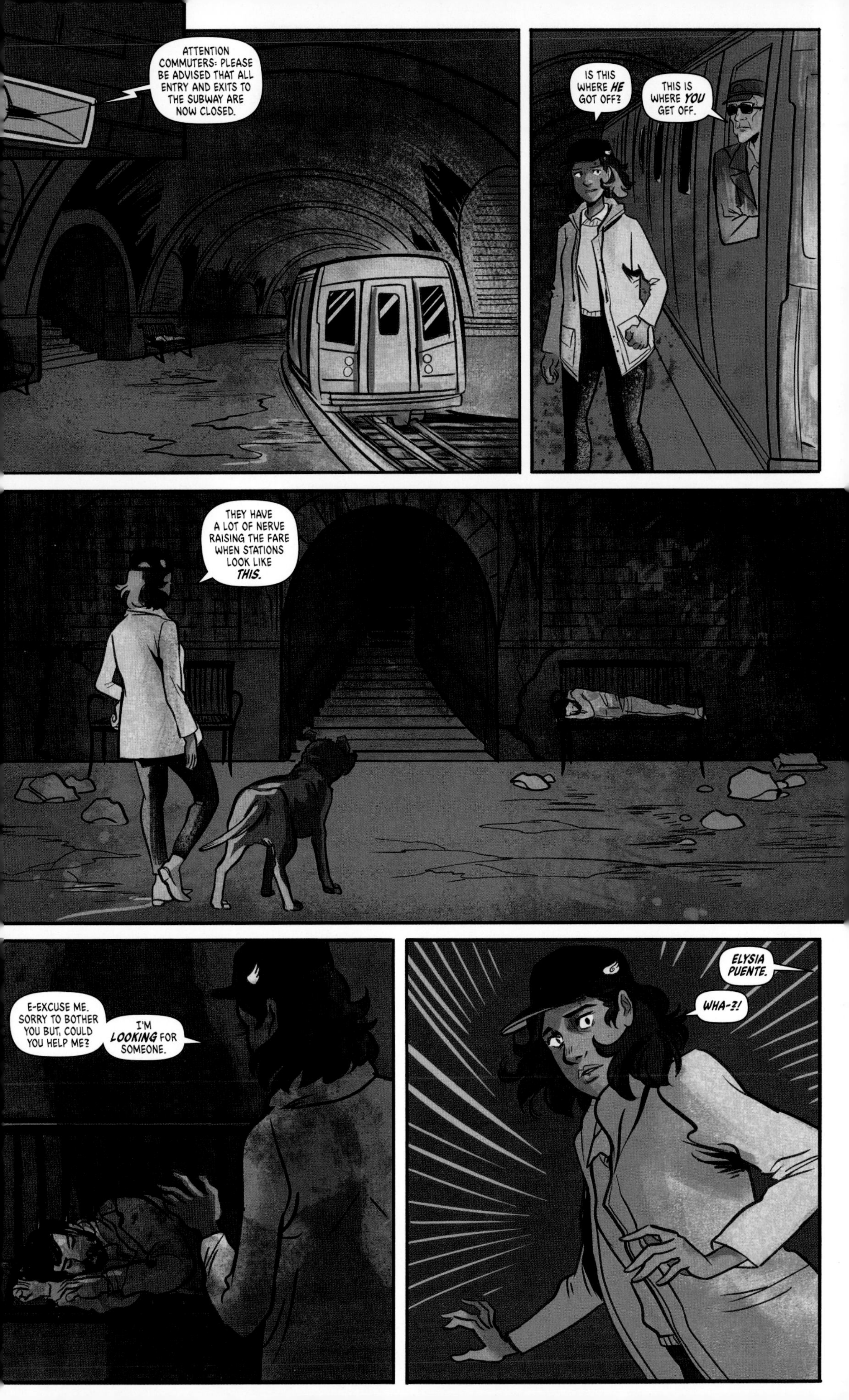
ATTENTION COMMUTERS: PLEASE BE ADVISED THAT ALL ENTRY AND EXITS TO THE SUBWAY ARE NOW CLOSED.
IS THIS WHERE HE GOT OFF?
THIS IS WHERE YOU GET OFF.
THEY HAVE A LOT OF NERVE RAISING THE FARE WHEN STATIONS LOOK LIKE THIS.
E-EXCUSE ME. SORRY TO BOTHER YOU BUT, COULD YOU HELP ME?
I'M LOOKING FOR SOMEONE.
ELYSIA PUENTE.
WHA-?!

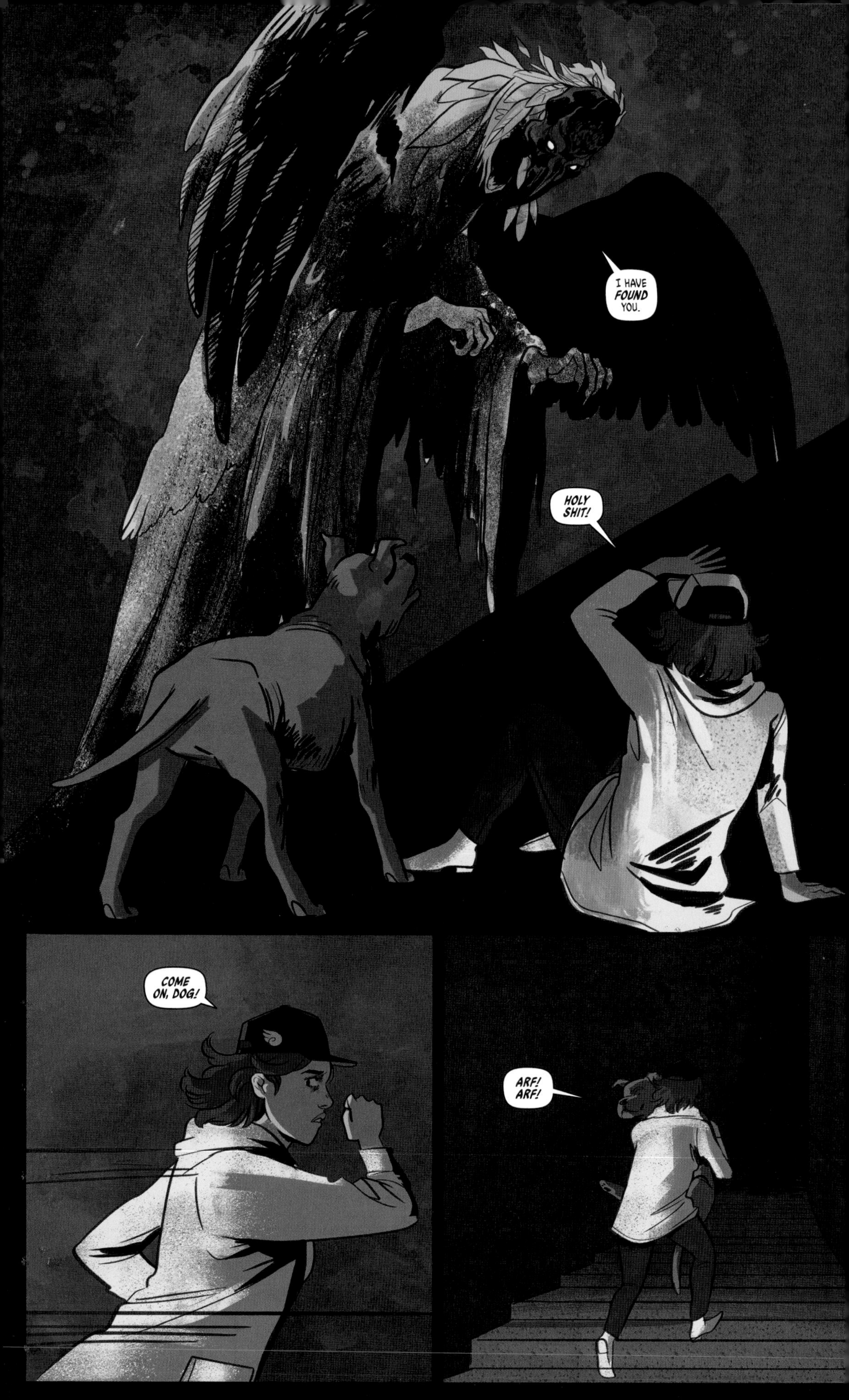
I HAVE FOUND YOU.
HOLY SHIT!
COME ON, DOG!
ARF! ARF!

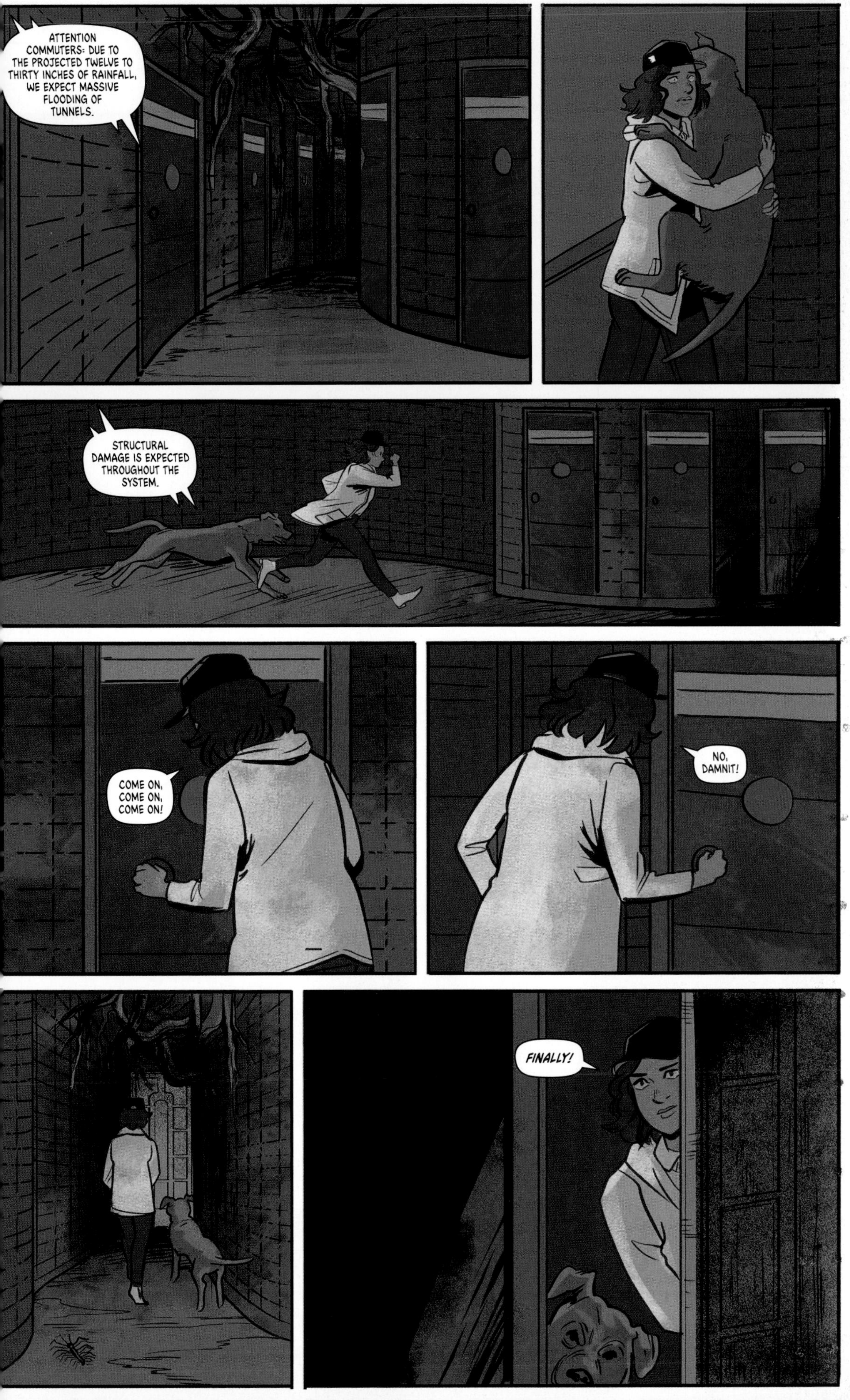
ATTENTION COMMUTERS: DUE TO THE PROJECTED TWELVE TO THIRTY INCHES OF RAINFALL, WE EXPECT MASSIVE FLOODING OF TUNNELS.
STRUCTURAL DAMAGE IS EXPECTED THROUGHOUT THE SYSTEM.
COME ON, COME ON, COME ON!
NO, DAMNIT!
FINALLY!

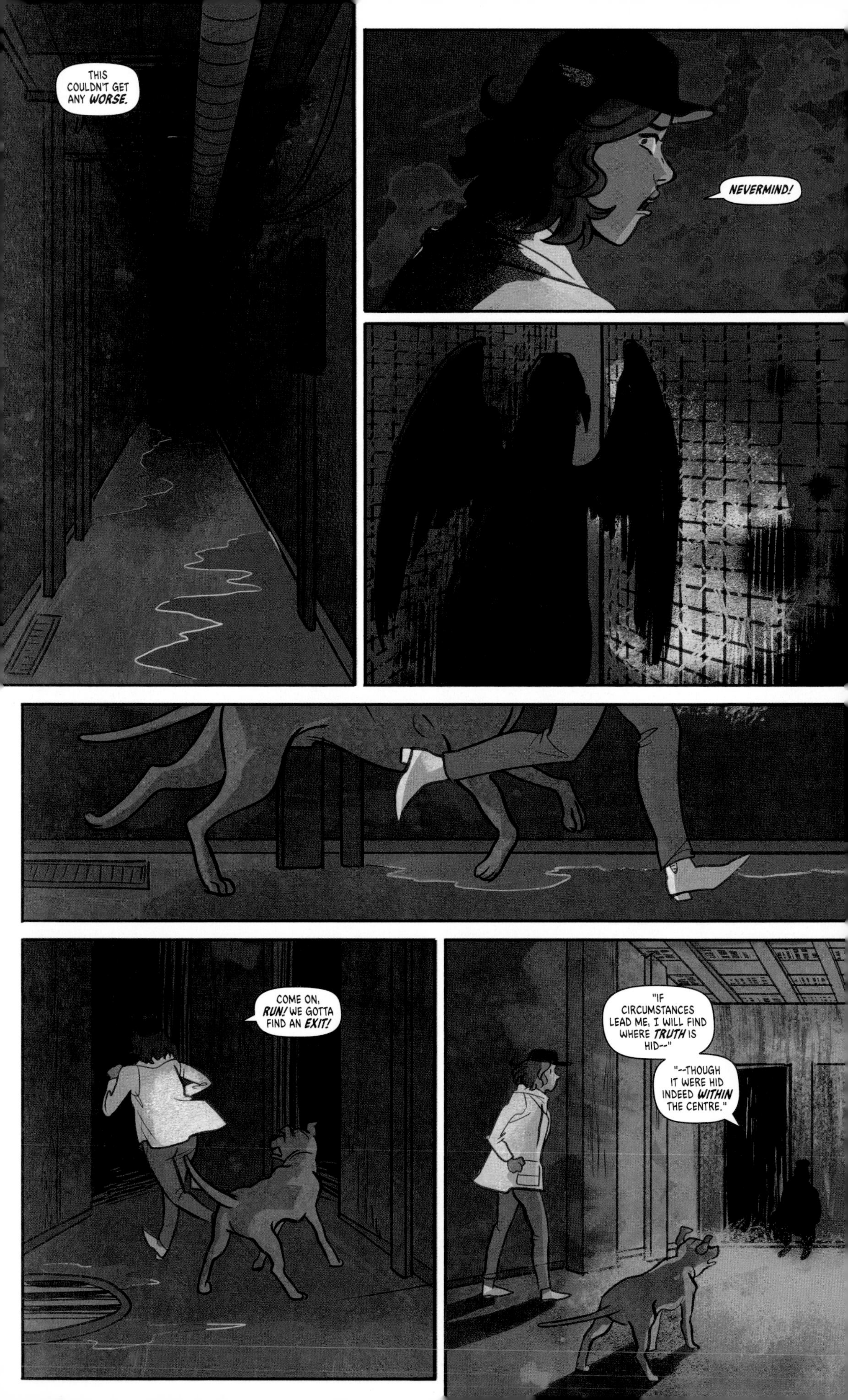
THIS COULDN'T GET ANY WORSE.
NEVERMIND!
COME ON, RUN! WE GOTTA FIND AN EXIT!
"IF CIRCUMSTANCES LEAD ME, I WILL FIND WHERE TRUTH IS HID--"
"--THOUGH IT WERE HID INDEED WITHIN THE CENTRE."

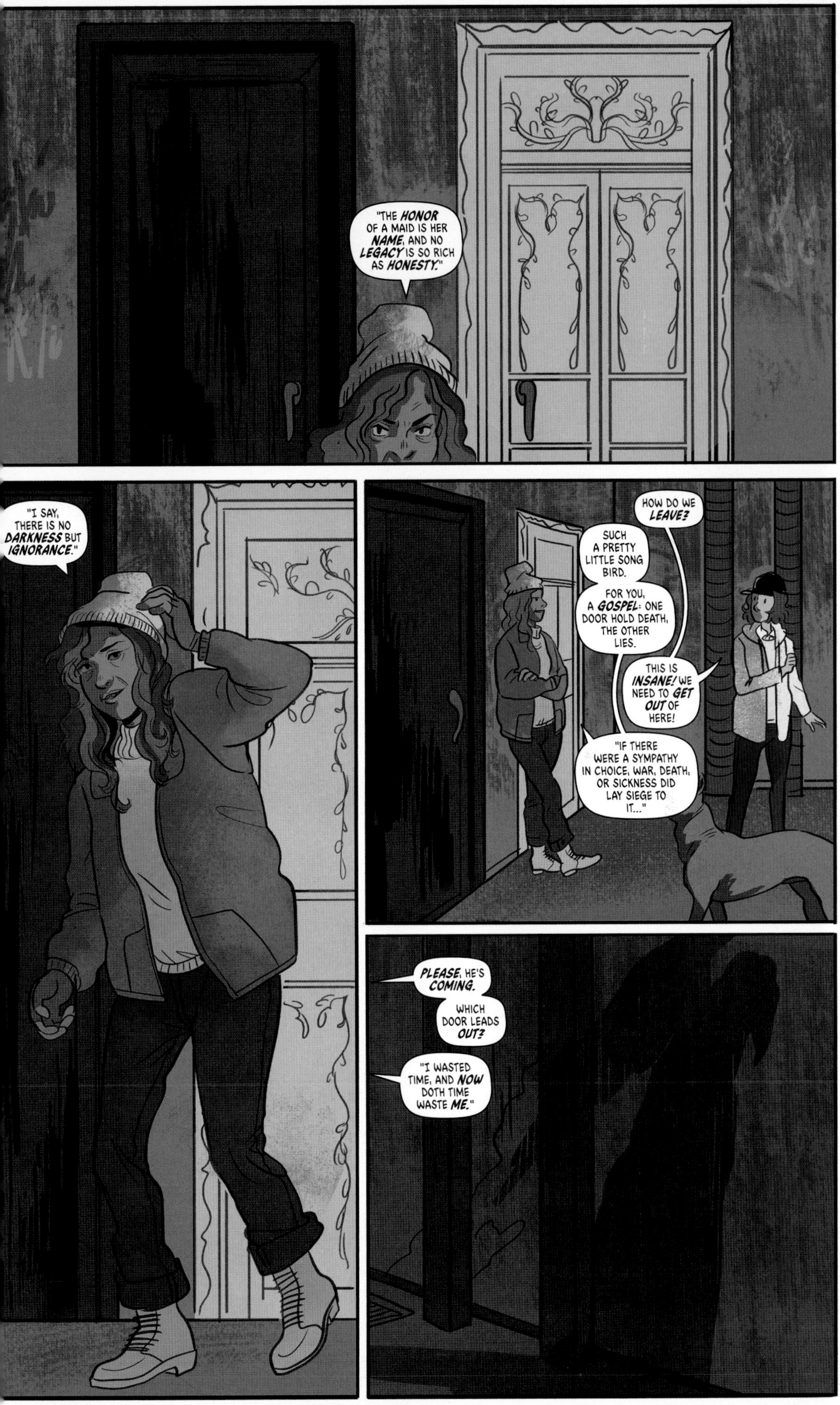
"THE HONOR OF A MAID IS HER NAME, AND NO LEGACY IS SO RICH AS HONESTY."
"I SAY, THERE IS NO DARKNESS BUT IGNORANCE."
HOW DO WE LEAVE?
SUCH A PRETTY LITTLE SONG BIRD.
FOR YOU, A GOSPEL: ONE DOOR HOLD DEATH, THE OTHER LIES.
THIS IS INSANE! WE NEED TO GET OUT OF HERE!
"IF THERE WERE A SYMPATHY IN CHOICE, WAR, DEATH, OR SICKNESS DID LAY SIEGE TO IT..."
PLEASE, HE'S COMING.
WHICH DOOR LEADS OUT?
"I WASTED TIME, AND NOW DOTH TIME WASTE ME."

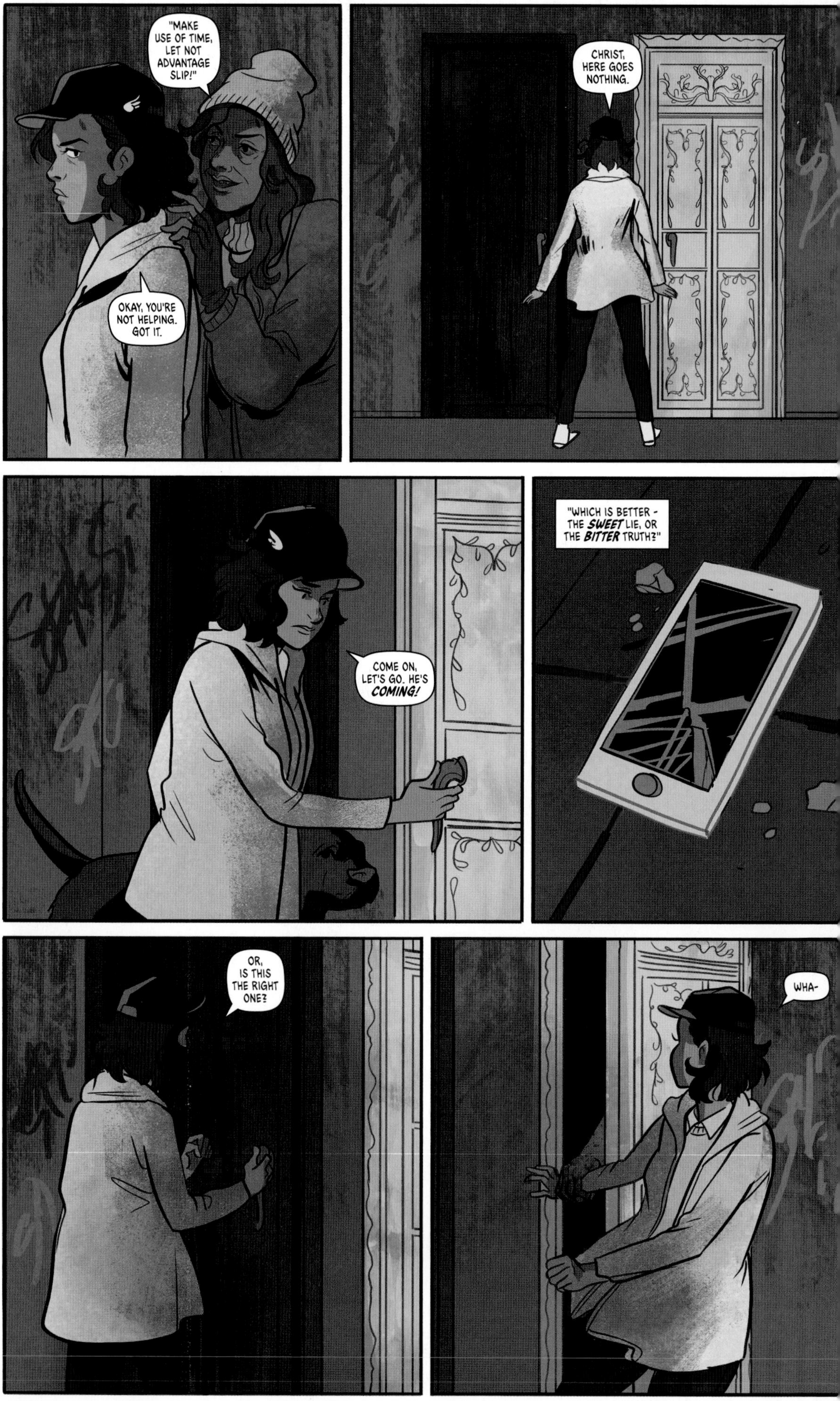
"MAKE USE OF TIME, LET NOT ADVANTAGE SLIP!"
OKAY, YOU'RE NOT HELPING. GOT IT.
CHRIST, HERE GOES NOTHING.
COME ON, LET'S GO. HE'S **COMING!**
"WHICH IS BETTER - THE **SWEET** LIE, OR THE **BITTER** TRUTH?"
OR, IS THIS THE RIGHT ONE?
WHA-

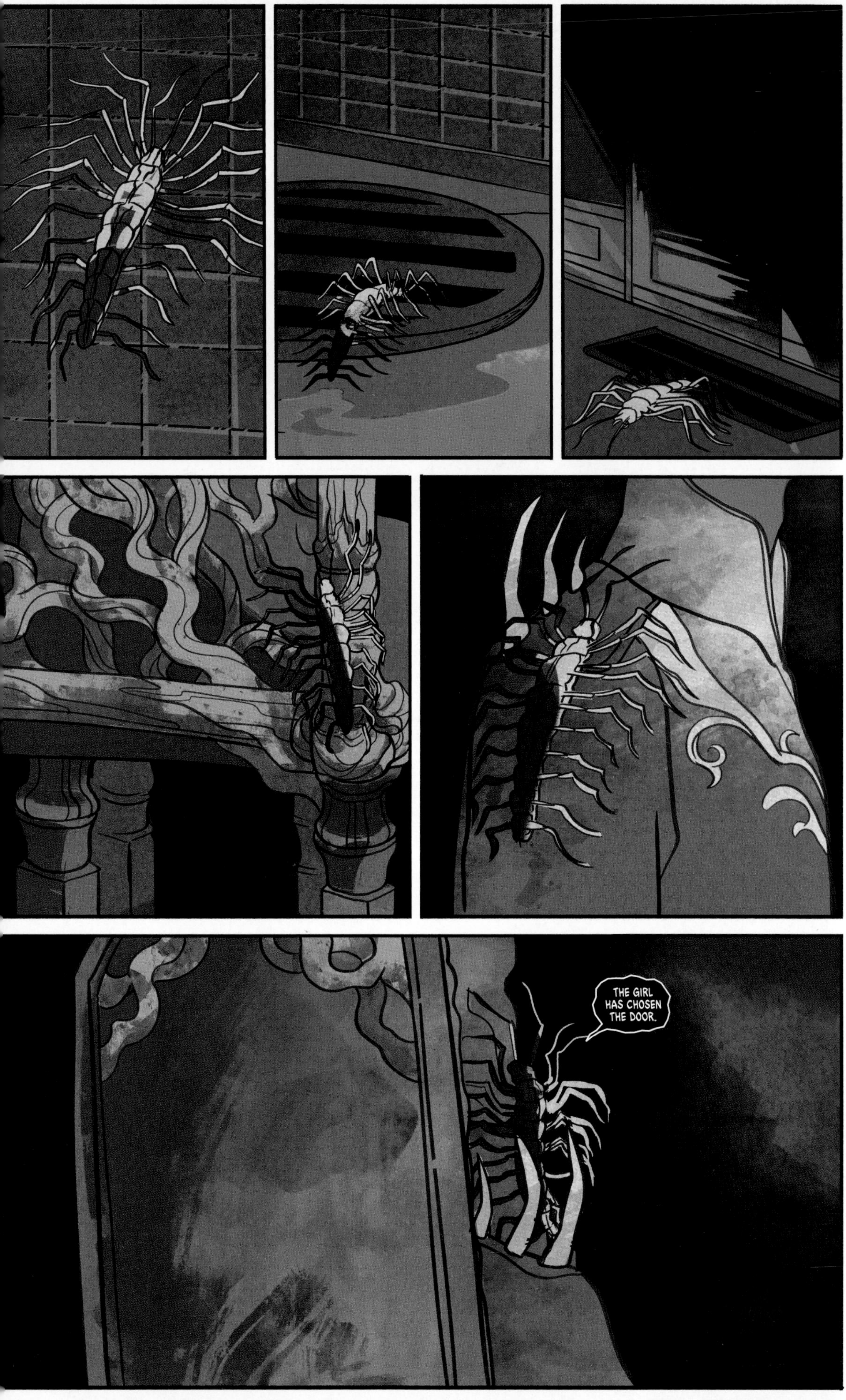
THE GIRL HAS CHOSEN THE DOOR.

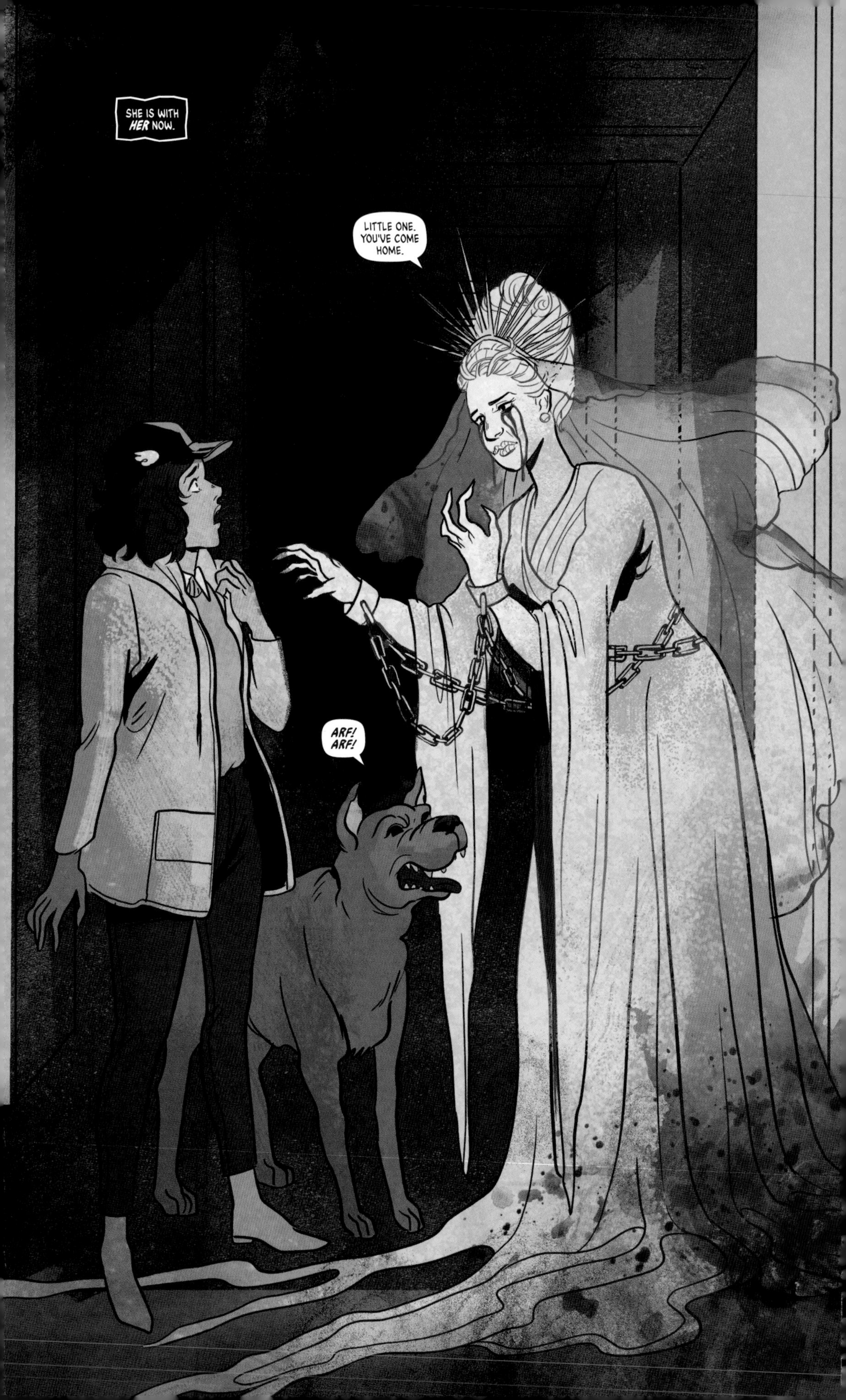
SHE IS WITH *HER* NOW.
LITTLE ONE. YOU'VE COME HOME.
ARF! ARF!

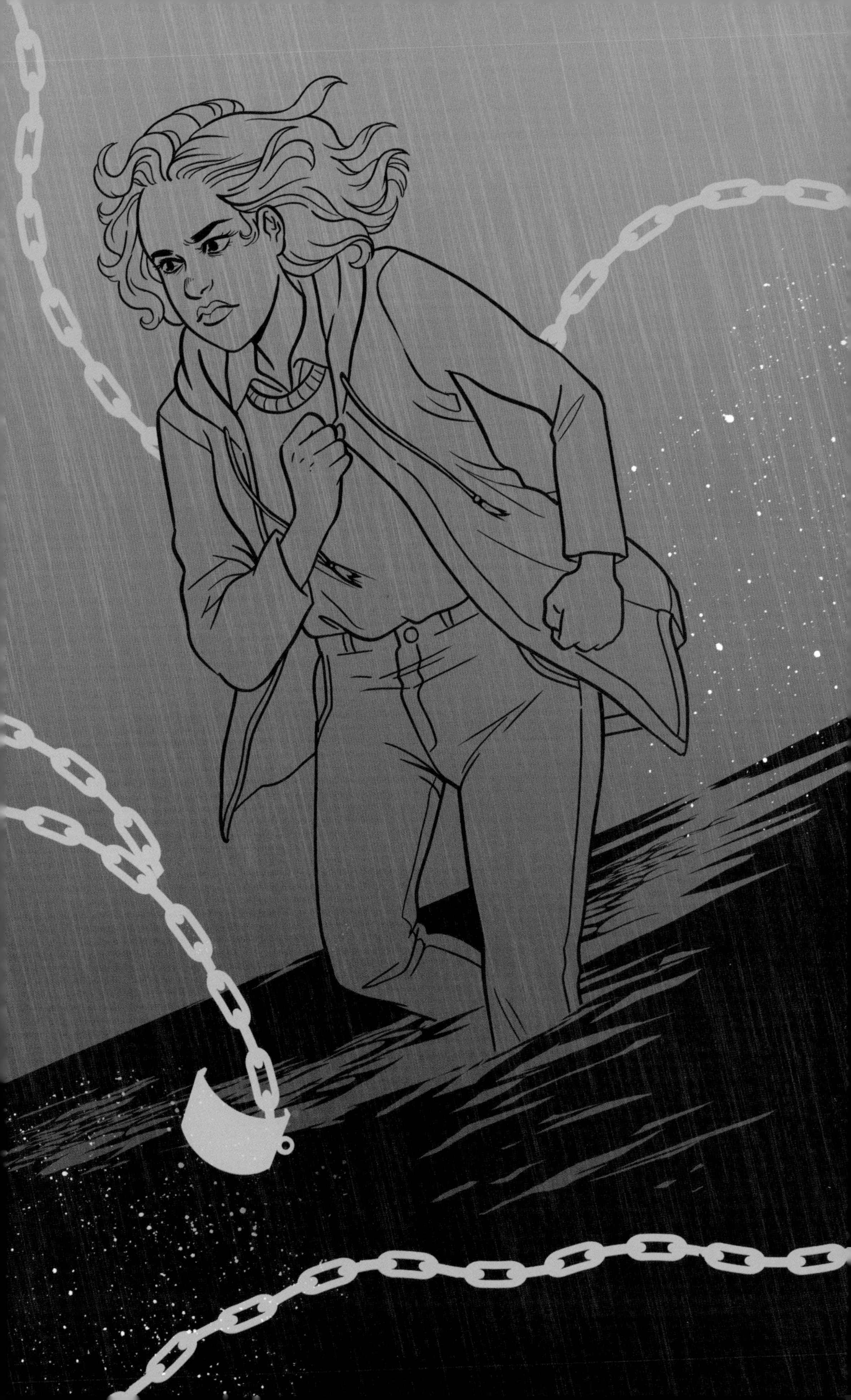

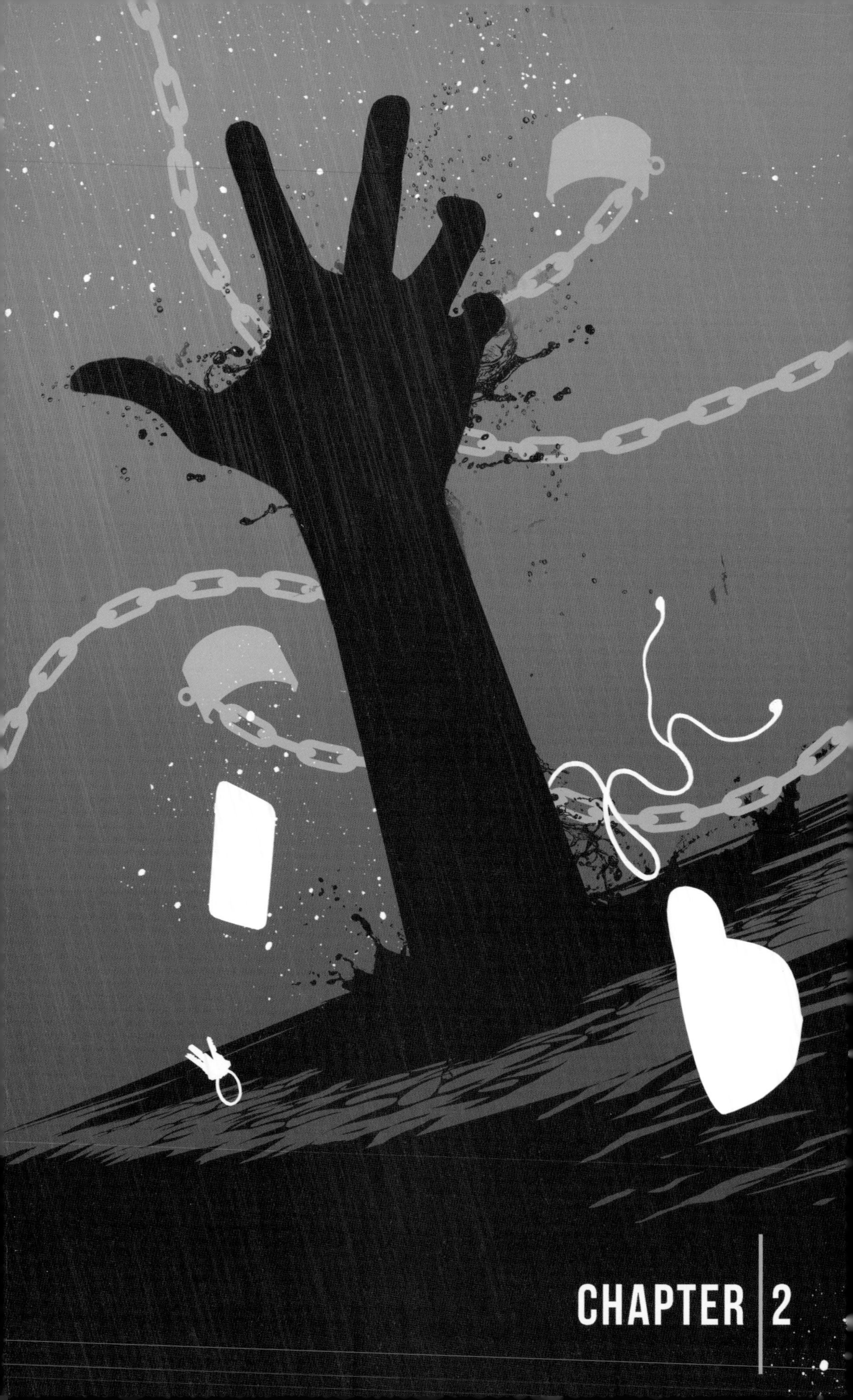

CHAPTER 2

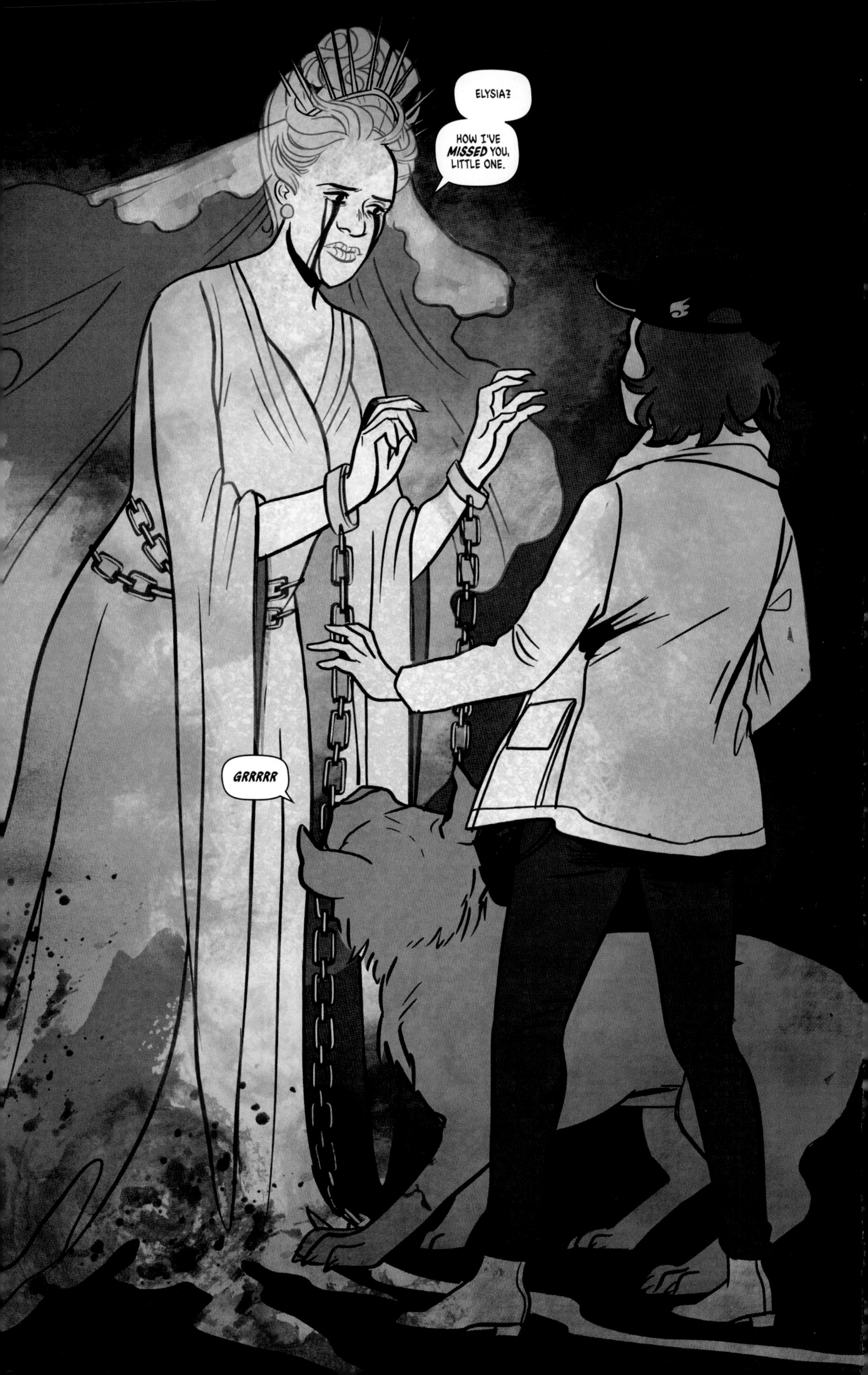
ELYSIA?
HOW I'VE MISSED YOU, LITTLE ONE.
GRRRRR

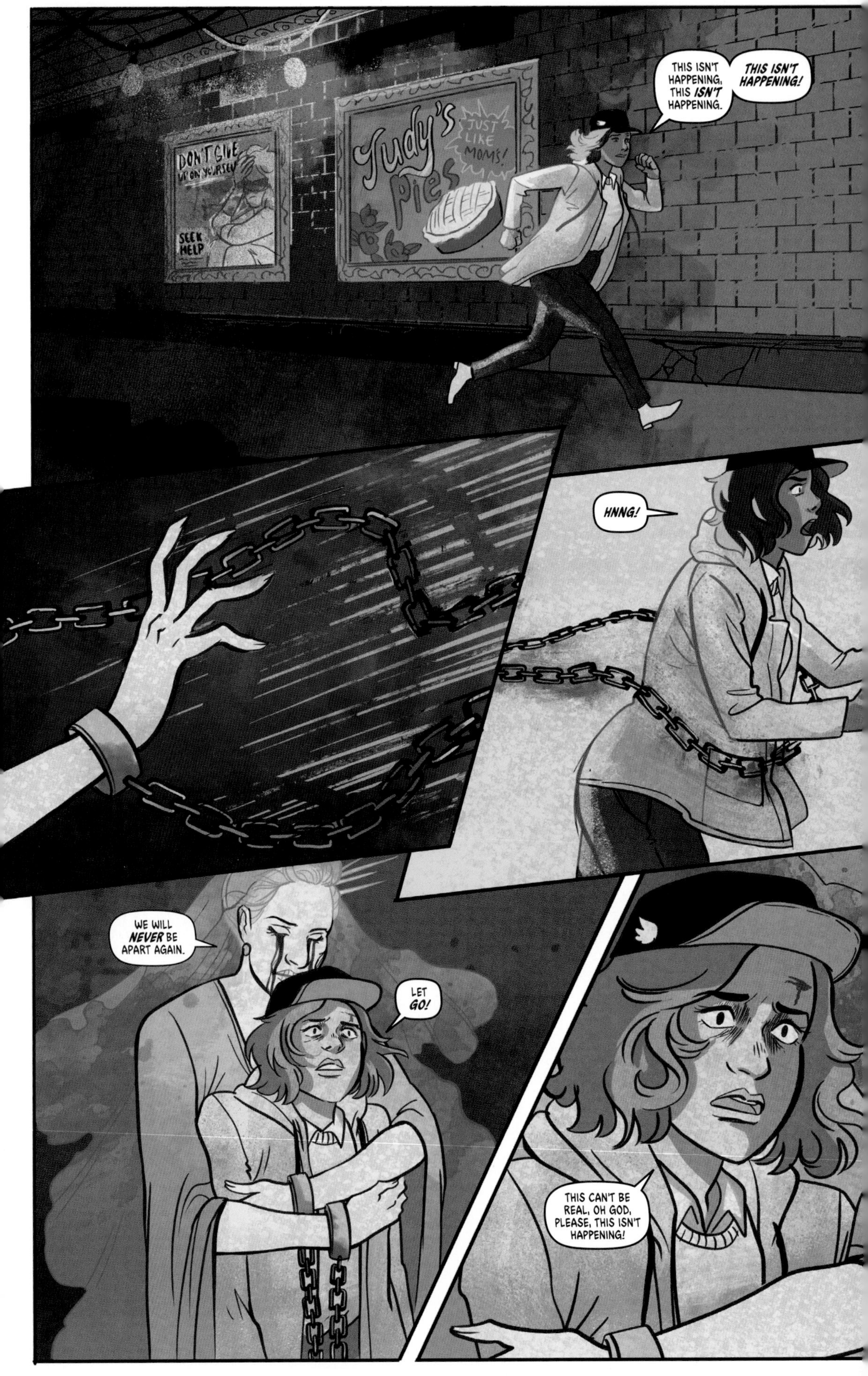

DON'T GIVE UP ON YOURSELF
SEEK HELP
Judy's pies
JUST LIKE MOM'S!
THIS ISN'T HAPPENING, THIS *ISN'T* HAPPENING.
THIS ISN'T HAPPENING!
HNNG!
WE WILL ***NEVER*** BE APART AGAIN.
LET ***GO!***
THIS CAN'T BE REAL, OH GOD, PLEASE, THIS ISN'T HAPPENING!

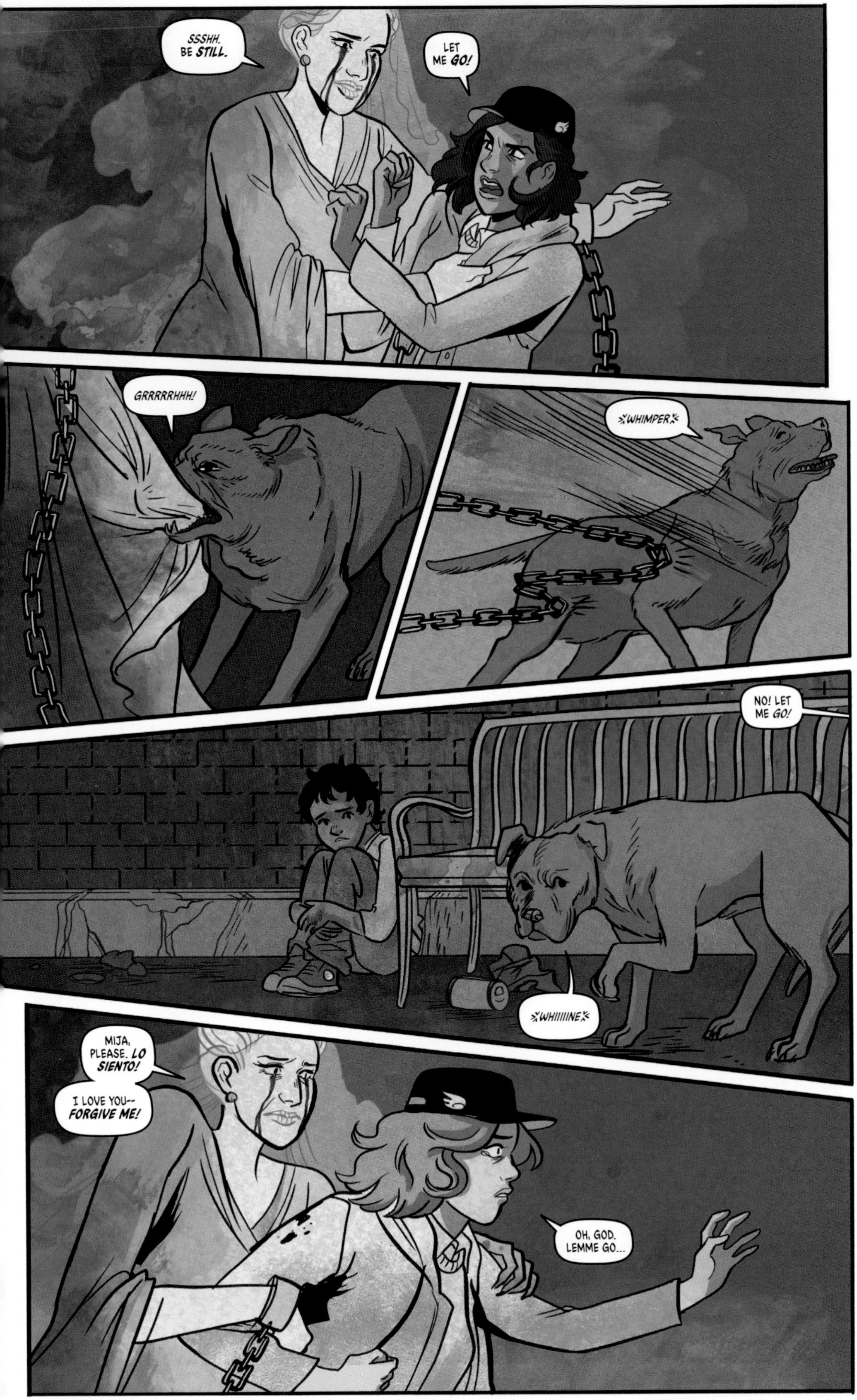
SSSHH. BE STILL.
LET ME GO!
GRRRRRHHH!
WHIMPER
NO! LET ME GO!
WHIIIIINE
MIJA, PLEASE. LO SIENTO!
I LOVE YOU-- FORGIVE ME!
OH, GOD. LEMME GO...

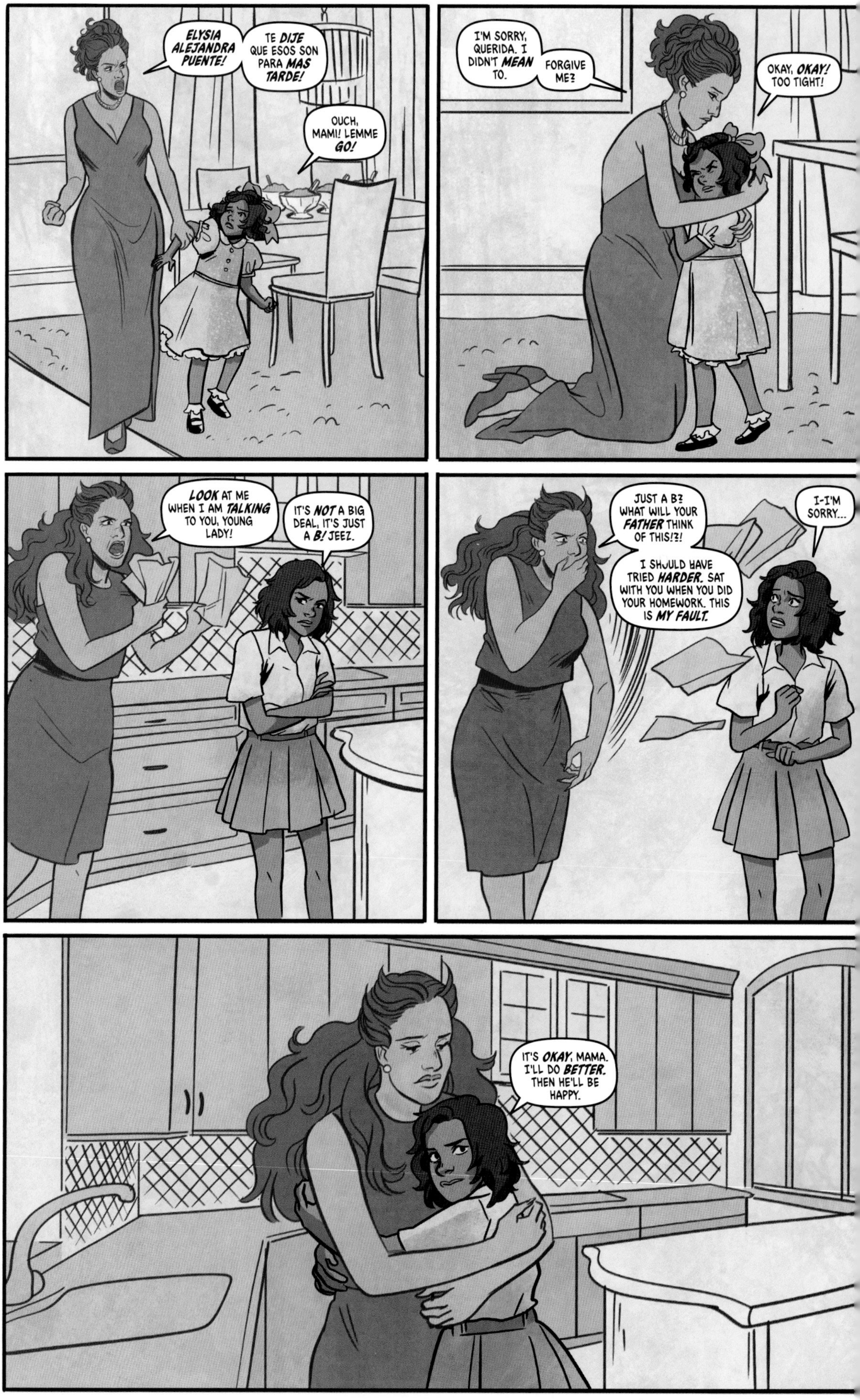
ELYSIA ALEJANDRA PUENTE!
TE DIJE QUE ESOS SON PARA MAS TARDE!
OUCH, MAMI! LEMME GO!
I'M SORRY, QUERIDA. I DIDN'T MEAN TO.
FORGIVE ME?
OKAY, OKAY! TOO TIGHT!
LOOK AT ME WHEN I AM TALKING TO YOU, YOUNG LADY!
IT'S NOT A BIG DEAL, IT'S JUST A B! JEEZ.
JUST A B? WHAT WILL YOUR FATHER THINK OF THIS!?!
I SHOULD HAVE TRIED HARDER. SAT WITH YOU WHEN YOU DID YOUR HOMEWORK. THIS IS MY FAULT.
I-I'M SORRY...
IT'S OKAY, MAMA. I'LL DO BETTER. THEN HE'LL BE HAPPY.

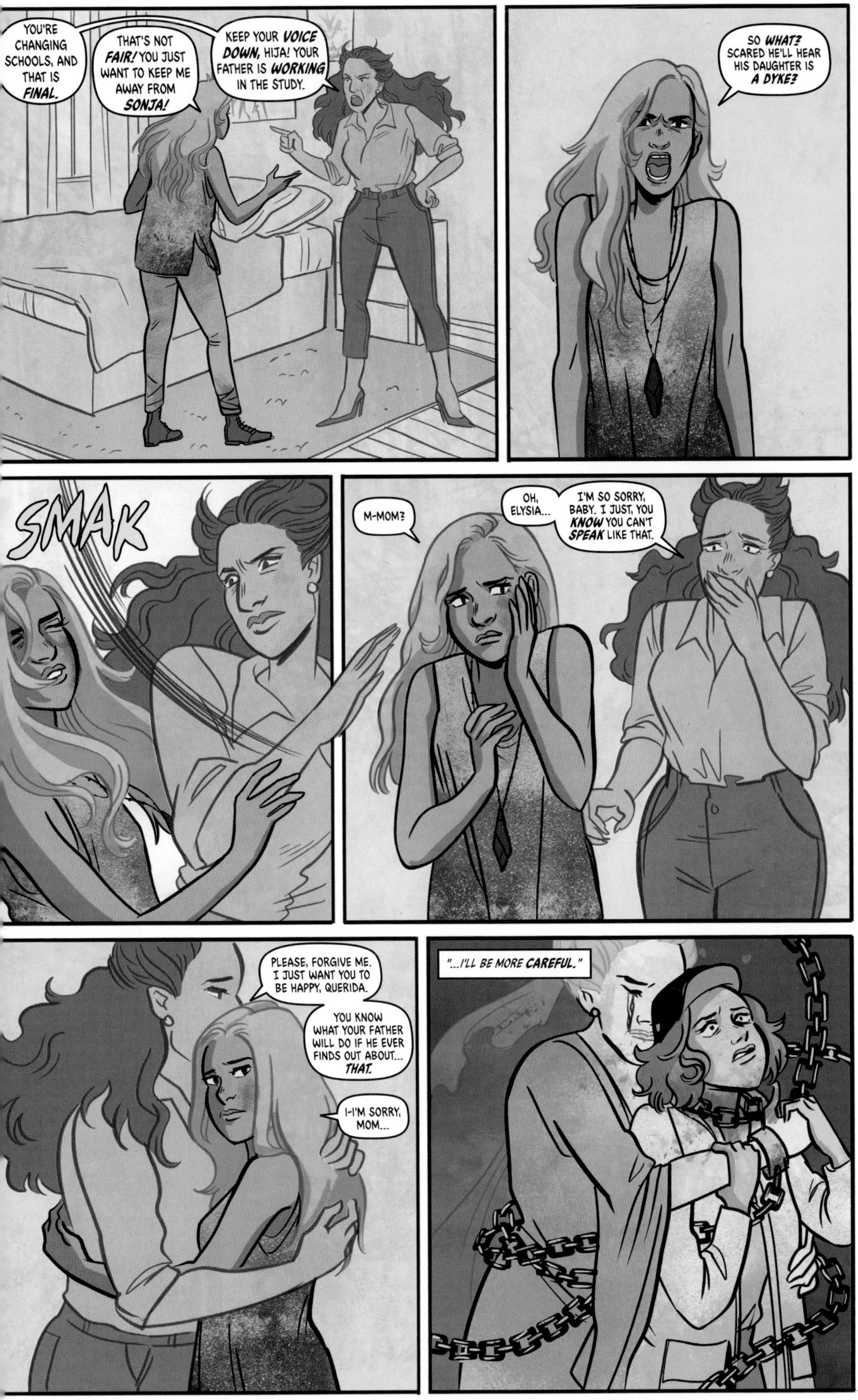
YOU'RE CHANGING SCHOOLS, AND THAT IS *FINAL.*
THAT'S NOT *FAIR!* YOU JUST WANT TO KEEP ME AWAY FROM *SONJA!*
KEEP YOUR *VOICE DOWN,* HIJA! YOUR FATHER IS *WORKING* IN THE STUDY.
SO *WHAT?* SCARED HE'LL HEAR HIS DAUGHTER IS *A DYKE?*
SMAK
M-MOM?
OH, ELYSIA...
I'M SO SORRY, BABY. I JUST, YOU *KNOW* YOU CAN'T *SPEAK* LIKE THAT.
PLEASE, FORGIVE ME. I JUST WANT YOU TO BE HAPPY, QUERIDA.
YOU KNOW WHAT YOUR FATHER WILL DO IF HE EVER FINDS OUT ABOUT... *THAT.*
I-I'M SORRY, MOM...
"...I'LL BE MORE *CAREFUL.*"

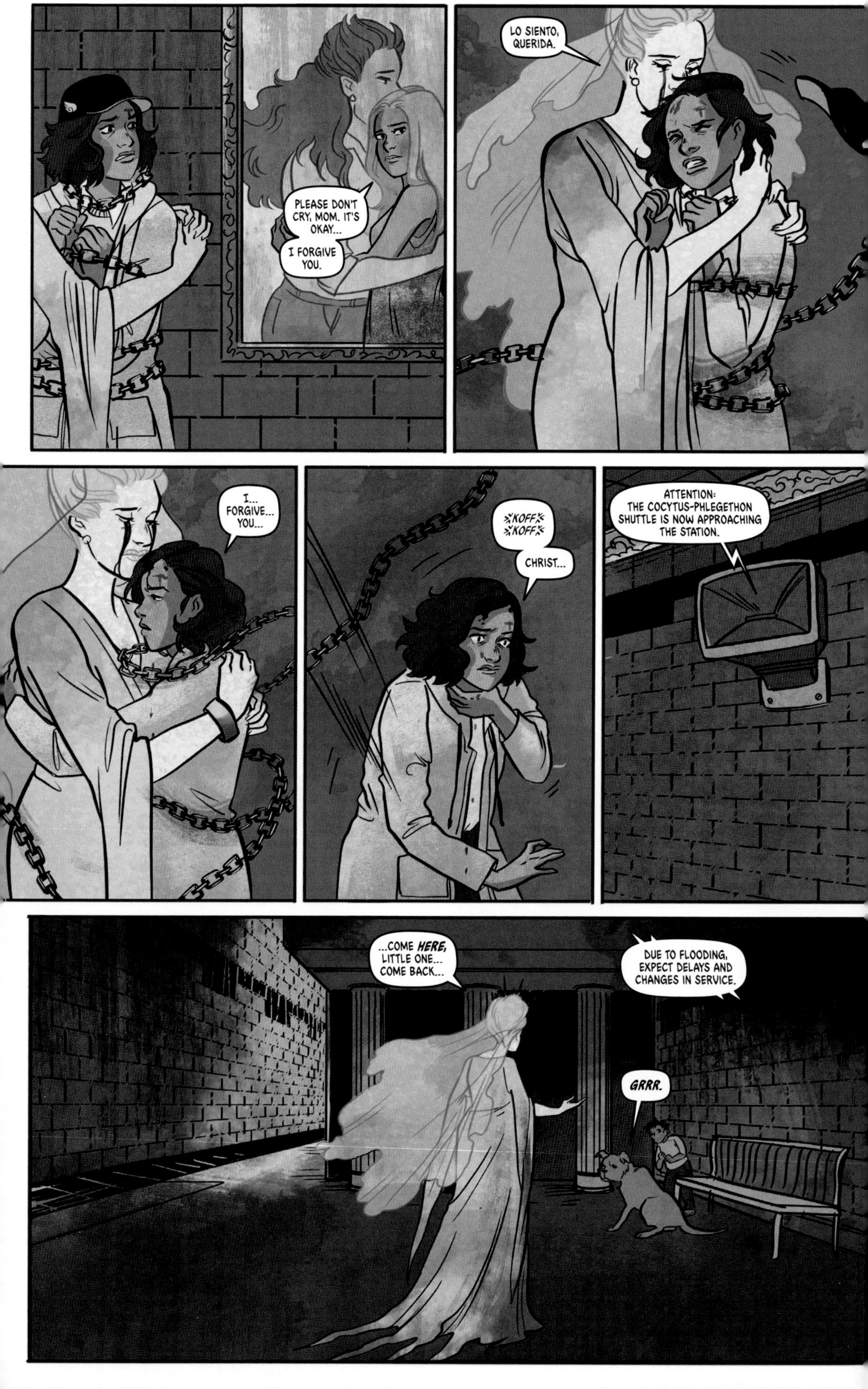
PLEASE DON'T CRY, MOM. IT'S OKAY...
I FORGIVE YOU.
LO SIENTO, QUERIDA.
I... FORGIVE... YOU...
KOFF KOFF
CHRIST...
ATTENTION: THE COCYTUS-PHLEGETHON SHUTTLE IS NOW APPROACHING THE STATION.
...COME HERE, LITTLE ONE... COME BACK...
DUE TO FLOODING, EXPECT DELAYS AND CHANGES IN SERVICE.
GRRR.

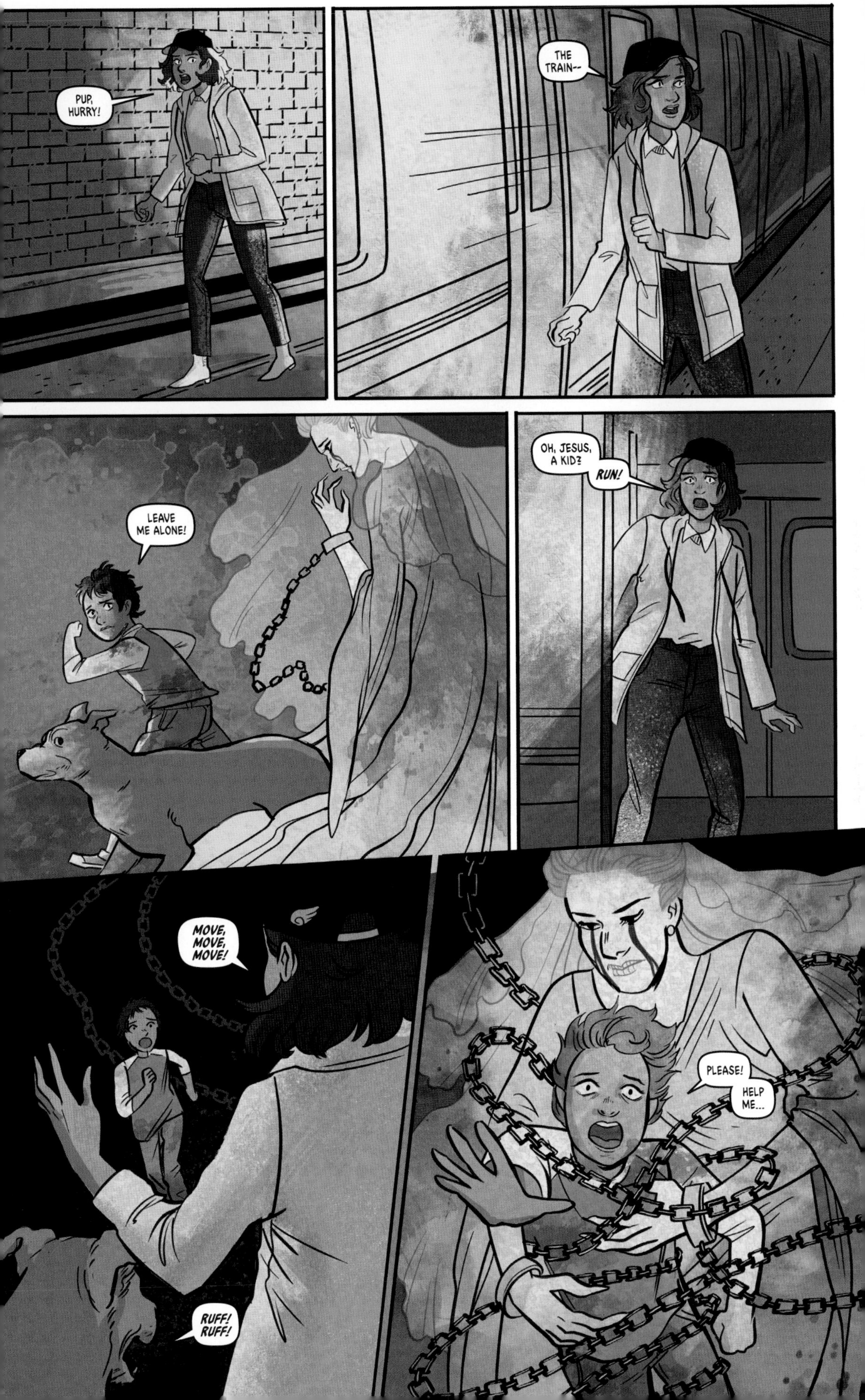
PUP, HURRY!
THE TRAIN--
LEAVE ME ALONE!
OH, JESUS, A KID?
RUN!
MOVE, MOVE, MOVE!
RUFF! RUFF!
PLEASE!
HELP ME...

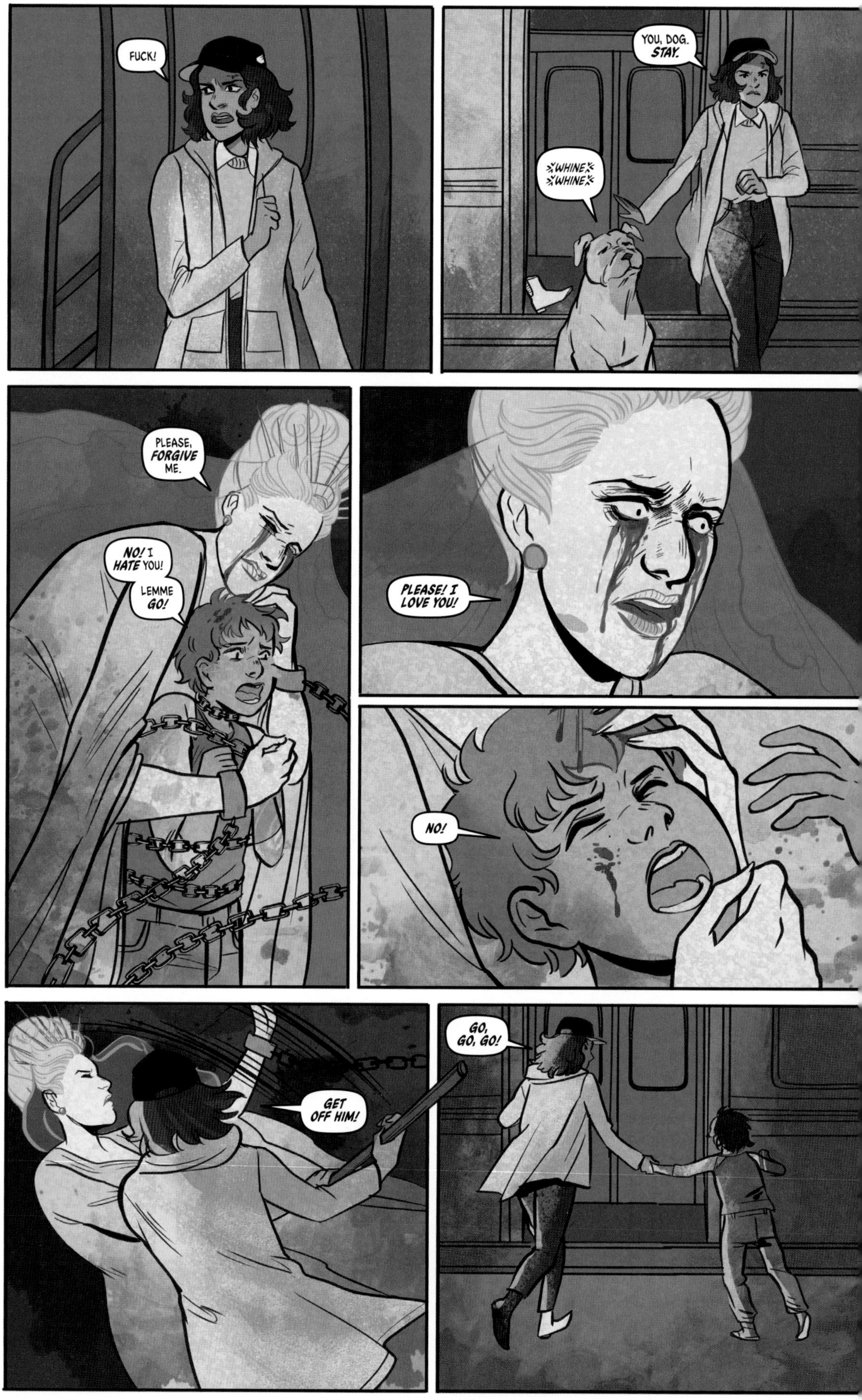
FUCK!
YOU, DOG. STAY.
WHINE WHINE
PLEASE, FORGIVE ME.
NO! I HATE YOU!
LEMME GO!
PLEASE! I LOVE YOU!
NO!
GET OFF HIM!
GO, GO, GO!

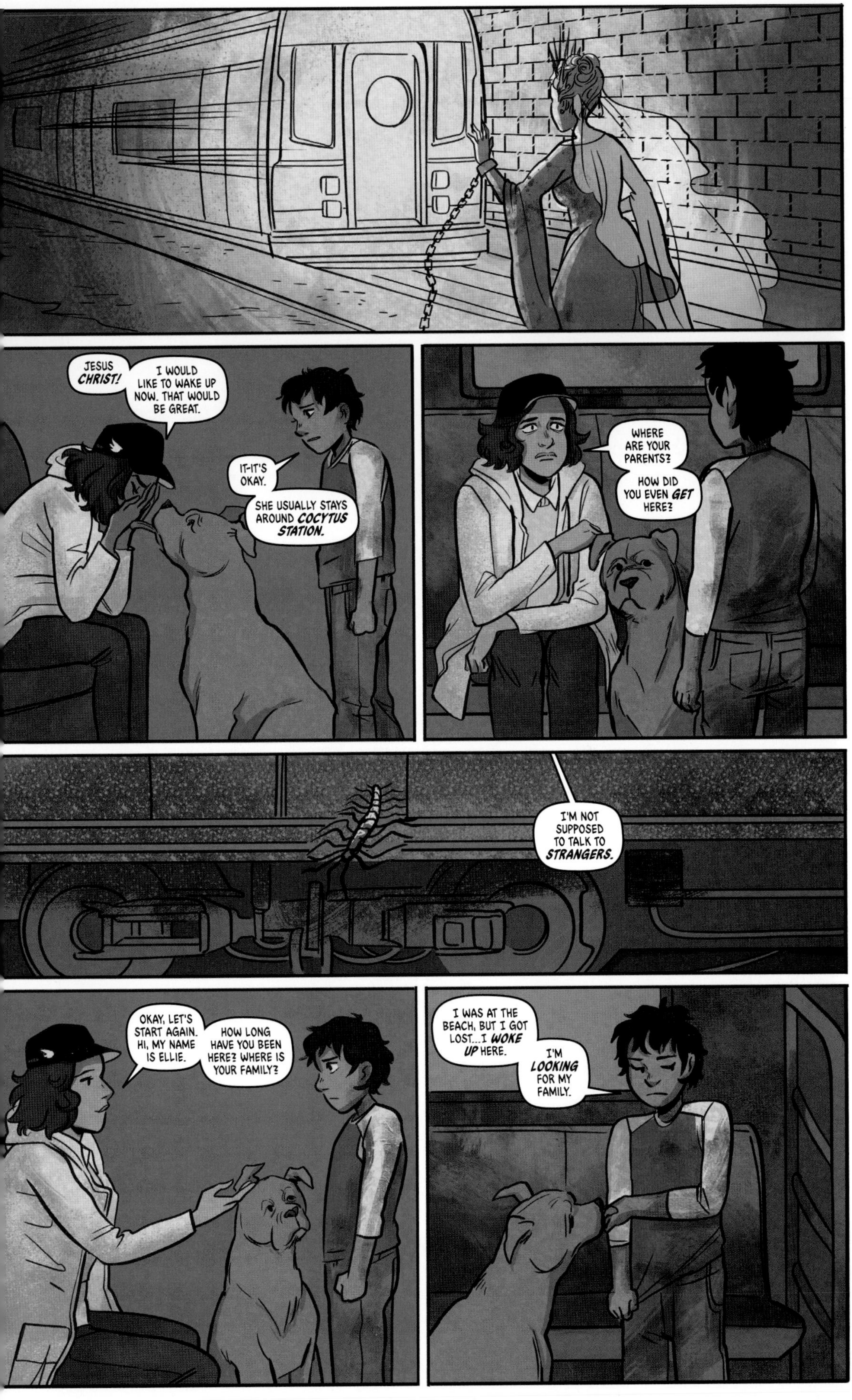
JESUS CHRIST!
I WOULD LIKE TO WAKE UP NOW. THAT WOULD BE GREAT.
IT-IT'S OKAY.
SHE USUALLY STAYS AROUND COCYTUS STATION.
WHERE ARE YOUR PARENTS?
HOW DID YOU EVEN GET HERE?
I'M NOT SUPPOSED TO TALK TO STRANGERS.
OKAY, LET'S START AGAIN. HI, MY NAME IS ELLIE.
HOW LONG HAVE YOU BEEN HERE? WHERE IS YOUR FAMILY?
I WAS AT THE BEACH, BUT I GOT LOST...I WOKE UP HERE.
I'M LOOKING FOR MY FAMILY.

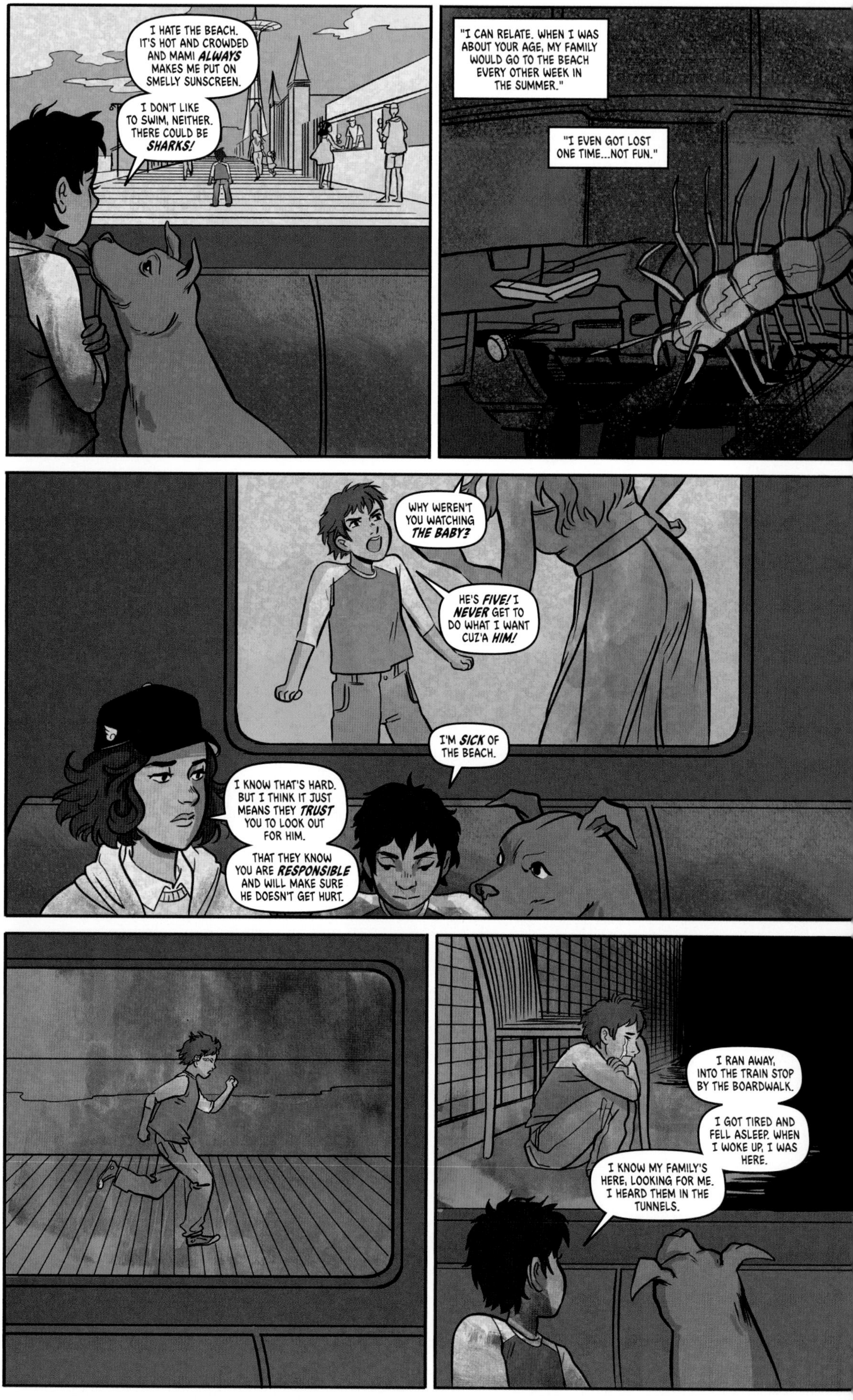
I HATE THE BEACH. IT'S HOT AND CROWDED AND MAMI ALWAYS MAKES ME PUT ON SMELLY SUNSCREEN.
I DON'T LIKE TO SWIM, NEITHER. THERE COULD BE SHARKS!
"I CAN RELATE. WHEN I WAS ABOUT YOUR AGE, MY FAMILY WOULD GO TO THE BEACH EVERY OTHER WEEK IN THE SUMMER."
"I EVEN GOT LOST ONE TIME...NOT FUN."
WHY WEREN'T YOU WATCHING THE BABY?
HE'S FIVE! I NEVER GET TO DO WHAT I WANT CUZ'A HIM!
I'M SICK OF THE BEACH.
I KNOW THAT'S HARD. BUT I THINK IT JUST MEANS THEY TRUST YOU TO LOOK OUT FOR HIM.
THAT THEY KNOW YOU ARE RESPONSIBLE AND WILL MAKE SURE HE DOESN'T GET HURT.
I RAN AWAY, INTO THE TRAIN STOP BY THE BOARDWALK.
I GOT TIRED AND FELL ASLEEP. WHEN I WOKE UP, I WAS HERE.
I KNOW MY FAMILY'S HERE, LOOKING FOR ME. I HEARD THEM IN THE TUNNELS.

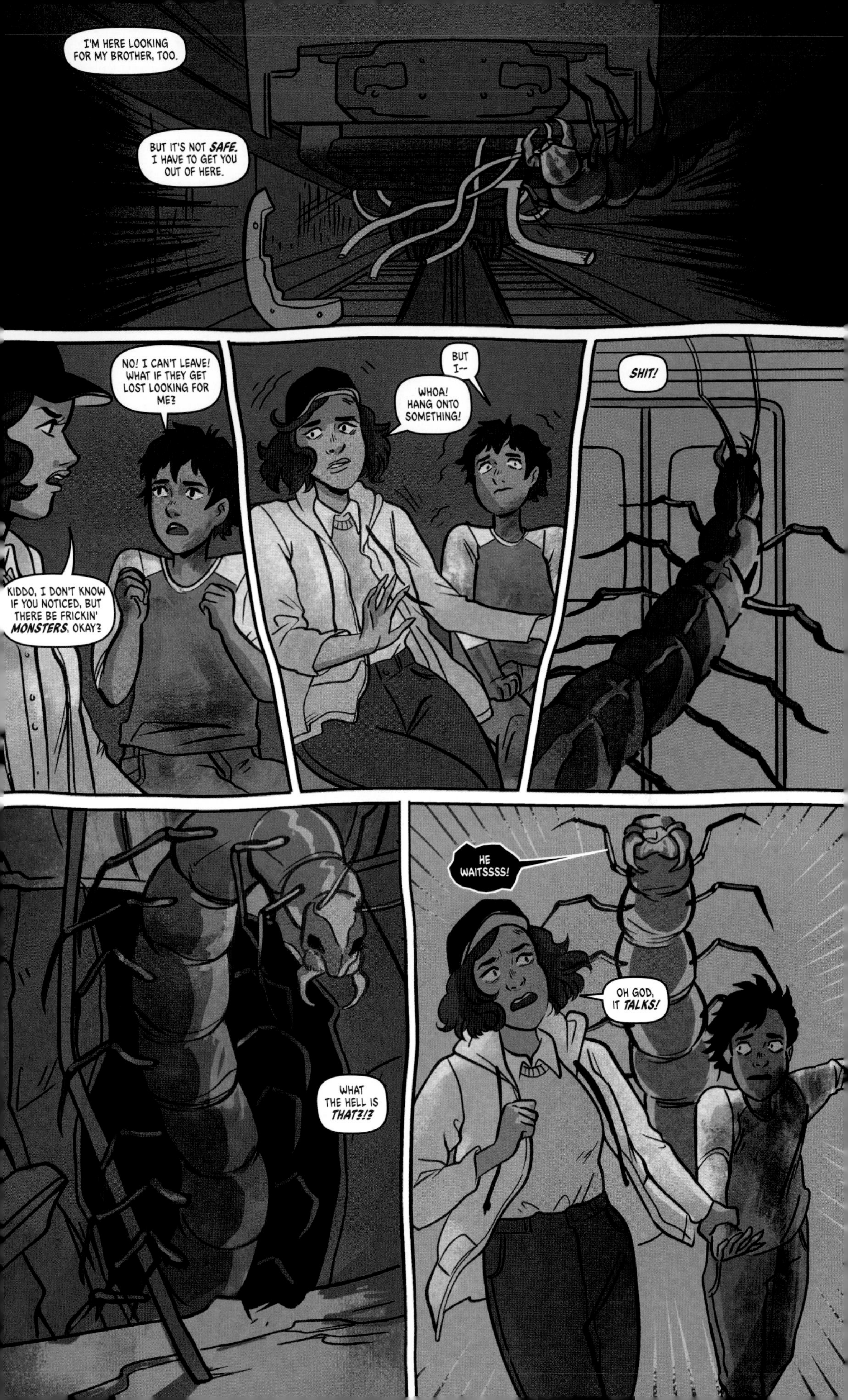
I'M HERE LOOKING FOR MY BROTHER, TOO.
BUT IT'S NOT SAFE. I HAVE TO GET YOU OUT OF HERE.
NO! I CAN'T LEAVE! WHAT IF THEY GET LOST LOOKING FOR ME?
KIDDO, I DON'T KNOW IF YOU NOTICED, BUT THERE BE FRICKIN' MONSTERS, OKAY?
BUT I--
WHOA! HANG ONTO SOMETHING!
SHIT!
WHAT THE HELL IS THAT?!?
HE WAITSSSS!
OH GOD, IT TALKS!

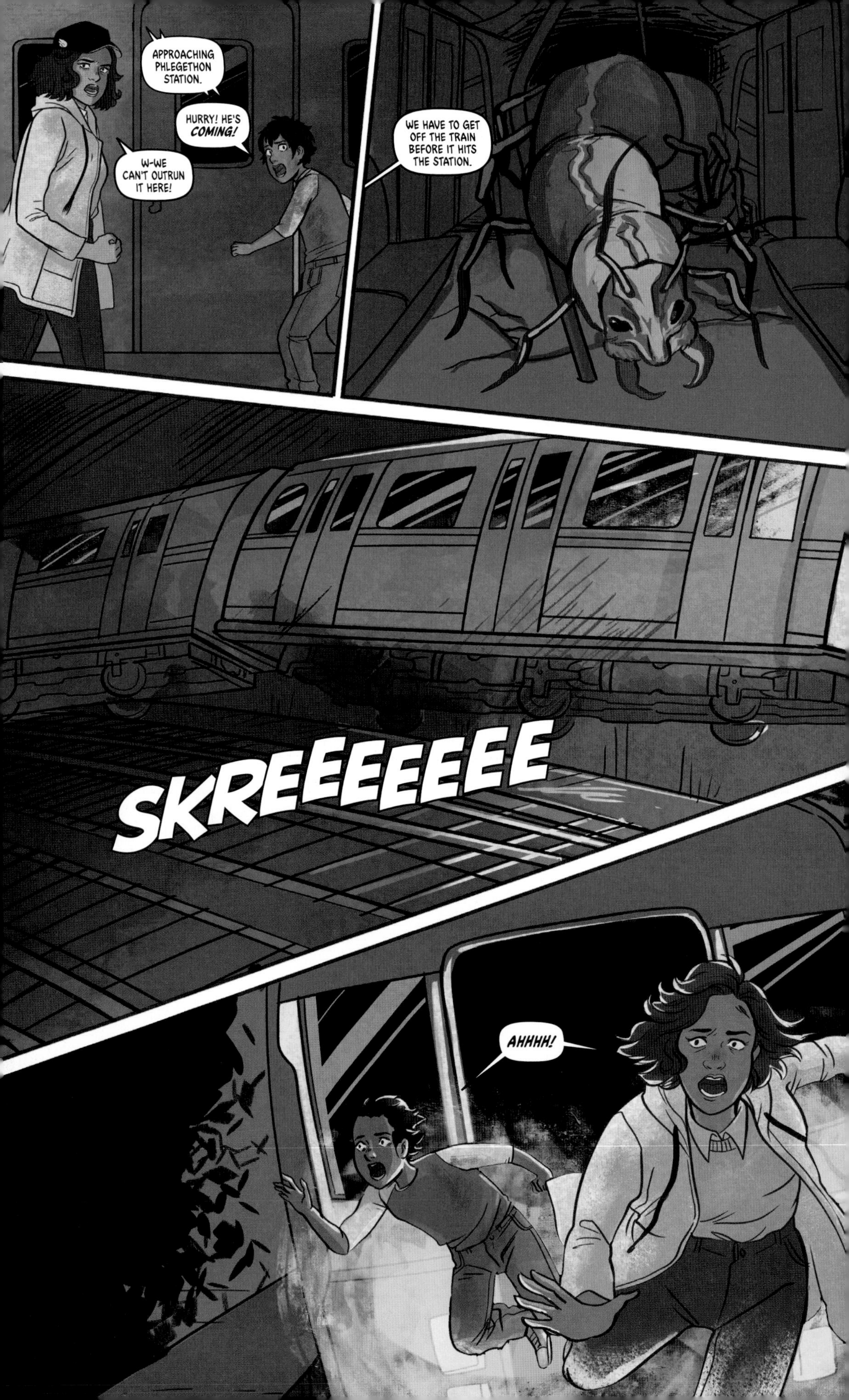
APPROACHING PHLEGETHON STATION.
HURRY! HE'S COMING!
W-WE CAN'T OUTRUN IT HERE!
WE HAVE TO GET OFF THE TRAIN BEFORE IT HITS THE STATION.
SKREEEEEEEE
AHHHH!

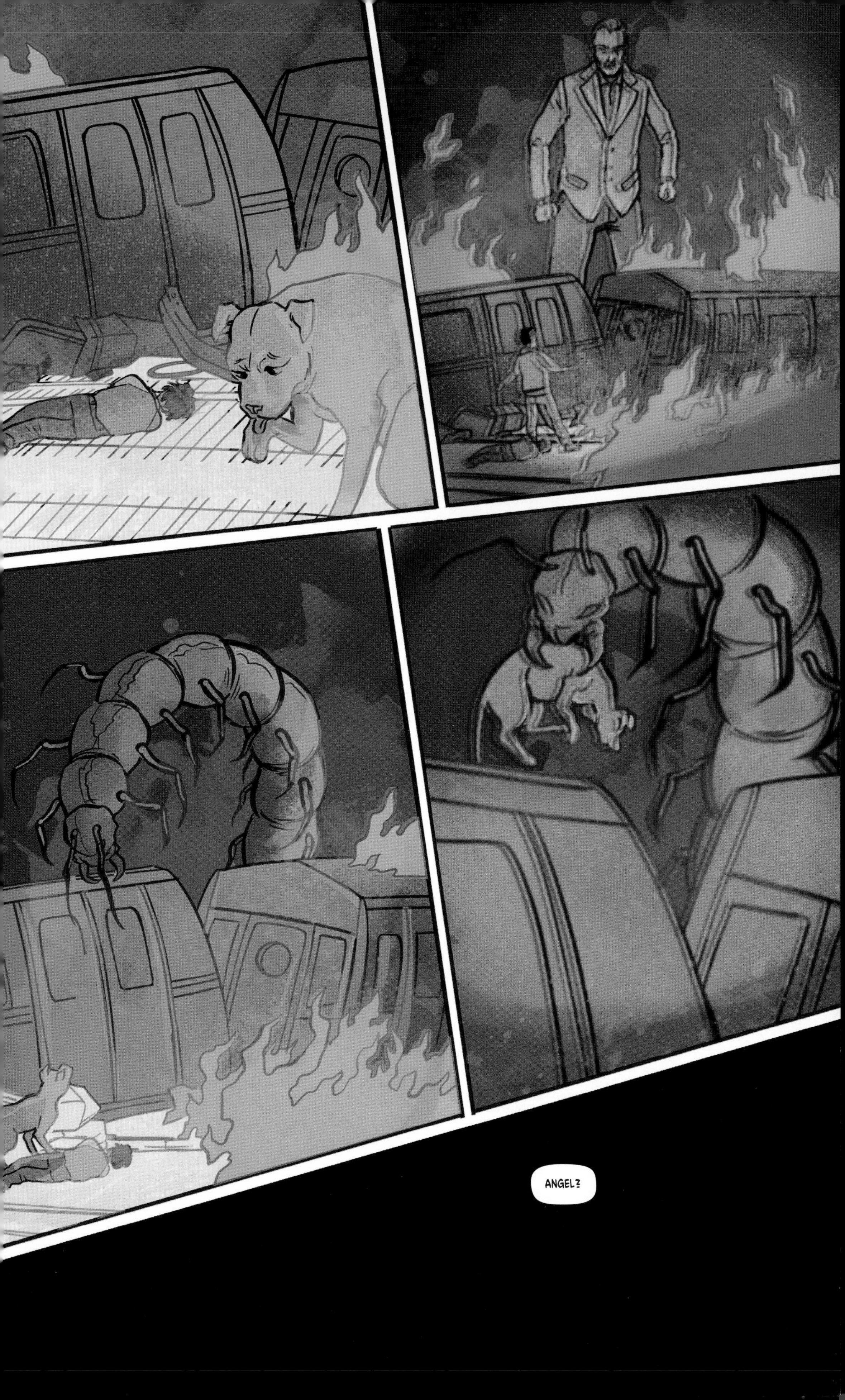
ANGEL?

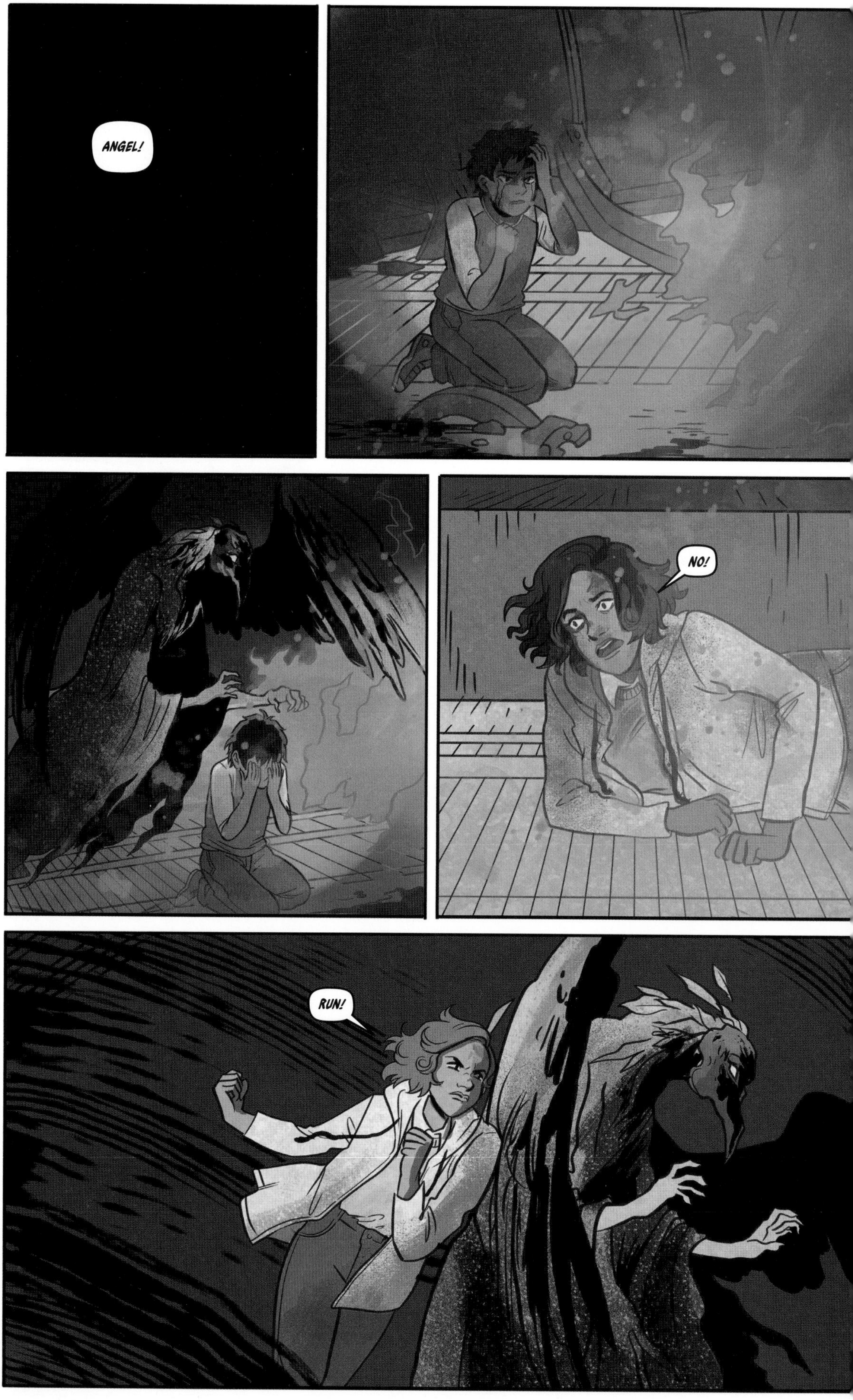
ANGEL!
NO!
RUN!

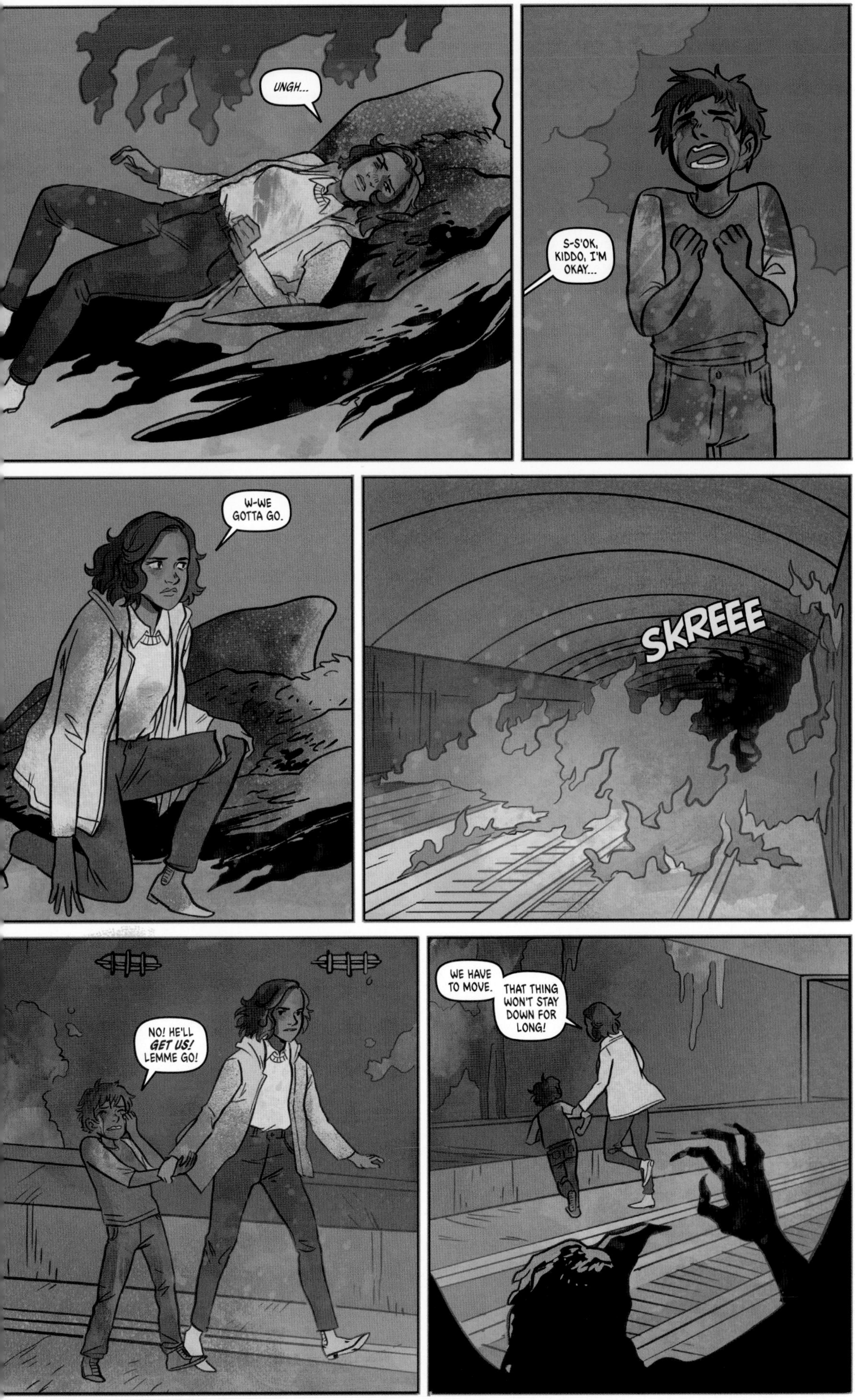
UNGH...
S-S'OK, KIDDO, I'M OKAY...
W-WE GOTTA GO.
SKREEE
NO! HE'LL GET US! LEMME GO!
WE HAVE TO MOVE.
THAT THING WON'T STAY DOWN FOR LONG!

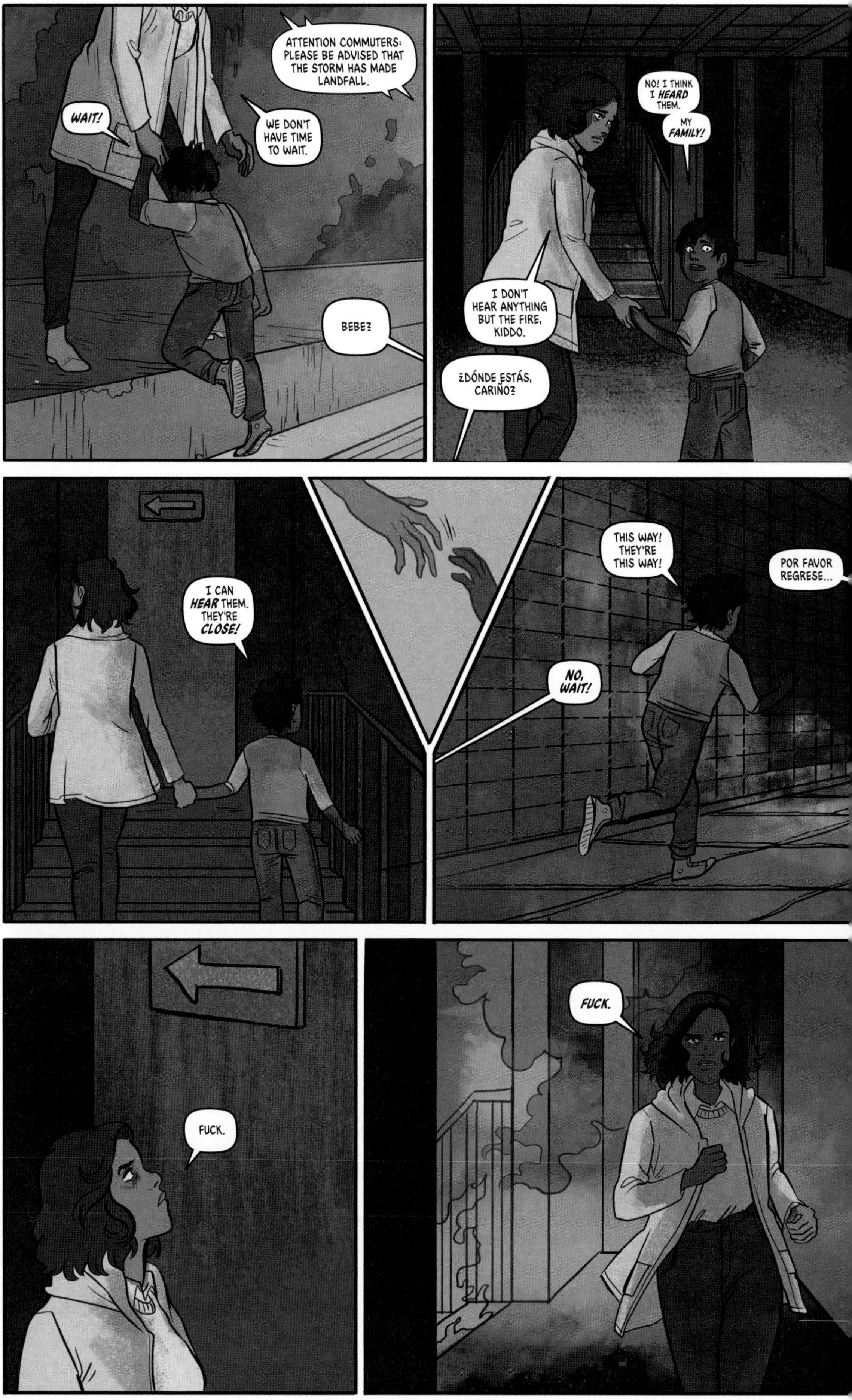
ATTENTION COMMUTERS: PLEASE BE ADVISED THAT THE STORM HAS MADE LANDFALL.
WAIT!
WE DON'T HAVE TIME TO WAIT.
BEBE?
NO! I THINK I HEARD THEM.
MY FAMILY!
I DON'T HEAR ANYTHING BUT THE FIRE, KIDDO.
¿DÓNDE ESTÁS, CARIÑO?
I CAN HEAR THEM. THEY'RE CLOSE!
THIS WAY! THEY'RE THIS WAY!
POR FAVOR REGRESE...
NO, WAIT!
FUCK.
FUCK.

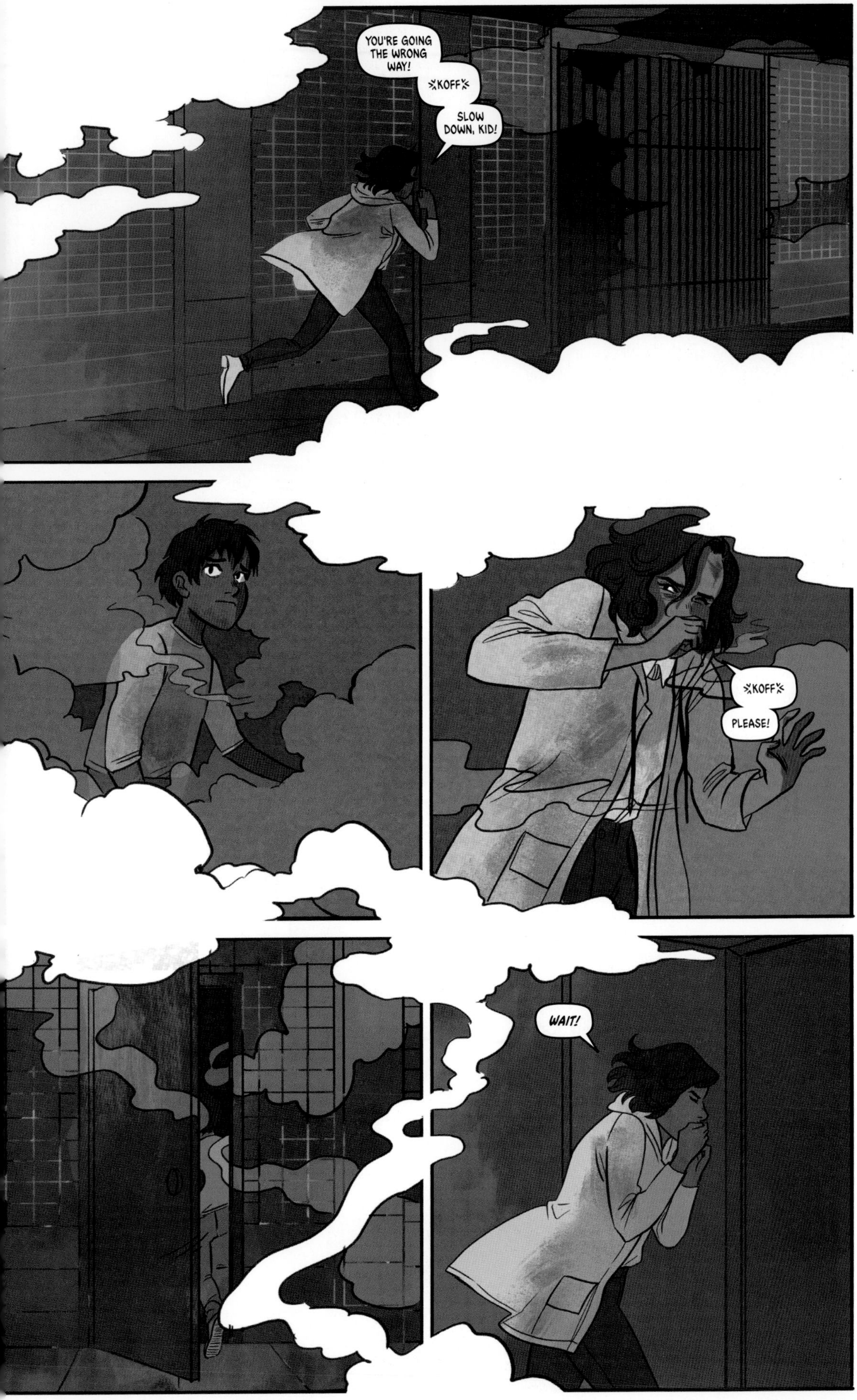
YOU'RE GOING THE WRONG WAY!
KOFF
SLOW DOWN, KID!
KOFF
PLEASE!
WAIT!

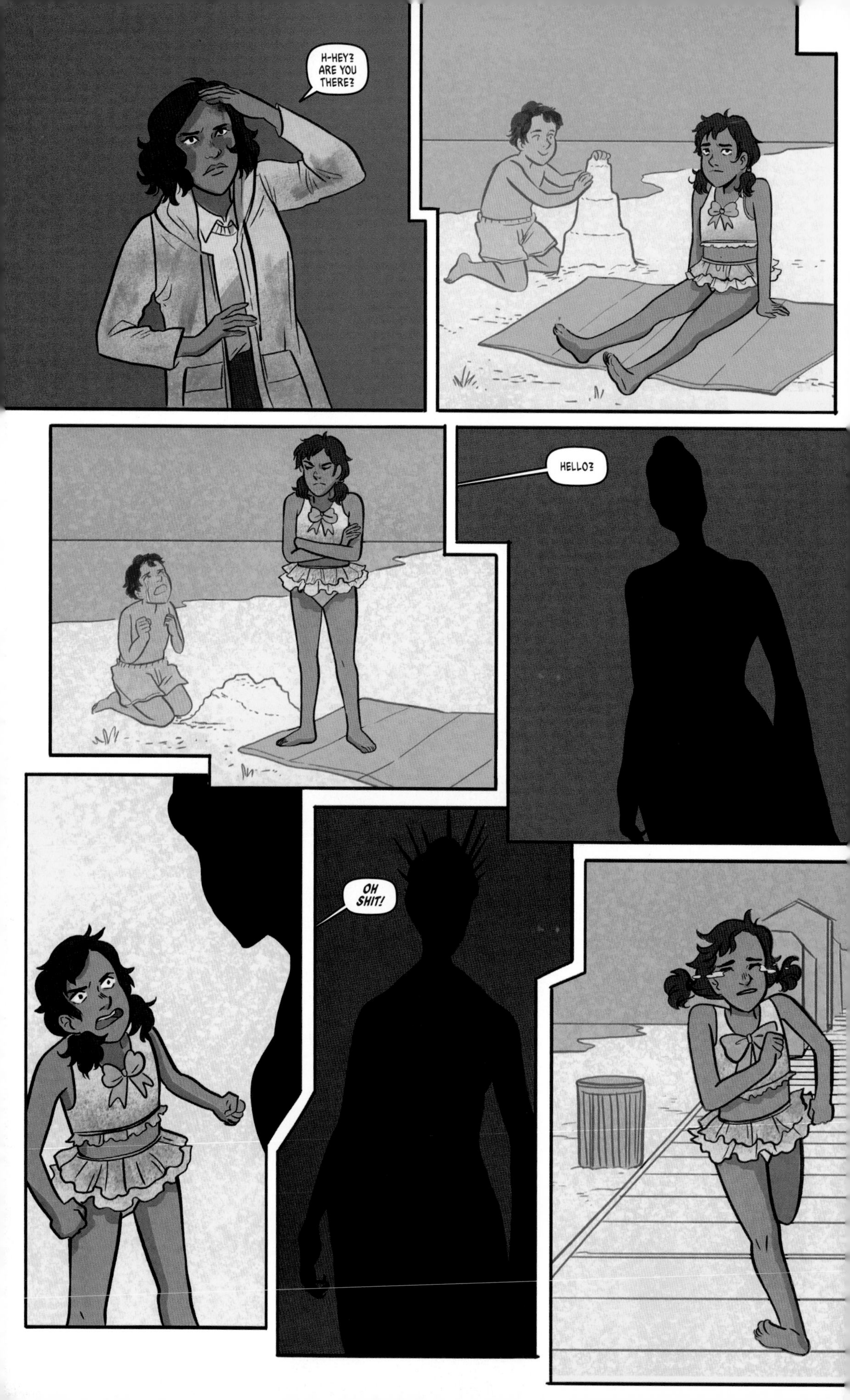
H-HEY?
ARE YOU
THERE?
HELLO?
OH
SHIT!

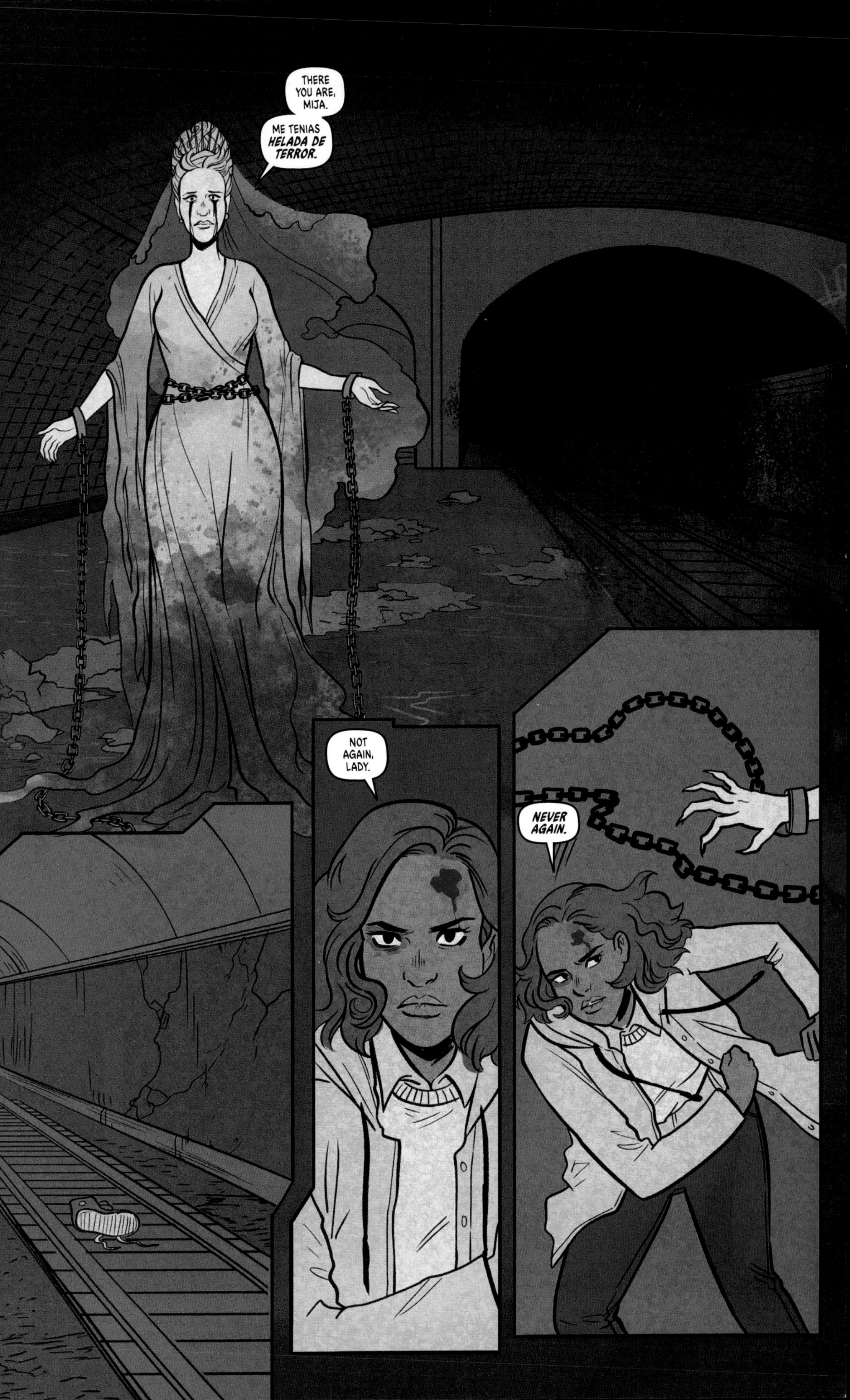
THERE YOU ARE, MIJA.
ME TENIAS *HELADA DE TERROR.*
NOT AGAIN, LADY.
NEVER AGAIN.

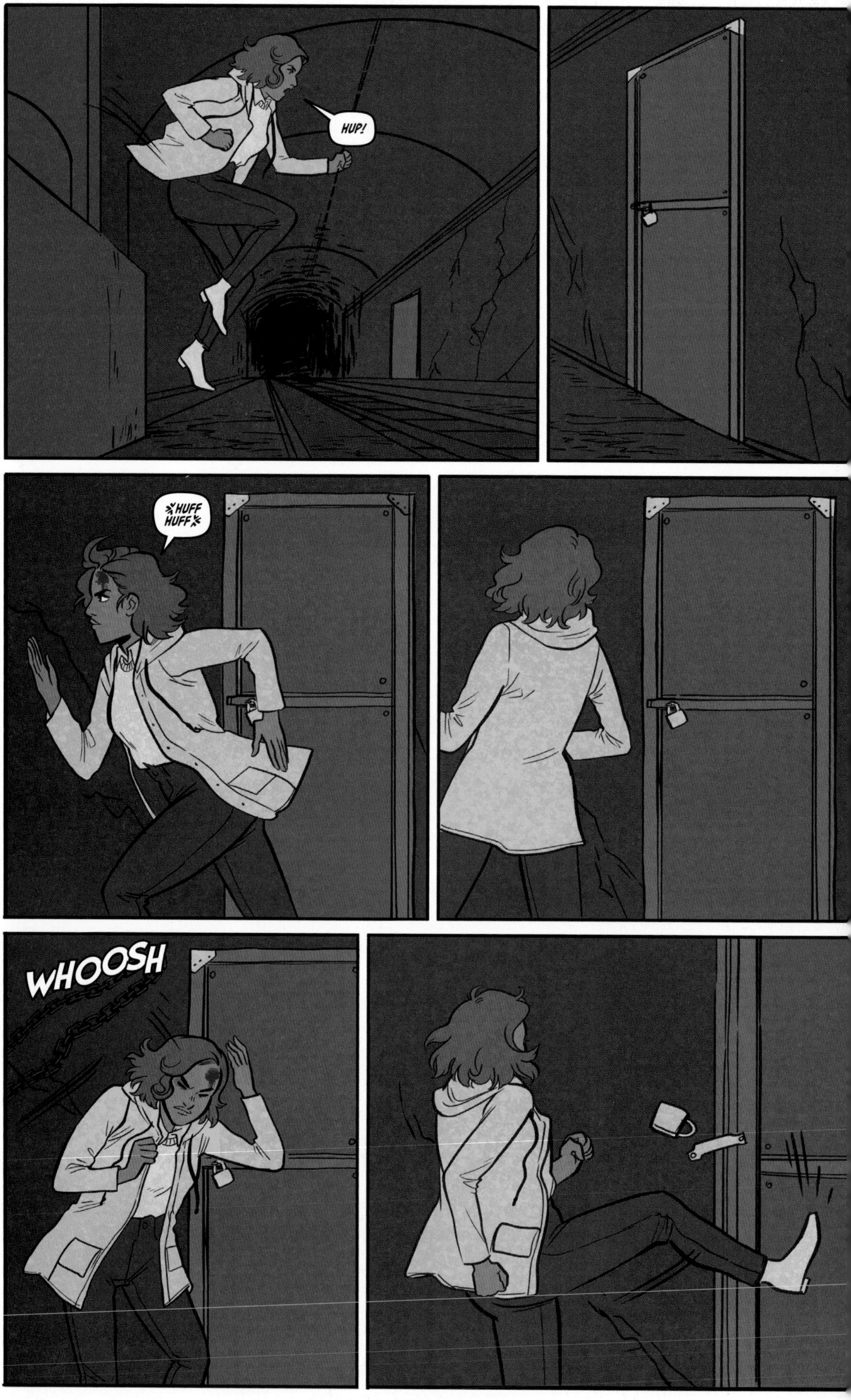
HUP!
HUFF HUFF
WHOOSH

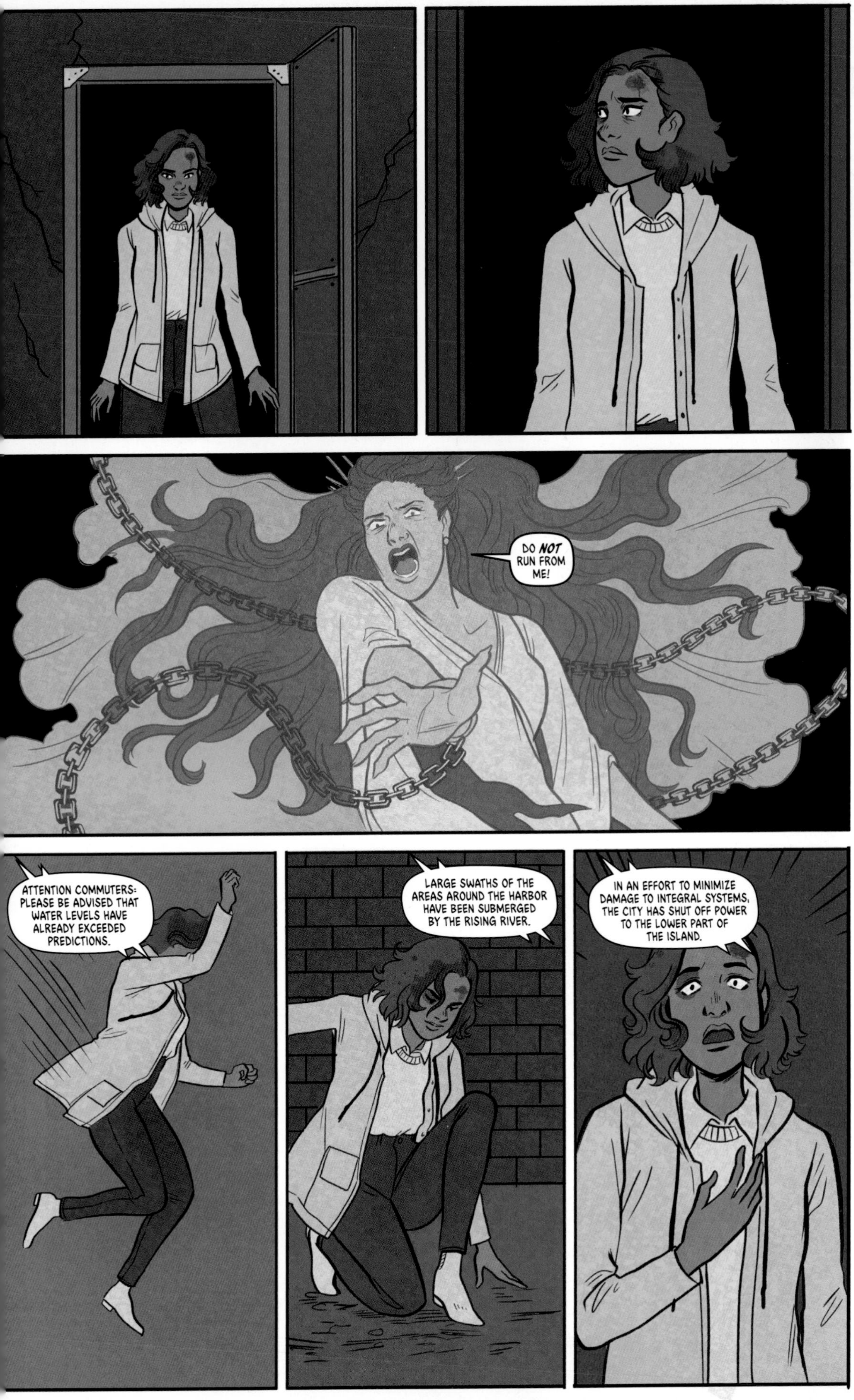
DO *NOT* RUN FROM ME!
ATTENTION COMMUTERS: PLEASE BE ADVISED THAT WATER LEVELS HAVE ALREADY EXCEEDED PREDICTIONS.
LARGE SWATHS OF THE AREAS AROUND THE HARBOR HAVE BEEN SUBMERGED BY THE RISING RIVER.
IN AN EFFORT TO MINIMIZE DAMAGE TO INTEGRAL SYSTEMS, THE CITY HAS SHUT OFF POWER TO THE LOWER PART OF THE ISLAND.

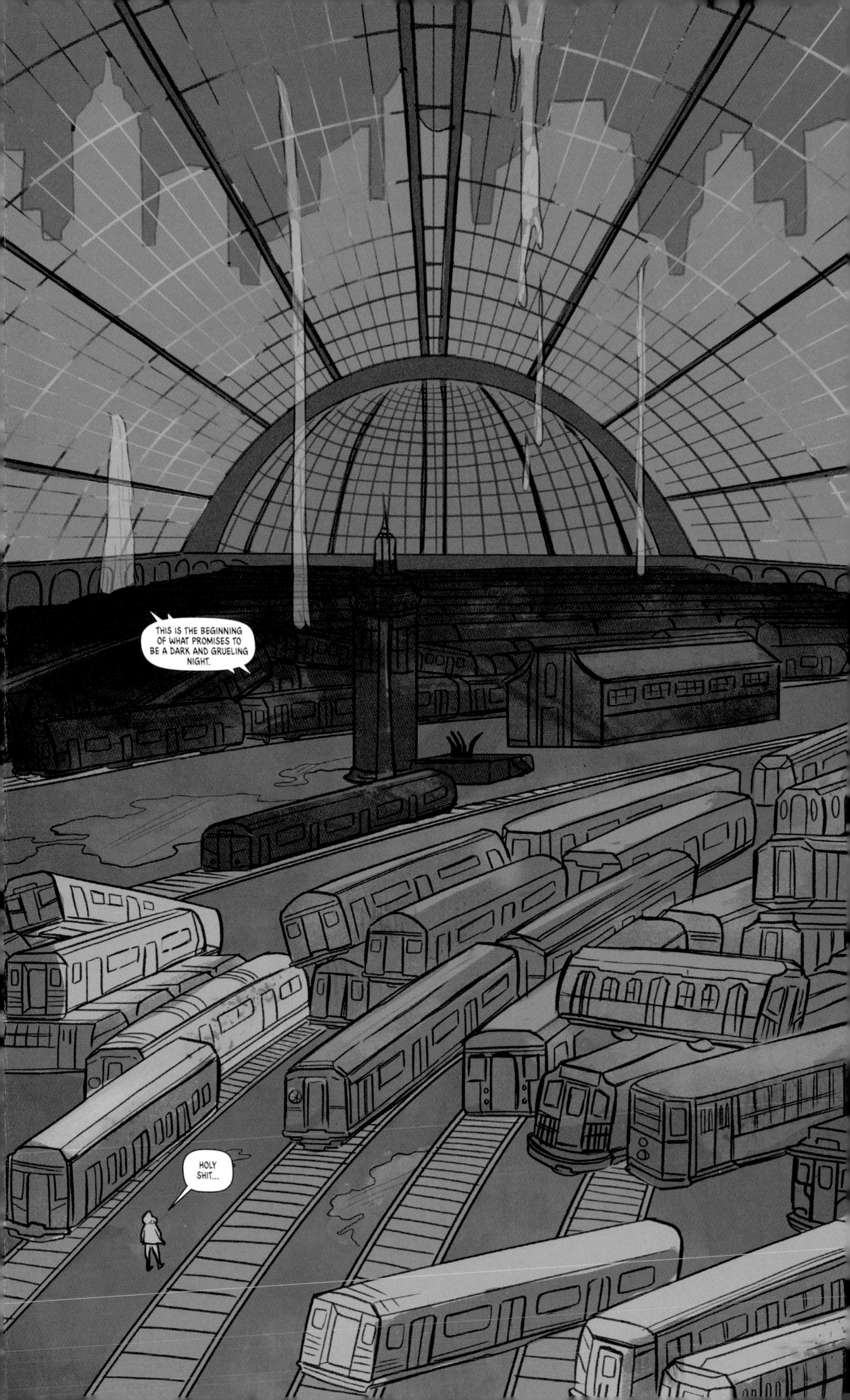
THIS IS THE BEGINNING OF WHAT PROMISES TO BE A DARK AND GRUELING NIGHT.
HOLY SHIT...

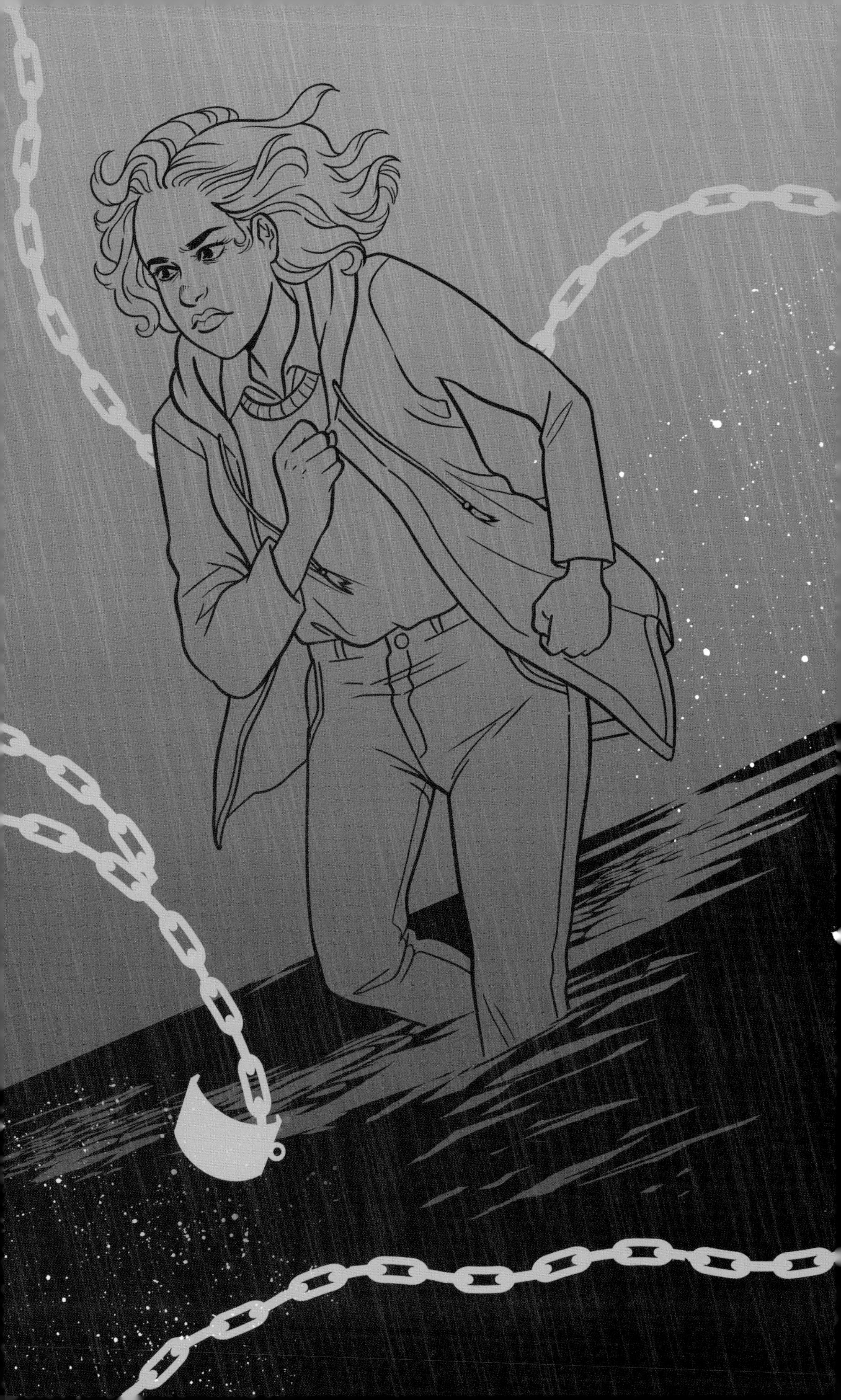

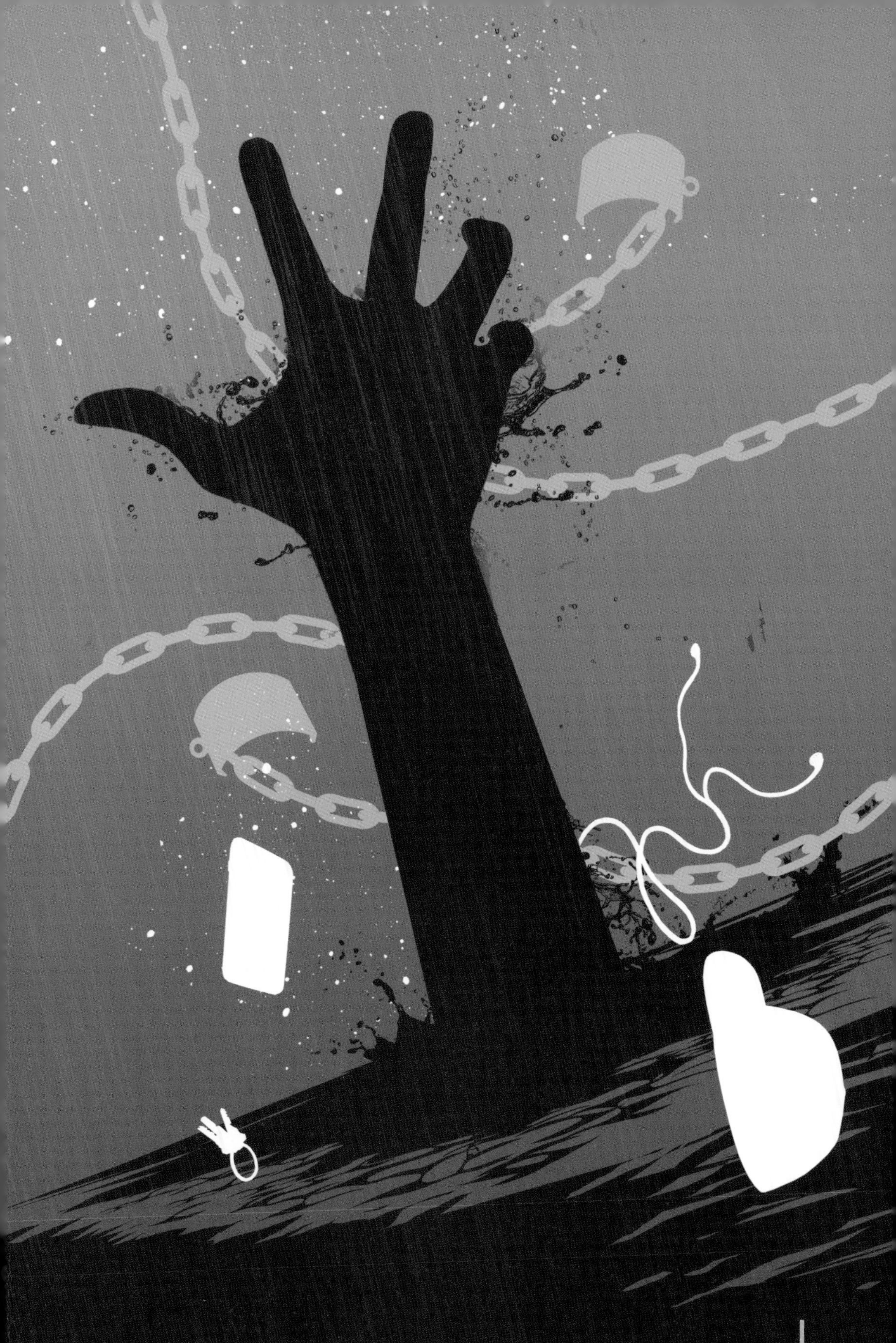

CHAPTER 3

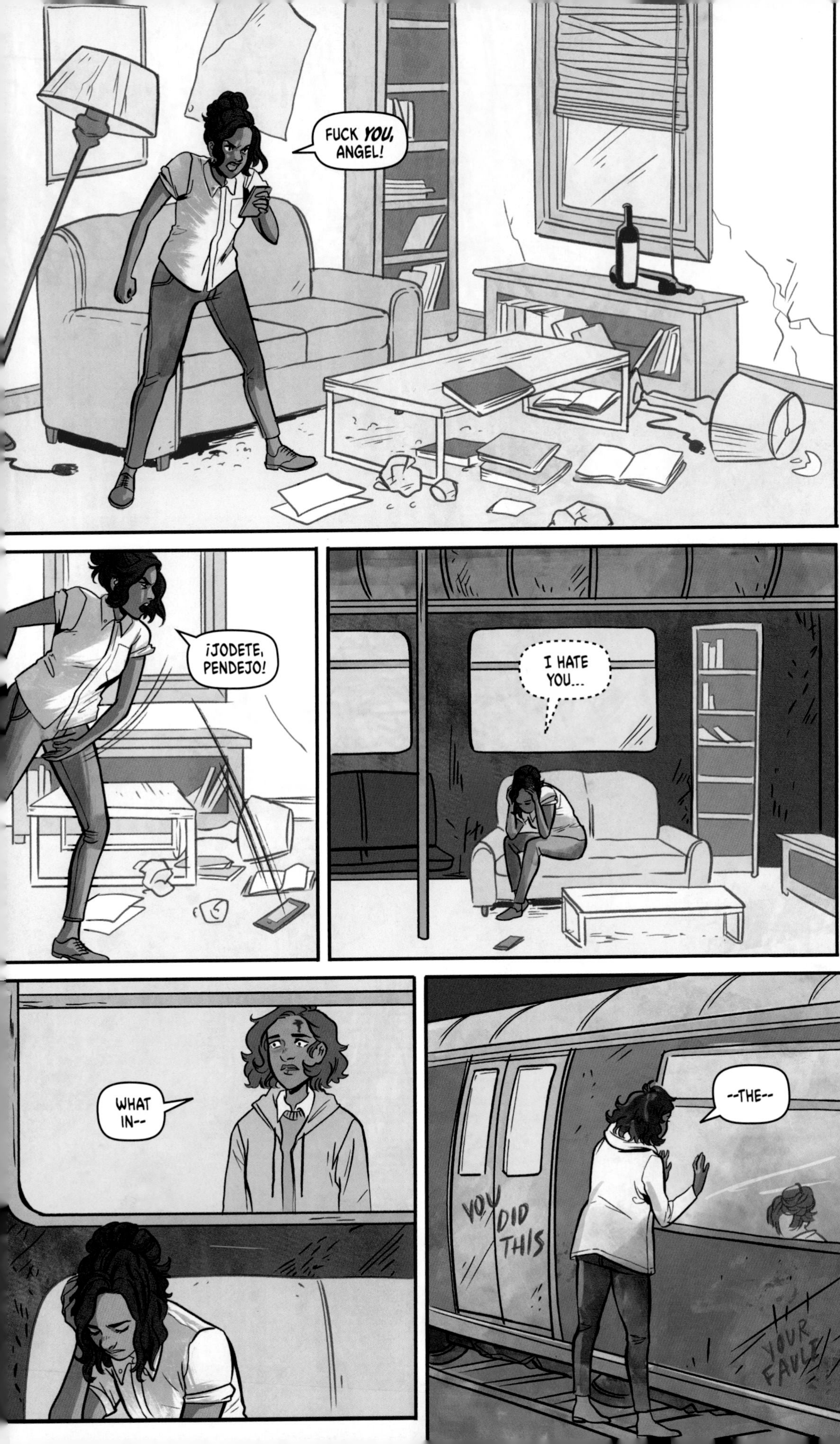
FUCK YOU, ANGEL!
¡JODETE, PENDEJO!
I HATE YOU...
WHAT IN--
--THE--
YOU DID THIS
YOUR FAULT!

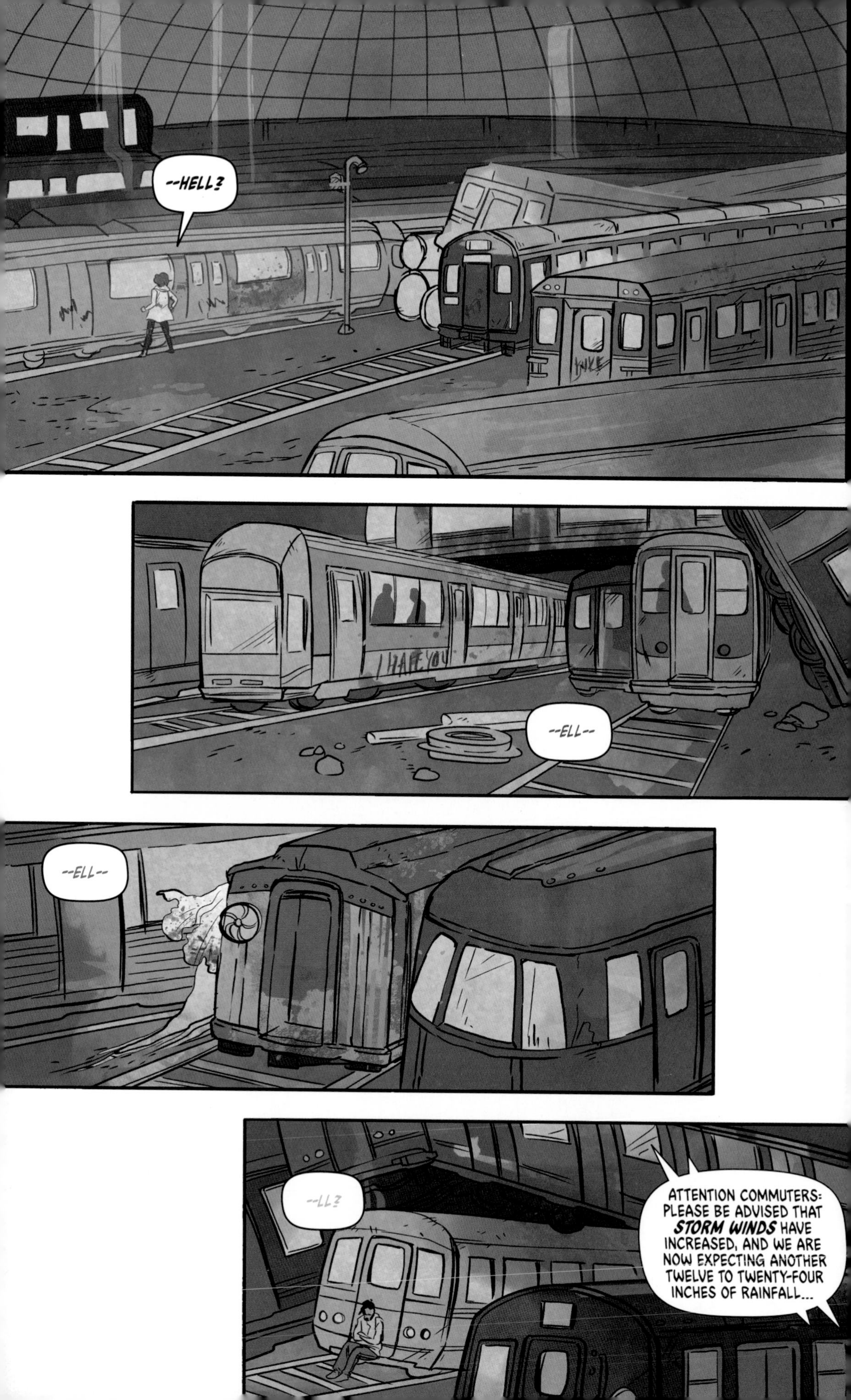
--HELL?
I HATE YOU
--ELL--
--ELL--
--LL?
ATTENTION COMMUTERS: PLEASE BE ADVISED THAT STORM WINDS HAVE INCREASED, AND WE ARE NOW EXPECTING ANOTHER TWELVE TO TWENTY-FOUR INCHES OF RAINFALL...

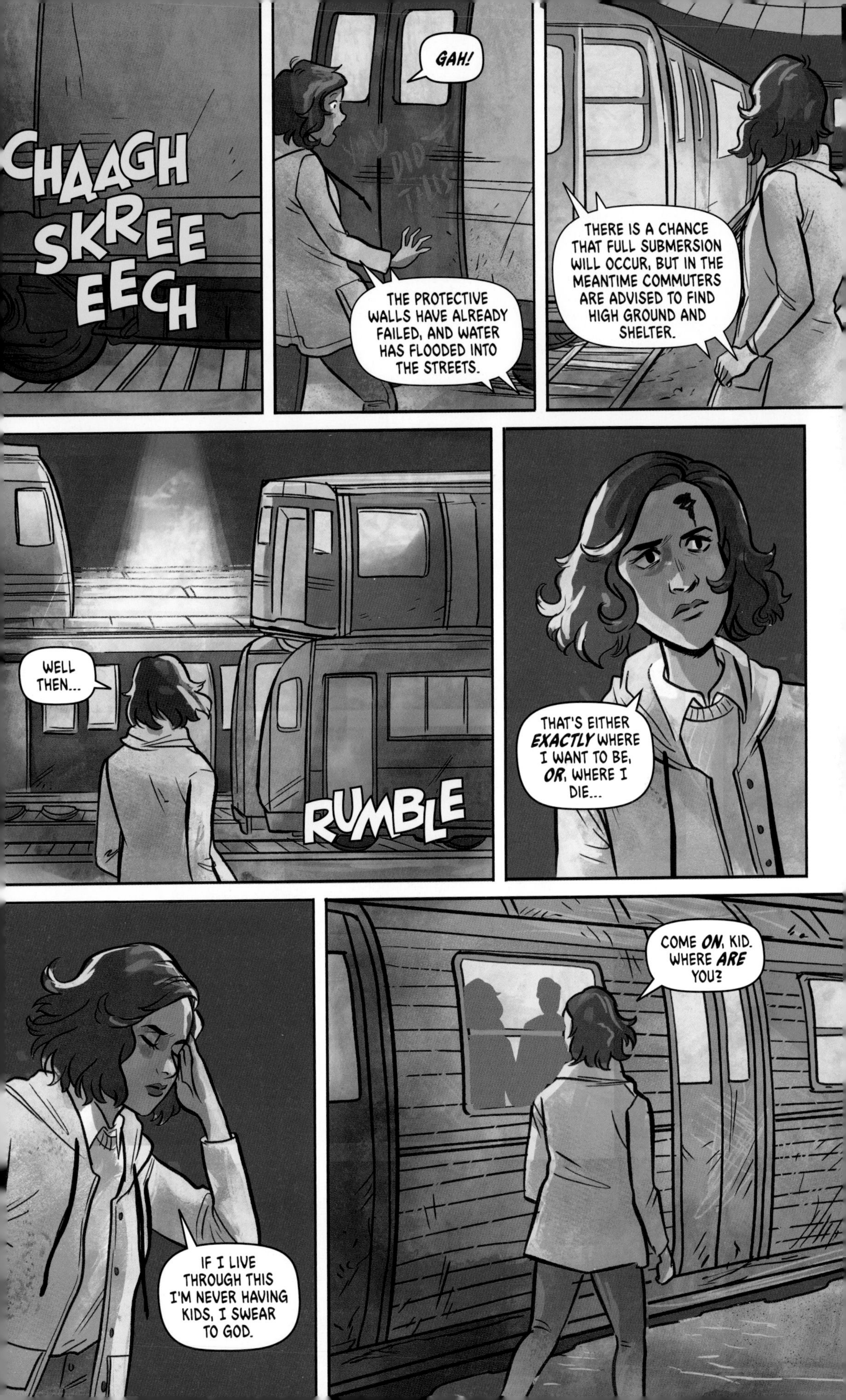

CHAAGH SKREE EECH
GAH!
YOU DID THIS
THE PROTECTIVE WALLS HAVE ALREADY FAILED, AND WATER HAS FLOODED INTO THE STREETS.
THERE IS A CHANCE THAT FULL SUBMERSION WILL OCCUR, BUT IN THE MEANTIME COMMUTERS ARE ADVISED TO FIND HIGH GROUND AND SHELTER.
WELL THEN...
RUMBLE
THAT'S EITHER *EXACTLY* WHERE I WANT TO BE, *OR*, WHERE I DIE...
IF I LIVE THROUGH THIS I'M NEVER HAVING KIDS, I SWEAR TO GOD.
COME *ON*, KID. WHERE *ARE* YOU?

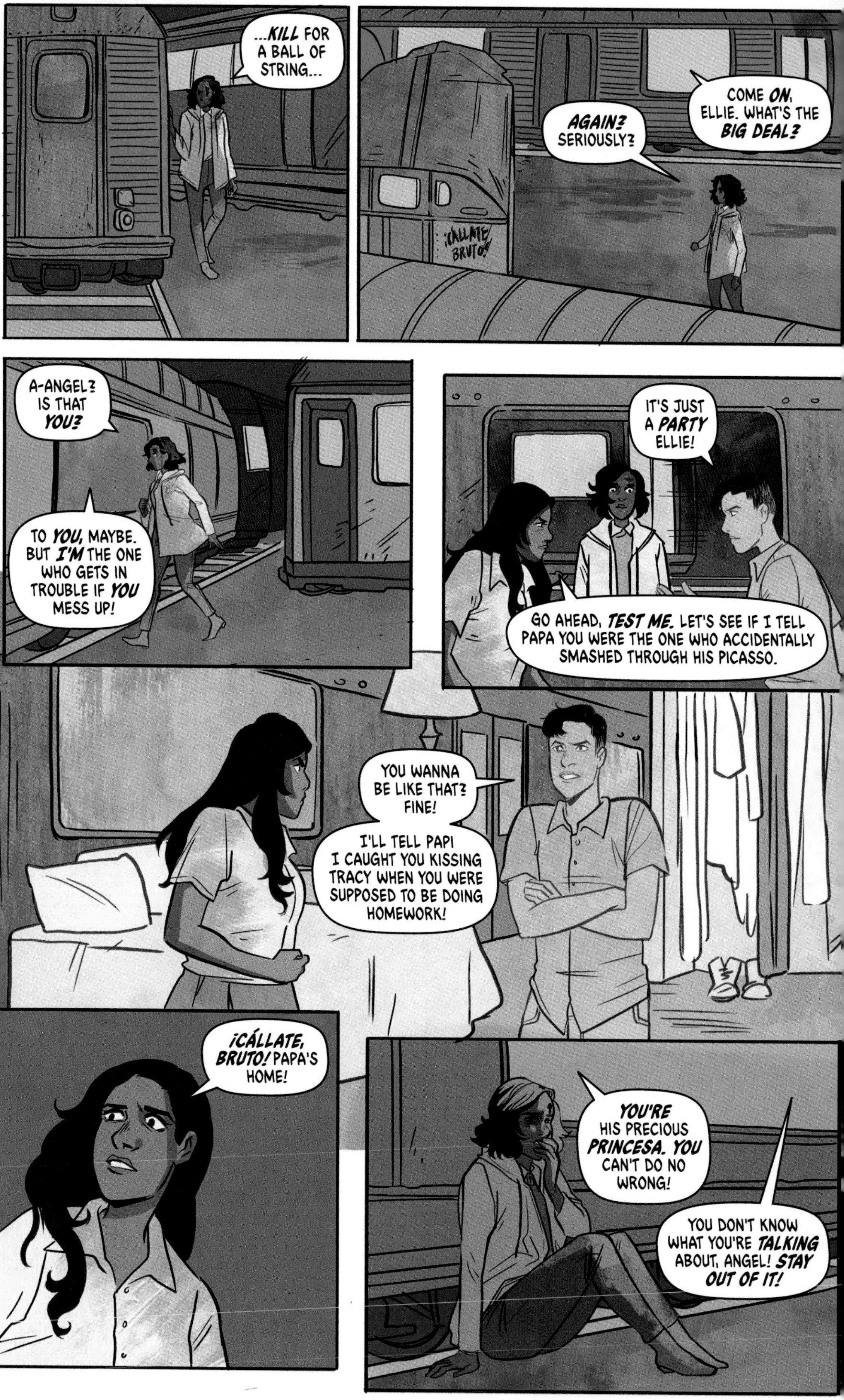
...KILL FOR A BALL OF STRING...
AGAIN? SERIOUSLY?
COME ON, ELLIE. WHAT'S THE BIG DEAL?
¡CÁLLATE BRUTO!
A-ANGEL? IS THAT YOU?
TO YOU, MAYBE. BUT I'M THE ONE WHO GETS IN TROUBLE IF YOU MESS UP!
IT'S JUST A PARTY ELLIE!
GO AHEAD, TEST ME. LET'S SEE IF I TELL PAPA YOU WERE THE ONE WHO ACCIDENTALLY SMASHED THROUGH HIS PICASSO.
YOU WANNA BE LIKE THAT? FINE!
I'LL TELL PAPI I CAUGHT YOU KISSING TRACY WHEN YOU WERE SUPPOSED TO BE DOING HOMEWORK!
¡CÁLLATE, BRUTO! PAPA'S HOME!
YOU'RE HIS PRECIOUS PRINCESA. YOU CAN'T DO NO WRONG!
YOU DON'T KNOW WHAT YOU'RE TALKING ABOUT, ANGEL! STAY OUT OF IT!

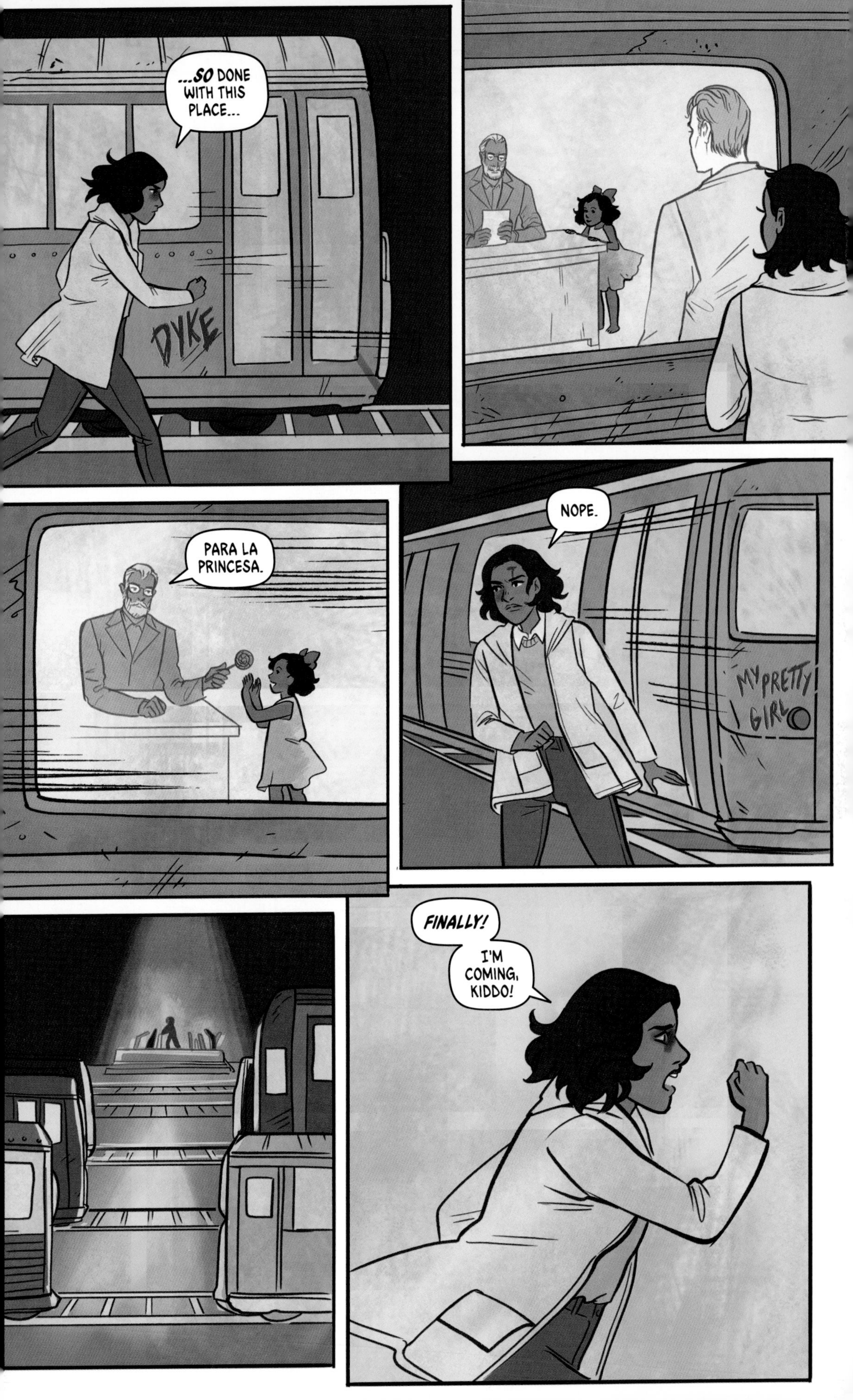
...SO DONE WITH THIS PLACE...
DYKE
PARA LA PRINCESA.
NOPE.
MY PRETTY GIRL
FINALLY!
I'M COMING, KIDDO!

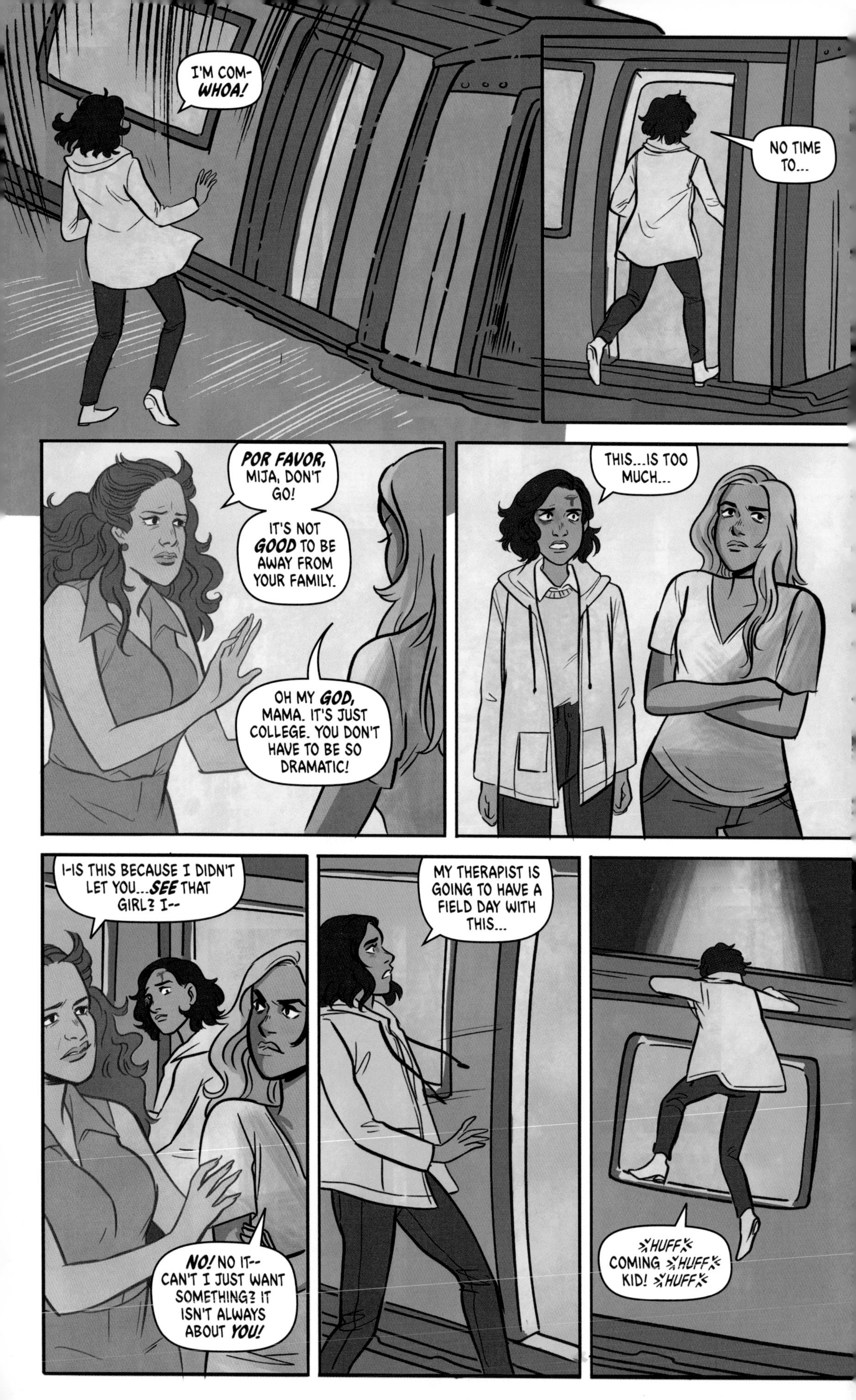
I'M COM-
WHOA!
NO TIME TO...
POR FAVOR, MIJA, DON'T GO!
IT'S NOT GOOD TO BE AWAY FROM YOUR FAMILY.
OH MY GOD, MAMA. IT'S JUST COLLEGE. YOU DON'T HAVE TO BE SO DRAMATIC!
THIS...IS TOO MUCH...
I-IS THIS BECAUSE I DIDN'T LET YOU...SEE THAT GIRL? I--
NO! NO IT-- CAN'T I JUST WANT SOMETHING? IT ISN'T ALWAYS ABOUT YOU!
MY THERAPIST IS GOING TO HAVE A FIELD DAY WITH THIS...
HUFF COMING *HUFF* KID! *HUFF*

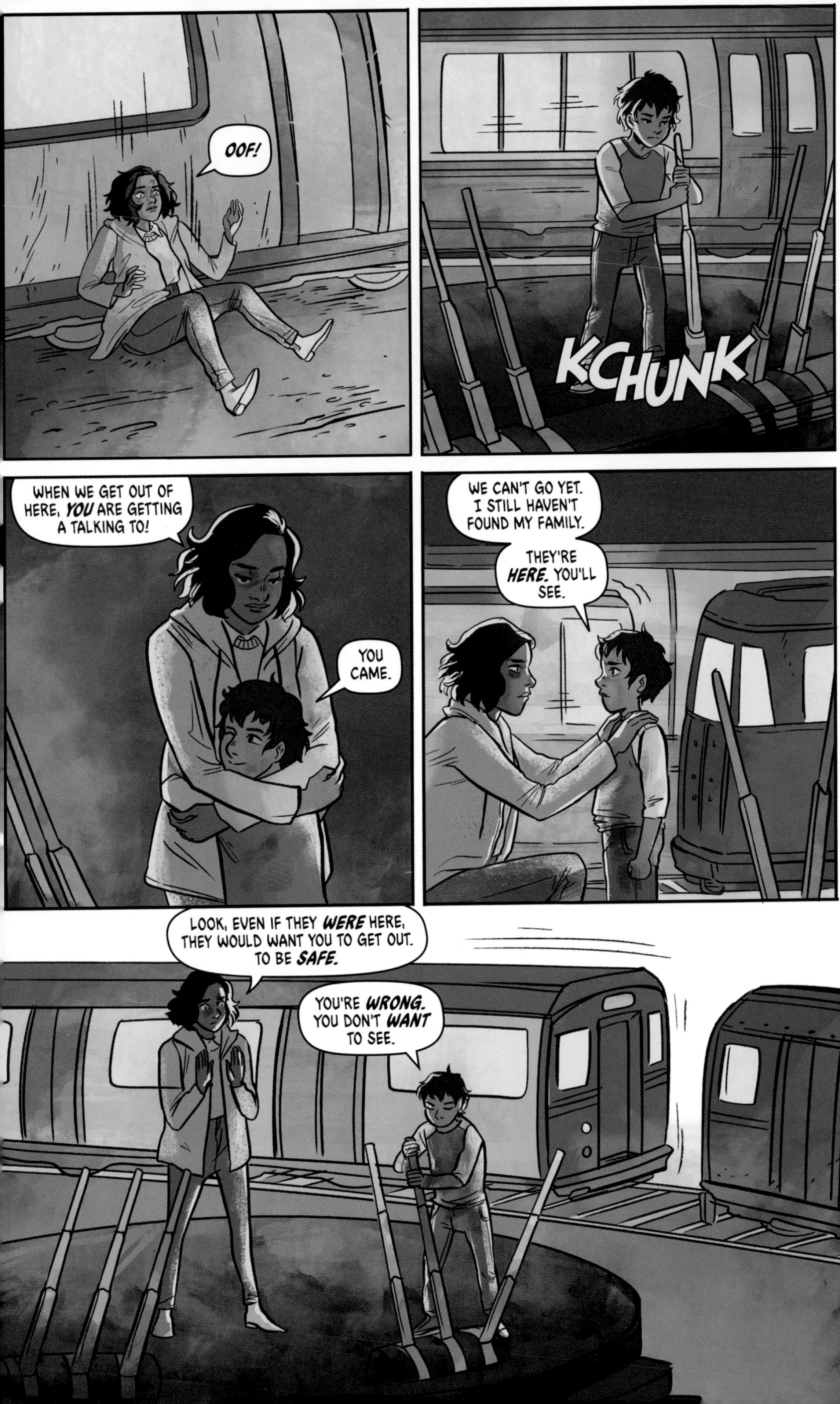
OOF!
KCHUNK
WHEN WE GET OUT OF HERE, YOU ARE GETTING A TALKING TO!
YOU CAME.
WE CAN'T GO YET. I STILL HAVEN'T FOUND MY FAMILY.
THEY'RE HERE. YOU'LL SEE.
LOOK, EVEN IF THEY WERE HERE, THEY WOULD WANT YOU TO GET OUT. TO BE SAFE.
YOU'RE WRONG. YOU DON'T WANT TO SEE.

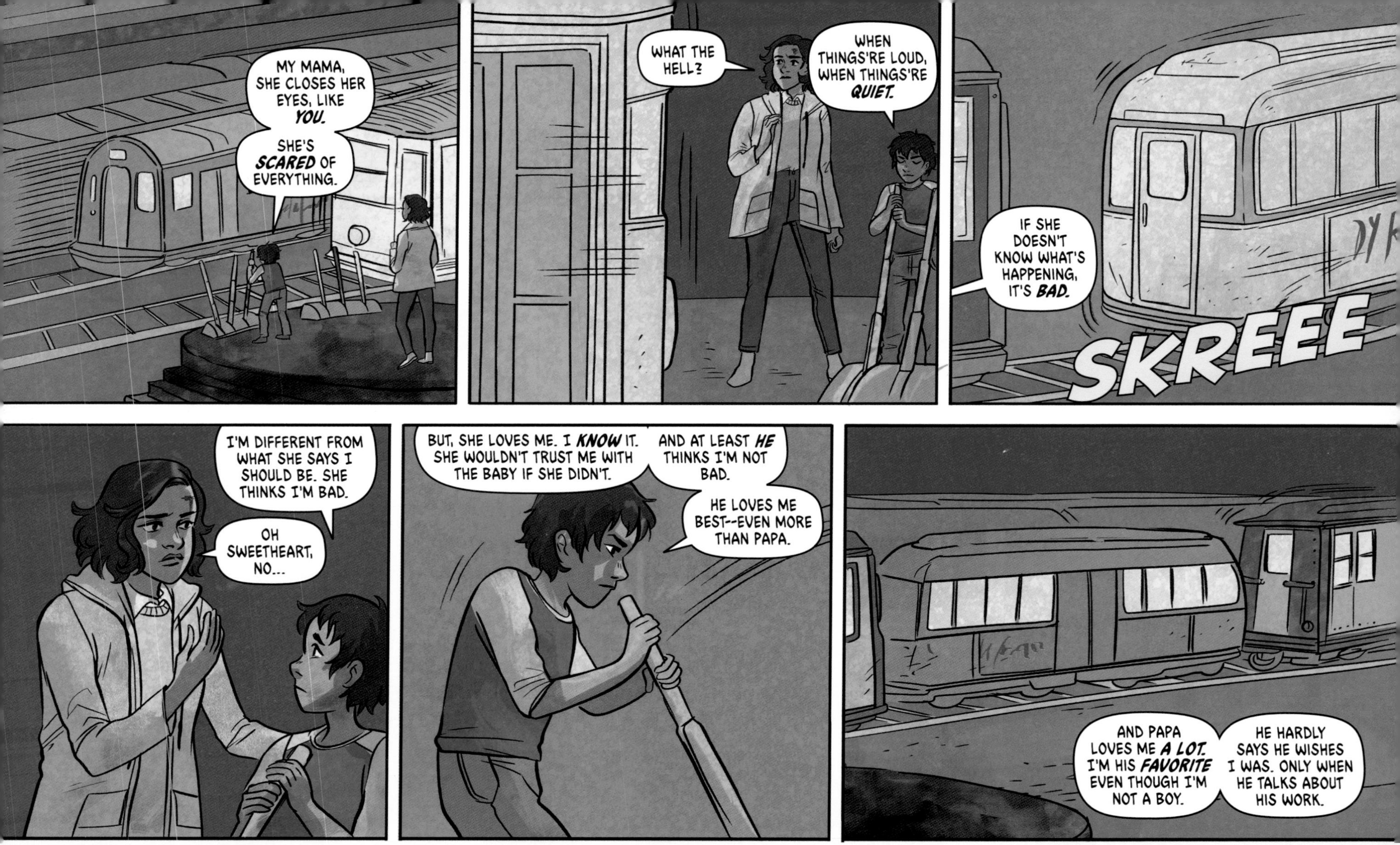
MY MAMA, SHE CLOSES HER EYES, LIKE *YOU.*
SHE'S *SCARED* OF EVERYTHING.
WHAT THE HELL?
WHEN THINGS'RE LOUD, WHEN THINGS'RE *QUIET.*
IF SHE DOESN'T KNOW WHAT'S HAPPENING, IT'S *BAD.*
SKREEE
I'M DIFFERENT FROM WHAT SHE SAYS I SHOULD BE. SHE THINKS I'M BAD.
OH SWEETHEART, NO...
BUT, SHE LOVES ME. I *KNOW* IT. SHE WOULDN'T TRUST ME WITH THE BABY IF SHE DIDN'T.
AND AT LEAST *HE* THINKS I'M NOT BAD.
HE LOVES ME BEST--EVEN MORE THAN PAPA.
AND PAPA LOVES ME *A LOT.* I'M HIS *FAVORITE* EVEN THOUGH I'M NOT A BOY.
HE HARDLY SAYS HE WISHES I WAS. ONLY WHEN HE TALKS ABOUT HIS WORK.

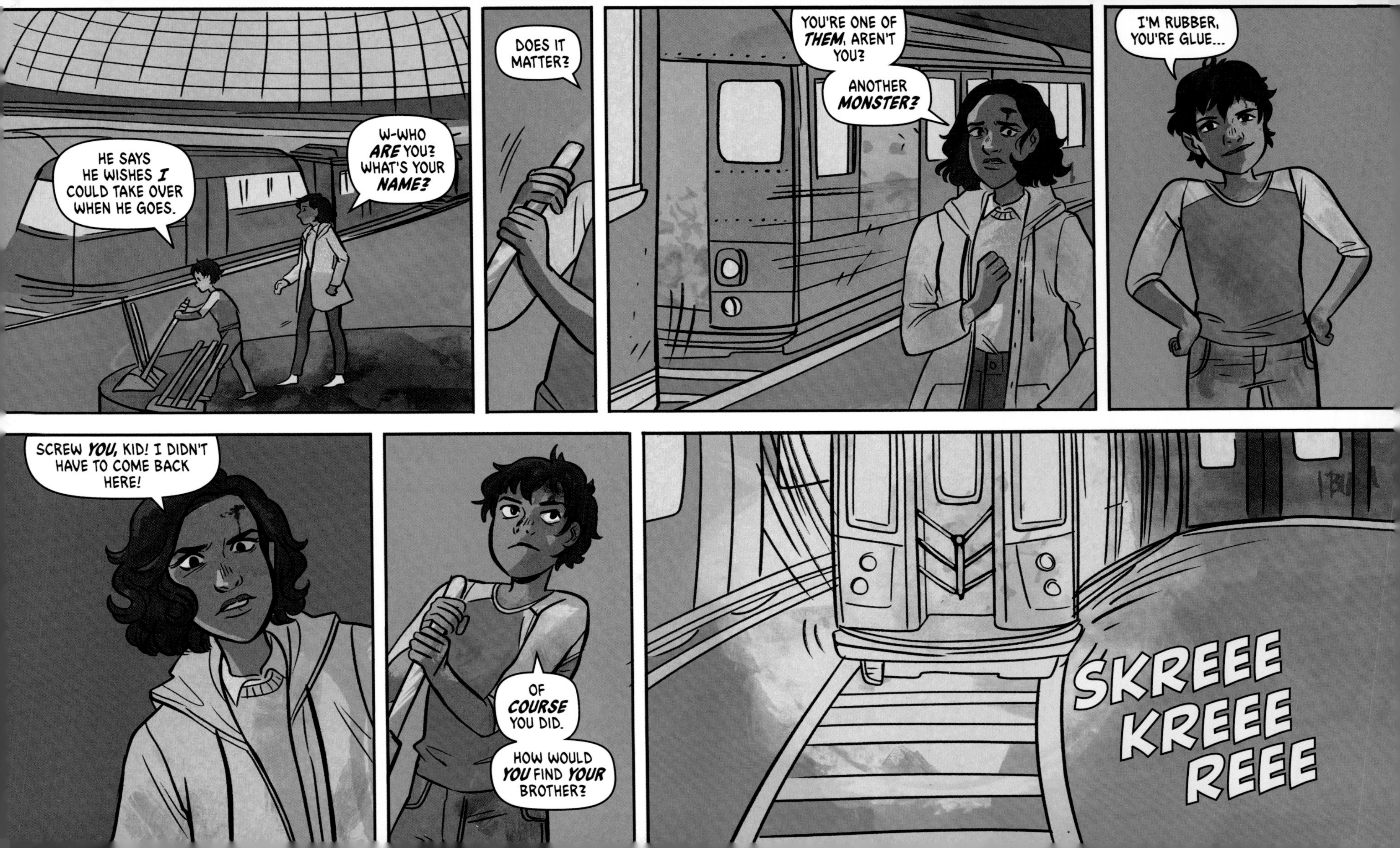
HE SAYS HE WISHES *I* COULD TAKE OVER WHEN HE GOES.
W-WHO *ARE* YOU? WHAT'S YOUR *NAME?*
DOES IT MATTER?
YOU'RE ONE OF *THEM*, AREN'T YOU?
ANOTHER *MONSTER?*
I'M RUBBER, YOU'RE GLUE...
SCREW *YOU,* KID! I DIDN'T HAVE TO COME BACK HERE!
OF *COURSE* YOU DID.
HOW WOULD *YOU* FIND *YOUR* BROTHER?
SKREEE
KREEE
REEE

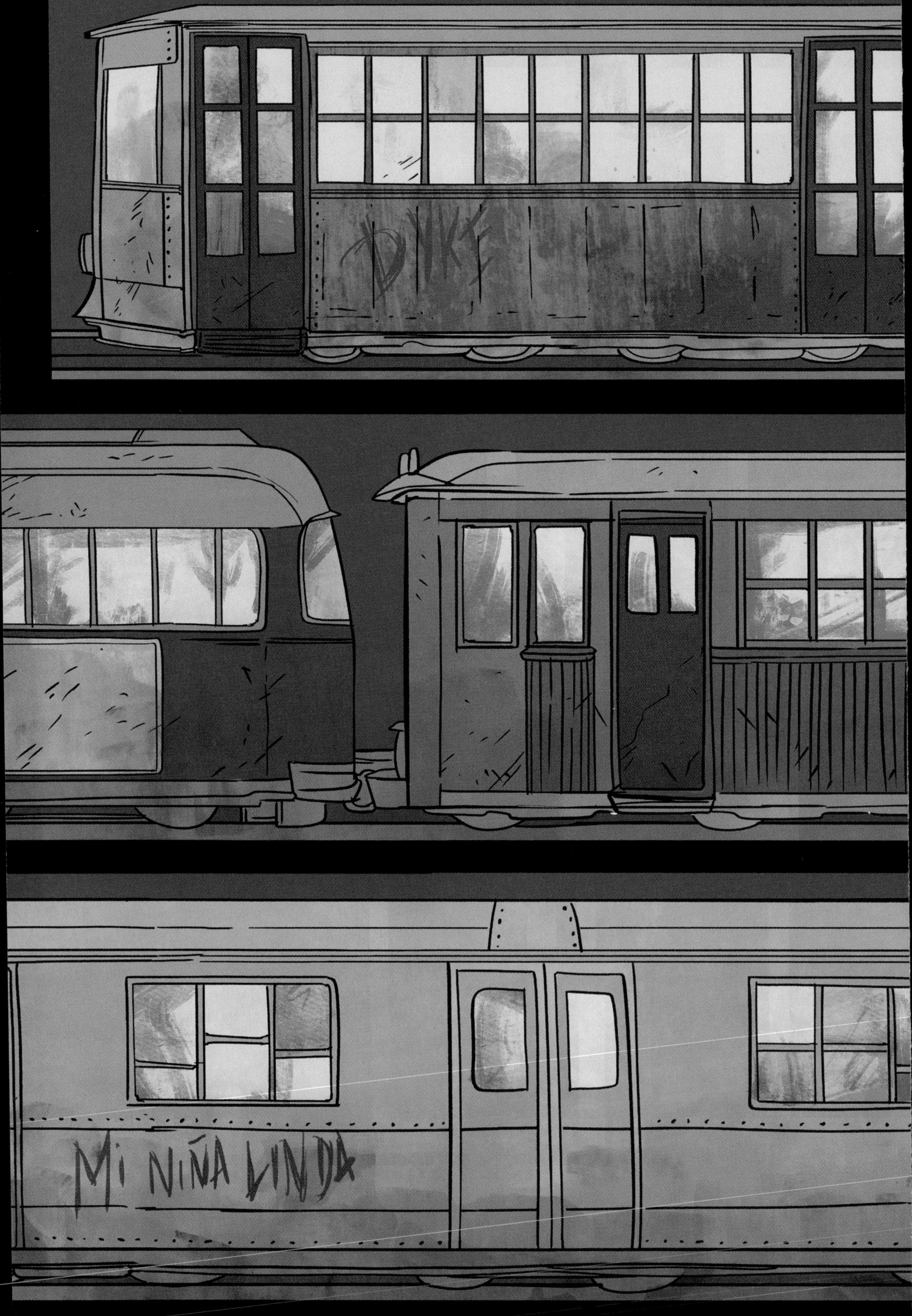
DYKE
MI NIÑA LINDA

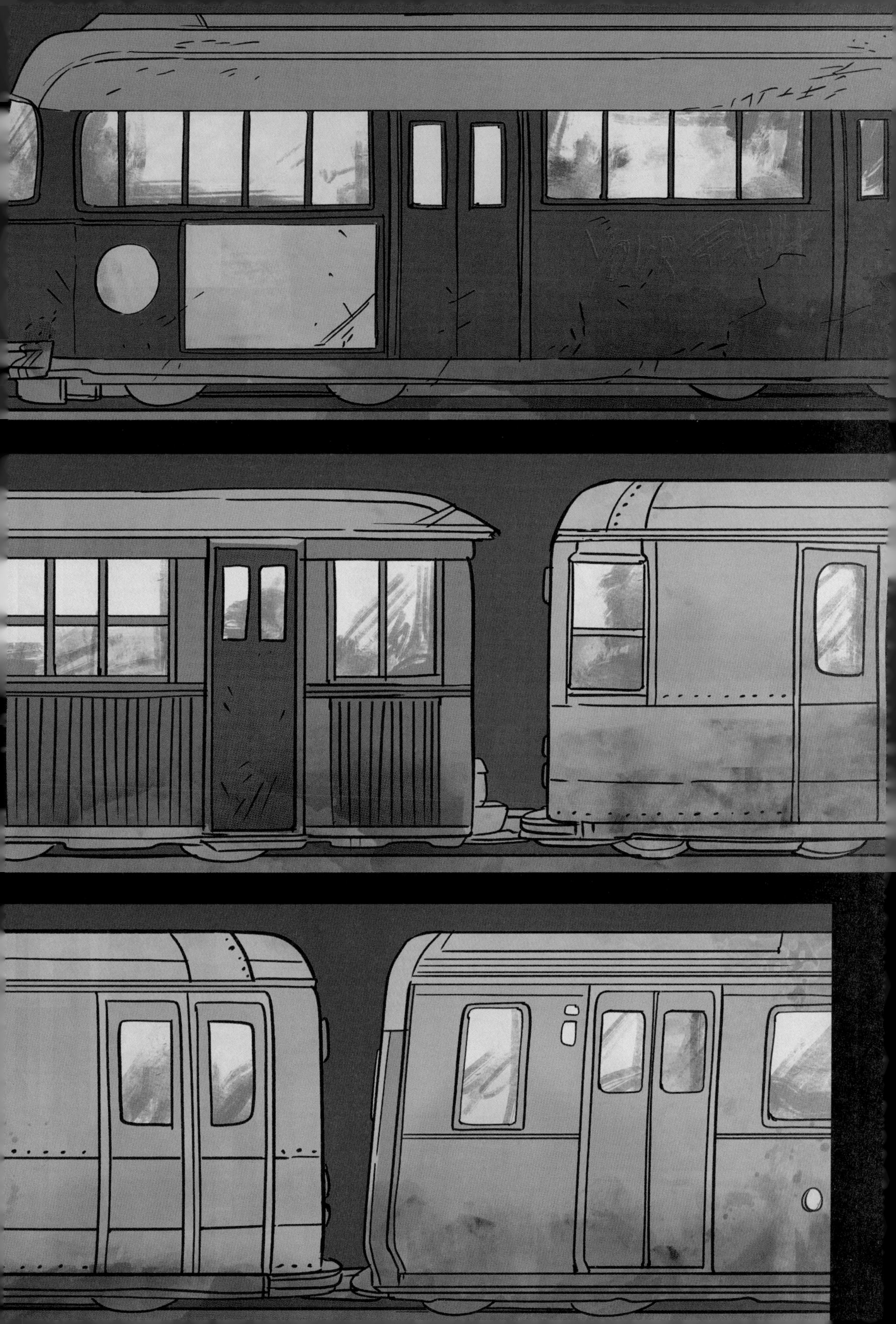

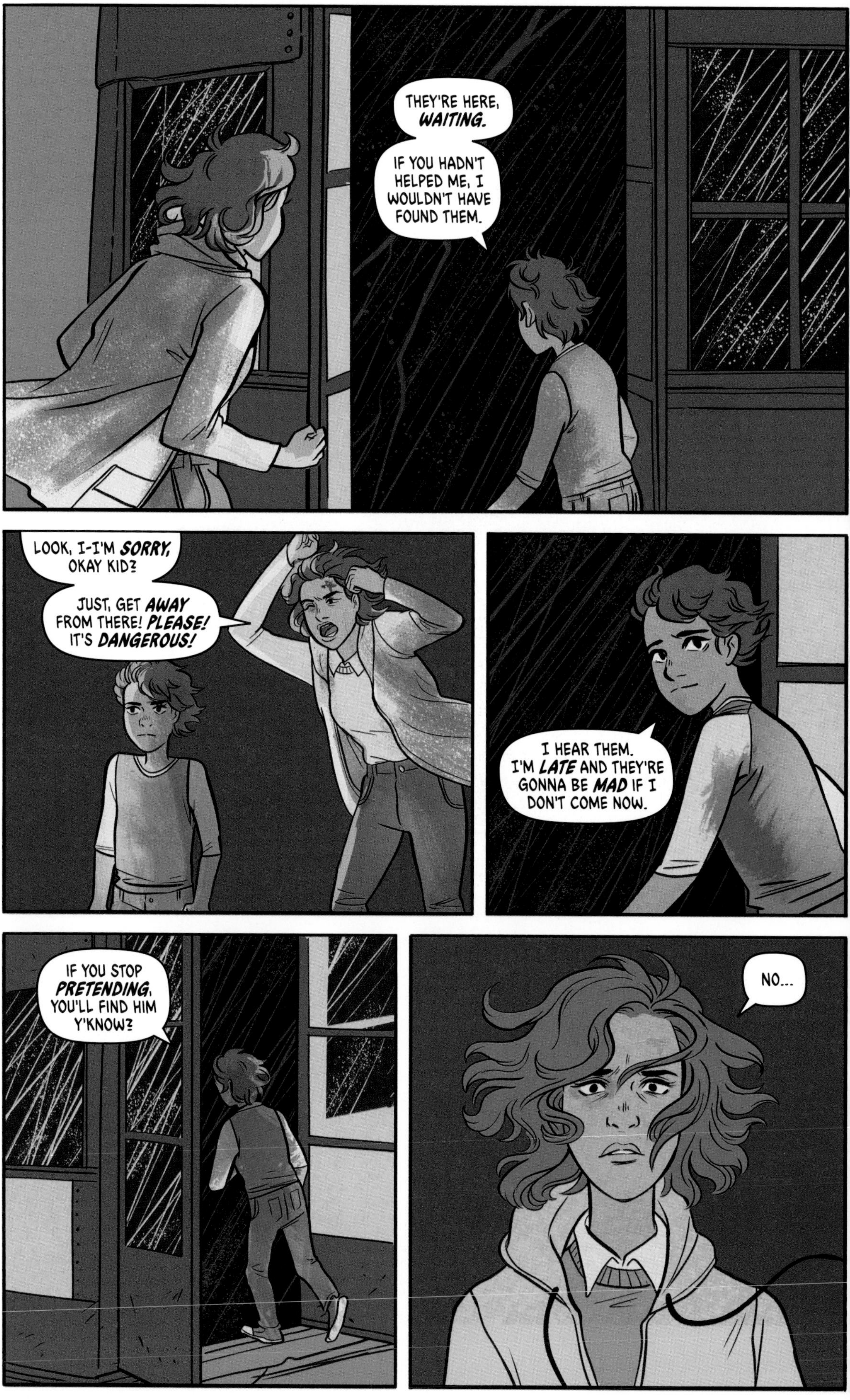
THEY'RE HERE, WAITING.
IF YOU HADN'T HELPED ME, I WOULDN'T HAVE FOUND THEM.
LOOK, I-I'M SORRY, OKAY KID?
JUST, GET AWAY FROM THERE! PLEASE! IT'S DANGEROUS!
I HEAR THEM. I'M LATE AND THEY'RE GONNA BE MAD IF I DON'T COME NOW.
IF YOU STOP PRETENDING, YOU'LL FIND HIM Y'KNOW?
NO...

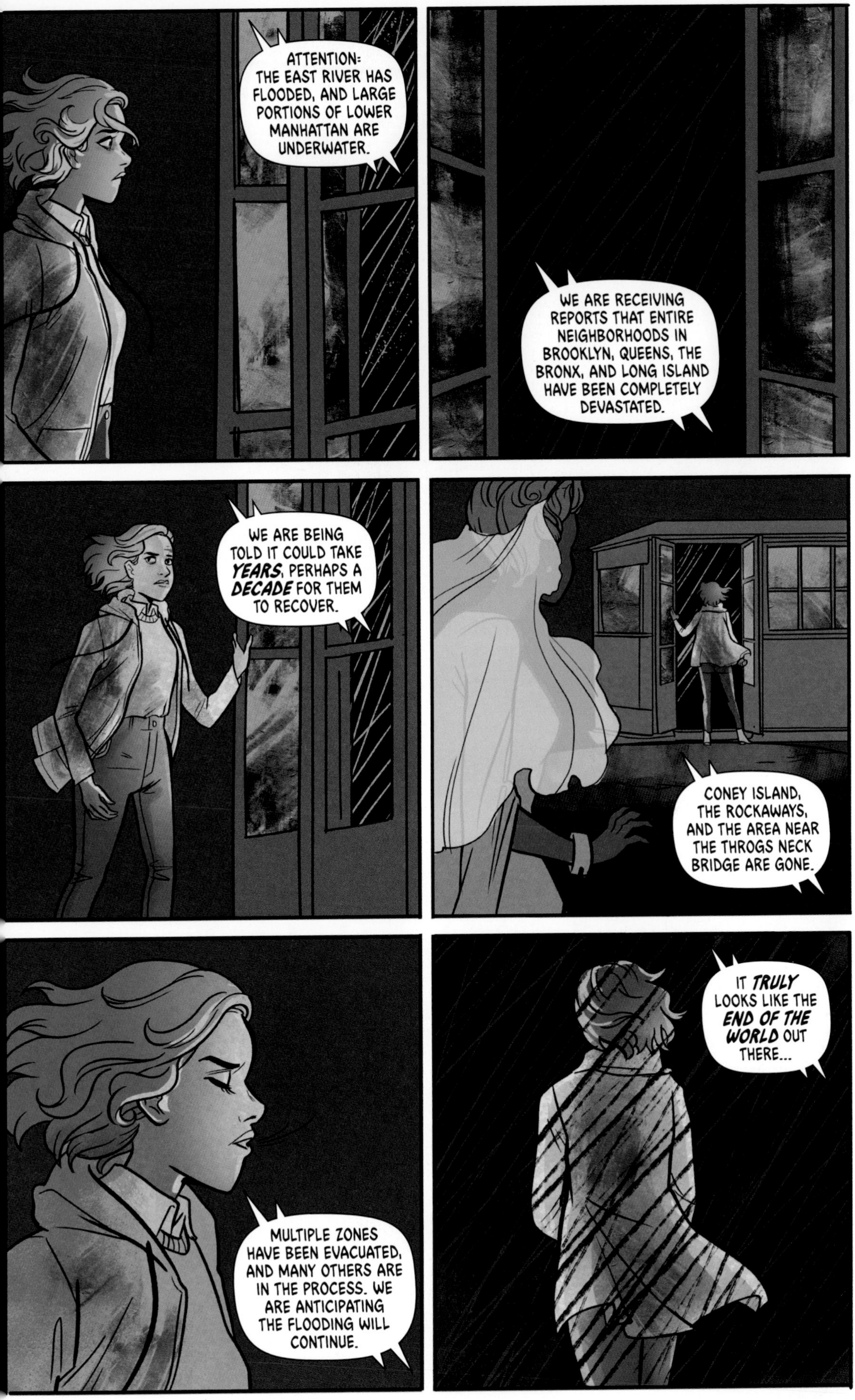
ATTENTION: THE EAST RIVER HAS FLOODED, AND LARGE PORTIONS OF LOWER MANHATTAN ARE UNDERWATER.
WE ARE RECEIVING REPORTS THAT ENTIRE NEIGHBORHOODS IN BROOKLYN, QUEENS, THE BRONX, AND LONG ISLAND HAVE BEEN COMPLETELY DEVASTATED.
WE ARE BEING TOLD IT COULD TAKE YEARS, PERHAPS A DECADE FOR THEM TO RECOVER.
CONEY ISLAND, THE ROCKAWAYS, AND THE AREA NEAR THE THROGS NECK BRIDGE ARE GONE.
MULTIPLE ZONES HAVE BEEN EVACUATED, AND MANY OTHERS ARE IN THE PROCESS. WE ARE ANTICIPATING THE FLOODING WILL CONTINUE.
IT TRULY LOOKS LIKE THE END OF THE WORLD OUT THERE...

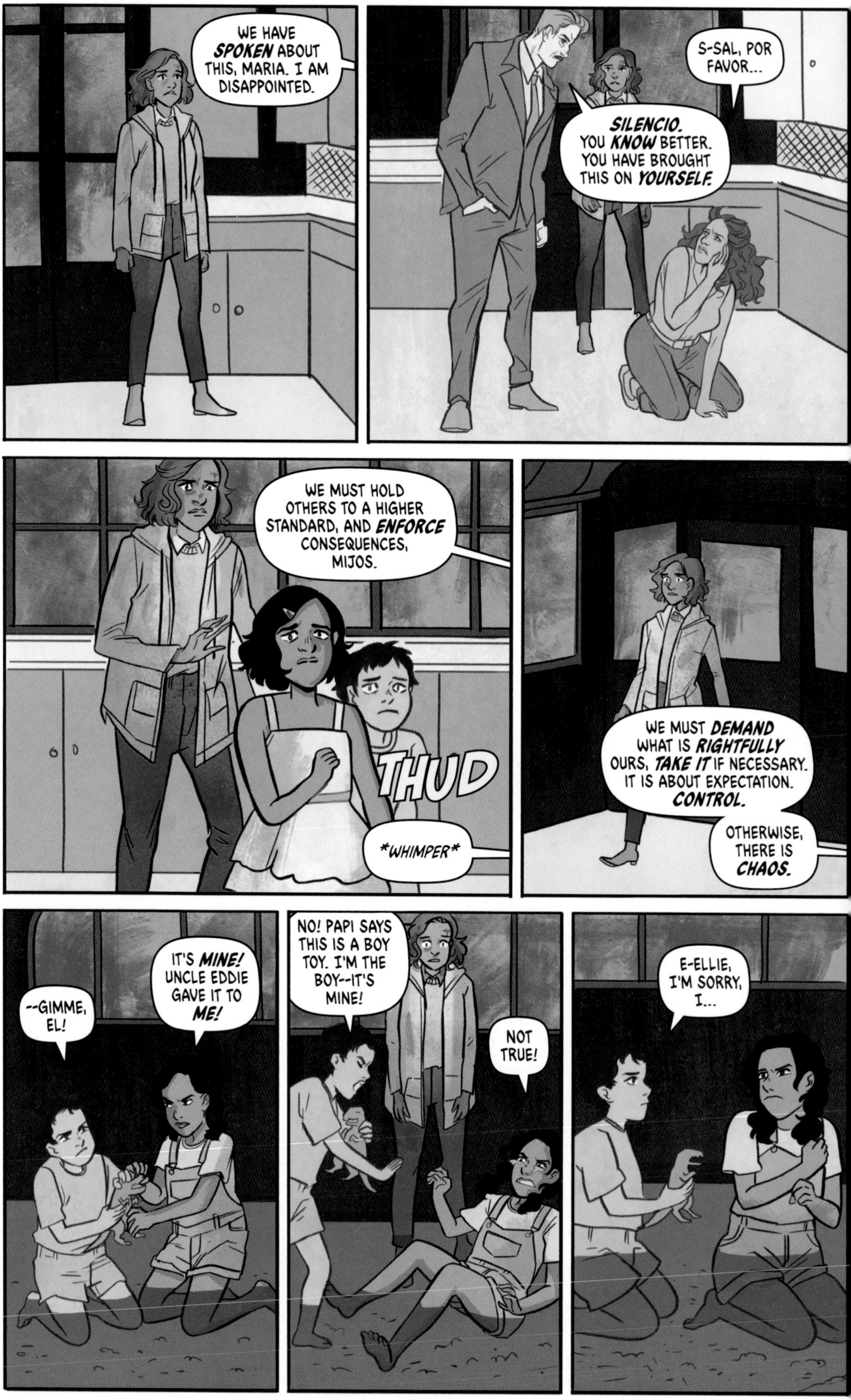
WE HAVE SPOKEN ABOUT THIS, MARIA. I AM DISAPPOINTED.
S-SAL, POR FAVOR...
SILENCIO. YOU KNOW BETTER. YOU HAVE BROUGHT THIS ON YOURSELF.
WE MUST HOLD OTHERS TO A HIGHER STANDARD, AND ENFORCE CONSEQUENCES, MIJOS.
THUD
WHIMPER
WE MUST DEMAND WHAT IS RIGHTFULLY OURS, TAKE IT IF NECESSARY. IT IS ABOUT EXPECTATION. CONTROL.
OTHERWISE, THERE IS CHAOS.
--GIMME, EL!
IT'S MINE! UNCLE EDDIE GAVE IT TO ME!
NO! PAPI SAYS THIS IS A BOY TOY. I'M THE BOY--IT'S MINE!
NOT TRUE!
E-ELLIE, I'M SORRY, I...

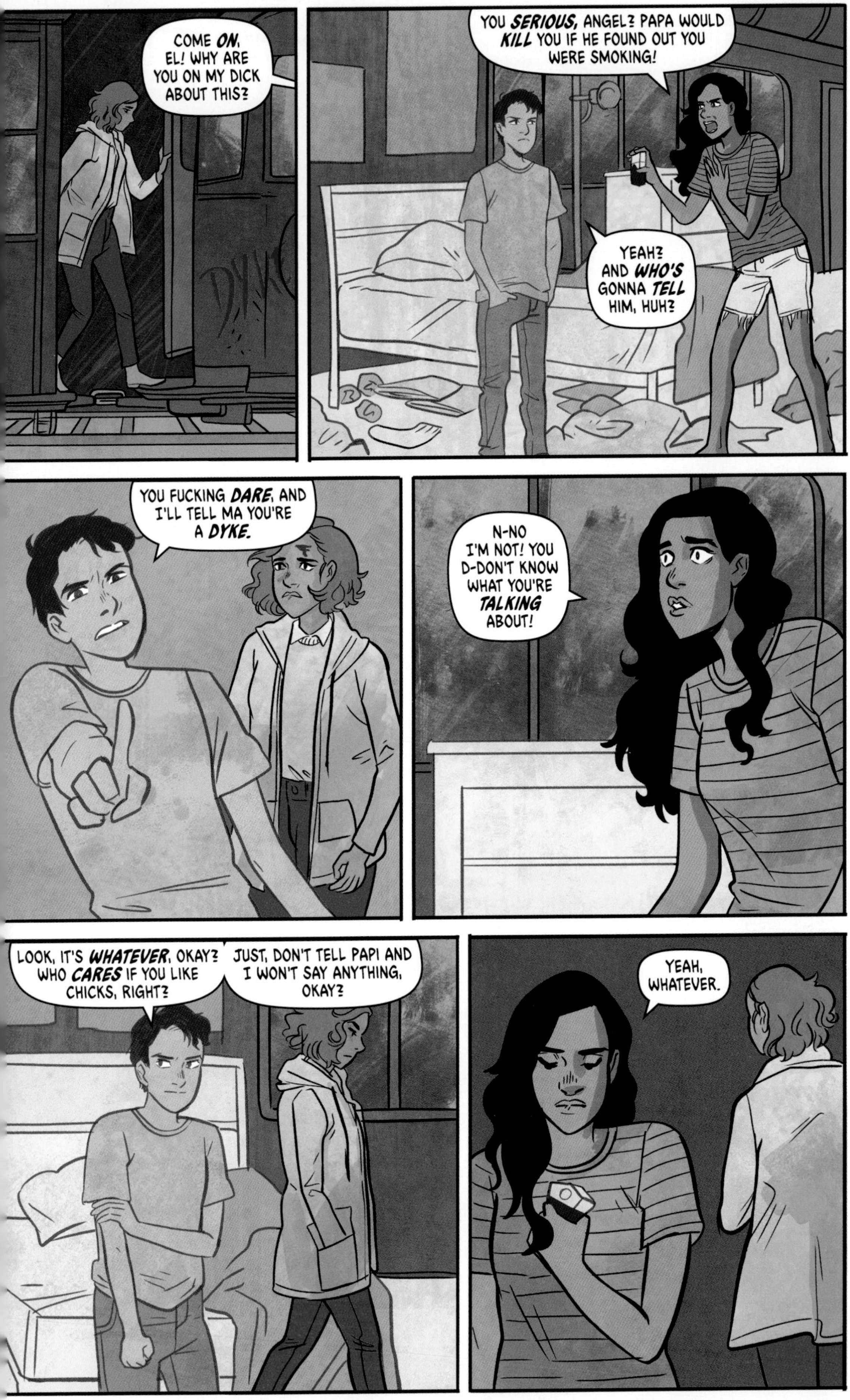
COME ON, EL! WHY ARE YOU ON MY DICK ABOUT THIS?
YOU SERIOUS, ANGEL? PAPA WOULD KILL YOU IF HE FOUND OUT YOU WERE SMOKING!
YEAH? AND WHO'S GONNA TELL HIM, HUH?
YOU FUCKING DARE, AND I'LL TELL MA YOU'RE A DYKE.
N-NO I'M NOT! YOU D-DON'T KNOW WHAT YOU'RE TALKING ABOUT!
LOOK, IT'S WHATEVER, OKAY? WHO CARES IF YOU LIKE CHICKS, RIGHT?
JUST, DON'T TELL PAPI AND I WON'T SAY ANYTHING, OKAY?
YEAH, WHATEVER.

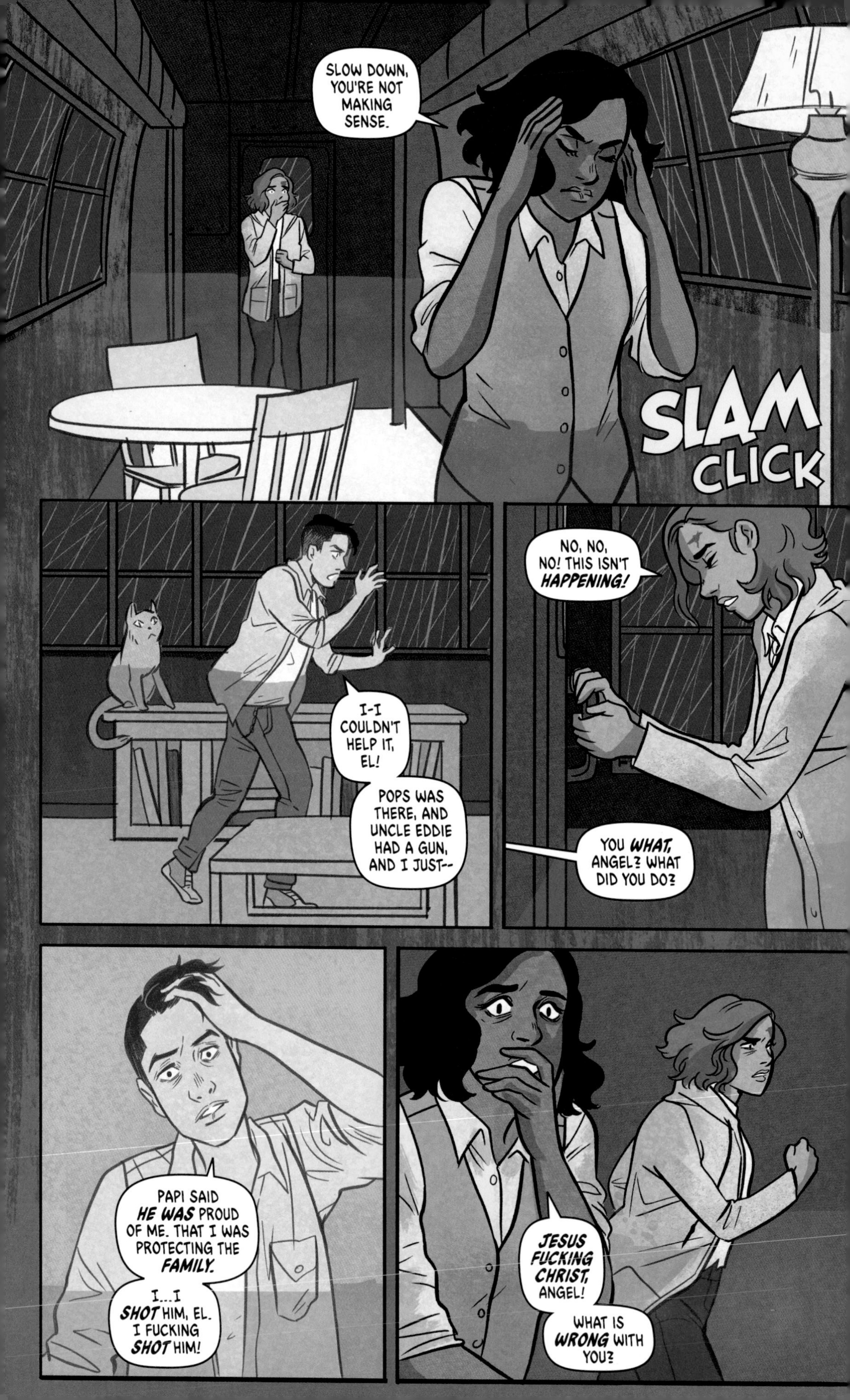
SLOW DOWN, YOU'RE NOT MAKING SENSE.
SLAM
CLICK
I-I COULDN'T HELP IT, EL!
POPS WAS THERE, AND UNCLE EDDIE HAD A GUN, AND I JUST--
NO, NO, NO! THIS ISN'T *HAPPENING!*
YOU *WHAT,* ANGEL? WHAT DID YOU DO?
PAPI SAID *HE WAS* PROUD OF ME. THAT I WAS PROTECTING THE *FAMILY.*
I... I *SHOT* HIM, EL. I FUCKING *SHOT* HIM!
JESUS FUCKING CHRIST, ANGEL!
WHAT IS *WRONG* WITH YOU?

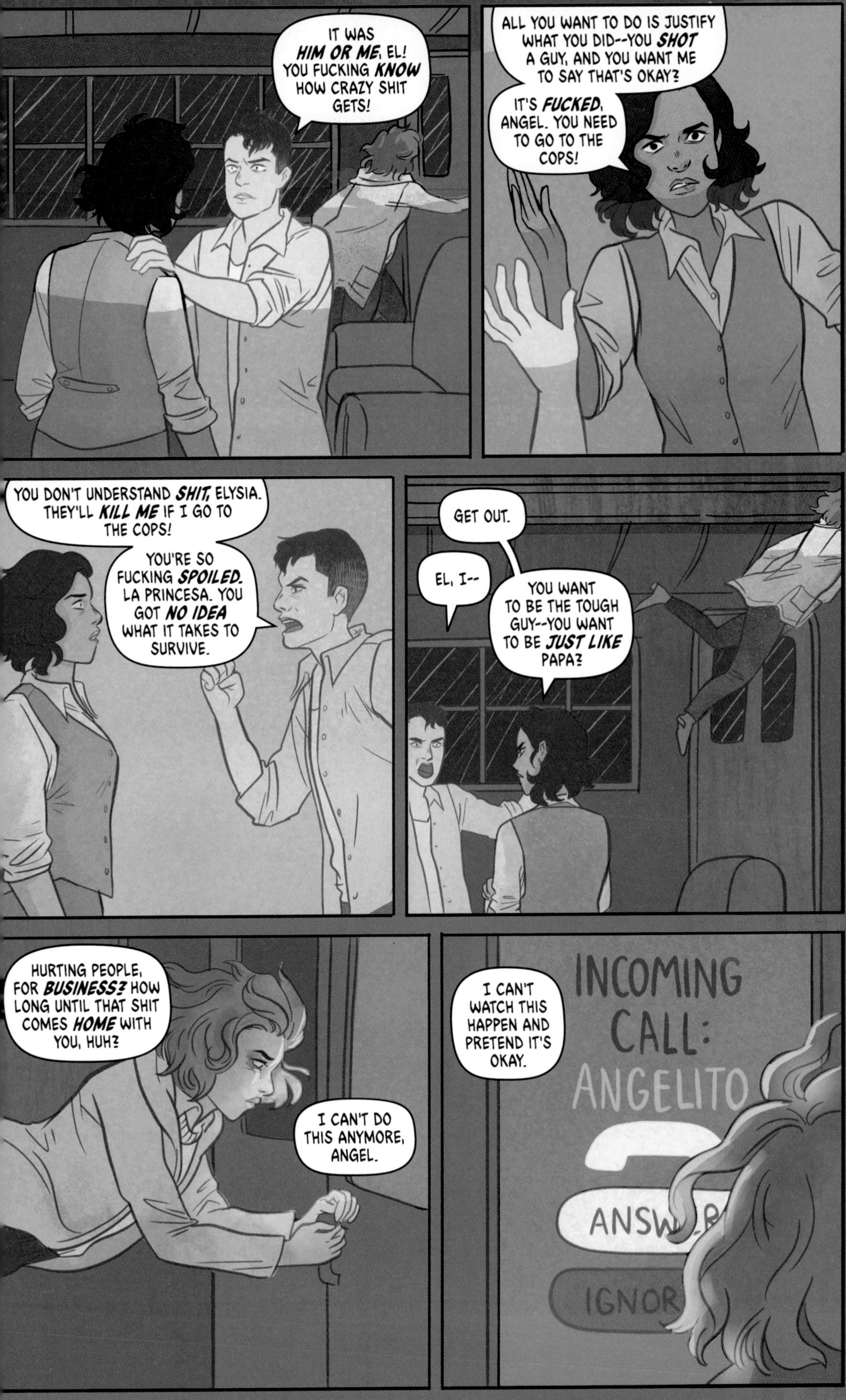
IT WAS HIM OR ME, EL! YOU FUCKING KNOW HOW CRAZY SHIT GETS!
ALL YOU WANT TO DO IS JUSTIFY WHAT YOU DID--YOU SHOT A GUY, AND YOU WANT ME TO SAY THAT'S OKAY?
IT'S FUCKED, ANGEL. YOU NEED TO GO TO THE COPS!
YOU DON'T UNDERSTAND SHIT, ELYSIA. THEY'LL KILL ME IF I GO TO THE COPS!
YOU'RE SO FUCKING SPOILED. LA PRINCESA. YOU GOT NO IDEA WHAT IT TAKES TO SURVIVE.
GET OUT.
EL, I--
YOU WANT TO BE THE TOUGH GUY--YOU WANT TO BE JUST LIKE PAPA?
HURTING PEOPLE, FOR BUSINESS? HOW LONG UNTIL THAT SHIT COMES HOME WITH YOU, HUH?
I CAN'T DO THIS ANYMORE, ANGEL.
I CAN'T WATCH THIS HAPPEN AND PRETEND IT'S OKAY.
INCOMING CALL:
ANGELITO

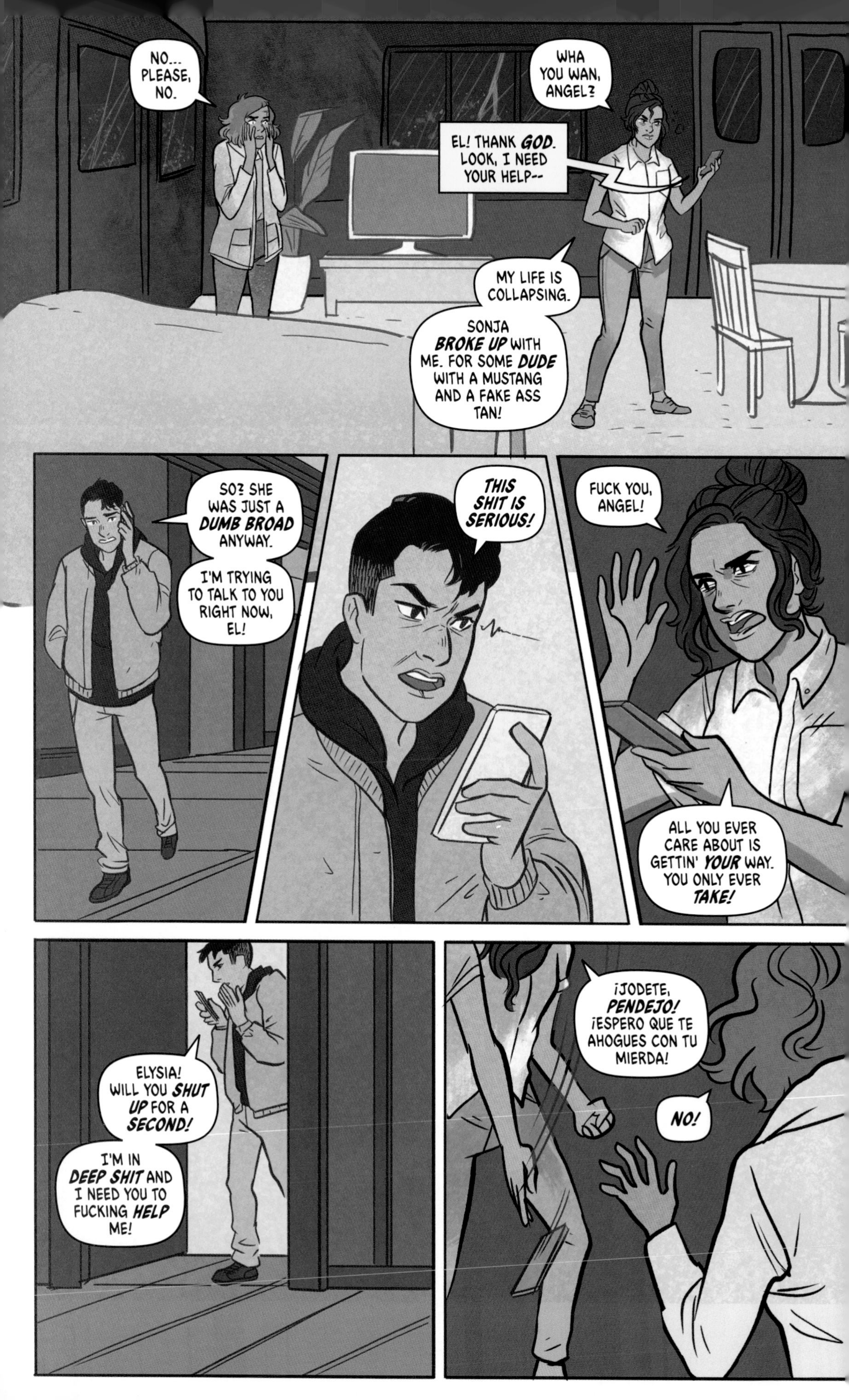
NO... PLEASE, NO.
WHA YOU WAN, ANGEL?
EL! THANK GOD. LOOK, I NEED YOUR HELP--
MY LIFE IS COLLAPSING.
SONJA BROKE UP WITH ME. FOR SOME DUDE WITH A MUSTANG AND A FAKE ASS TAN!
SO? SHE WAS JUST A DUMB BROAD ANYWAY.
I'M TRYING TO TALK TO YOU RIGHT NOW, EL!
THIS SHIT IS SERIOUS!
FUCK YOU, ANGEL!
ALL YOU EVER CARE ABOUT IS GETTIN' YOUR WAY. YOU ONLY EVER TAKE!
ELYSIA! WILL YOU SHUT UP FOR A SECOND!
I'M IN DEEP SHIT AND I NEED YOU TO FUCKING HELP ME!
¡JODETE, PENDEJO! ¡ESPERO QUE TE AHOGUES CON TU MIERDA!
NO!

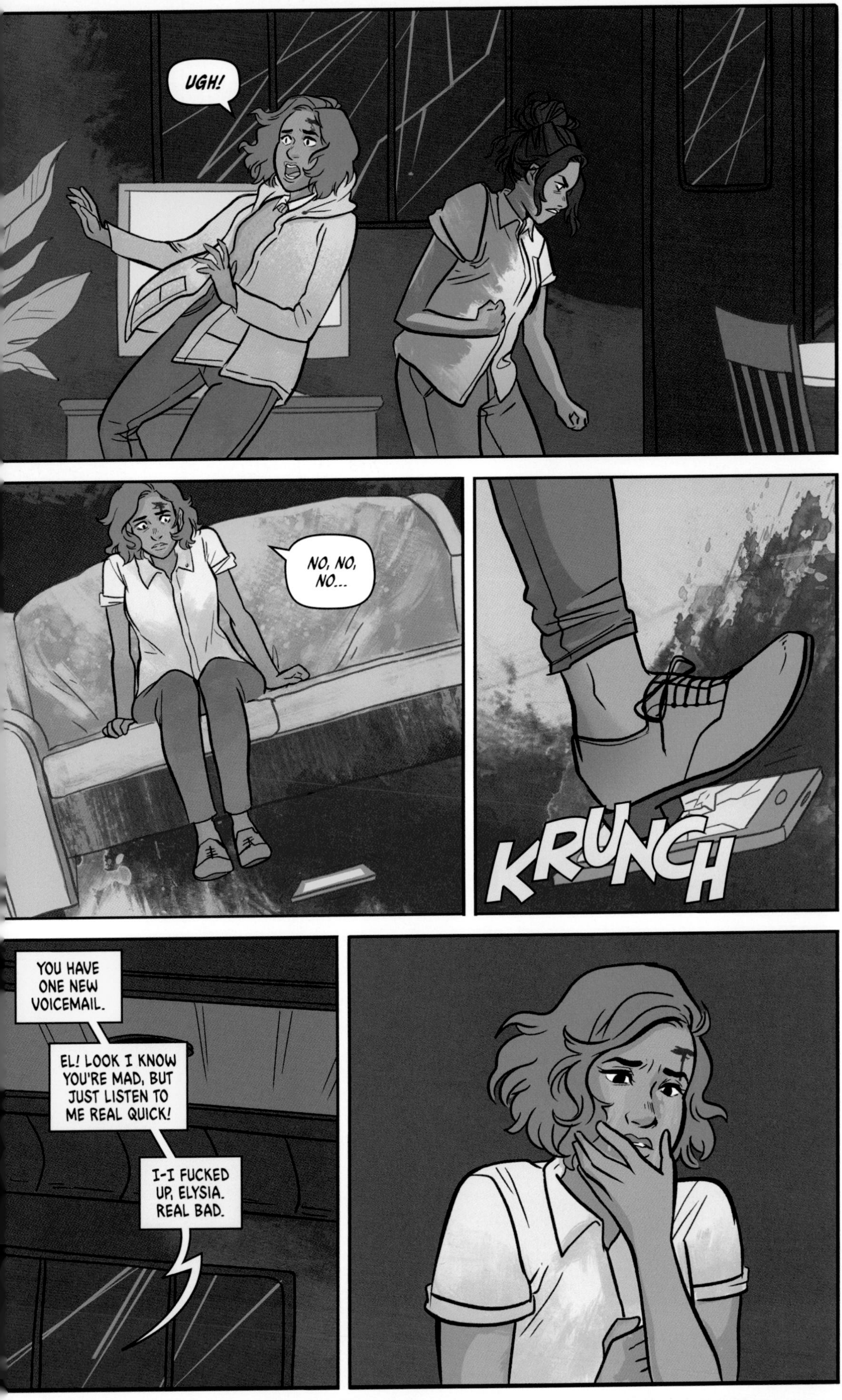
UGH!
NO, NO, NO...
KRUNCH
YOU HAVE ONE NEW VOICEMAIL.
EL! LOOK I KNOW YOU'RE MAD, BUT JUST LISTEN TO ME REAL QUICK!
I-I FUCKED UP, ELYSIA. REAL BAD.

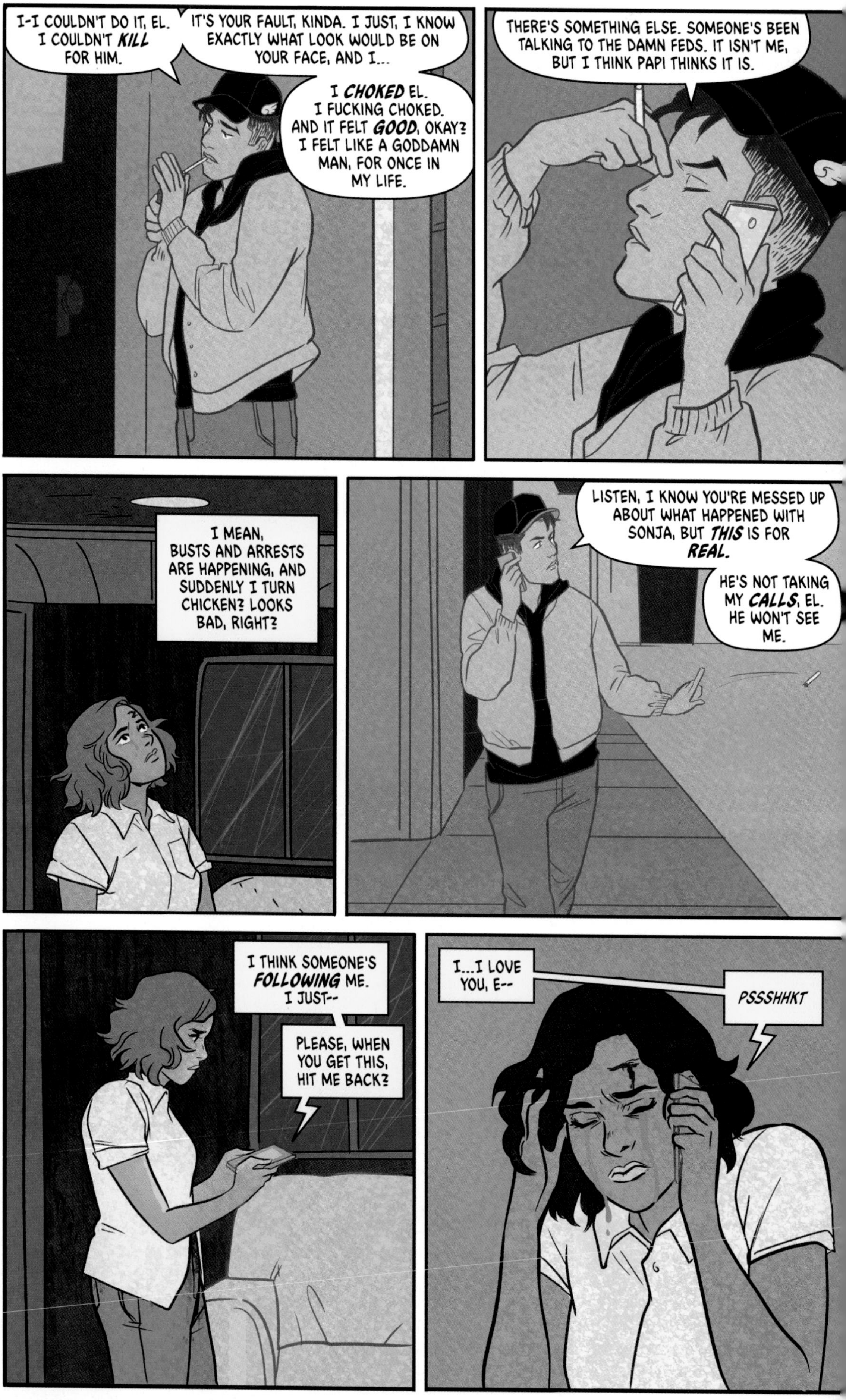

I-I COULDN'T DO IT, EL. I COULDN'T *KILL* FOR HIM.
IT'S YOUR FAULT, KINDA. I JUST, I KNOW EXACTLY WHAT LOOK WOULD BE ON YOUR FACE, AND I...
I *CHOKED* EL. I FUCKING CHOKED. AND IT FELT *GOOD*, OKAY? I FELT LIKE A GODDAMN MAN, FOR ONCE IN MY LIFE.
THERE'S SOMETHING ELSE. SOMEONE'S BEEN TALKING TO THE DAMN FEDS. IT ISN'T ME, BUT I THINK PAPI THINKS IT IS.
I MEAN, BUSTS AND ARRESTS ARE HAPPENING, AND SUDDENLY I TURN CHICKEN? LOOKS BAD, RIGHT?
LISTEN, I KNOW YOU'RE MESSED UP ABOUT WHAT HAPPENED WITH SONJA, BUT *THIS* IS FOR *REAL.*
HE'S NOT TAKING MY *CALLS*, EL. HE WON'T SEE ME.
I THINK SOMEONE'S *FOLLOWING* ME. I JUST--
PLEASE, WHEN YOU GET THIS, HIT ME BACK?
I...I LOVE YOU, E--
PSSSHHKT

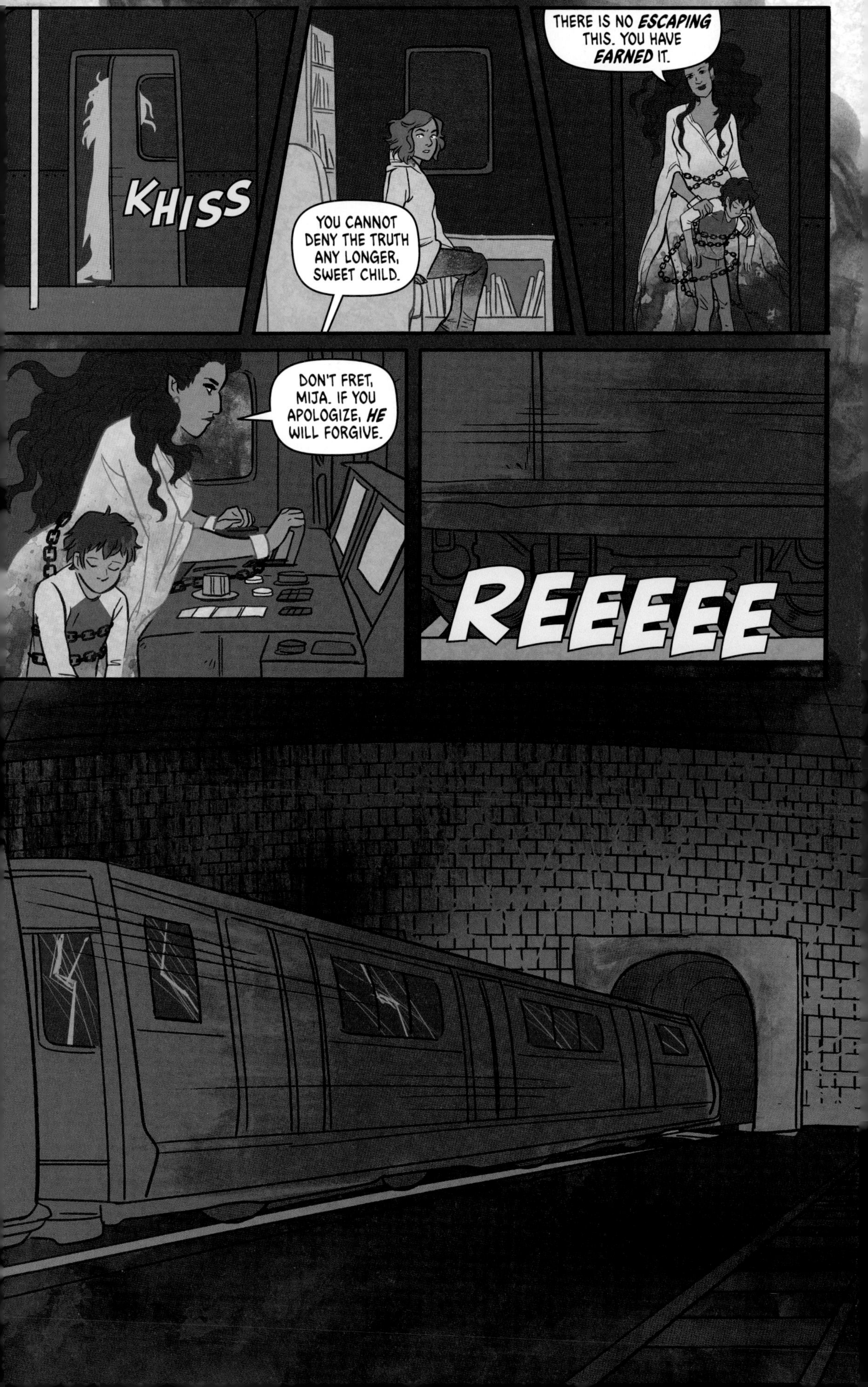
KHISS
YOU CANNOT DENY THE TRUTH ANY LONGER, SWEET CHILD.
THERE IS NO ESCAPING THIS. YOU HAVE EARNED IT.
DON'T FRET, MIJA. IF YOU APOLOGIZE, HE WILL FORGIVE.
REEEEE

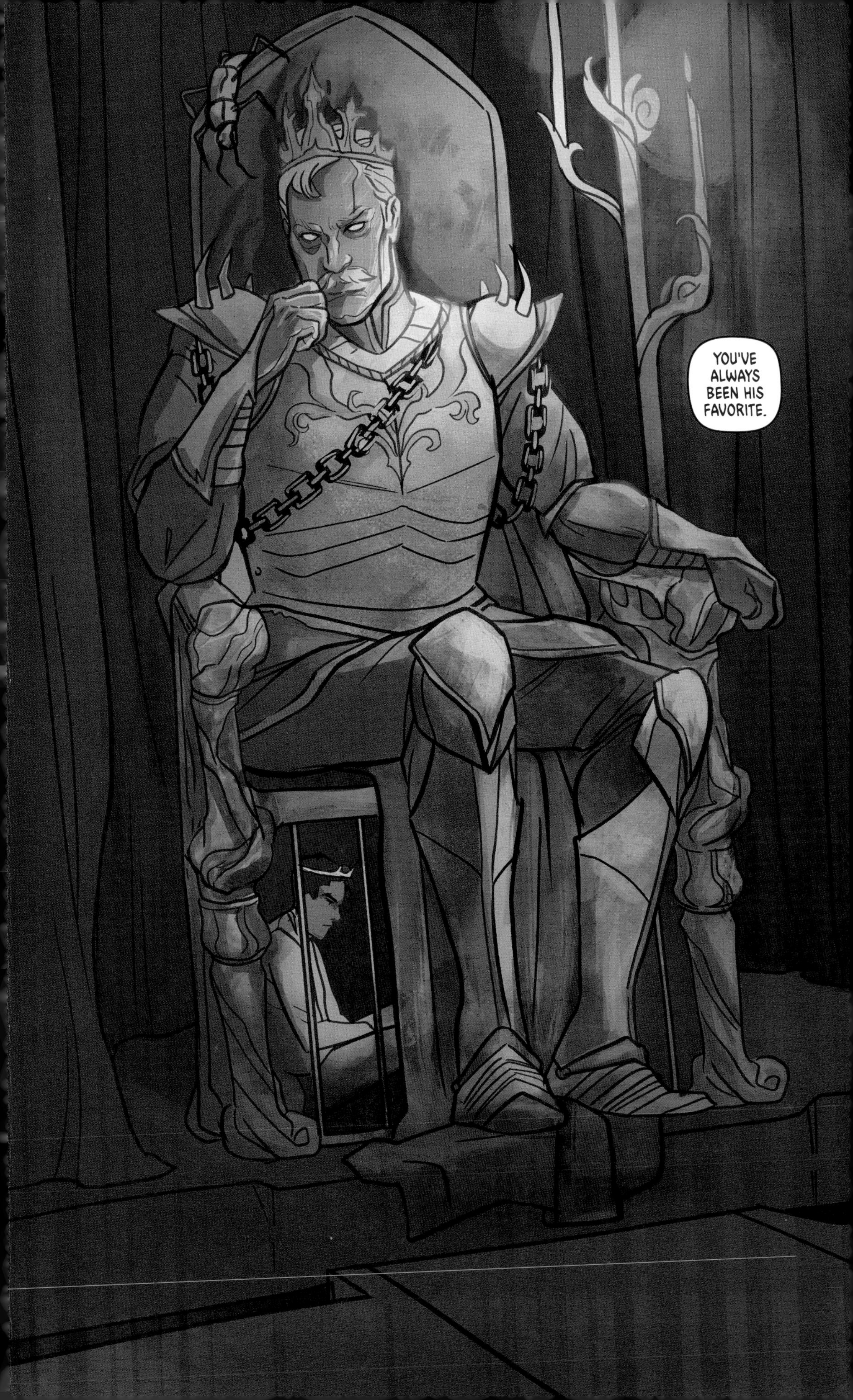
YOU'VE ALWAYS BEEN HIS FAVORITE.

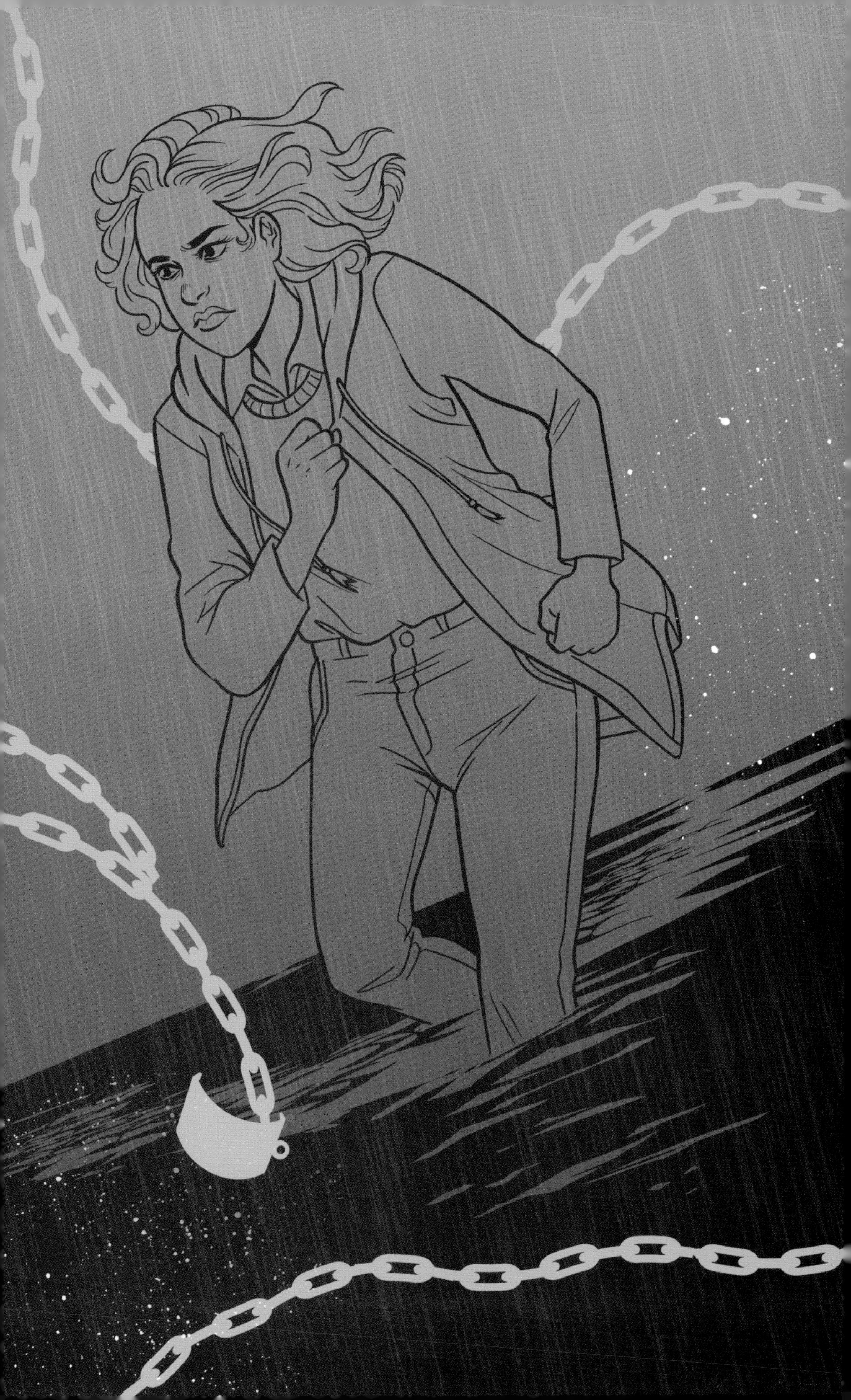

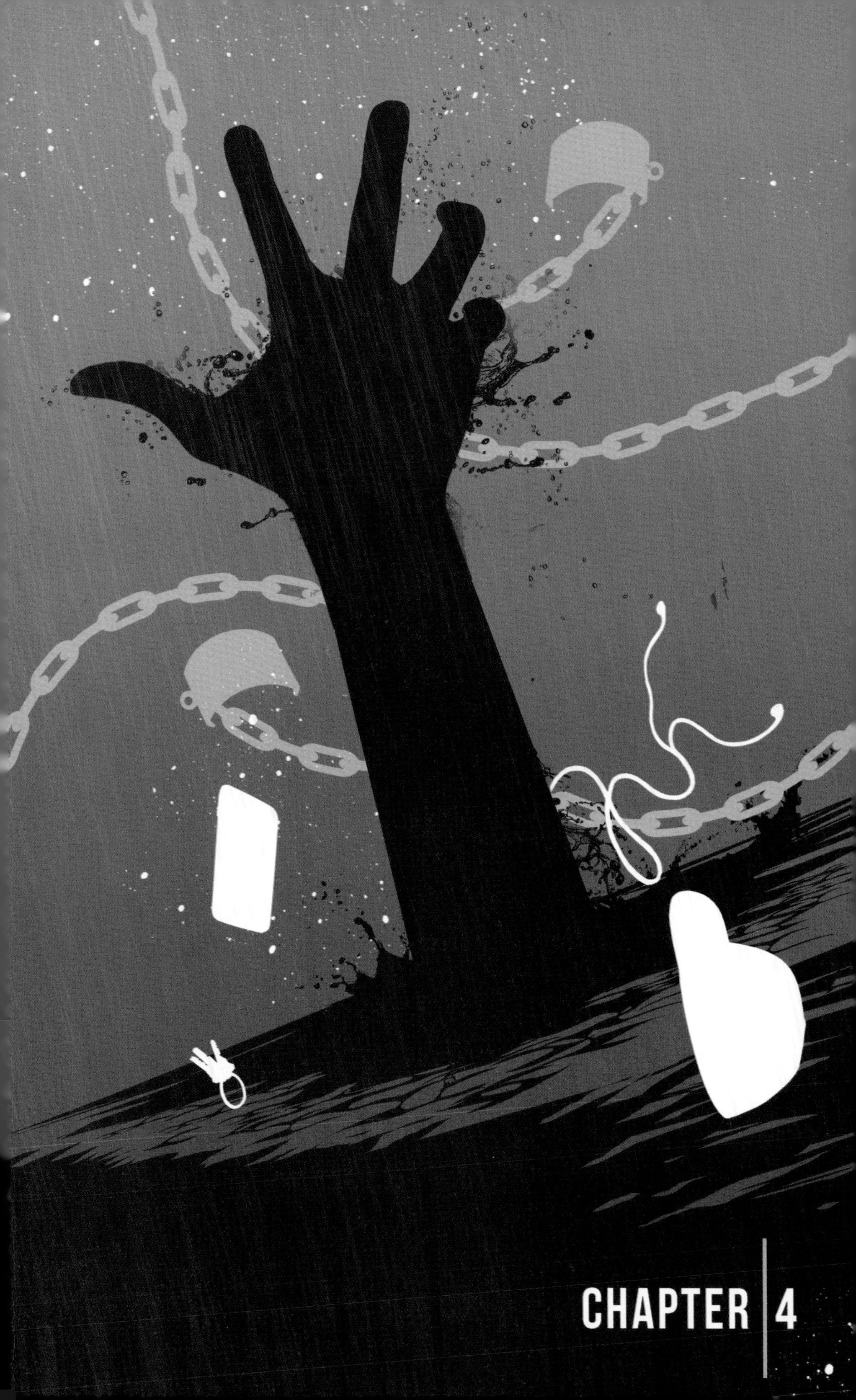

CHAPTER 4

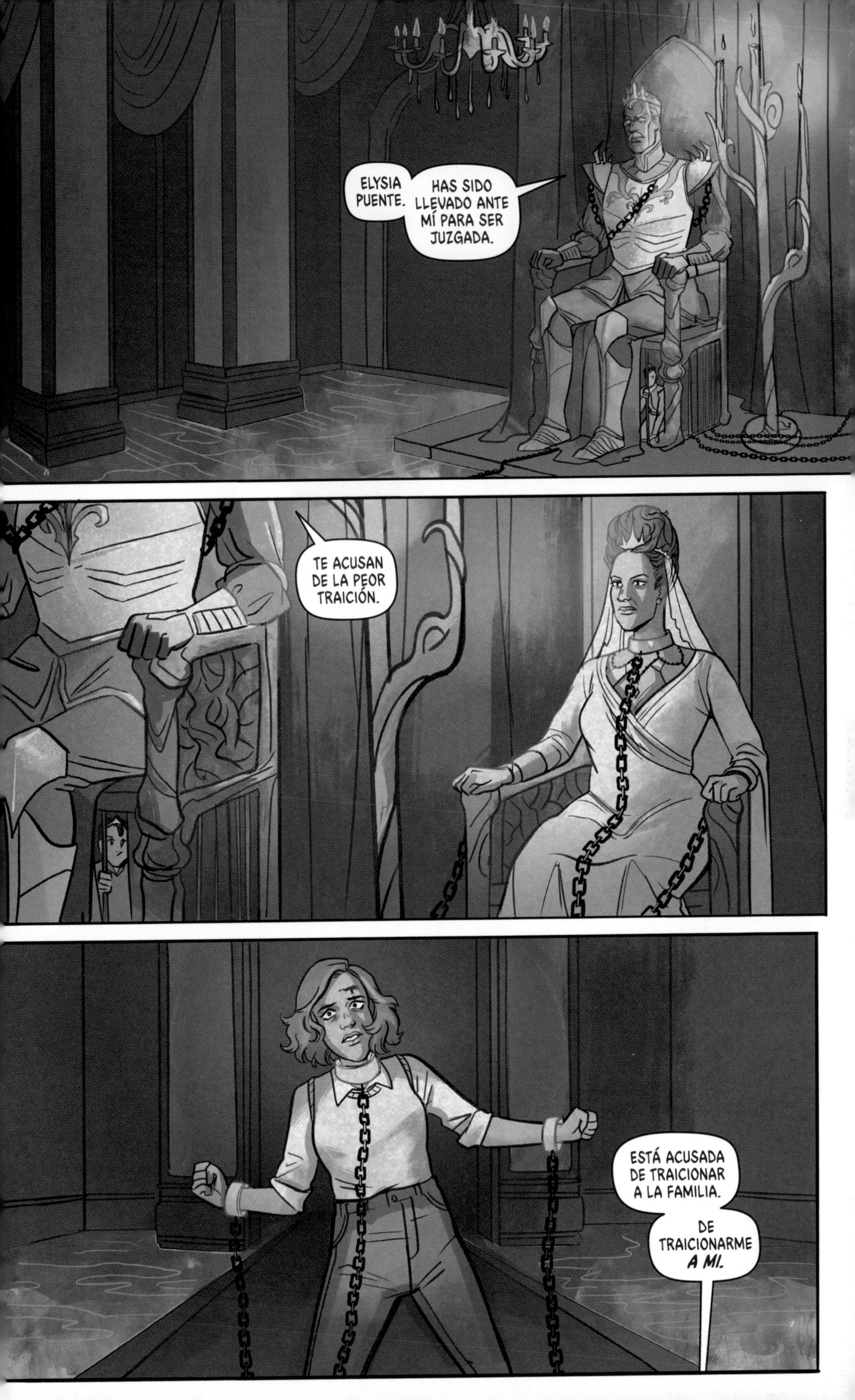
ELYSIA PUENTE.
HAS SIDO LLEVADO ANTE MÍ PARA SER JUZGADA.
TE ACUSAN DE LA PEOR TRAICIÓN.
ESTÁ ACUSADA DE TRAICIONAR A LA FAMILIA.
DE TRAICIONARME *A MÍ.*

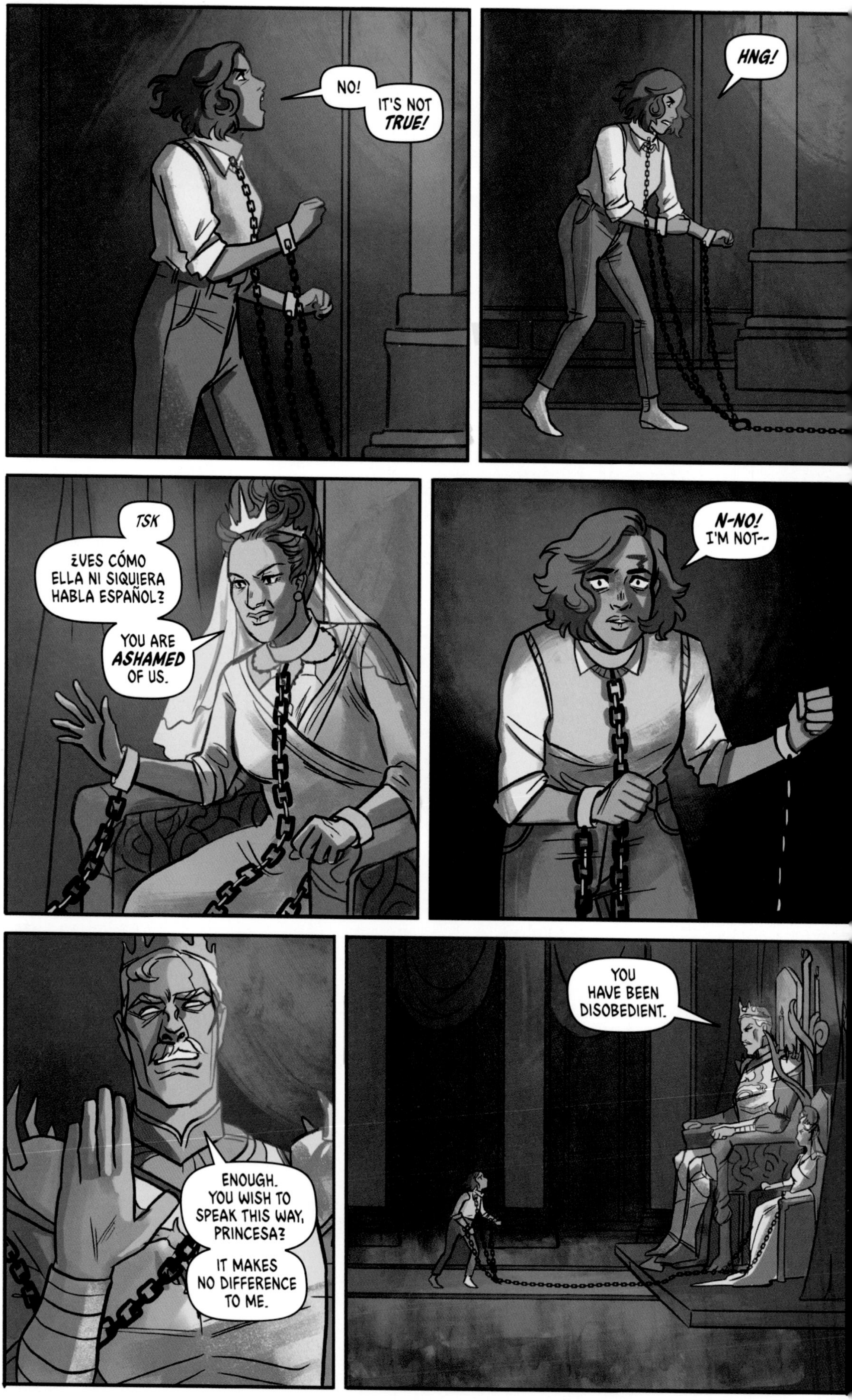

NO!
IT'S NOT TRUE!
HNG!
TSK
¿VES CÓMO ELLA NI SIQUIERA HABLA ESPAÑOL?
YOU ARE ASHAMED OF US.
N-NO! I'M NOT--
ENOUGH. YOU WISH TO SPEAK THIS WAY, PRINCESA?
IT MAKES NO DIFFERENCE TO ME.
YOU HAVE BEEN DISOBEDIENT.

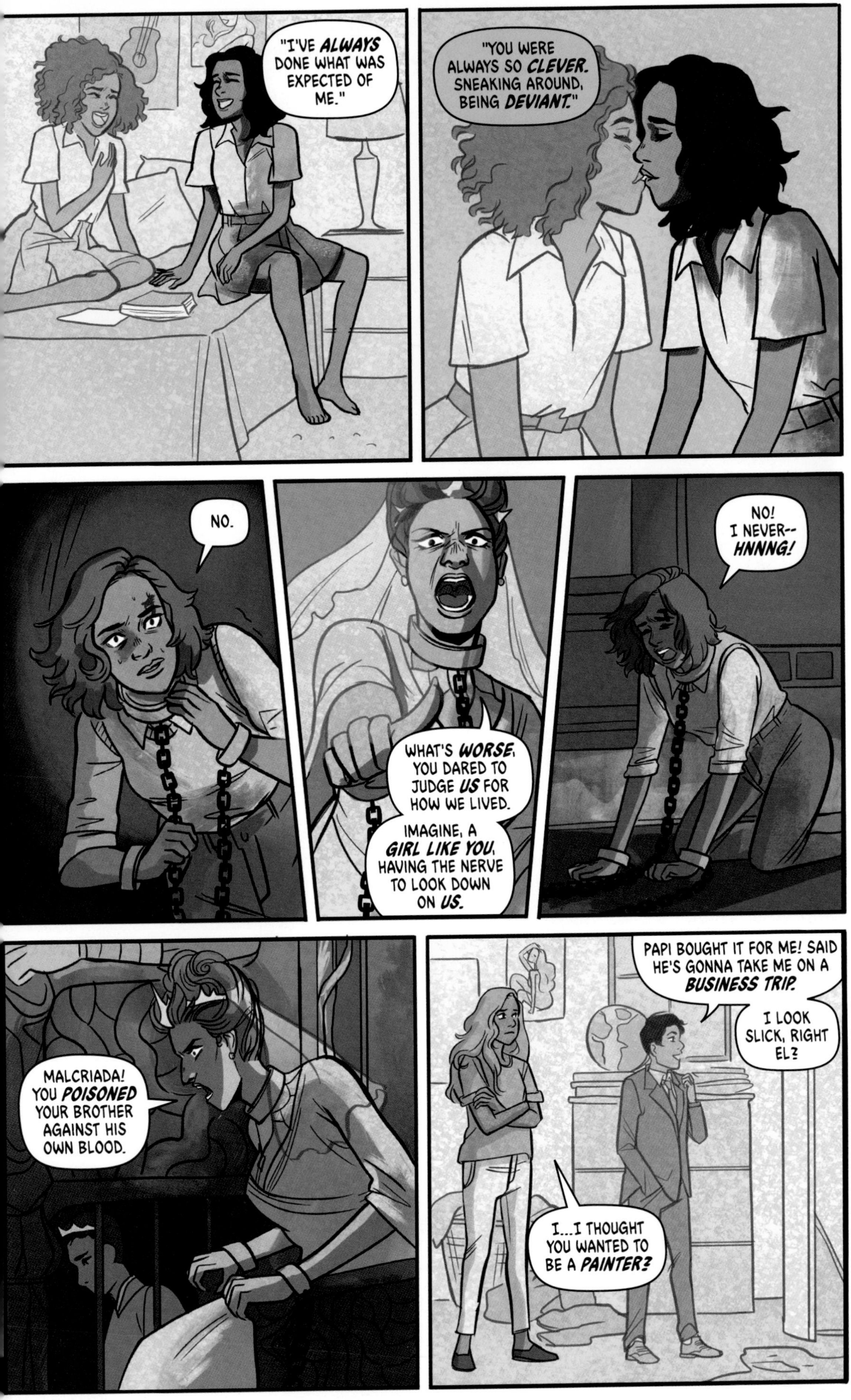
"I'VE ALWAYS DONE WHAT WAS EXPECTED OF ME."
"YOU WERE ALWAYS SO CLEVER. SNEAKING AROUND, BEING DEVIANT."
NO.
WHAT'S WORSE, YOU DARED TO JUDGE US FOR HOW WE LIVED.
IMAGINE, A GIRL LIKE YOU, HAVING THE NERVE TO LOOK DOWN ON US.
NO! I NEVER-- HNNNG!
MALCRIADA! YOU POISONED YOUR BROTHER AGAINST HIS OWN BLOOD.
PAPI BOUGHT IT FOR ME! SAID HE'S GONNA TAKE ME ON A BUSINESS TRIP.
I LOOK SLICK, RIGHT EL?
I...I THOUGHT YOU WANTED TO BE A PAINTER?

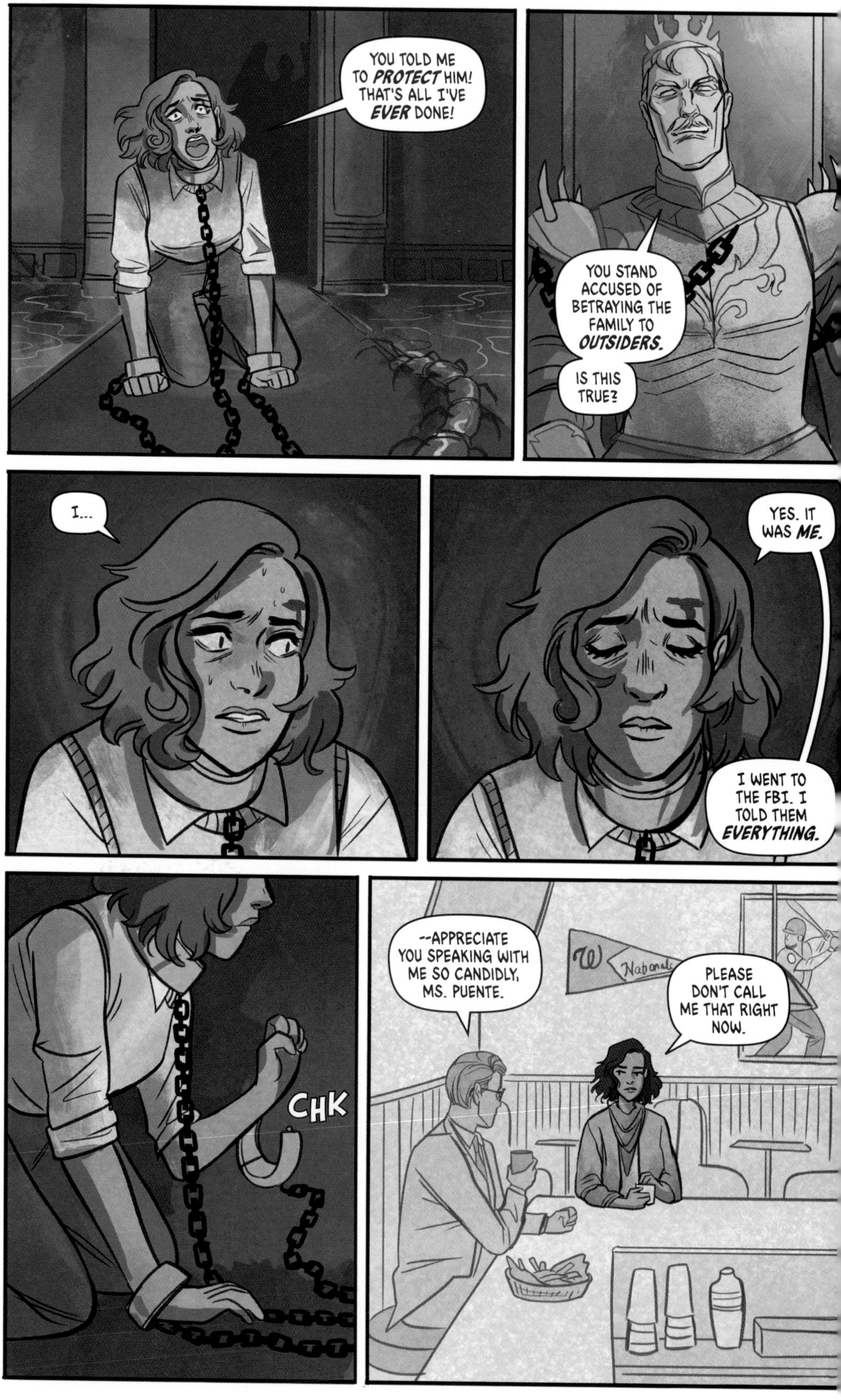
YOU TOLD ME TO *PROTECT* HIM! THAT'S ALL I'VE *EVER* DONE!
YOU STAND ACCUSED OF BETRAYING THE FAMILY TO *OUTSIDERS.*
IS THIS TRUE?
I...
YES. IT WAS *ME.*
I WENT TO THE FBI. I TOLD THEM *EVERYTHING.*
CHK
--APPRECIATE YOU SPEAKING WITH ME SO CANDIDLY, MS. PUENTE.
PLEASE DON'T CALL ME THAT RIGHT NOW.

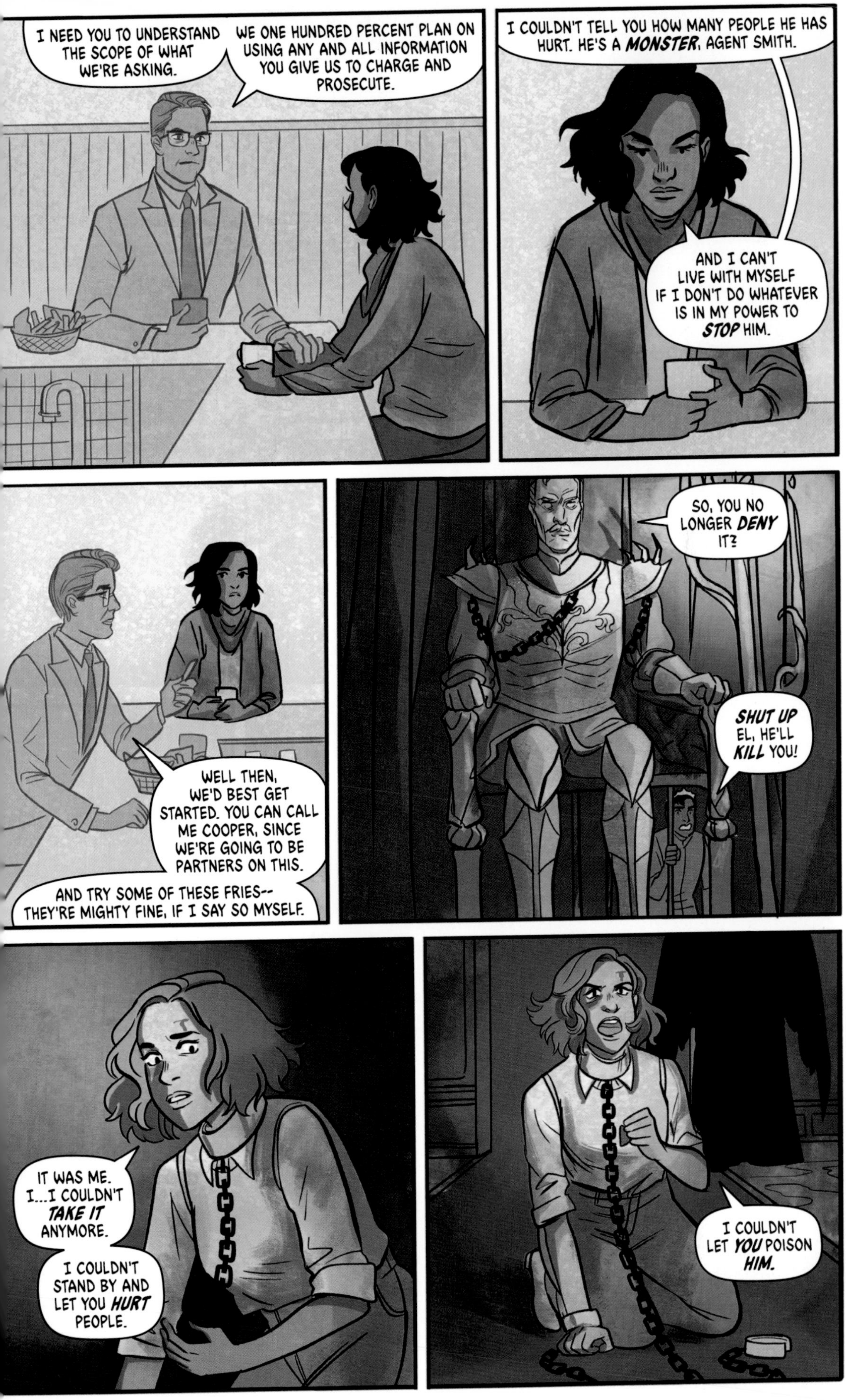
I NEED YOU TO UNDERSTAND THE SCOPE OF WHAT WE'RE ASKING.
WE ONE HUNDRED PERCENT PLAN ON USING ANY AND ALL INFORMATION YOU GIVE US TO CHARGE AND PROSECUTE.
I COULDN'T TELL YOU HOW MANY PEOPLE HE HAS HURT. HE'S A MONSTER, AGENT SMITH.
AND I CAN'T LIVE WITH MYSELF IF I DON'T DO WHATEVER IS IN MY POWER TO STOP HIM.
WELL THEN, WE'D BEST GET STARTED. YOU CAN CALL ME COOPER, SINCE WE'RE GOING TO BE PARTNERS ON THIS.
AND TRY SOME OF THESE FRIES-- THEY'RE MIGHTY FINE, IF I SAY SO MYSELF.
SO, YOU NO LONGER DENY IT?
SHUT UP EL, HE'LL KILL YOU!
IT WAS ME. I...I COULDN'T TAKE IT ANYMORE.
I COULDN'T STAND BY AND LET YOU HURT PEOPLE.
I COULDN'T LET YOU POISON HIM.

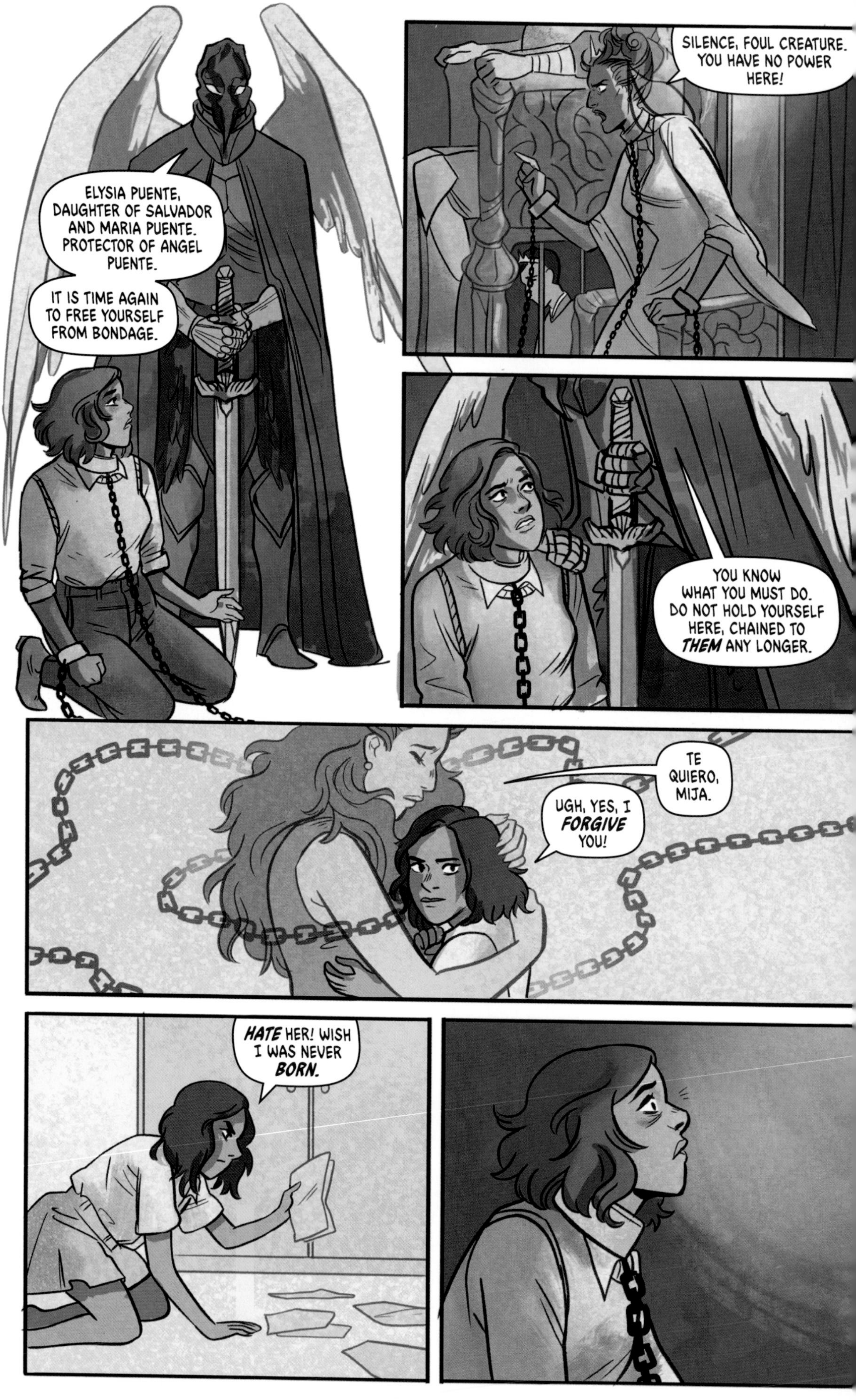
ELYSIA PUENTE, DAUGHTER OF SALVADOR AND MARIA PUENTE. PROTECTOR OF ANGEL PUENTE.
IT IS TIME AGAIN TO FREE YOURSELF FROM BONDAGE.
SILENCE, FOUL CREATURE. YOU HAVE NO POWER HERE!
YOU KNOW WHAT YOU MUST DO. DO NOT HOLD YOURSELF HERE, CHAINED TO *THEM* ANY LONGER.
TE QUIERO, MIJA.
UGH, YES, I *FORGIVE* YOU!
HATE HER! WISH I WAS NEVER *BORN.*

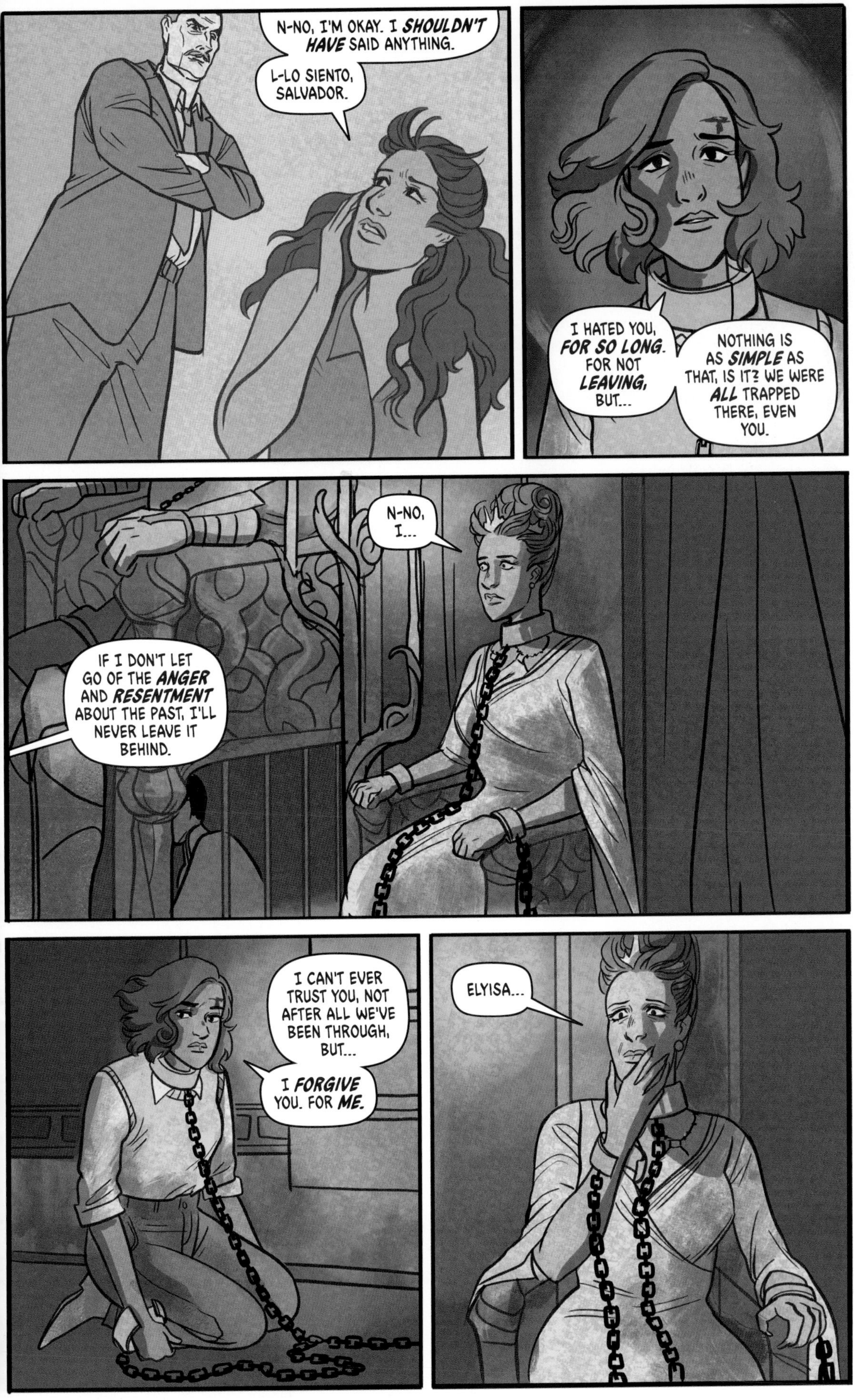
N-NO, I'M OKAY. I SHOULDN'T HAVE SAID ANYTHING.
L-LO SIENTO, SALVADOR.
I HATED YOU, FOR SO LONG. FOR NOT LEAVING, BUT...
NOTHING IS AS SIMPLE AS THAT, IS IT? WE WERE ALL TRAPPED THERE, EVEN YOU.
N-NO, I...
IF I DON'T LET GO OF THE ANGER AND RESENTMENT ABOUT THE PAST, I'LL NEVER LEAVE IT BEHIND.
I CAN'T EVER TRUST YOU, NOT AFTER ALL WE'VE BEEN THROUGH, BUT...
I FORGIVE YOU. FOR ME.
ELYISA...

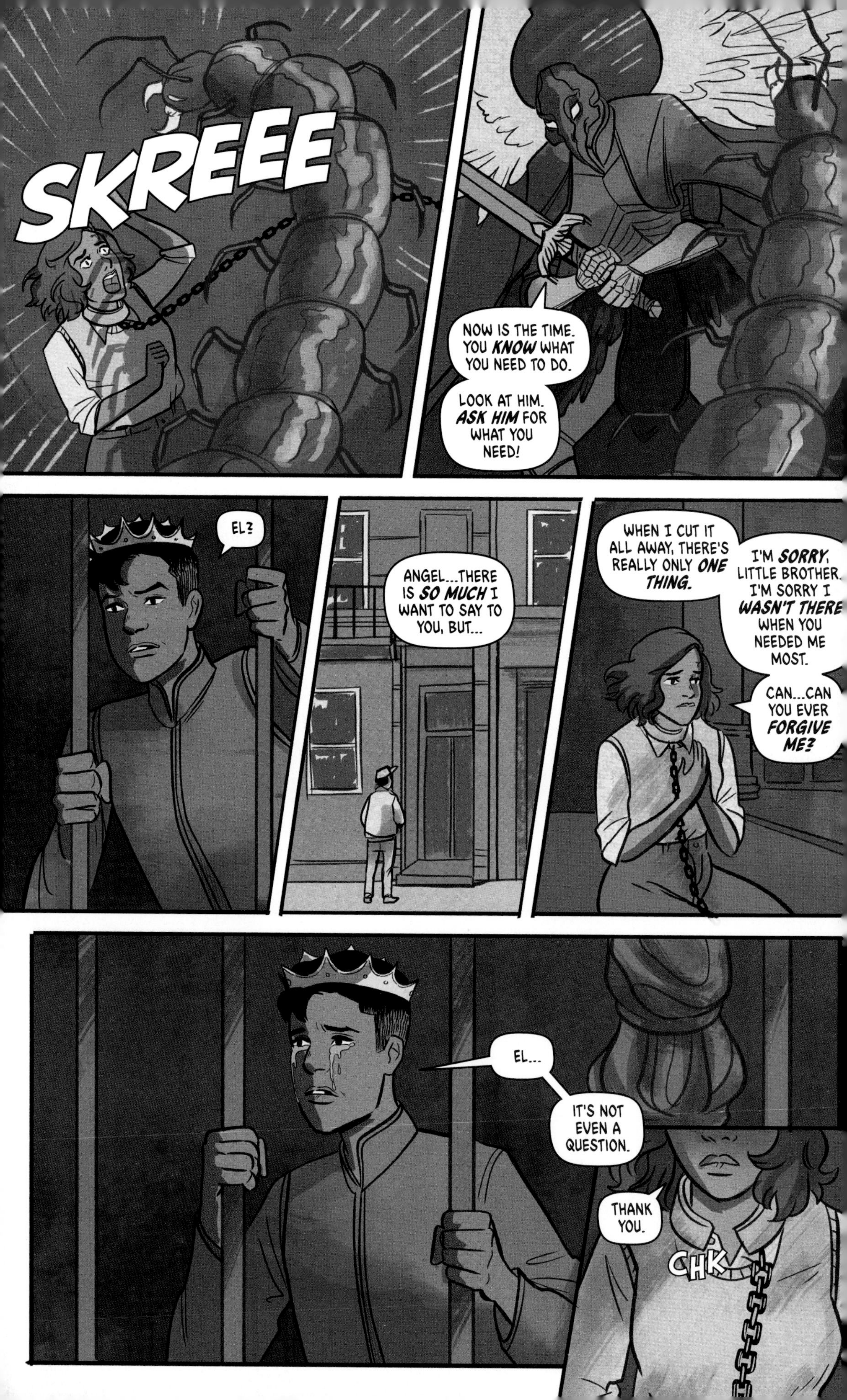
SKREEE
NOW IS THE TIME. YOU KNOW WHAT YOU NEED TO DO.
LOOK AT HIM. ASK HIM FOR WHAT YOU NEED!
EL?
ANGEL...THERE IS SO MUCH I WANT TO SAY TO YOU, BUT...
WHEN I CUT IT ALL AWAY, THERE'S REALLY ONLY ONE THING.
I'M SORRY, LITTLE BROTHER. I'M SORRY I WASN'T THERE WHEN YOU NEEDED ME MOST.
CAN...CAN YOU EVER FORGIVE ME?
EL...
IT'S NOT EVEN A QUESTION.
THANK YOU.
CHK

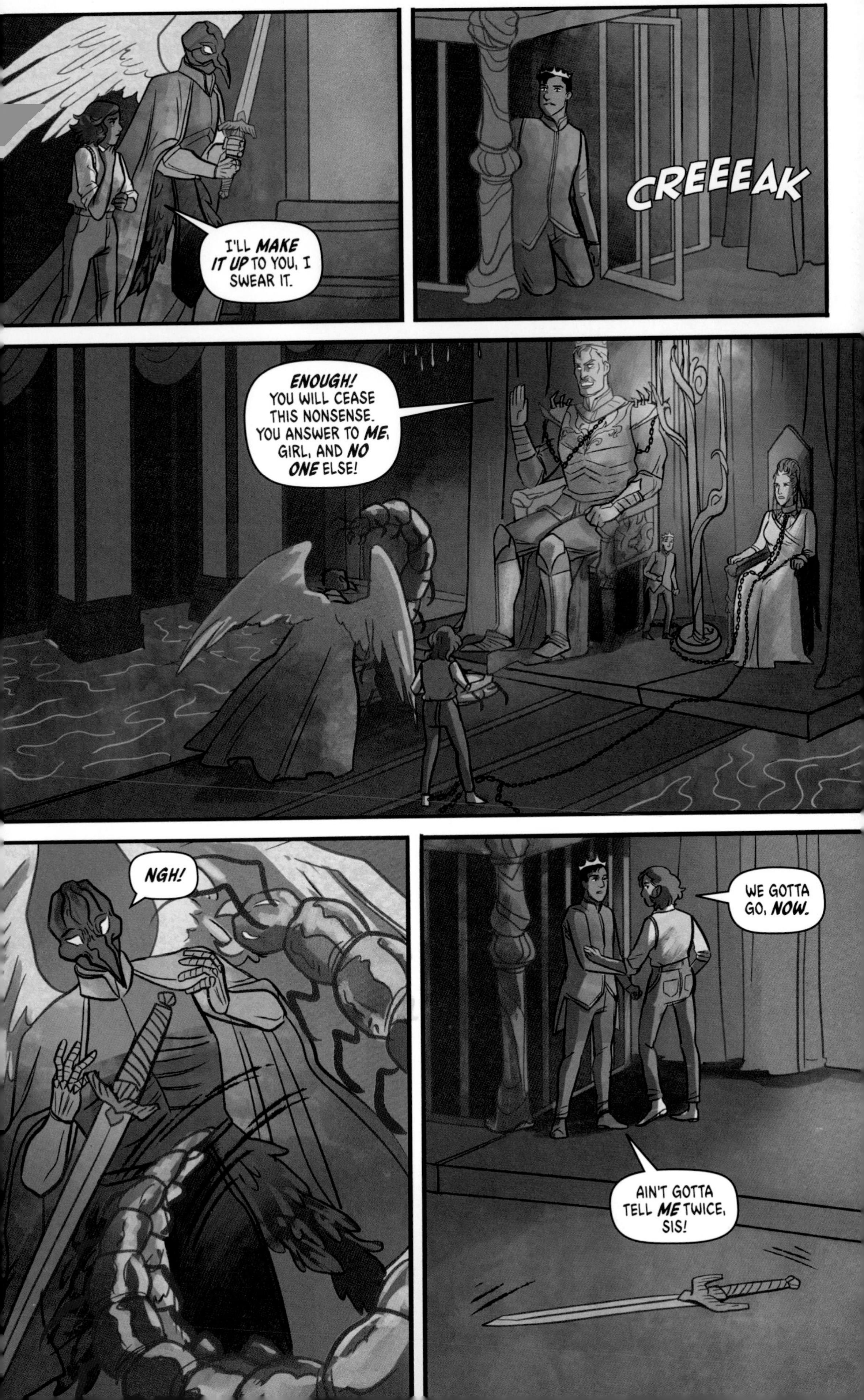
I'LL MAKE IT UP TO YOU, I SWEAR IT.
CREEEAK
ENOUGH! YOU WILL CEASE THIS NONSENSE. YOU ANSWER TO ME, GIRL, AND NO ONE ELSE!
NGH!
WE GOTTA GO, NOW.
AIN'T GOTTA TELL ME TWICE, SIS!

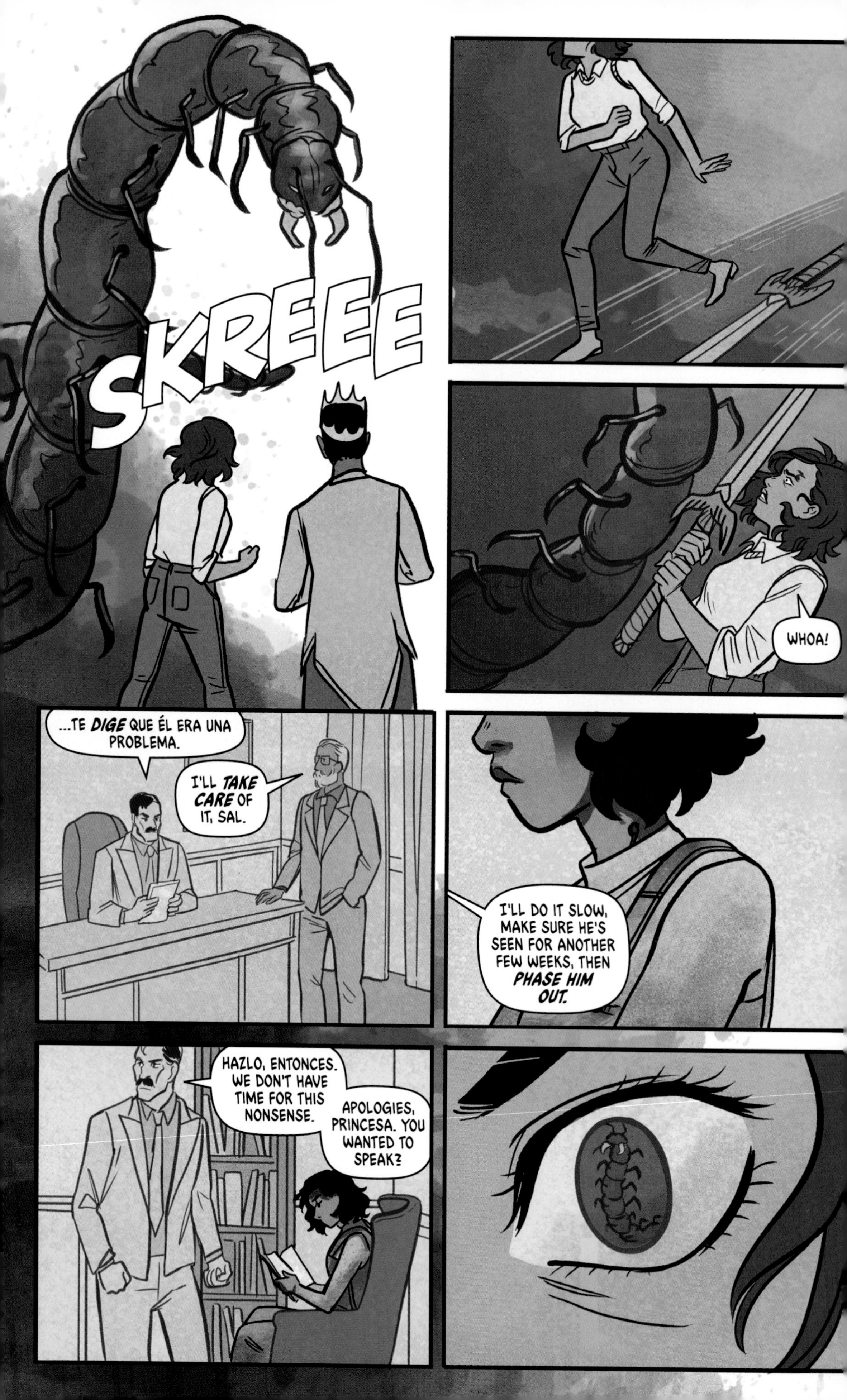
SKREEE
WHOA!
...TE DIGE QUE ÉL ERA UNA PROBLEMA.
I'LL TAKE CARE OF IT, SAL.
I'LL DO IT SLOW, MAKE SURE HE'S SEEN FOR ANOTHER FEW WEEKS, THEN PHASE HIM OUT.
HAZLO, ENTONCES. WE DON'T HAVE TIME FOR THIS NONSENSE.
APOLOGIES, PRINCESA. YOU WANTED TO SPEAK?

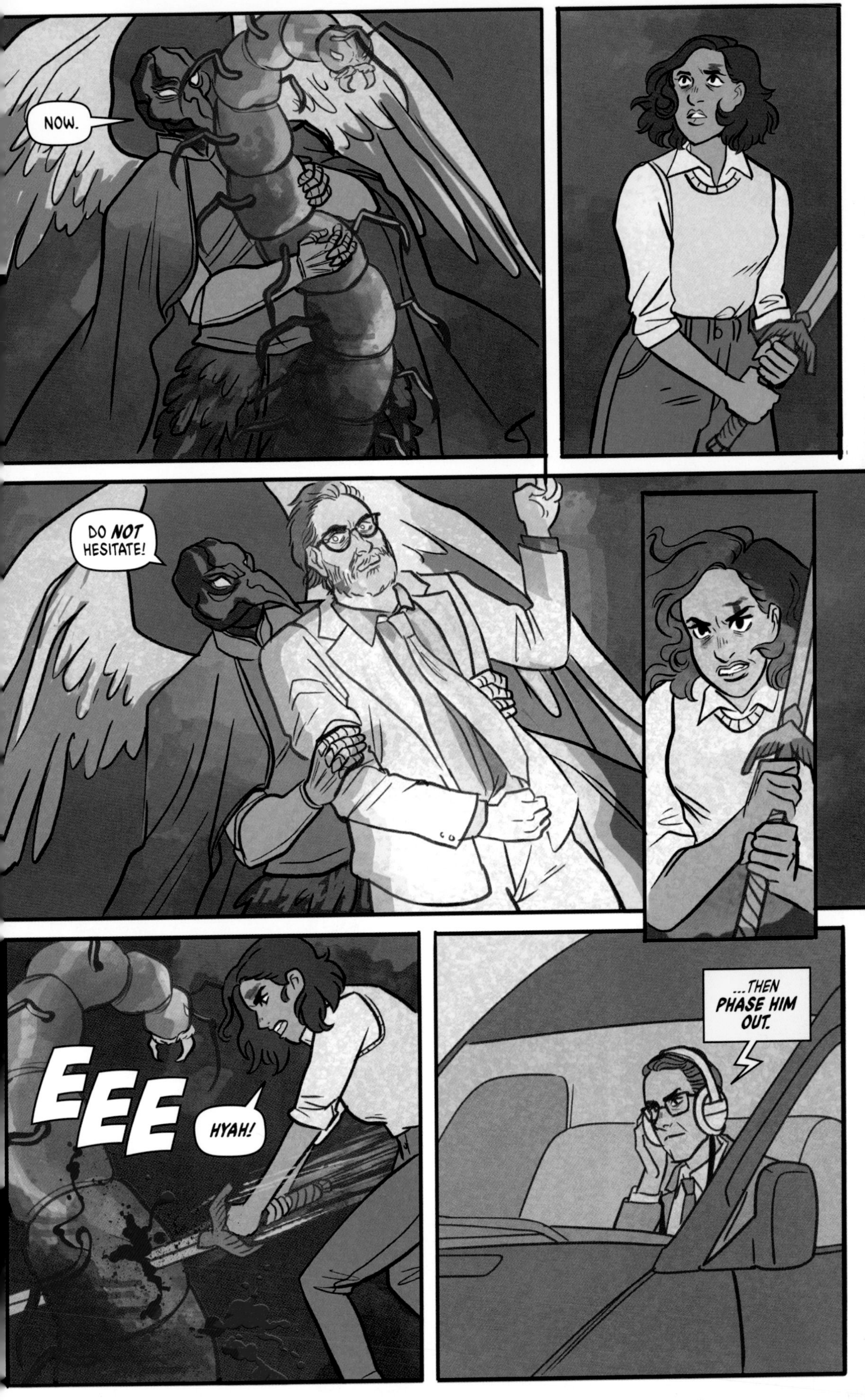
NOW.
DO NOT HESITATE!
EEE
HYAH!
...THEN PHASE HIM OUT.

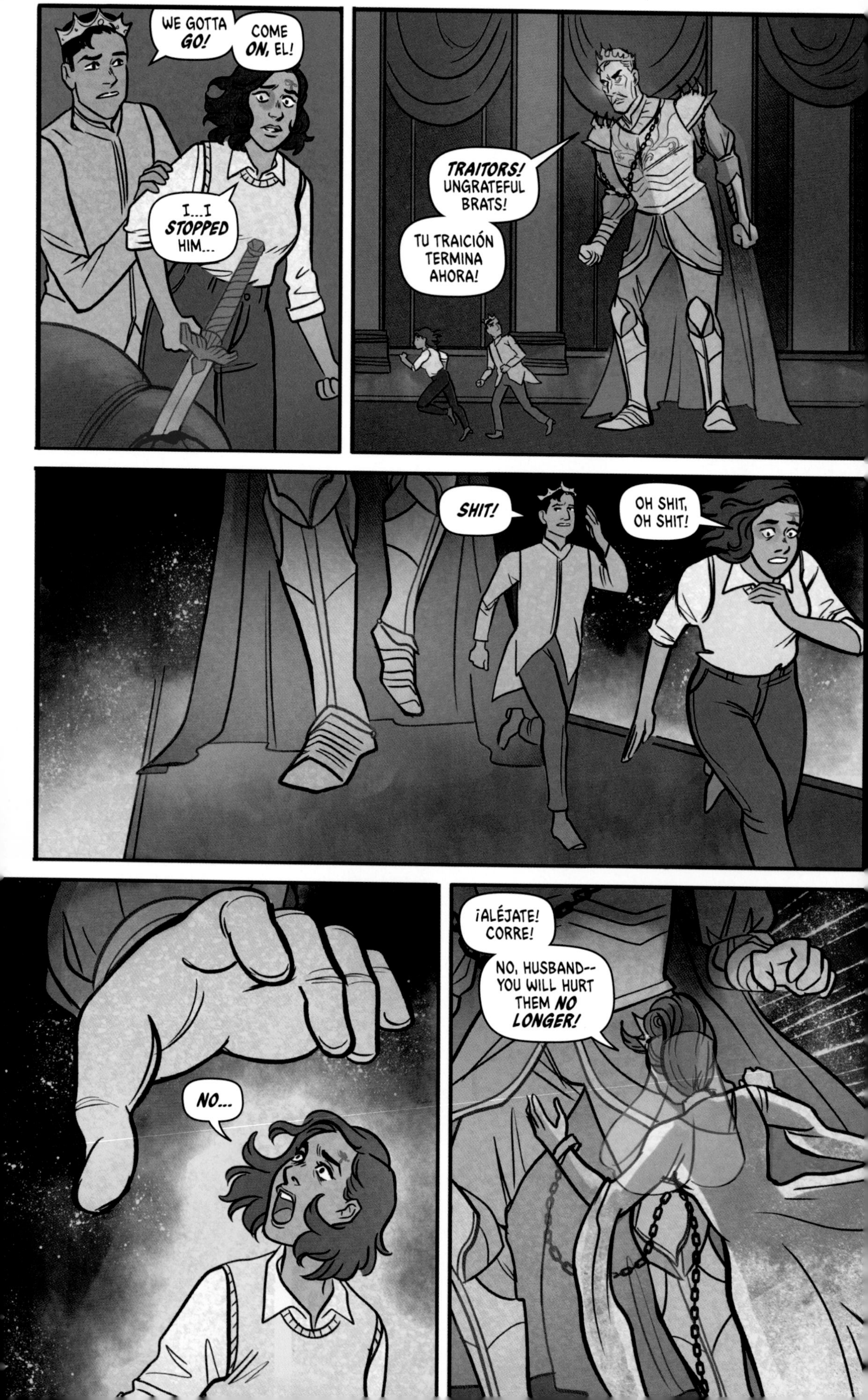

WE GOTTA GO!
COME ON, EL!
I...I STOPPED HIM...
TRAITORS! UNGRATEFUL BRATS!
TU TRAICIÓN TERMINA AHORA!
SHIT!
OH SHIT, OH SHIT!
NO...
¡ALÉJATE! CORRE!
NO, HUSBAND-- YOU WILL HURT THEM NO LONGER!

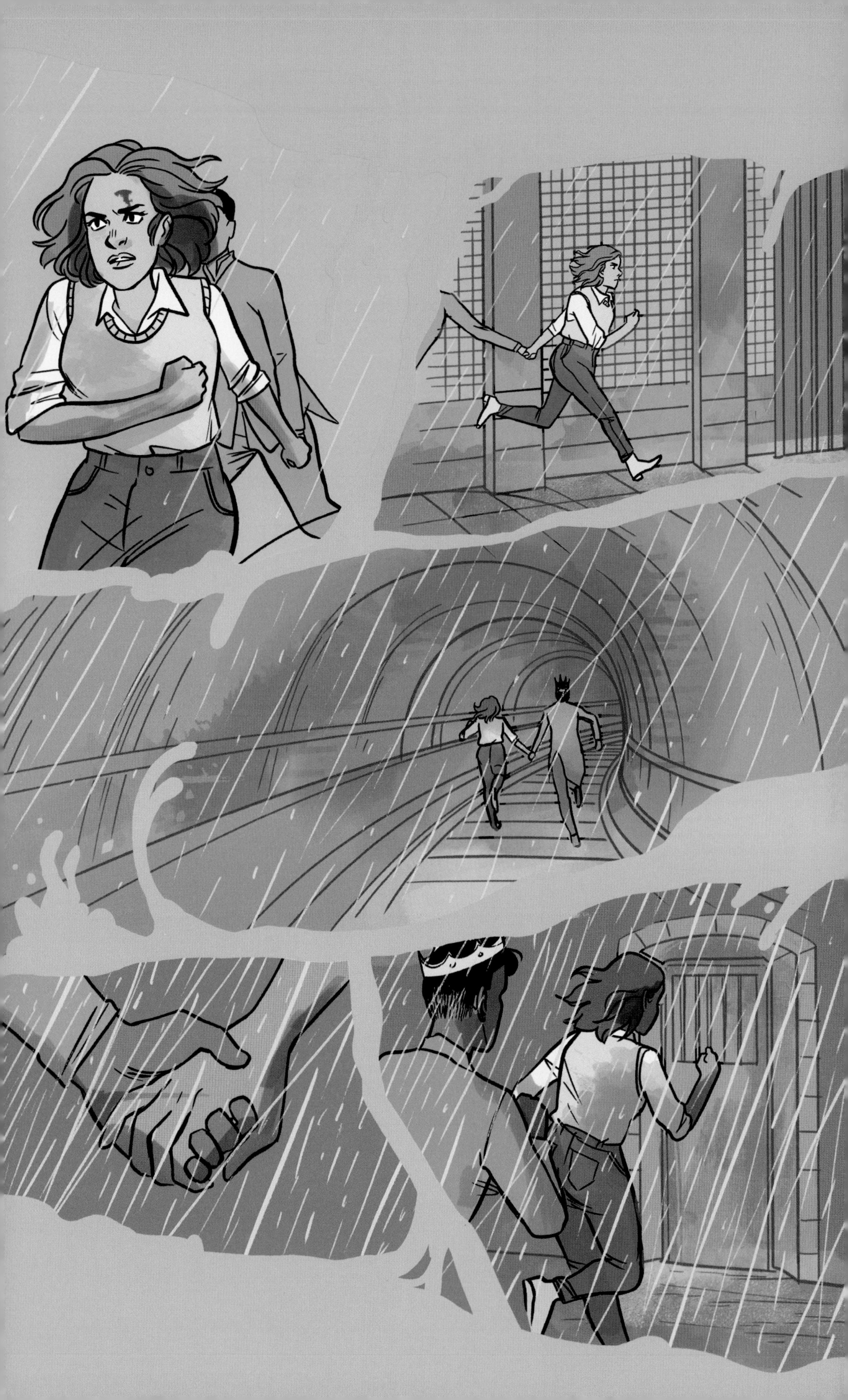

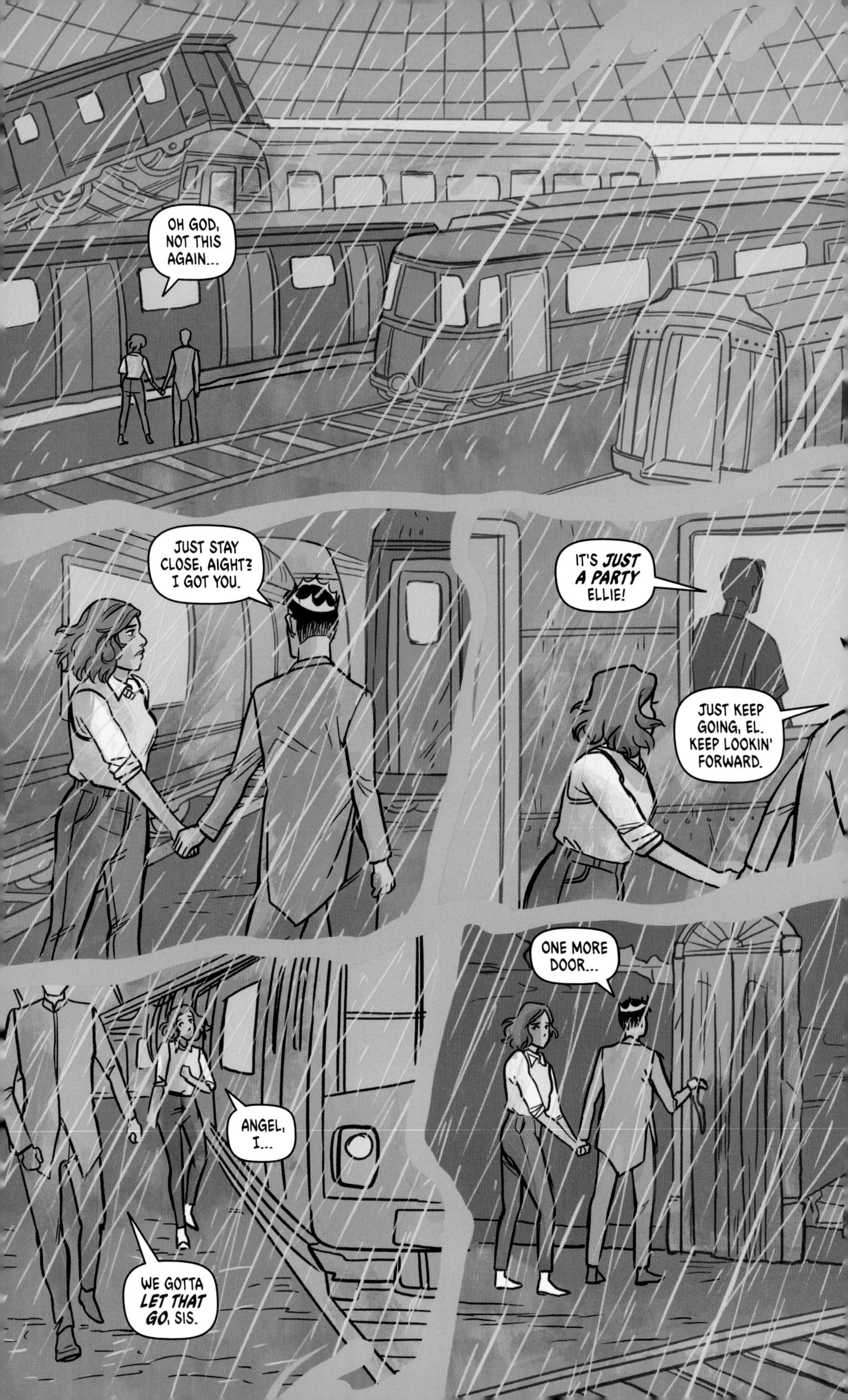
OH GOD, NOT THIS AGAIN...
JUST STAY CLOSE, AIGHT? I GOT YOU.
IT'S *JUST A PARTY* ELLIE!
JUST KEEP GOING, EL. KEEP LOOKIN' FORWARD.
ANGEL, I...
WE GOTTA *LET THAT GO*, SIS.
ONE MORE DOOR...

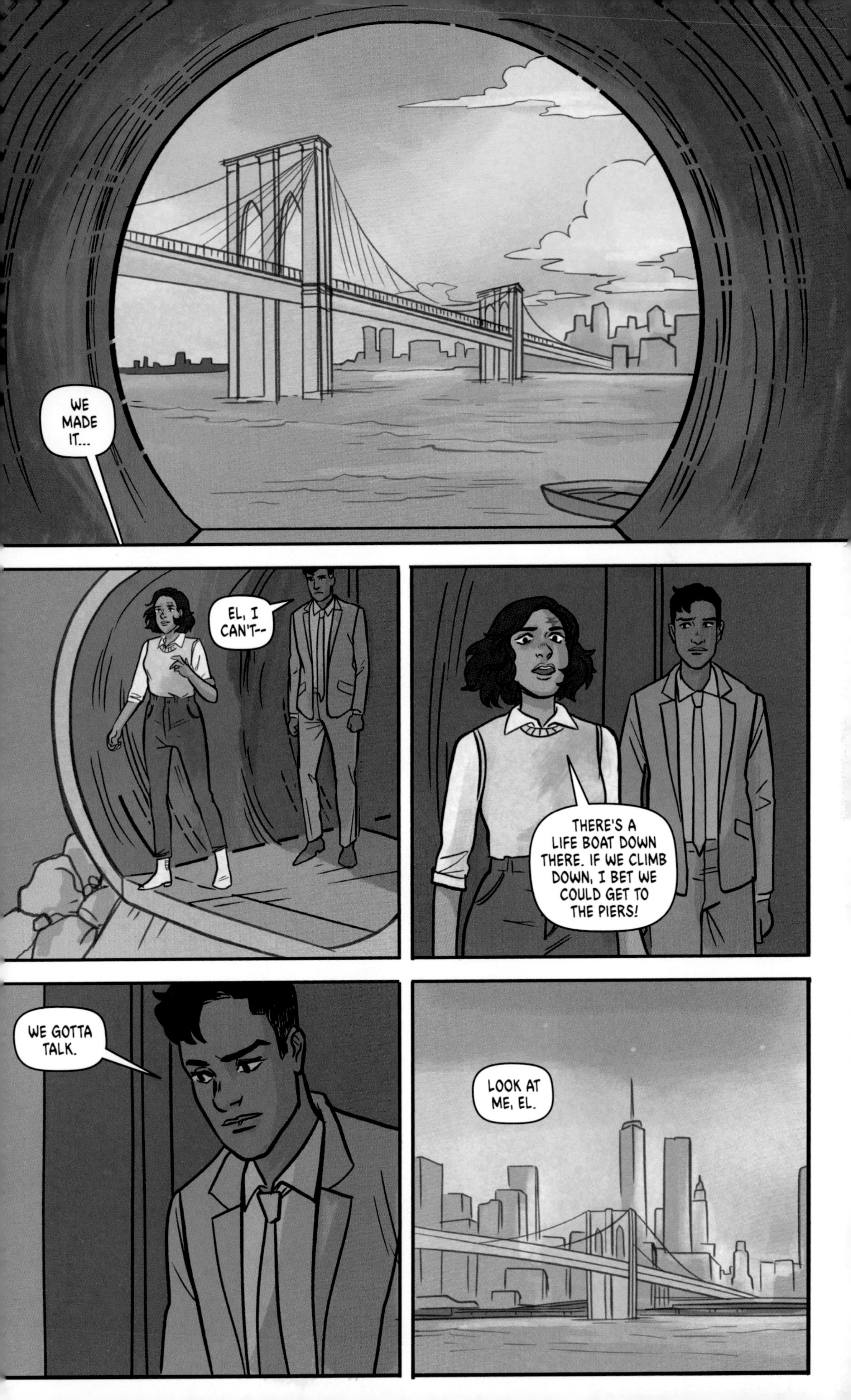
WE MADE IT...
EL, I CAN'T--
THERE'S A LIFE BOAT DOWN THERE. IF WE CLIMB DOWN, I BET WE COULD GET TO THE PIERS!
WE GOTTA TALK.
LOOK AT ME, EL.

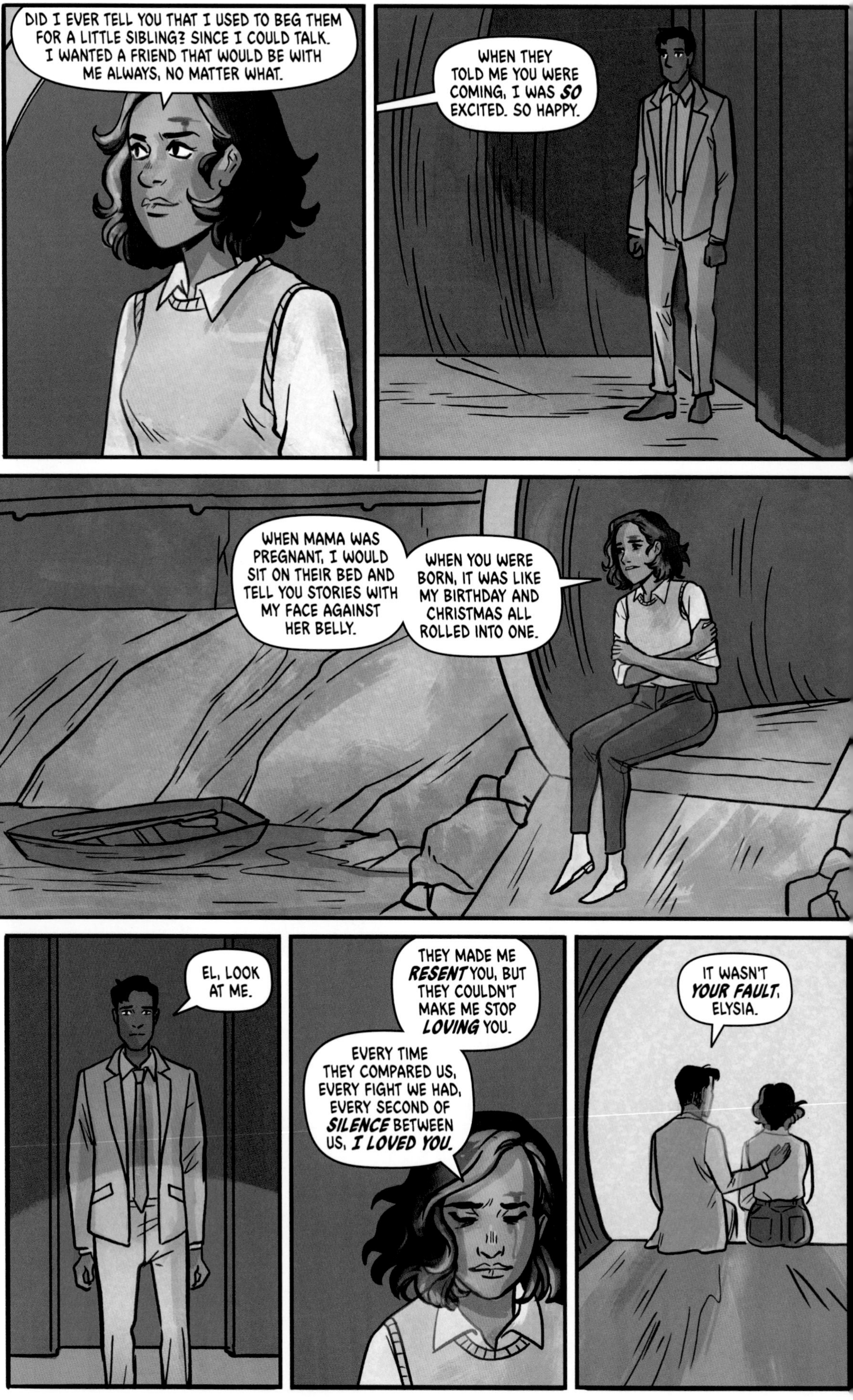
DID I EVER TELL YOU THAT I USED TO BEG THEM FOR A LITTLE SIBLING? SINCE I COULD TALK. I WANTED A FRIEND THAT WOULD BE WITH ME ALWAYS, NO MATTER WHAT.
WHEN THEY TOLD ME YOU WERE COMING, I WAS *SO* EXCITED. SO HAPPY.
WHEN MAMA WAS PREGNANT, I WOULD SIT ON THEIR BED AND TELL YOU STORIES WITH MY FACE AGAINST HER BELLY.
WHEN YOU WERE BORN, IT WAS LIKE MY BIRTHDAY AND CHRISTMAS ALL ROLLED INTO ONE.
EL, LOOK AT ME.
THEY MADE ME *RESENT* YOU, BUT THEY COULDN'T MAKE ME STOP *LOVING* YOU.
EVERY TIME THEY COMPARED US, EVERY FIGHT WE HAD, EVERY SECOND OF *SILENCE* BETWEEN US, *I LOVED YOU.*
IT WASN'T *YOUR FAULT*, ELYSIA.

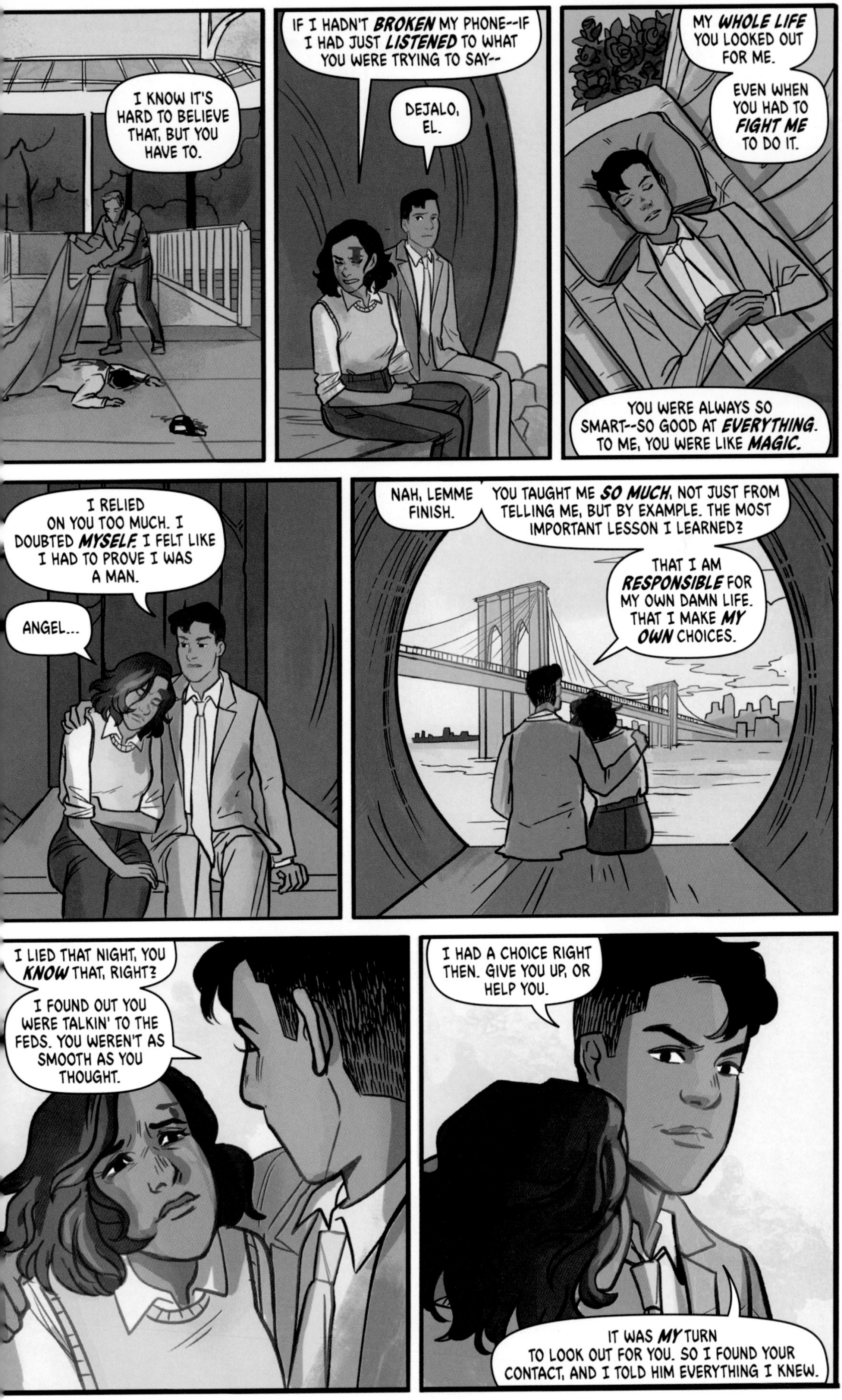
I KNOW IT'S HARD TO BELIEVE THAT, BUT YOU HAVE TO.
IF I HADN'T BROKEN MY PHONE--IF I HAD JUST LISTENED TO WHAT YOU WERE TRYING TO SAY--
DEJALO, EL.
MY WHOLE LIFE YOU LOOKED OUT FOR ME.
EVEN WHEN YOU HAD TO FIGHT ME TO DO IT.
YOU WERE ALWAYS SO SMART--SO GOOD AT EVERYTHING. TO ME, YOU WERE LIKE MAGIC.
I RELIED ON YOU TOO MUCH. I DOUBTED MYSELF. I FELT LIKE I HAD TO PROVE I WAS A MAN.
ANGEL...
NAH, LEMME FINISH.
YOU TAUGHT ME SO MUCH, NOT JUST FROM TELLING ME, BUT BY EXAMPLE. THE MOST IMPORTANT LESSON I LEARNED?
THAT I AM RESPONSIBLE FOR MY OWN DAMN LIFE. THAT I MAKE MY OWN CHOICES.
I LIED THAT NIGHT, YOU KNOW THAT, RIGHT?
I FOUND OUT YOU WERE TALKIN' TO THE FEDS. YOU WEREN'T AS SMOOTH AS YOU THOUGHT.
I HAD A CHOICE RIGHT THEN. GIVE YOU UP, OR HELP YOU.
IT WAS MY TURN TO LOOK OUT FOR YOU. SO I FOUND YOUR CONTACT, AND I TOLD HIM EVERYTHING I KNEW.

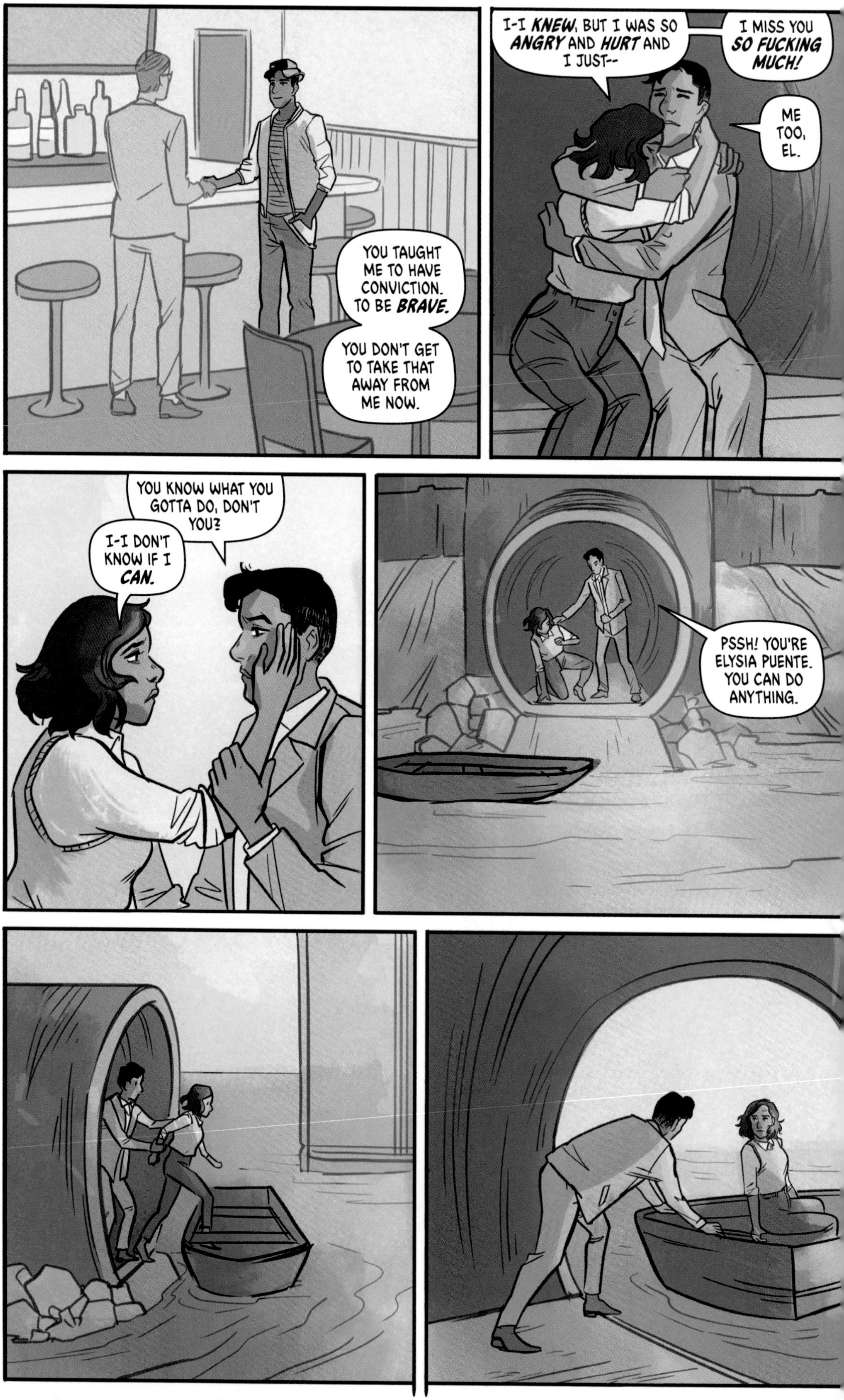
YOU TAUGHT ME TO HAVE CONVICTION. TO BE BRAVE.
YOU DON'T GET TO TAKE THAT AWAY FROM ME NOW.
I-I KNEW, BUT I WAS SO ANGRY AND HURT AND I JUST--
I MISS YOU SO FUCKING MUCH!
ME TOO, EL.
YOU KNOW WHAT YOU GOTTA DO, DON'T YOU?
I-I DON'T KNOW IF I CAN.
PSSH! YOU'RE ELYSIA PUENTE. YOU CAN DO ANYTHING.

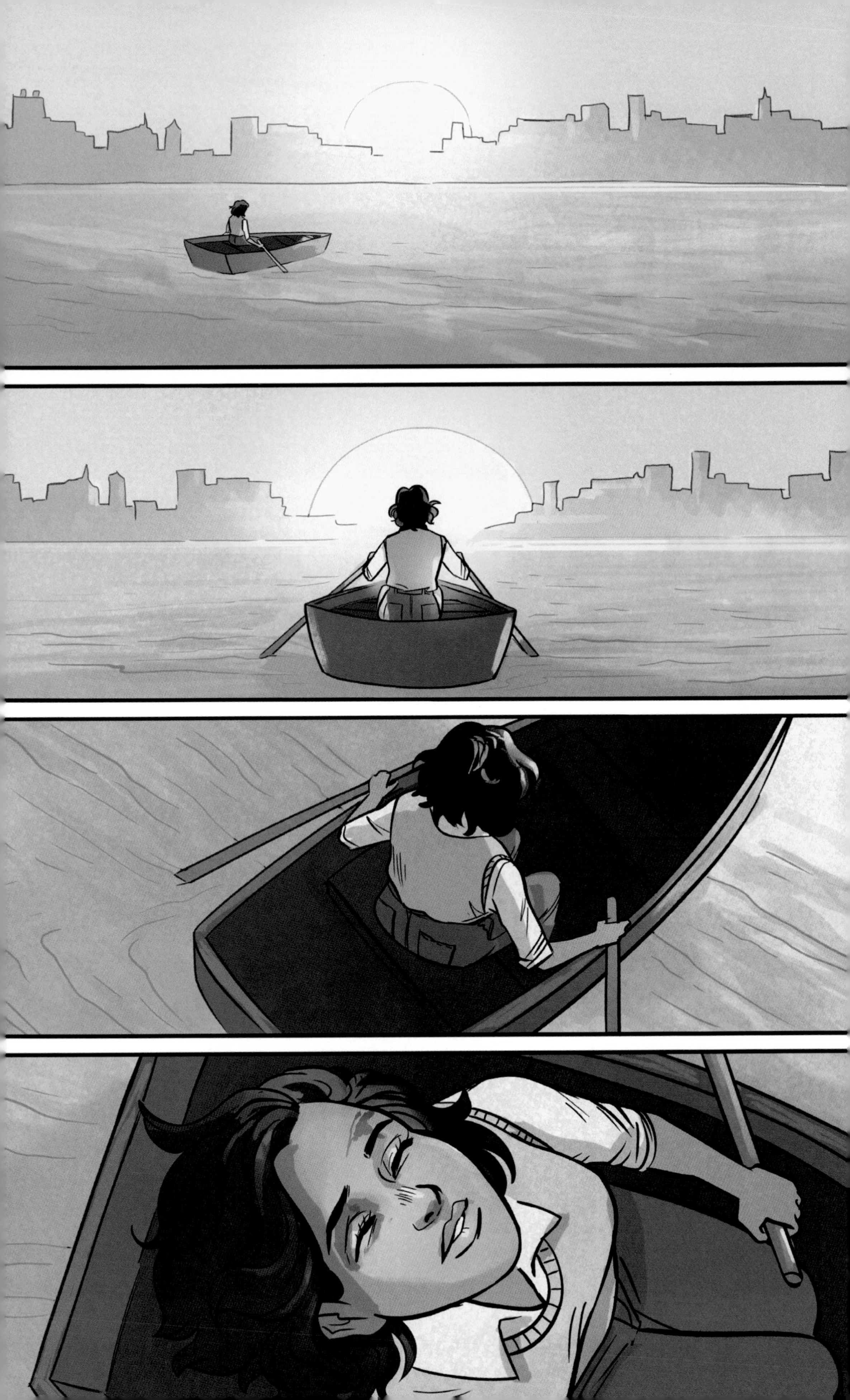

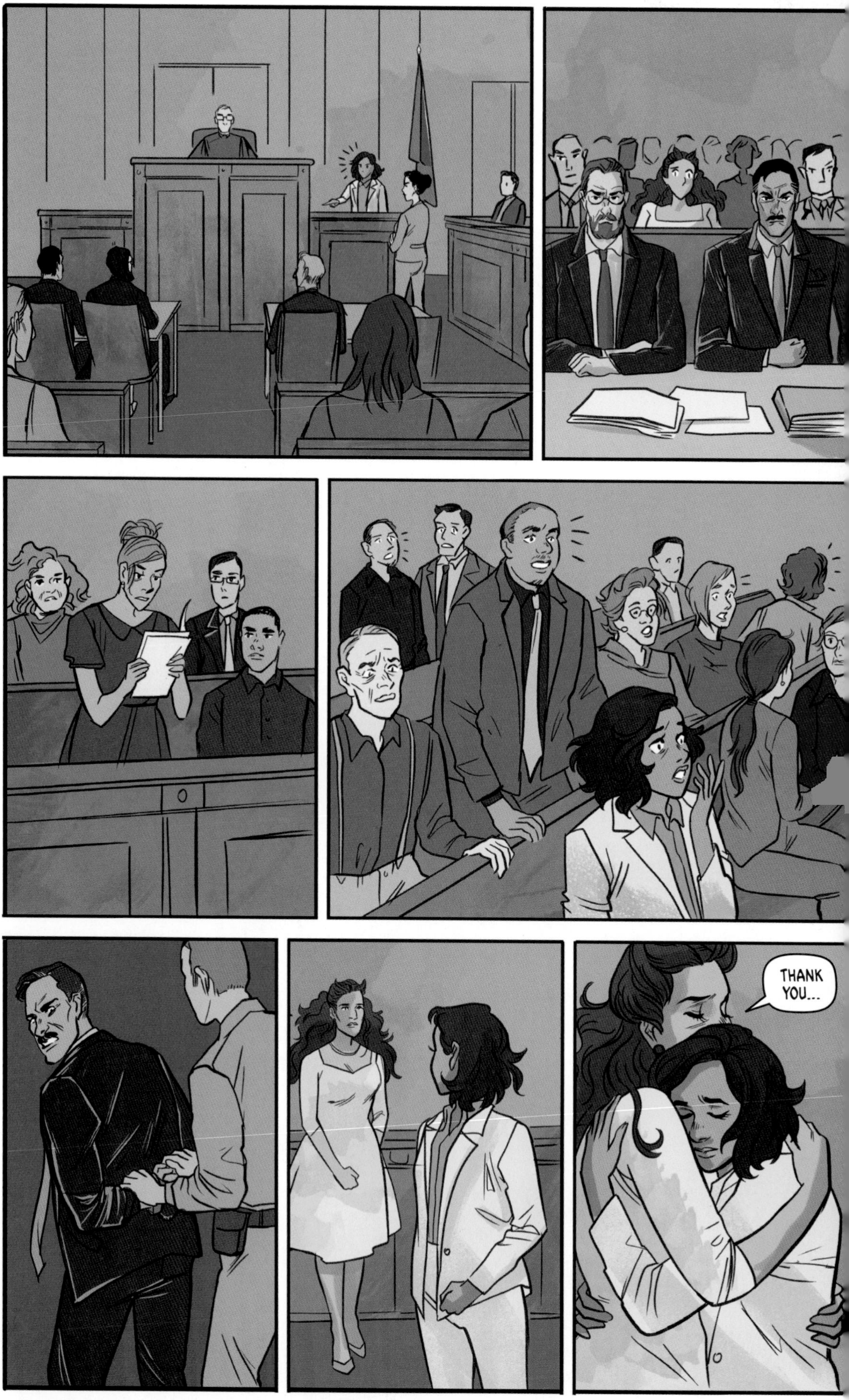
THANK YOU...

..ANY COMMENTS ABOUT THE VERDICT...

WE PLAN TO APPEAL!

"IF MONEY GO BEFORE, ALL WAYS DO LIE OPEN..."

OH, UM, LEMME SEE.

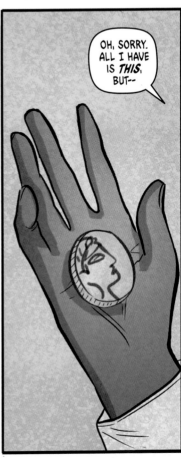

OH, SORRY. ALL I HAVE IS THIS, BUT--

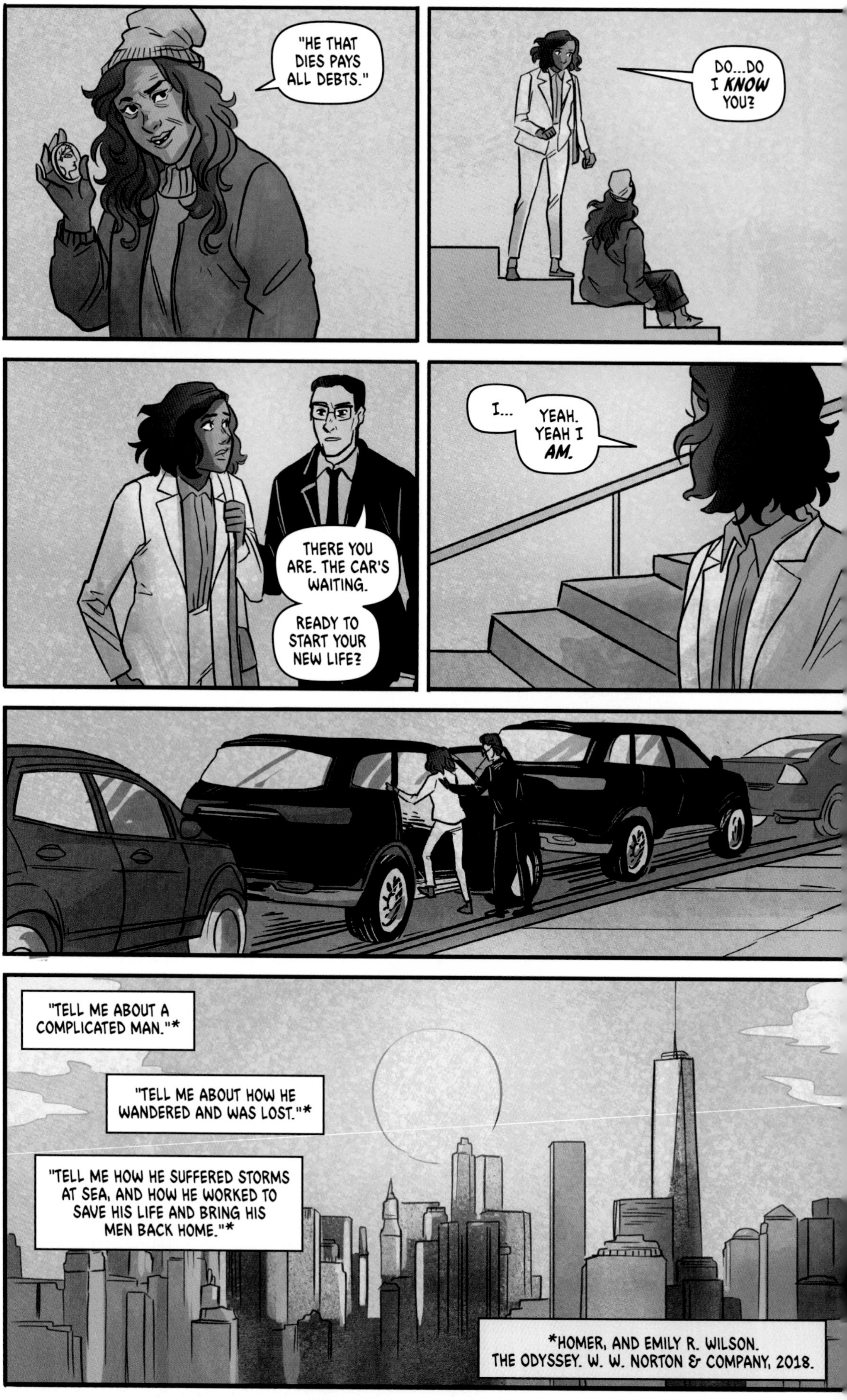
"HE THAT DIES PAYS ALL DEBTS."
DO...DO I KNOW YOU?
THERE YOU ARE. THE CAR'S WAITING.
READY TO START YOUR NEW LIFE?
I...
YEAH. YEAH I AM.
"TELL ME ABOUT A COMPLICATED MAN."*
"TELL ME ABOUT HOW HE WANDERED AND WAS LOST."*
"TELL ME HOW HE SUFFERED STORMS AT SEA, AND HOW HE WORKED TO SAVE HIS LIFE AND BRING HIS MEN BACK HOME."*
*HOMER, AND EMILY R. WILSON. THE ODYSSEY. W. W. NORTON & COMPANY, 2018.

SUB
MERGED

COVER GALLERY FEATURING THE ART OF

JEN BARTEL

LISA STERLE

CASPAR WIJNGAARD

TRIONA FARRELL

TIM DANIEL

COVER ISSUE 1 - JEN BARTEL & TRIONA FARRELL

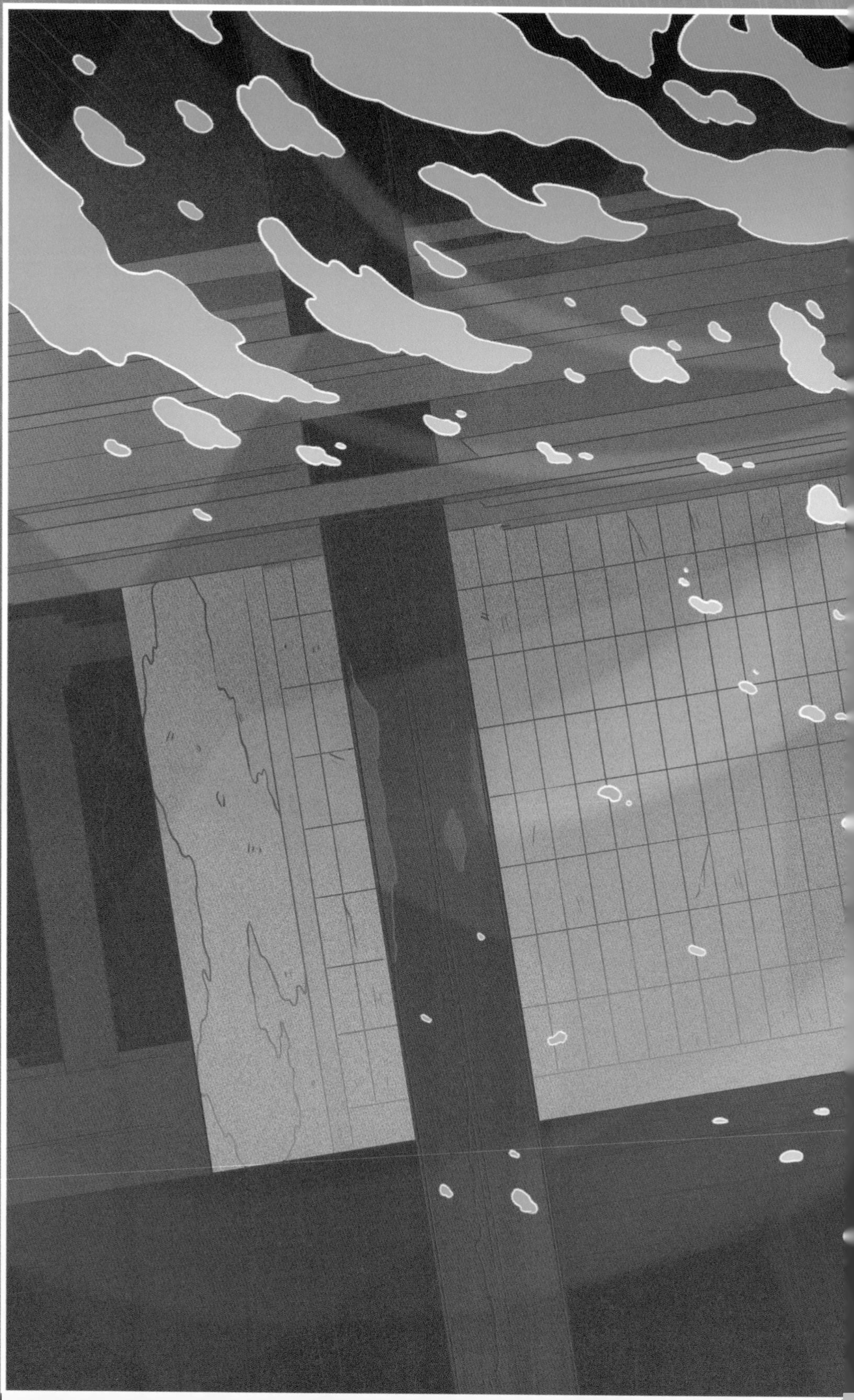

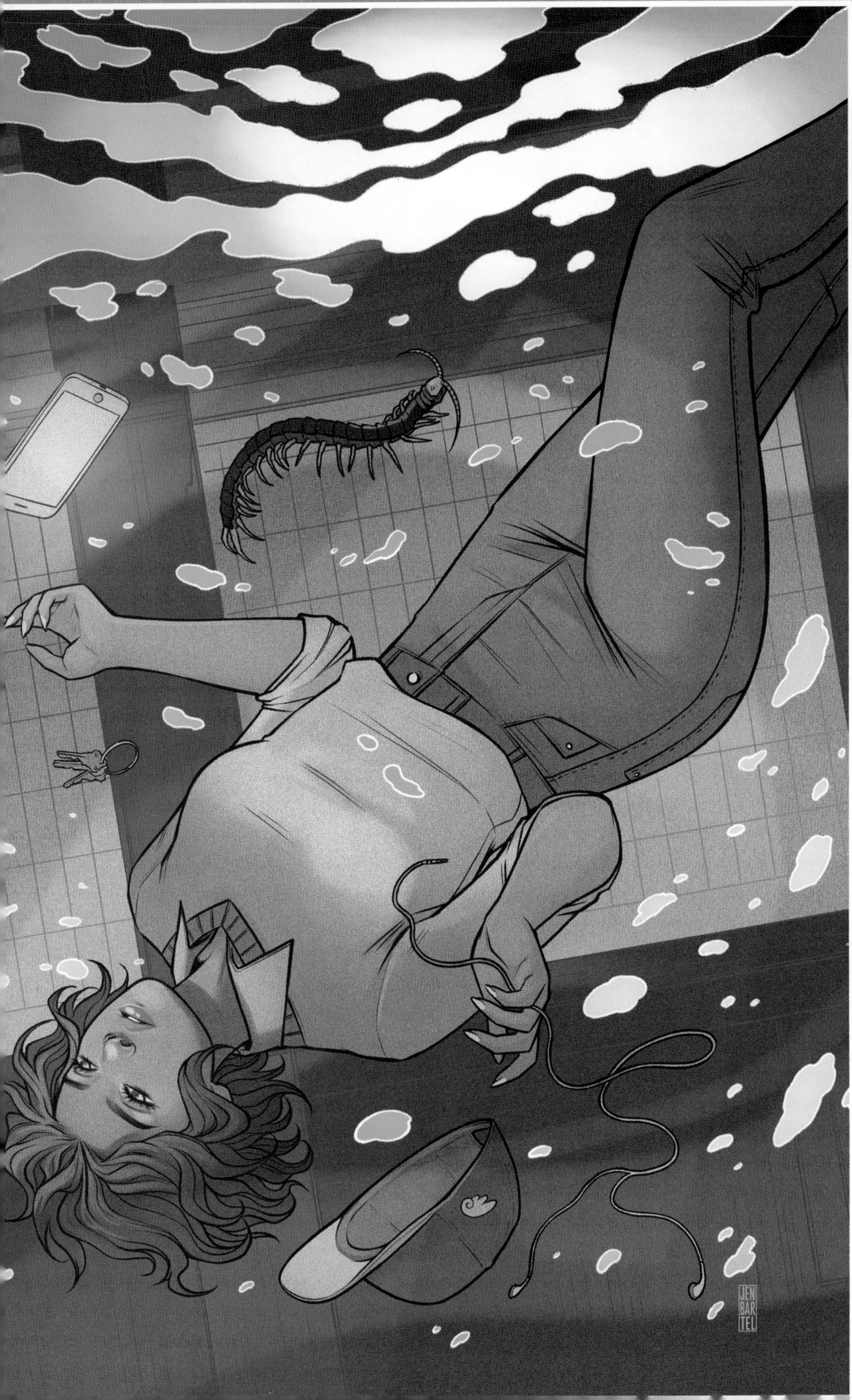
JEN BARTEL

COVER ISSUE 2 - JEN BARTEL & TRIONA FARRELL

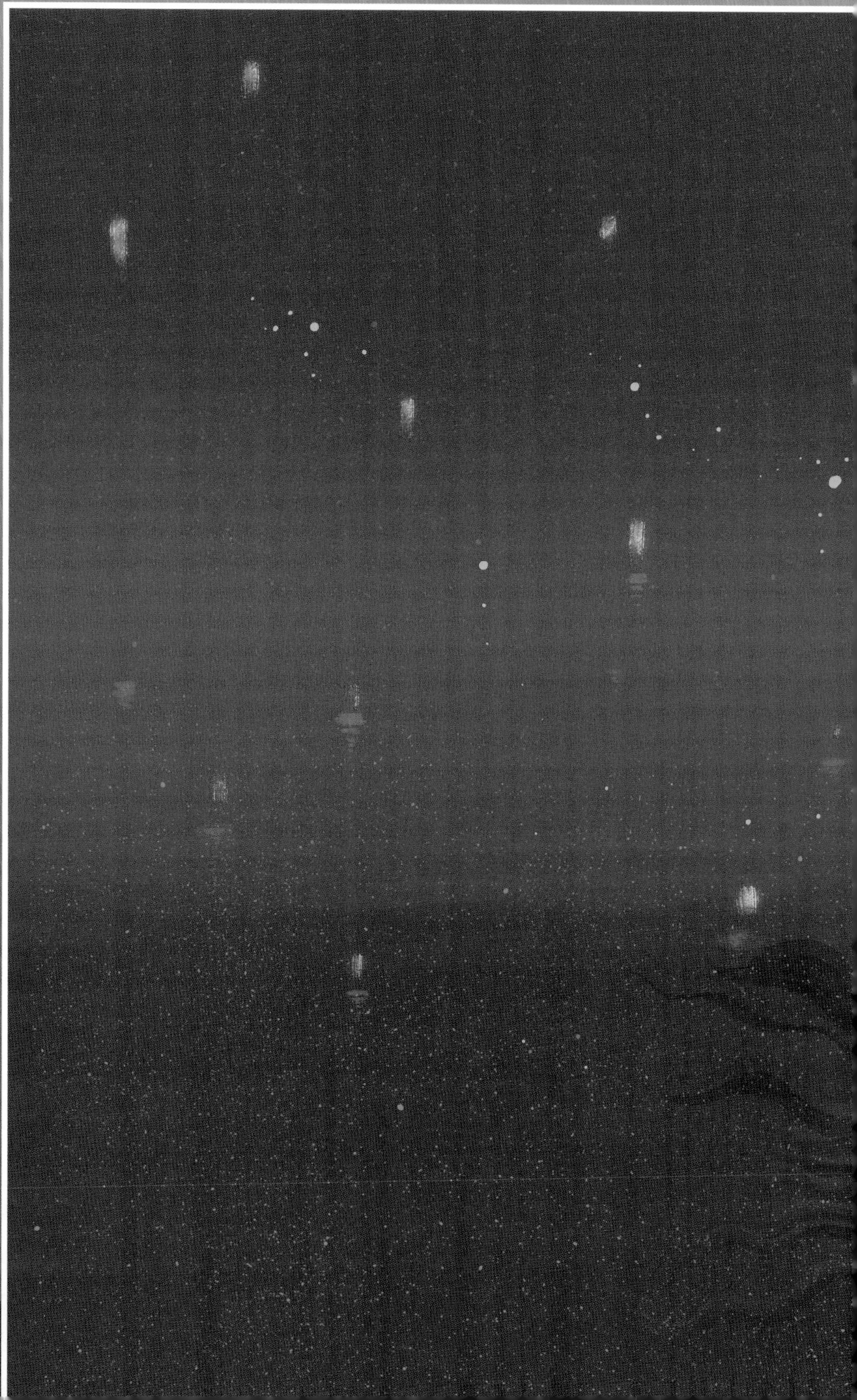

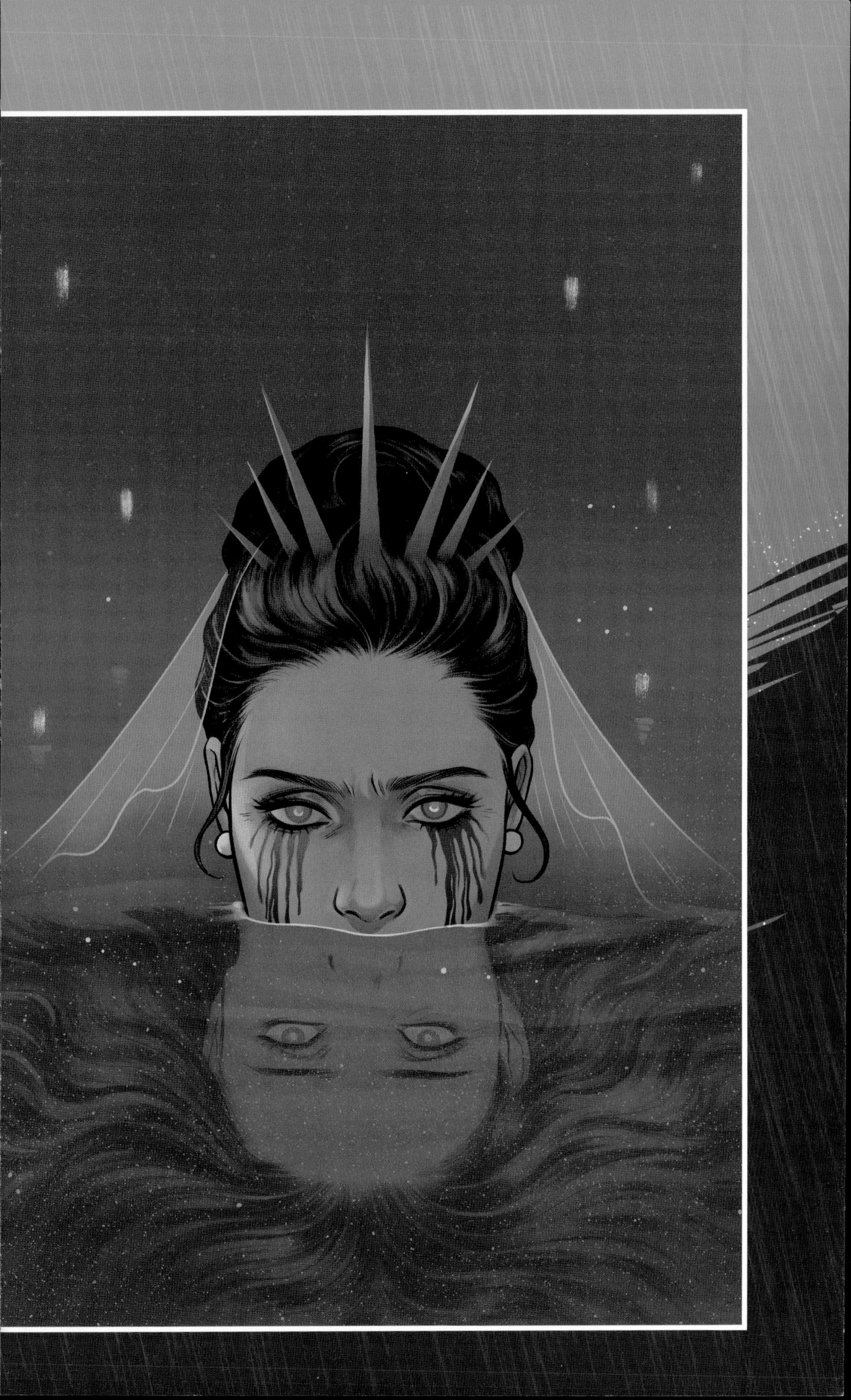

COVER ISSUE 3 - JEN BARTEL & TRIONA FARRELL

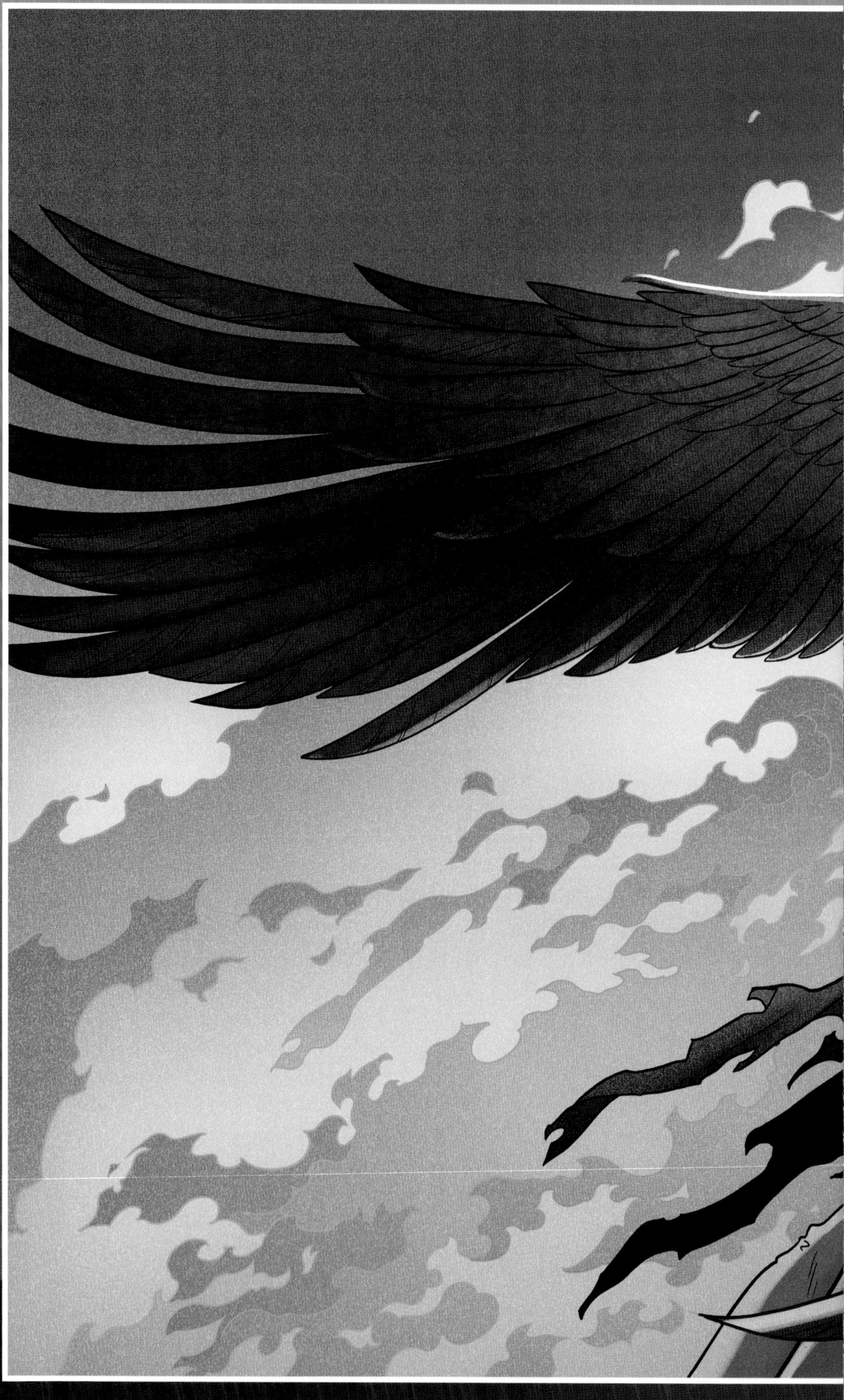

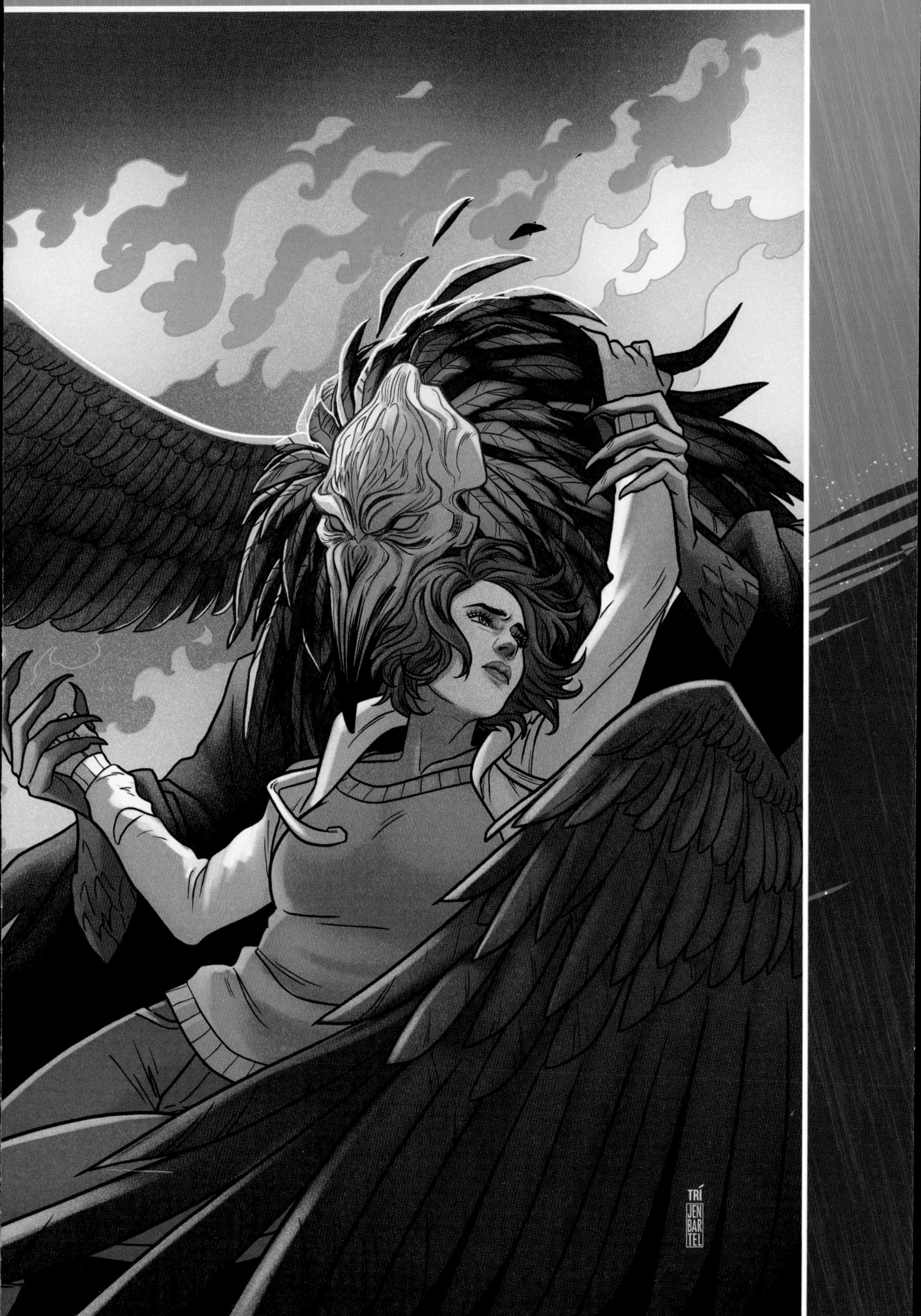
TRÍ
JEN
BAR
TEL

COVER ISSUE 4 - JEN BARTEL & TRIONA FARRELL

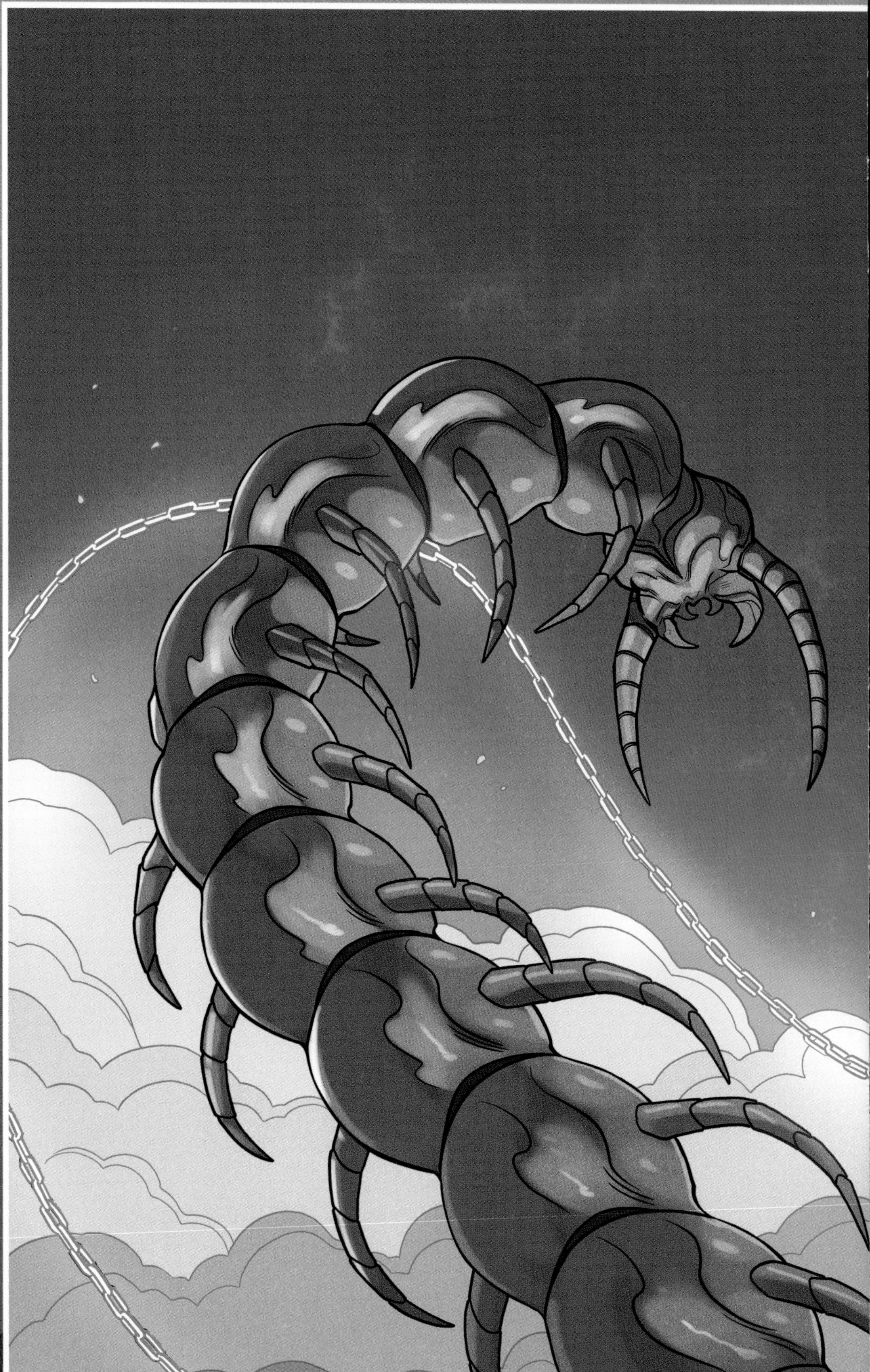

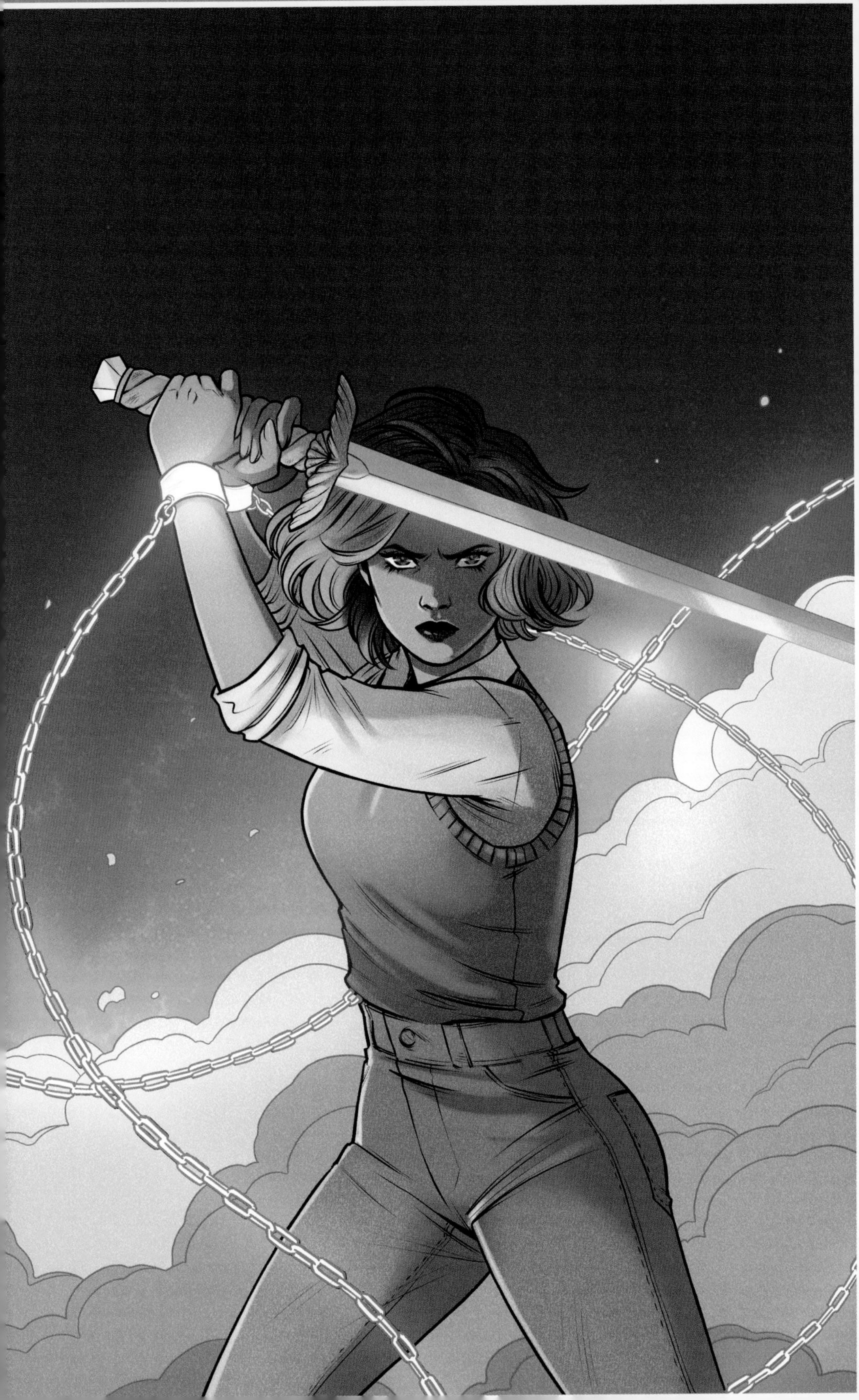

COVER ISSUE 1 - LISA STERLE

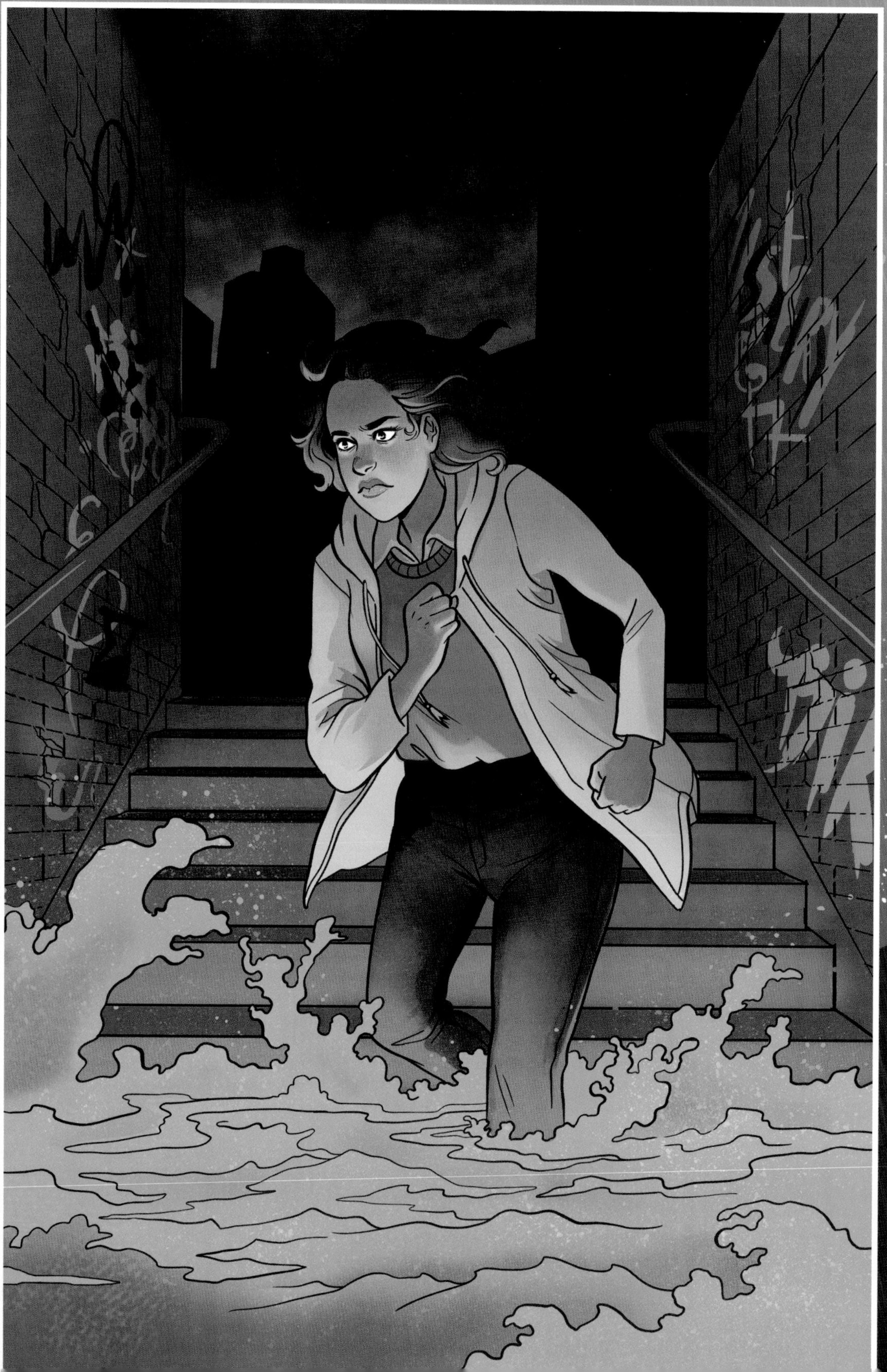

COVER ISSUE 2 - LISA STERLE

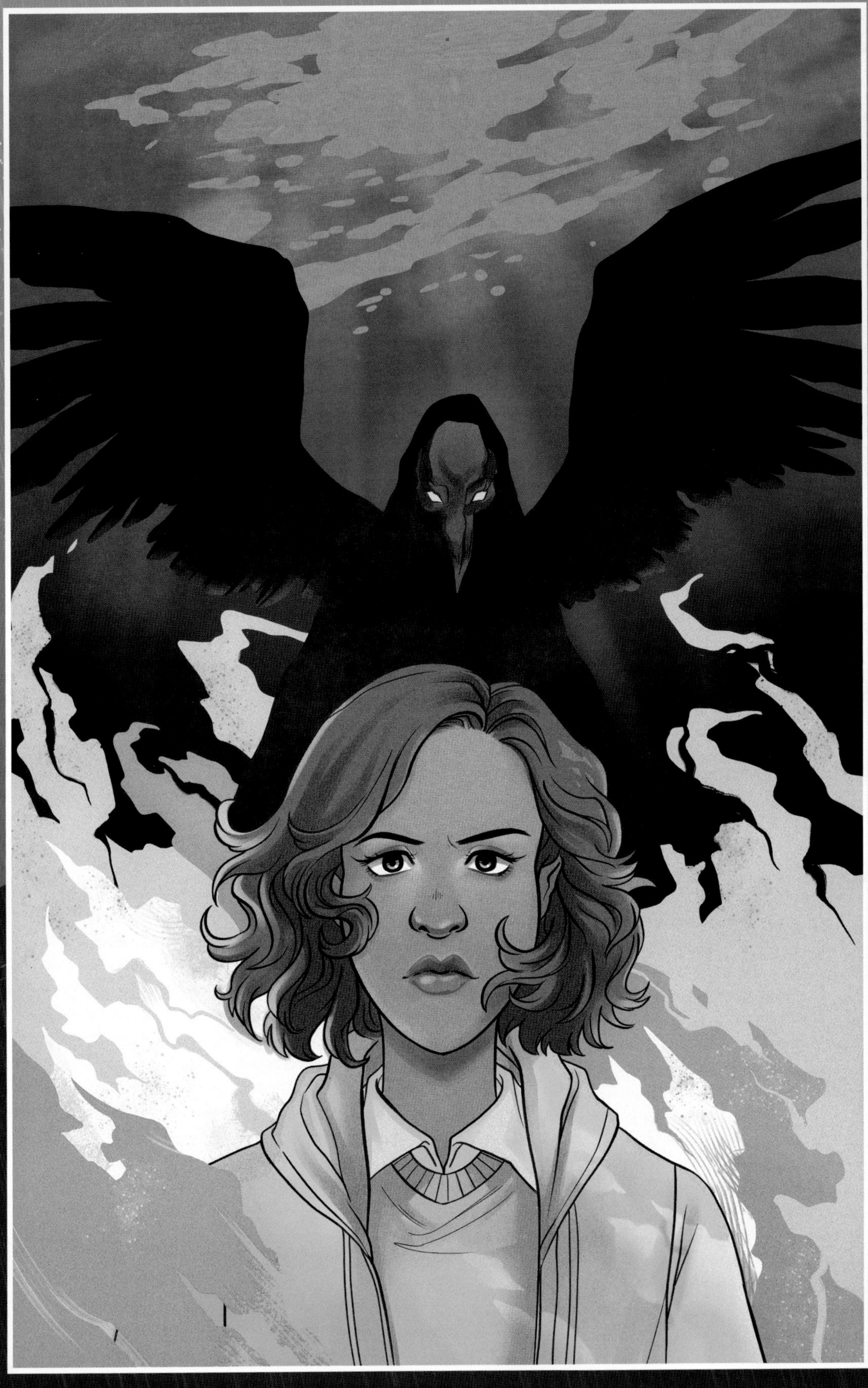

COVER ISSUE 3 - LISA STERLE

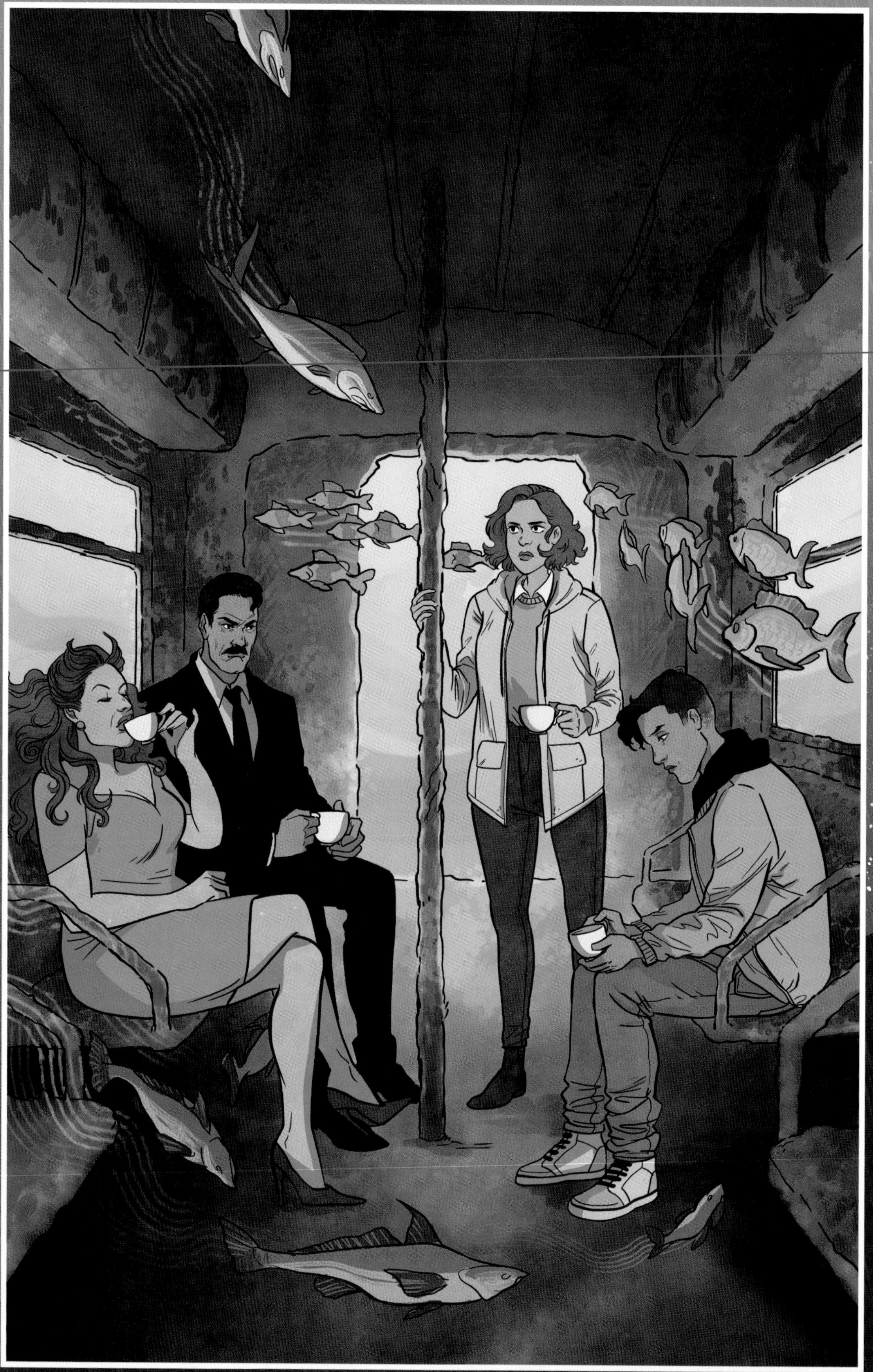

COVER ISSUE 4 - LISA STERLE

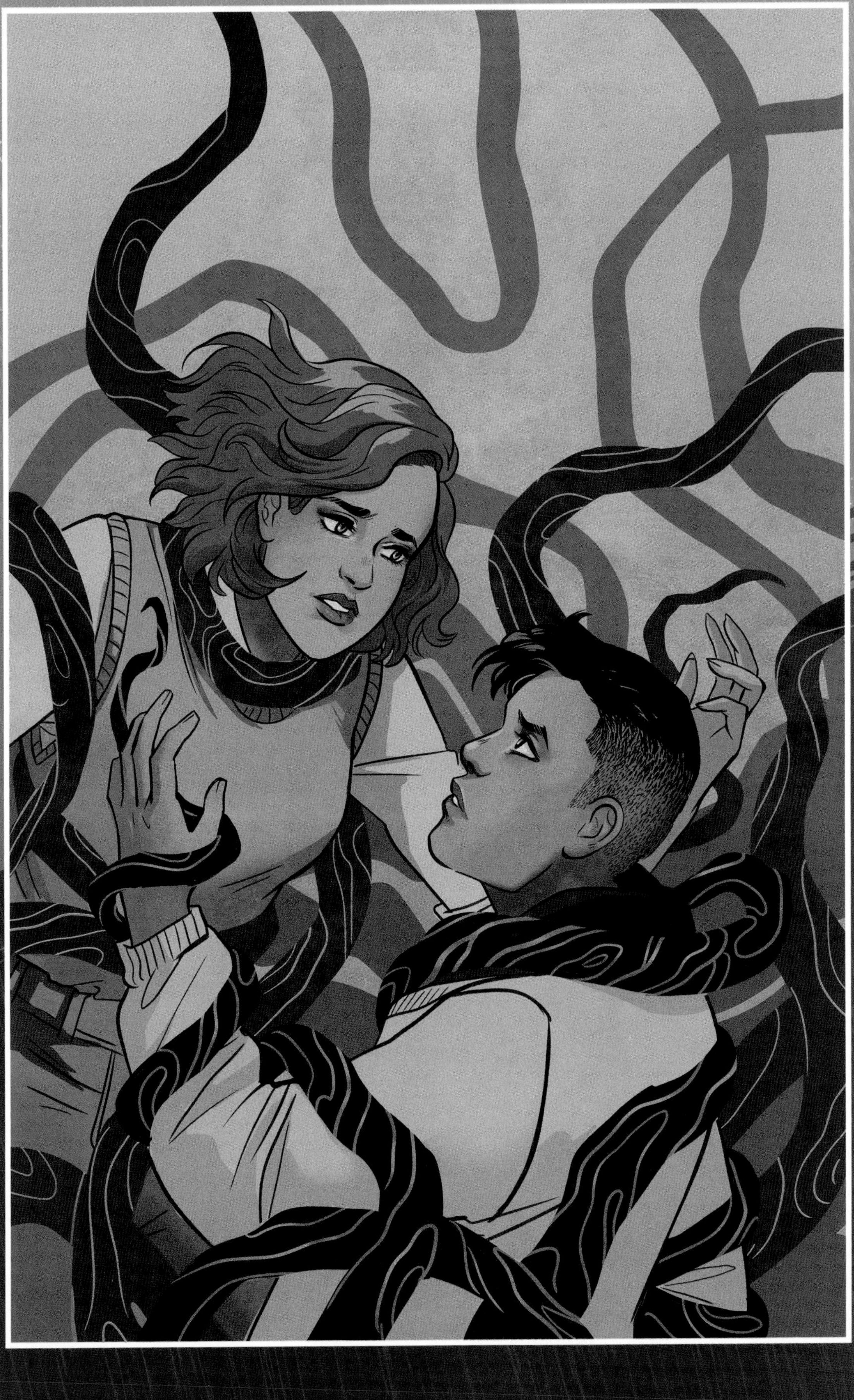

COVER ISSUE 1: VAULT VINTAGE- CASPAR WIJNGAARD

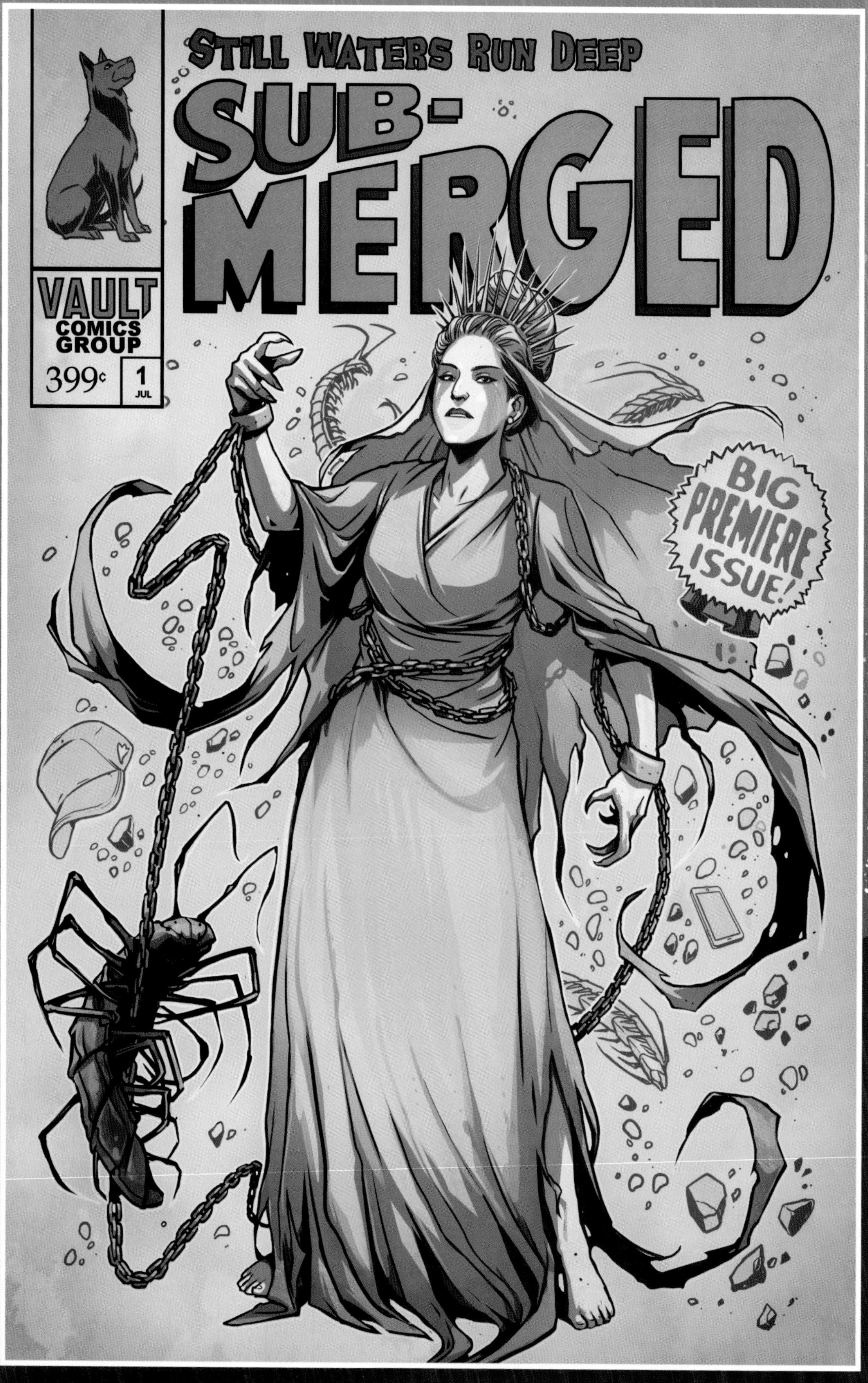
STILL WATERS RUN DEEP
SUB-
MERGED
VAULT
COMICS
GROUP
399¢
1
JUL
BIG
PREMIERE
ISSUE!

COVER ISSUE 1: VAULT VINTAGE - TIM DANIEL

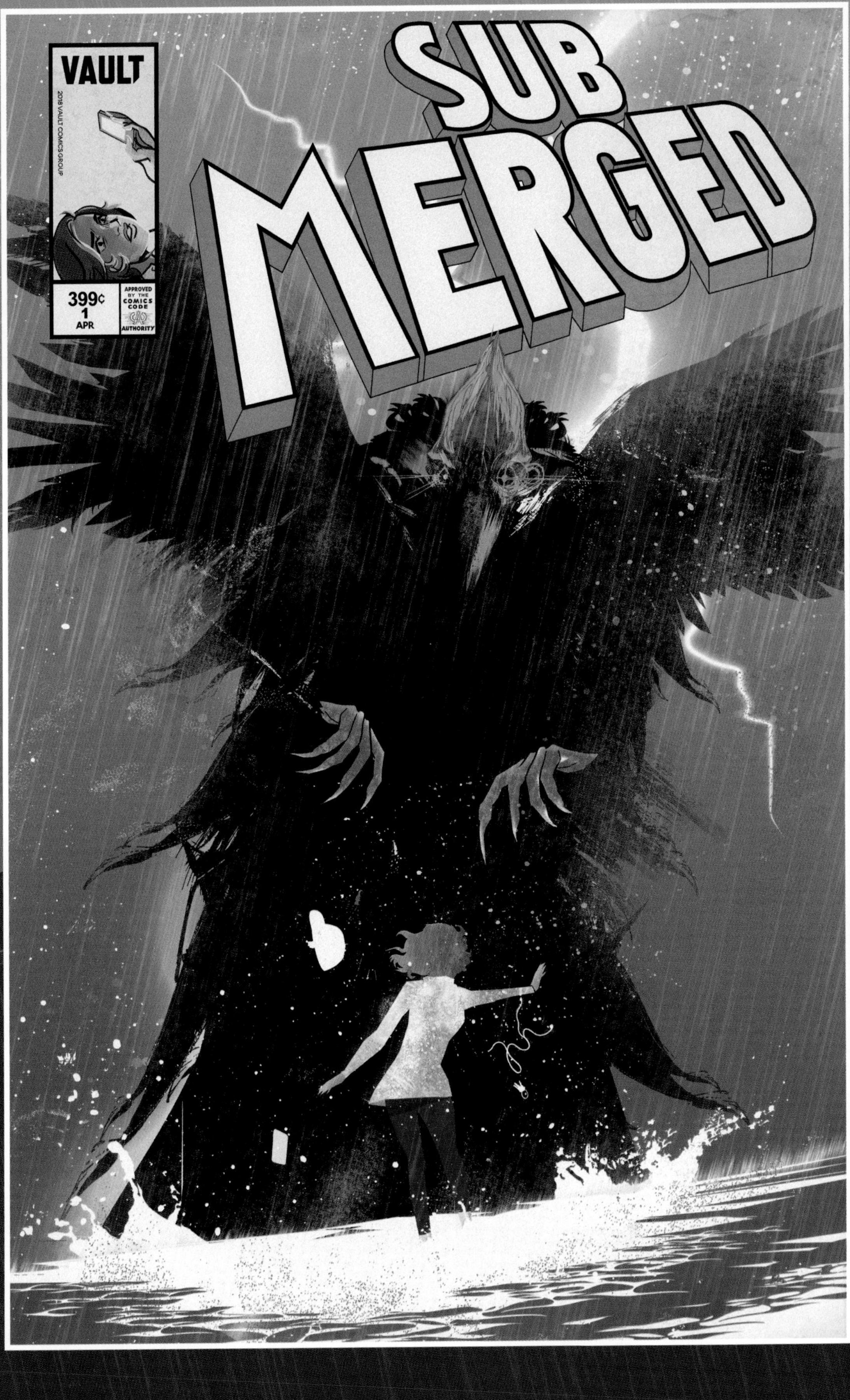

VAULT
2018 VAULT COMICS GROUP
399¢
1
APR
APPROVED BY THE COMICS CODE AUTHORITY
SUB
MERGED

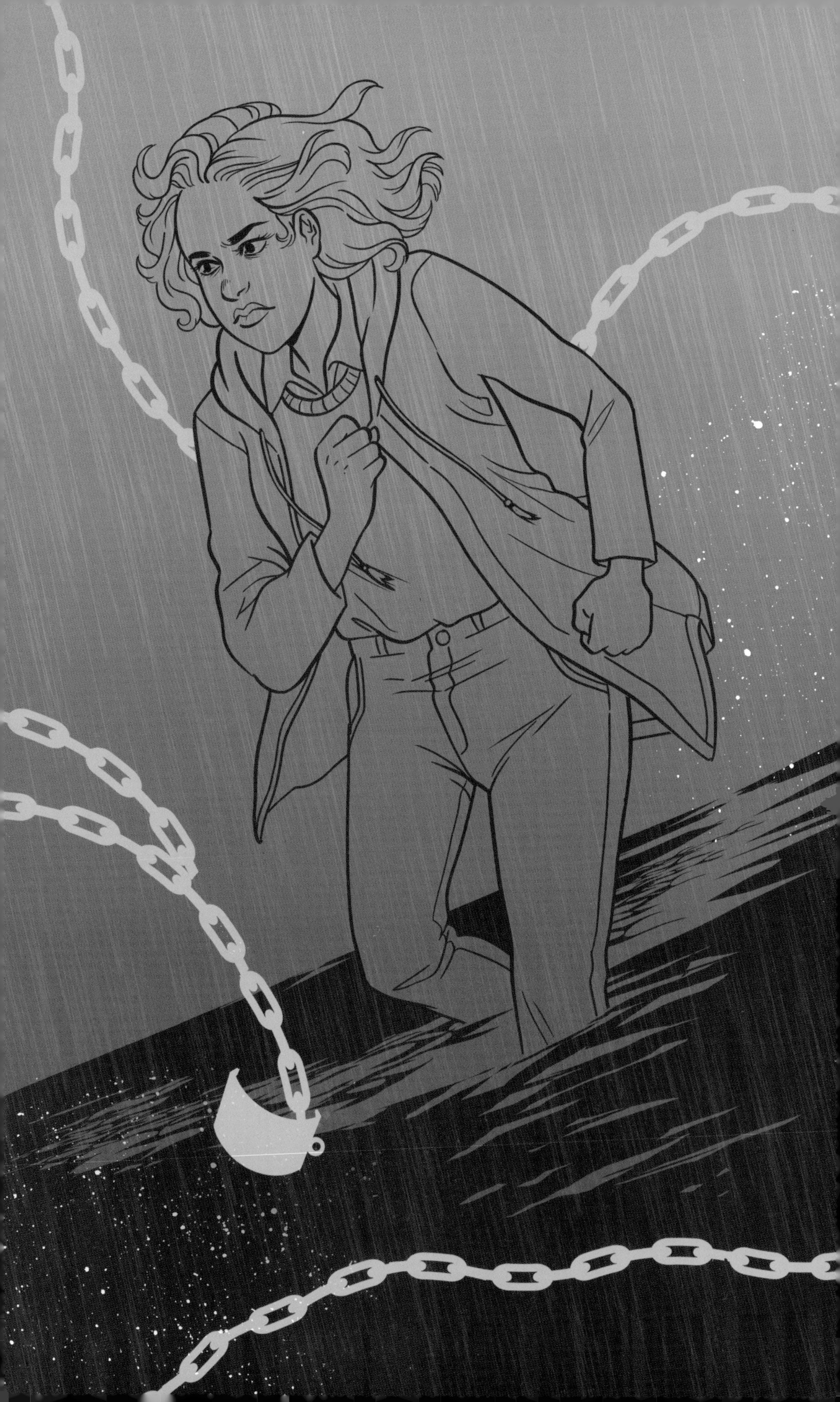

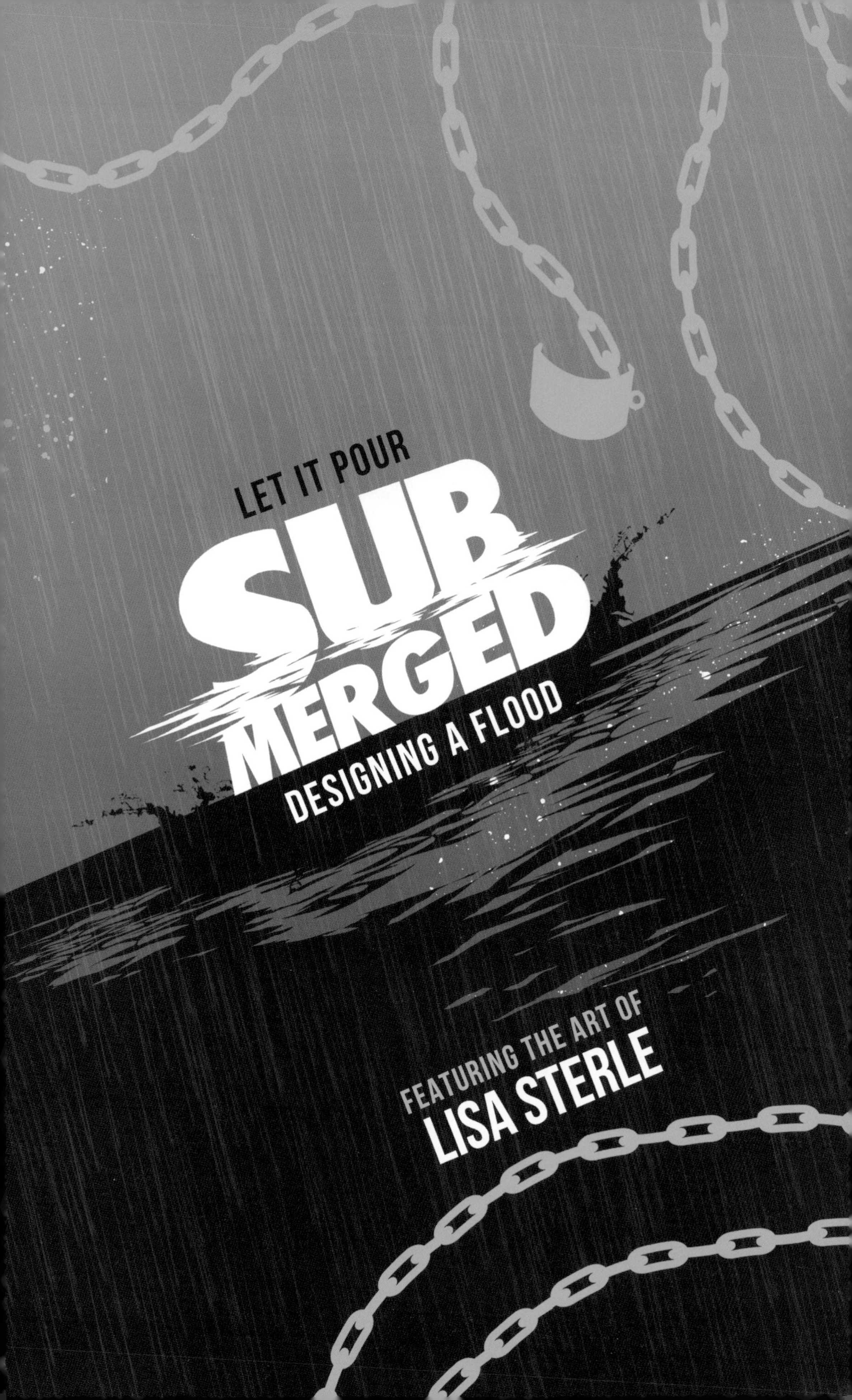
LET IT POUR
SUB
MERGED
DESIGNING A FLOOD
FEATURING THE ART OF
LISA STERLE

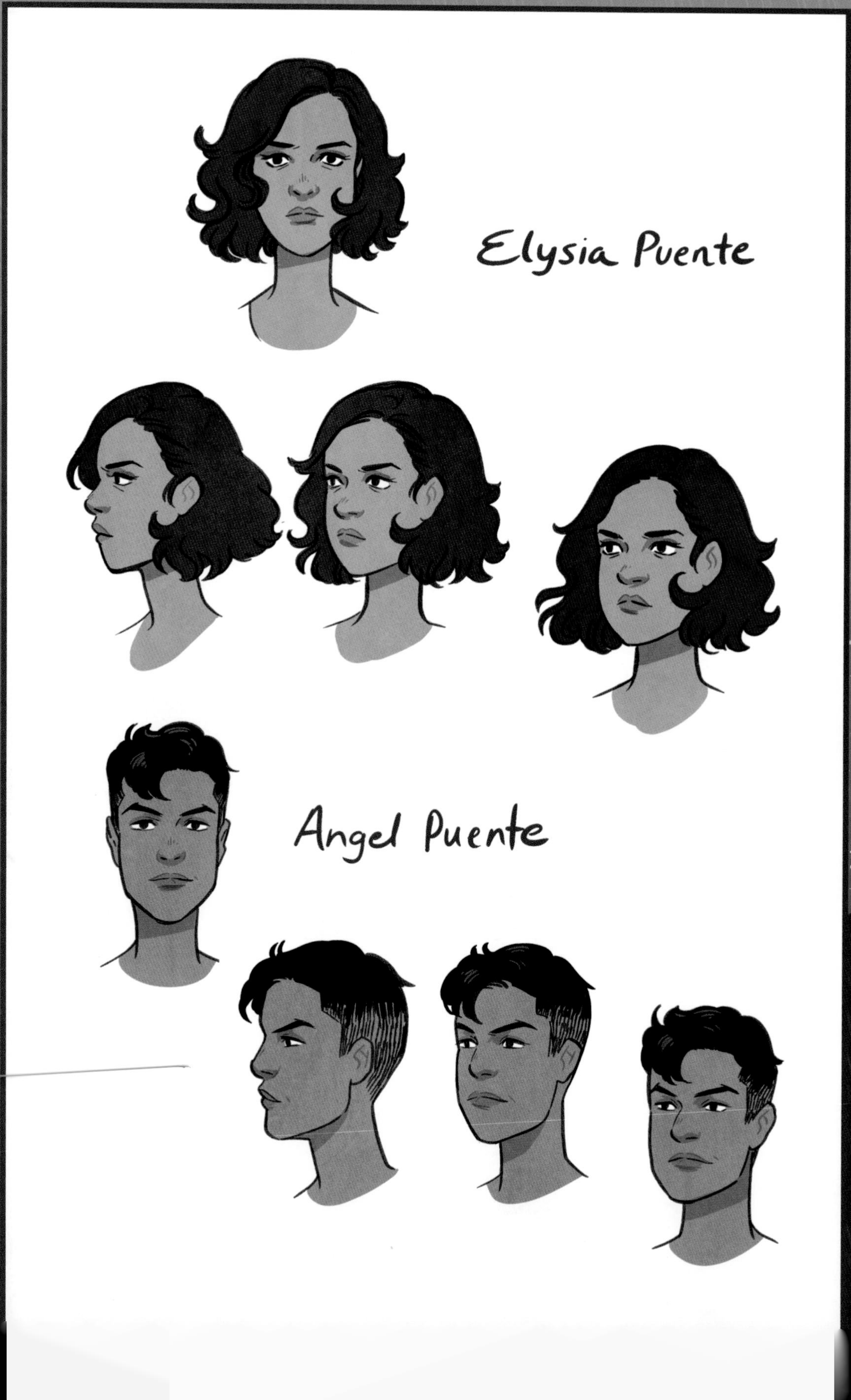
Elysia Puente
Angel Puente

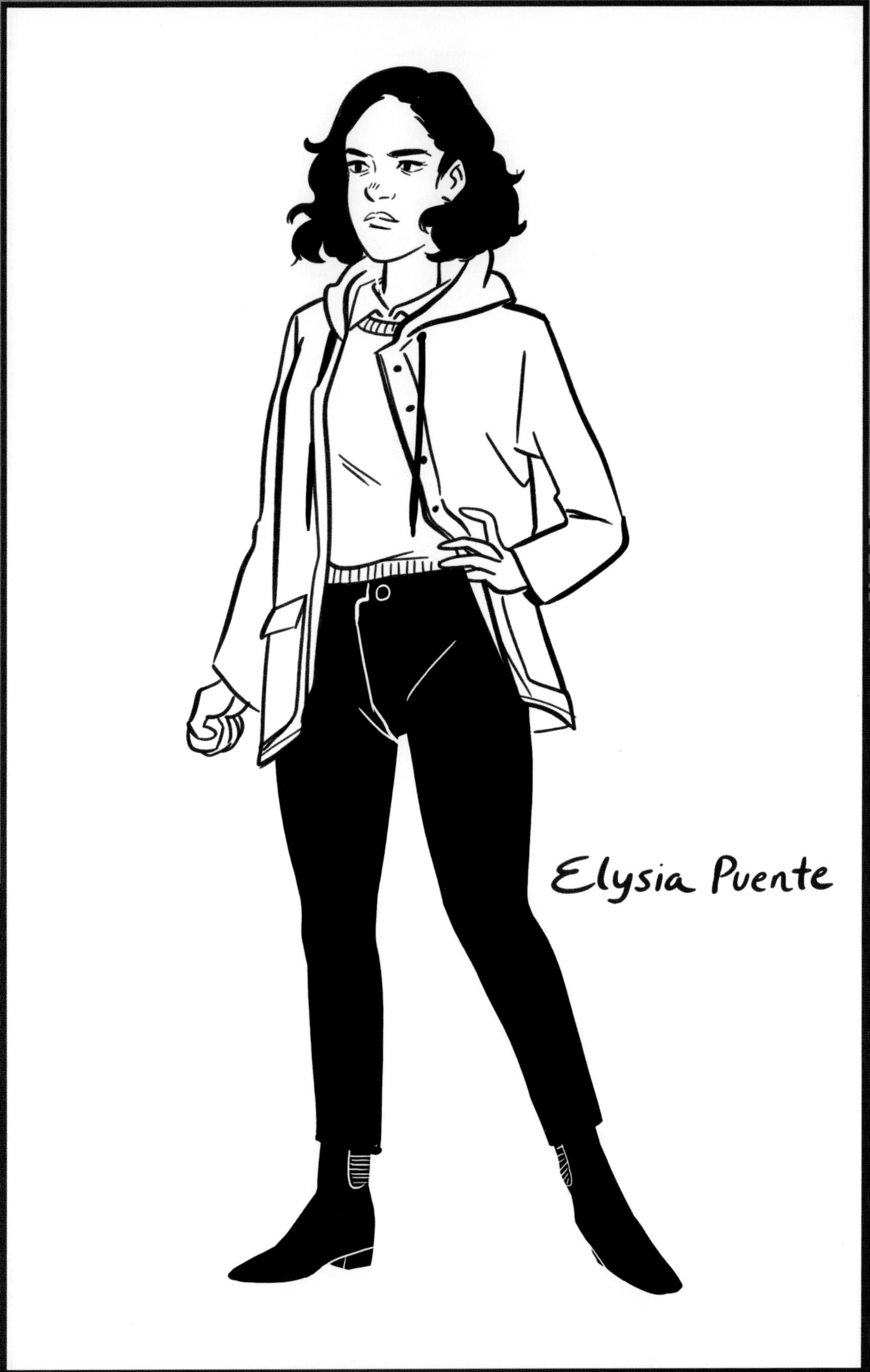
Elysia Puente

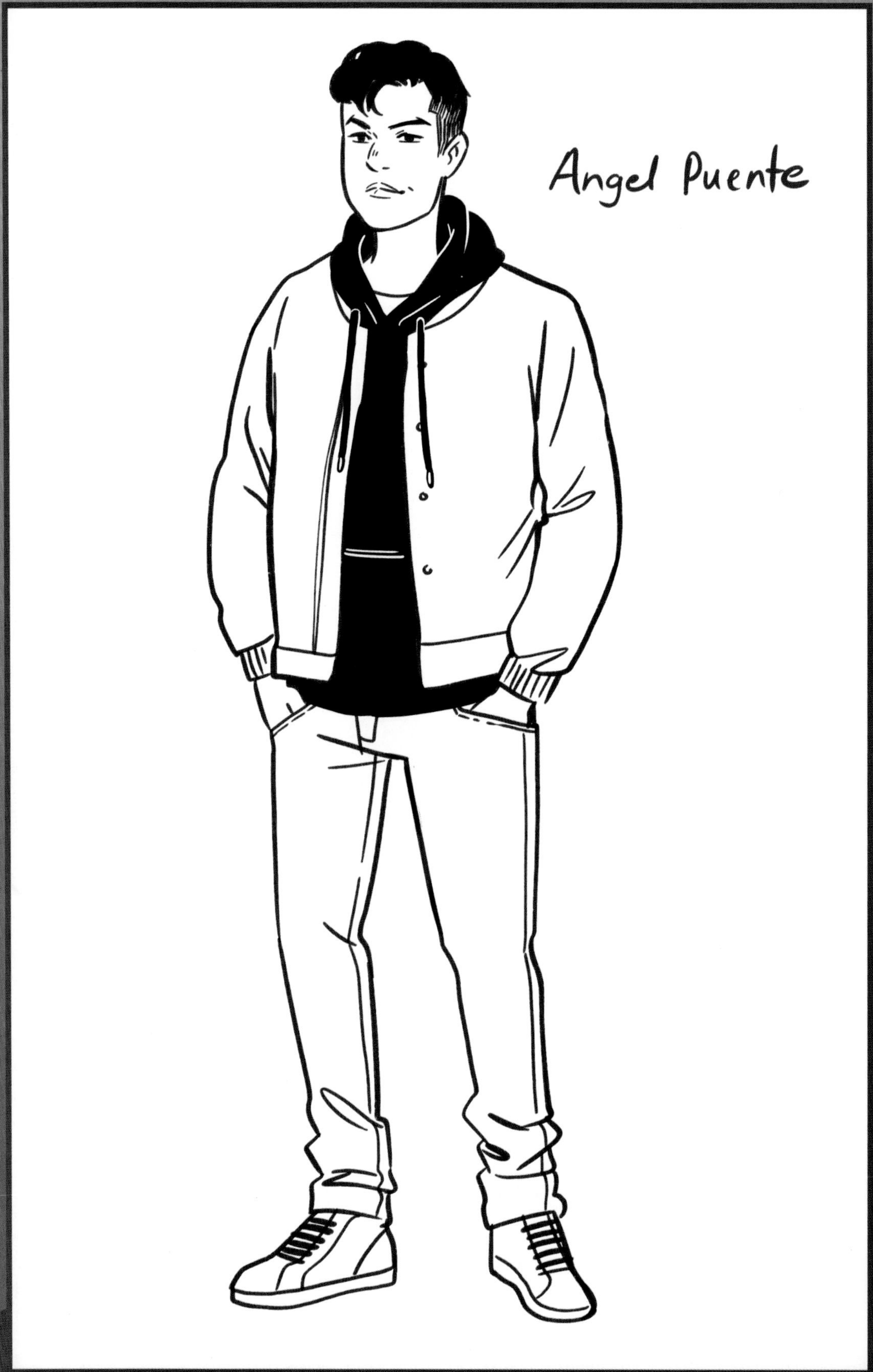
Angel Puente

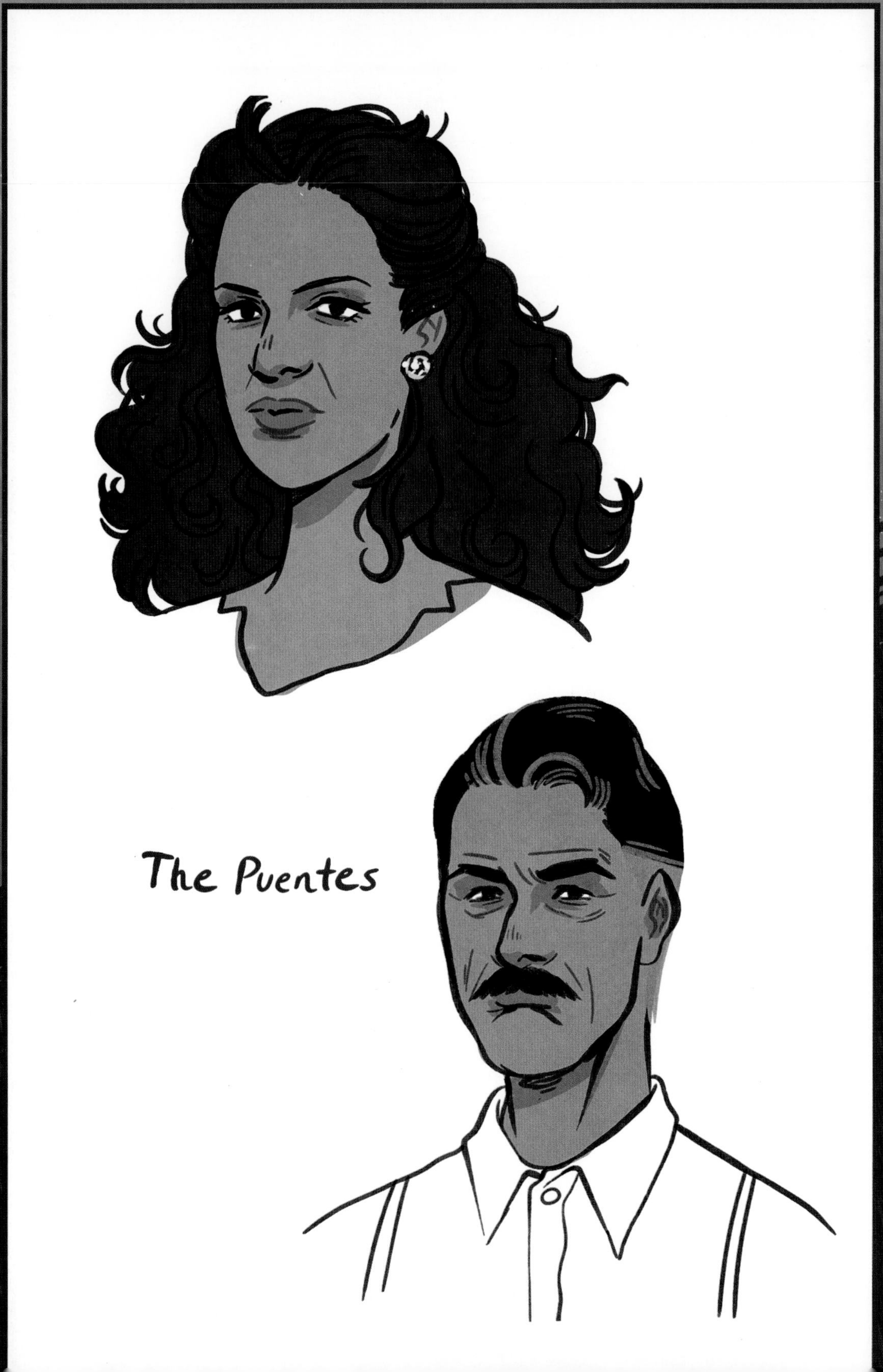
The Puentes

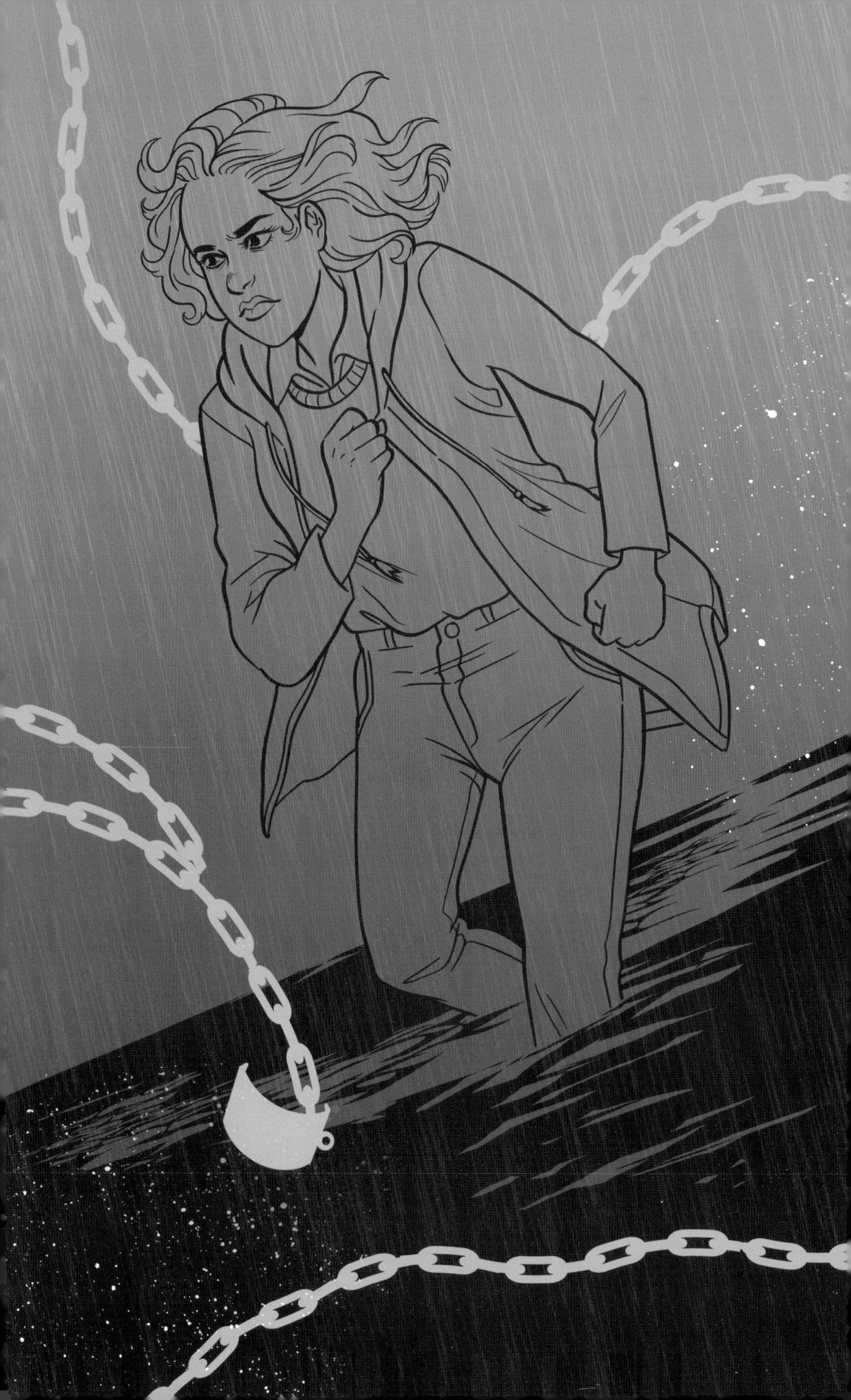